AGE OF SECESSION : VINDIC

ROSICK

For my mum
For the support and encouragement in all things

AGE OF SECESSION : VINDICATOR TRILOGY PART II

ROSICRUX

Third Edition
Published in Great Britain by Roger Ruffles, February 2018

www.ageofsecession.com

First published by Roger Ruffles, October 2013

Printed by CreateSpace, An Amazon.com Company

ISBN : 978-1493728244

Chapter I

All was peaceful in the planetary system, the low-grade, dying sun at its centre peacefully nearing the end of its life. A number of planets continued on in their slow dance around the ageing star. There were numerous asteroid fields with the system, which would have been hazards to heavy interstellar shipping if humanity had ever considered colonising this lonely, unwanted place. Humanity had only ever wanted one thing from this system, though, and it had it in abundance.

Despite never colonising the system, a space station was located between the orbital tracks of the third and fourth planets. It moved in a geosynchronous orbit with a large, many-ringed gas giant, numerous intra-stellar ships on a permanent conveyor belt to and from the rings to the station. The regular and predictable movements of the conveyances, day after day, week after week, merely added to the timelessness of the peaceful and relaxed atmosphere of the system.

In the heavier asteroid fields out towards the second half of the solar system, numerous mining ships grazed gently. They were the stellar equivalents of bovine animals harvesting the rich metals and precious resources within the fields. The giant maws of collecting ram-scoops swallowed asteroids whole, the internal processes within the large ships breaking down the collected material, and then ejecting the unwanted detritus in another parody of organic life. The antennae-like extensions of the mining lasers occasionally fired at short-range to break up larger targets, whilst the many mining ships drifted gently on their pre-planned courses.

It all seemed like any other day in the Graviticus System, but only because the warships that had jumped into the peaceful vista hours before had arrived completely undetected.

Mining Captain Feder Lahtinen took a long sip from his cup of real tea. He insisted on the real stuff and his ship carried a special reserve just for him, as he was unable to bear any of the synthesised stock. There were precious few luxuries aboard a mining ship, and he was determined he would have this one.

He yawned. It was early morning according to Imperial Standard time, not that there was a Red Imperium anymore to set the time. The changes in the galaxy had mostly passed him by, and his life had not changed greatly at least in its day-to-day routine. He counted himself fortunate, as he had contacts elsewhere in the galaxy who had suffered in the dissolution of the Empire.

"Johann," he demanded of his First Officer, "do you have the projected take for today?"

"Aye, sir," Johann appeared at his side, passing a data-slate over to him. "We're ahead of schedule for the week, Captain."

"Then this is our chance to get ahead for the month," said Captain Lahtinen, thinking of his end-of-month bonus. The inter-galactic mining operation of Ventaxa Industries had been majorly disrupted by the StarCom invasions, and the bonuses had been cut. He was determined to obtain as great a bonus as he could. In that respect, the dissolution of the Empire had affected him greatly.

He and most of the crew aboard the *Gandolf* were un-augmented, being humans who had not received cybernetic implants. Ventaxa Industries had a policy of trying to keep the crews on its ships either fully human, or fully cyborg, to prevent any problems aboard ship. The pogroms by the False Emperor had only accentuated centuries of hatred between the augmented and the un-augmented, and many of the sanctioned wars between Houses before the dissolution of the Empire, and the secession wars following its break-up, had been caused by this hatred. House Lindholm itself was classified as a free-thinking house in this clash of opinions, one which did not match the extreme anti-cybernetic humanist view, or the polar opposite but equally extreme anti-implant borgite view, and was officially neutral on the subject.

There was a holographic image of the *SS Gandolf* mining ship rotating by the left side of his command seat. The ship was huge, and had a couple of hundred crew to man its various operations, as well as droids and drones in support. Ventaxa Industries had contracted this ship and many others to the noble House of Lindholm, and he himself was a Lindholm national recruited specifically because of his experience in stellar mining. He had been on this ship for nearly three decades.

House Lindholm was a small, independent territory in the north-eastern segment of galaxy, just beyond the boundary between the Core and the Mid-Sector regions of space. It had yet to declare whether it was joining one of the many conglomerations of houses that were forming their own nations, or go it alone, but Captain Feder Lahtinen did not much care.

All he cared about was his quiet life, and the money.

Captain Dolf Reichenburg breathed shallowly, using his implants to regulate his breathing. He was jacked into the datasphere of the warship by the internal modem implanted into his brain, allowing him instant access to any part of the ship and even any mind of his cybernetic crew. They were all ex-Praetorian Guard, once the best and most elite military force in the galaxy, sworn to protect the Emperors of the Red Imperium.

The ship he commanded, the SS *Vengeance*, was a former Praetorian ship. It was running on silent, one of many under his command, and one that had jumped into the Graviticus System undetected. It had coasted on reduced power for hours, chameleonic fields engaged to bend light around its immense structure, electrical and magnetic signals dampened.

It had stealthily crept up on its target, passively scanning the system for any sign of any military defences. There were none. The uninhabited system had any number of small intra-stellar and larger inter-stellar starships, but none were a threat to the forces he had brought into Graviticus.

<We have reached the nominated assault time, Captain,> his second-in-command, Commander Jan Alvarez said unnecessarily. It was more of an impatient prompt, Reichenburg guessed. He had served with Alvarez for years, since before they had turned traitor against the False Emperor.

<All weapons locked and loaded,> his senior tactical officer confirmed.

Reichenburg used his connection to the datasphere to call an image of the forward targeting sensors into his minds-eye. The forward torpedo launchers were locked onto a precise location on the mining ship SS *Gandolf*. The beast of a civilian ship, moving sedately through the upper ranges of the asteroid field, had no idea they were moving ever closer to his hidden battlecruiser.

When Reichenburg gave the signal, the other warships he had in-system would attack their targets.

<Fire,> he ordered calmly.

Out in space, the lines of the V-class SS *Vengeance* battlecruiser were revealed as the torpedoes rocketed out of their forward launch tubes. The backlight caused by their launch disrupted the chameleonic field hiding the ship, playing along its rounded head-like prow as the four lethal projectiles sped away.

"Er – Captain?" his scanners officer said.

"Yes?" Captain Lahtinen asked around the cup of tea at his lips.

"We have an odd energy signature just picked up. I think there's something out there."

"Really? Show me," he demanded, curiosity piqued. This was highly unusual.

He looked up above the bridge as the main holoprojector flared into life, showing him and the entire bridge crew a forward view ahead of the *Gandolf* mining ship. The image came on-line just as the backlit prow of what looked like some large ship was disappearing behind some kind of stealth force field. There were a number of small objects highlighted on the display, coming in towards them.

"What are they?" he asked.

Johann, his second-in-command, who had served in the house military of Lindholm for some years, shouted, "Torpedoes!"

"Torpedoes?" Lahtinen questioned. His eyes widened in fear as the rapidly-moving objects were now close enough for him to recognise. They looked almost exactly like the things he had seen in holo-vids.

"Evasive –" he began, but it was too late. Even as he was speaking, his eyes had focused through the holo-image to the open metaglass windows of his bridge, and he saw the torpedo that was heading directly for them.

The ship rocked violently, Lahtinen crying out, but then the windows of the bridge shattered as the torpedo crashed in. The bridge and a number of surrounding decks were turned into a gigantic inferno, and Lahtinen's quiet life came to a violent end.

Reichenburg watched dispassionately as the torpedoes tracked in a series of hits along the length of the mining ship. The first struck the ram-scoop, destroying it, forcing the ship's automated computers to bring the ship to a halt as a safety precaution, even as the second ploughed into the bridge. A third torpedo exploded along the spine, a special warhead attached which allowed it to penetrate deeper than the others before detonating, wiping out the main crew quarters in the bowels of the *Gandolf*. For good measure, the fourth took out the boxy rear engines.

<Target is dead-in-the-water,> his tactical officer announced.

<Launch marines, board the target> Captain Reichenburg ordered.

<Marines away,> mission control said.

<Come about, full speed to the space station,> he ordered.

A number of mining ships were pulling away from the asteroid fields, trying desperately to get clear so they could engage jump capacitors and leap to safety. A couple of others had come under attack, first attacked by unseen assailants and then boarded by marines aboard fast-moving strike-pods, the pods crashing into the metal hulls of their targets.

Massive cargo-freighters began jumping openly in-system, ready to take the mining ships' cargo-tanks. All mining operations in the Graviticus System had been violently disrupted.

Aboard the commercial space station, all was in panic. They had no weaponry, no shields, no way of defending themselves. They could not even jump out-system. Besides some of the larger mining ships such as the *Gandolf* that had been struck, they were the single largest target in-system.

A number of warships appeared, their chameleonic fields unable to hide them any longer as they neared the station. It was not necessary to remain in hiding any longer. The first of the ships to reach the space station was the *SS Vengeance*, the ship which had launched the attack.

It began to pummel the space station with torpedoes, turbolasers and other weaponry. All was chaos in the system, the smaller ships on their runs from the gas giant's rings desperately trying to escape, like flies disturbed from their meal. Life-pods began to eject from the space station, and thankfully the hostile warships ignored them.

They were intent on disrupting all operations in the Graviticus System, stealing what they could, and the utter destruction of the space station.

Under the combined fire-power of several warships, the space station split apart.

*

Some hours later, the House Lindholm battlecruiser *LhSS Emperor's Fist* jumped into the Graviticus System. It was accompanied by the rest of the small squadron of battlecruisers and strikecruisers attached to the Admiral Jakub Halvorssen, all of them translating out of the warp-jump in unison, exiting the terminus point in a battle-ready V-formation.

Admiral-of-the-Fleet Jakub Halvorssen sat on the bridge of the *LhSS Emperor's Fist*, leaning forwards in his chair.

"There's no sign of the attackers?" he demanded once again of his scanners officer.

"None detected, sir."

"Order the squadron to spread out, I want a search pattern for any survivors," he ordered. "Keep lively people – they may still be here, running silent."

He stood up and began to pace the bridge, receiving report after report. Some of the interstellar mining ships had jumped to Lindholm systems with hyper-pulse communications generators, and so the message had flashed light-years across space to where he had been located on a training exercise with his squadron. It had taken them only two jumps to make it here to Graviticus, a mere four hours after the attack in real-time and a half-hour after they had received the message about the assault, but in transit-time through hyper-space it had been the equivalent of nearly a week and a half out of his life.

The space station had been utterly destroyed. The system was awash with small lifeboats and life-pods, transmitting distress signals now the unknown enemy had disappeared. The highly lucrative mining operations in the Graviticus System had been permanently disrupted. All the interstellar mining ships had jumped out, and the ones not capable of interstellar travel had retreated to safe distances. Many would doubtless be awaiting pick-up, to leave the system, their parent companies unhappy with the events that had unfolded here.

"Admiral," his second-in-command approached him with a data-slate.

"Yes, Commodore?"

"We have picked up this image from the *SS Gandolf*, a mining ship out on the edge of the largest asteroid field here. The image has been found on a couple of other targets too, etched into the hulls with low-powered turbolasers."

Admiral Halvorssen experienced a sinking feeling. He had seen this before. He wordlessly held out a hand for the data-slate, depressed a small button, and the data-pad projected a holographic image into the air.

It was a cross, in the style of the old Christian religion, with a very simple skull outlined on the traverse length.

"It's the Pirates of the Cross," his Commodore said quietly.

"They've struck us – again!" Admiral Halvorssen slammed the data-pad down onto the floor in disgust.

*

The young man opened his eyes slowly. His head was banging, a result of the alcohol from the night before. He stretched in bed and yawned, sleepily relaxed, before the events from last night came back to him. Jerked more awake by the recollection, he turned his head to the side, seeing the depression in the pillow. He felt the warmth still coming from that side of the bed.

He sat up in the small room of the apartment. The kitchen unit was recessed into its alcove, and the small bureau table had been extended out. A naked woman sat at the table, the person he had met last night, her clothing over the back of the single chair in the room.

"Morning," he said, a silly grin on his face.

"Hey," she replied. She turned slowly, "sorry, what's your name again?"

Feeling slightly taken aback, then realising he could not recall her name either, he shrugged and said, "Juan Ramirez."

"Nice to meet ya," said the woman. She was about the same age as him, late twenties or early thirties, which was nothing in a time when people could live for centuries with rejuvenation treatments and advanced surgical medicine. "You a spacer?"

He swung his legs out of bed and stood up, equally as naked as her. He collected his clothes from the floor, and waved his hand over the sensor. He stepped out of the pit, the suspensor bed rising up into ceiling as the living area – a three-seater sofa and a table – rose up out of the recess. "Yeah," he said groggily, waving again to bring the kitchen unit out.

"Which ship?" she asked.

"None," he sighed. "I'm looking for a berth. You wouldn't happen to know anyone taking on?"

"No. Try the IMG boards."

"I do. Every day."

He walked over to her and went to kiss her neck, but she moved, standing up. "I'd better go," she said. She had a number of docker tattoos on her arm, obviously employed at the local space-port. "I've got to start my shift in half an hour."

"Oh, OK," he said. "I'll see you around then." On the bureau was the hololith she had activated, carrying his credentials. There was the licence from the Interstellar Merchants Guild, which was due to expire in less than three months, and his certificate from the Guild's School of Navigation. His passport was on display as well, the new issue from his home nation of Cervantia. House Cervantes had been one of the first Houses to declare itself independent following the Battle of Mars and the death of the False Emperor.

He felt as if some of his privacy had been invaded, but then, he guessed she had woken up with some rough kid she had never met before and it was only natural to wonder who he was. He looked at himself in the mirror over the desk; his youthful features were tired, strained with stress and hangover, his mousy brown hair ruffled and cheeks unshaven. He considered once again whether he should grow a small goatee in the typical Cervantian style, to make himself look older. He was far too young and inexperienced a Navigator for many ships to hire him on.

"I doubt it," she laughed.

He pulled out the coffee from the synthesiser unit, and when he turned, she was fully clothed. As a rough docker, she was heavy-set, bearing the bruises and marks of the straps from a lifter-walker. "Shit little pad you've got," she said.

"It's my last day," he replied, "I've not got much more money. I'm on the streets tonight," he said, half-hoping she would pick up on the hint.

"Good luck with that, spacer-boy," she laughed. She caught his look and meaning. "There's always the homeless hostels run by the Interstellar Red Cross and Crescent Society. You won't be on the streets."

He really did not want to go to one of the charity hostels, but he had no other option. "Were you born to natural parents, or vat-grown?" she asked.

"I was vat-grown," he replied.

"Can't you go back to the vathouse then?"

"I've no money to get there, and I wouldn't go back to that hell-hole anyway." Many people were vatgrown, created out of molecular soup from different donors or even synthesised genetic material, to provide populations for colonised planets. The family unit did not really exist anymore, and the workers of the vathouses acted as surrogate parents for many. It was not unknown for vatgrown adults down on their luck to go back to their vathouse, but not every vathouse welcomed their former children with open arms, and his certainly would not. He would not go back there if he was paid to.

"Well ..." said the woman, trailing off, lost as to what to say. He thought she looked a little guilty. Not that much of a hardened docker then. She was looking at his desk again, "What's the fascination with the borgs?" she asked. "The Hero of the Levitican Union?"

"Them?" he asked. He had no intention whatsoever of telling her. "I just like keeping interested in what's going on."

"I'd worry more about your own life, than the lives of these fucking augmented half-humans," she said. The use of the words sent a chill down his spine, and whatever attraction he felt towards her went. Cervantia was a very humanist nation, and very anti-borg. Most Cervantians were pure human, unaugmented.

That was why he worked so hard to keep his cybernetic nature a secret. Anti-borg sentiment was on the rise in Cervantia again, a back-lash against the pogroms of the False Emperor.

"I'll be seeing you," he said, as a way of seeing her out.

She took the hint there as well. "I doubt it," she said again, laughing, and walked out of the small room he had rented.

Juan Ramirez collected his bag of clothes from the floor – he was too poor to afford a hovering travel-droid. He had a rucksack too, and he began to clear the desk as he prepared to leave. He picked up the hologram she had looked at – it was a representation of the *SS Vindicator*, the battlecruiser commanded by Admiral James Gavain. Stories of his heroic actions in the Levitican Union had gained massive popularity across the galaxy, mainly because he had been successful against the StarCom Federation, seen by many as attempting to forge their own second Red Empire.

He had all number of hololiths, holograms and holorettas about the Vindicator Mercenary Corporation, James Gavain, and the *Vindicator* battlecruiser. He had a huge interest in the borg ex-Praetorian Guard mercenaries.

He put it all in the rucksack, had one last check to make sure he had everything, and then left the small apartment he could no longer afford.

Juan Ramirez walked along the wide walkway up to the space-port. Hover- and repulsorcraft flew by overhead, decelerating for their entrance into the large commercial docks. The planet of Costa Biancia had a thriving tourist industry, as well as having a strong heavy industry, being an agricultural exporter, and a commercial hub. He still could not get work here.

He looked up and saw a space-ship taking off, heading up to the skies. Another two were coming down. Despite the economic woes the dissolution of the Red Imperium had caused, trade still flowed.

He thought again about the *Vindicator*. As soon as Gavain and his mercenaries had become poster-boys and –girls for the Levitican Union, as well as celebrated for standing up to the might of StarCom, he had recognised the images of the ship.

It had been the *Vindicator* that had attacked the convoy he had been a part of. He had been a navigations officer aboard a small cargo-freighter, one of thirty-six crew, and very proud to have such a position at such a young age. They had been running military supplies to the front, back when Cervantia had been at war with Hausenhof and also Korhonen. The *Vindicator* had changed all that, capturing the *Featherlight* cargo-freighter, and dispossessing him and the crew he served with. They may still have the ship for all he knew. The last he had seen of it had been through the port-hole of their life-pod as they span away from the stricken freighter.

They had eventually been rescued by the Cervantian military, although much too late to be of any use. They had been brought back here, to the Costa System, but otherwise abandoned to their own devices. The crew had scattered, the Captain unable to keep them together.

That had been nearly six months ago, and Juan Ramirez had finally run out of his carefully safe-guarded money. The wars with Korhonen and Hausenhof had left many dispossessed spacers, many with more experience than him. He was also restricted in what he could apply for because as a Borg, he could not risk detection, as many companies and ships used the stricter medical checks that would 'out' him. Being a borg was not illegal, but it was becoming more and more inadvisable in the increasingly-humanist nation of Cervantia.

As if to underline the point, as he crossed into the main entrance hall, his eyes lit upon a scene at one of the customs checkpoints. Two Cervantian enforcers had wandered up to the checkpoint, pushing past the queue of people, and stood there watching, but not interfering.

There was a man on the floor, bleeding profusely. Two or three people were kicking him. There had been some kind of disagreement in the queue, and when the man had got to the front, his passport had marked him out as a borg. Juan was just thankful that his implants had been added after birth, and his passport did not carry any such identifiers.

The birth-borg was being set upon by a number of humanists. One of them wore a stylised 'H' armband, above the symbol of the Cervantian nation, proclaiming him as a hardline extremist. Juan shivered and walked on, ignoring the scene, reflecting that it was just one more example of how more extreme the Cervantian nation was becoming.

After a short journey through the space-port, he came to the offices of the Interstellar Merchants Guild. Showing his ID, he was permitted through security, and he made his way along the familiar path that he had taken every day for the last six months to the Hiring Office.

He walked in. It was a fairly average day, with the same disappointed faces before him. As he walked up to a free terminal booth, he waved his hand over the sensor. He had paid for a month's access to the IMG Hiring Boards, and had about two weeks worth left.

He scrolled through the adverts, and applied for a couple that he knew might not have the stringent medical checks he was desperate to avoid. After he had finished, he felt suddenly exhausted and overcome with emotion. He was so tired of having to do this, day after day, and not getting anywhere. He collapsed his head into his hands.

"Are you alright, sir?" a voice said.

He looked up. Instead of droids, the Interstellar Merchant Guild tended to prefer real live humans to man their various offices. He was looking into the face of one of the most handsome men he had seen for a while.

He could not help but smile as he saw the man's eyes widen. The mutual attraction was obvious.

By the time he was walking out of the Hiring Office, he did not have a job, but he did have somewhere to sleep that night, at least.

*

"The mercenary Admiral James Gavain, my lady," the man stood at the door announced.

"See him in," said Lady Sophia Towers, putting down the data-pad she was reading. She stood as the servant moved aside, bowing, as the tall mercenary leader entered her private chambers.

He was of an athletic build, which was only accentuated by the trim black military jacket he wore. It was modelled on the old Praetorian Guard uniform, black with red trim, but it had the stylised logo of the Vindicator Mercenary Corporation sewn into the breast and a huge V across the back. He bore the Imperial rank of a full Admiral, five crimson red stars between two red bars, on each short Nehru-style collar. The mercenaries were in business for themselves, but they had not forgotten their roots as Praetorian Guard elite.

He had short hazel brown hair, revealed as he removed his cap and bowed in her presence. As he straightened, he subjected her to the full force of his icy blue-grey eyed stare. He was incredibly hard to read, impassive, frosty, in most circumstances, although she had seen the warmer side of him that he reserved for people he counted as friends. She hoped she was a friend, although she was not sure; at best, she was the co-Director of the Vindicator Mercenary Corporation, his business partner.

"My lady," he greeted her, "Hope you are well," he added with typical brusqueness.

"Indeed one is, James. Please, take a seat."

He strode forwards and sat before her, looking around the chambers before he did so. Her suite of rooms was located in the Tahr Citadel, a fortified city within a city, which had seen much damage during the StarCom invasion. It was the new capital of House Towers, one of the founding members of the Levitican Union. The rooms had survived the war intact, and were as ostentatious and richly decorated as she could make them. Precious little had survived the destruction of the former capital of House Towers.

"You summoned me, my lady?"

"Not quite. Thank you for making the journey over in person," she said. "One could have had this discussion via hyper-pulse, however."

"I wanted to check on the repair of my ships," he said, "and the progress on the Tahrir Base," he referred to his secret base, located on the southern pole of the planet Tahrir.

"All goes well?"

"Tahrir Base is almost completed, and the ship repair is proceeding to schedule," he replied. "Although it is too slow. We have been out of action for almost two months."

"Many ships require the use of one's shipyards," Lady Sophia pointed up at the sky. "One has to serve the Levitican Union military, as well as one's mercenary company, equally. We have made enough of a hero out of you, without being accused of favouritism."

"I am uncomfortable with this hero-worship," Gavain said, grimacing.

"It was necessary. The Levitican Union needs time to recover, and heroes to stand behind. You were instrumental in devising the strategy for saving us, James, as well as recovering Blackheath from the enemy and defending it once re-taken. One would not have her capital system if it were not for you."

He merely nodded his head, accepting the praise, clearly uncomfortable at the way the conversation was going. That was unfortunate, she thought. Her perverse nature was going to enjoy this.

"We still have need of you," she said.

He looked up, one eyebrow raised. "A new contract?" he asked. Technically, although the Vindicator Mercenary Corporation called the Blackheath System and House Towers space a home, they had no tie to the House, or the Levitican Union. He had defended them under a major, very expensive contract. Even though Lady Sophia was a co-Director, she could not command them into defending the Levitican Union without his say-so. She would have to offer terms.

"No, it is not a new contract one wishes to discuss with you," she replied serenely. "Rather, the nature of your hero-status to the Levitican Union."

"I am not interested, my Lady," he replied.

"Please hear one out. We need heroes, as said, and the galaxy now views you with some worship. Many hated the StarCom Federation under Nielsen, and all it stood for. We need something to recognise you, Admiral. We in the Levitican Union have re-instated the old Imperial Knighthoods declared obsolete by the Second Emperor, especially for you and some other war-heroes. One would be highly honoured to knight you oneself."

She laughed out loud at the look on his face.

"You are enjoying this too much," said Admiral Gavain. "I am tempted to say no."

Here it comes, thought Lady Sophia. The green military man had taken very well to the mercenary business. "Only tempted?" she asked.

"Such a thing does not interest me at all," he said. "But I can see your need for it, perhaps, although the logic is distressing to me. I would only say yes if there was something in it for my mercenaries, of course. So what are you willing to offer?"

"What are you willing to accept?"

He paused, but she could read him to this extent. He had obviously been waiting for an opportunity to ask this, and had taken the opportunity when it presented himself. "We need our own shipyards," he said. "I now have fifteen ships-of-the-line, and fourteen support ships. In return for accepting this knighthood, I want your permission and resources to build a shipyards and military station above the south pole of Tahrir."

"This can be afforded can it?" asked Lady Sophia, amused. She laughed again. "You know, most people would be highly honoured to be knighted. You turn it into an opportunity."

"You taught me well." Gavain suddenly smiled, his icy demeanour melting. "We can afford it, my Lady, and we need it. We can build most of it ourselves, but will need some of the resources from your other companies."

"They will be provided at preferential rates," Lady Sophia nodded. "Show me the business plan, and the drawings, and we can agree it."

"Excellent," said Admiral Gavain. "Then you shall have your knight to parade around the galaxy. Just remember I still maintain my independence from the Levitican Union and House Towers."

"Although this will tie you closer to us," she pointed out.

"We were tied to you the day I agreed to the building of Tahrir Base, and the contract to defend the Union," Gavain shrugged. "But we still need this distinction, my Lady. I do not speak of it, but I do keep abreast of the politics of the Levitican Union. I have no wish to be dragged into its affairs."

"Certainly not," she said.

He hesitated, and then said, "But as a friend, Lady Sophia, I must ask – how are things between you and Lord Micalek Zupanic?"

She smiled, but she was sure the man read the fact it was false. "One's husband-to-be?" she asked. "They are good. Why do you ask the question?"

"House Zupanic and House Towers may have called the marriage pact to bind your houses together, but I know much has changed since it was first proposed," said Admiral Gavain. "I am asking after your happiness, Lady Sophia, and to ensure that it still suits you."

"It does," she said. She was aware that she had been terser in this conversation than Gavain, almost as if they had traded their usual roles, and her last reply had been too defensive.

He paused for a long time. "I do not believe you," he sighed, standing up. "Lady Sophia, I have a few friends left. I lost some in the civil war, others in the end of the Empire, more still recently in the Levitican War. You are one of the few people I know, left alive, that I count as a friend. If you need to talk, then please do. At any time."

She was taken aback. Such an emotional speech was something she had never expected from James Gavain. "Th – thank you, James."

"You are welcome," he said, affixing his cap. "Until you need me, my Lady," he saluted the Imperial way, right fist thumping on left breast.

Chapter II

Lord Principal Ramicek Zupanic tapped the metal ball onto the small disc in front of him, a musical chime ringing out across the Council Chamber. Lord Minister Luke Towers was careful to behave as he always did in front of the ruler of the Levitican Union, giving no indication as to his true feelings. He made sure he did not stare, made sure to keep himself professional and statesmanlike at all times. In some ways, he still felt it should be his half-sister, House Lady Sophia, here in the Council of the Union rather than him, but they were where they were.

"Order in the Chamber," the Lord Principal called out. The various conversations and mutterings died down.

Since the destruction of the capital on Leviticus, a new seat for the government of the Levitican Union had been chosen. A hasty amendment to the Charter of the Union, its constitution, had decided that the capital of the Union should be a planet within the territory of the House of the Lord Principal. As the Council had fled to Zubrenica XIX, a moon in orbit around Zubrenic Prime, that was the new home of the Council for the foreseeable future.

It was not as grand as Leviticus Megapolis had been, and certainly less comfortable, but the six council members and their entourages had settled in on the moon of Zubrenica XIX. Lord Minister Luke had the senior members of his ministry, the Ministry of Military Defence, around him, as did the other Ministers around the circular table.

"The recess is over," said Lord Principal Ramicek. "We have all had an extremely long day, so we move into any other business. I do have something I wish to propose to the council, but first, I open the floor."

I move to you have you replaced and tried for treason, you murderous bastard, thought Lord Minister Luke vehemently.

"I have a matter I wish to raise," said Lady Minister Monique Lapointe.

"You have the floor," said Lord Principal Ramicek Zupanic.

Lady Minister Monique stood, tall and imposing with the raven-black hair and sharp features of her mother, who was the ruling Lady of House Lapointe. Lady Monique was Minister for the Ministry of Economic Affairs and Trade.

"We are seeing increased piracy along the Galetti and Claes borders, which is severely affecting trade. It has been relatively minor so far, certainly in comparison to the piracy which is spreading throughout the Mid-Sectors and the Core, but it is escalating rapidly. It is beginning to threaten trade in the easterly to southerly parts of the Union. I wish to ask Lord Minister Luke what he intends to do about it, and to propose that we increase military presence along the affected region."

She sat back down, and Lord Principal Ramicek focused his evil eyes upon Lord Minister Luke.

Luke stood up. "I am aware of the piracy, but as Lady Minister Monique pointed out, we are not suffering as badly as some other states in the Eastern Segment. We are still repairing and rebuilding after our considerable losses during the war with StarCom. We just do not have the forces to spare, particularly in view of the potential aggression of House Jorgensson on our Lapointe, Towers, and Obamu borders. For the moment I propose to do nothing, but see if it escalates. We must withstand the losses, and concentrate our efforts elsewhere."

He sat back down, and Lady Minister Aria Galetti merely commented loudly, "We must defend your borders, Lord Luke, but not that of House Galetti?"

He rocketed back to his feet. "This is not about House politics or any self interest on my part, Lady Aria. This is about defending the Union. House Jorgensson views the Union with hungry eyes, and we are greatly weakened. They have a huge appetite to annex parts of our territory, and have done for nearly a century. They believe they have the opportunity. I protect us against the greater threat – hostile House invasion, compared to the relative pin-prick attacks of the pirates."

"Lady Minister Aria's assertion was unfair, and shall be struck from the record," Lord Principal Ramicek announced. "However keep the answer in the record. We do not have the appropriate information to take a vote – Lord Minister Luke, I charge you with presenting an analysis for how best to deal with the piracy with our limited resources, with a number of options for potential response, and Lady Minister Monique, please provide an analysis of the economic impact of the attacks for our session in two days time. I now open the floor again. Is there anyone else?"

Luke sat back down, somewhat surprised that the hated Ramicek Zupanic had called an end to the debate that quickly.

Luke sat quietly with little to contribute as the discussions continued. Lord Brin Claes, the worm that was definitely in Lord Ramicek's pocket, wanted to introduce a new law in relation to immigration, the nuances of which escaped Luke. They did vote on that, and it was accepted, although Luke abstained. Lady Monique took the floor again, to propose the raising of taxes, something which was vehemently opposed by Lady Aria on the basis that the people could not withstand higher taxation. This debate was shelved again by Ramicek, who requested more data from both in support of their arguments.

Lord Ramicek eventually revealed the reason for his impatience. "If there are no more, then I shall speak," he said. "I wish to propose something entirely new. The houses of we six formed the Levitican Union on the planet of Leviticus. We have already faced many trials and tribulations, we continue to do so, and we no doubt will face them in the future. However, we may not have to do this alone. I wish to propose something radical ..." he hesitated for effect, "the joining to the Union of a new House."

The other ministers, Lords and Ladies of the Houses, began to speak at once, but Luke remained silent. He carefully controlled his reactions, but wondered what new Machiavellian plan Lord Principal Ramicek was throwing upon them now. Anything Ramicek brought to the Council Luke automatically viewed with suspicion, despite the fact his sister and leader of House Towers was about to marry Ramicek's son, Micalek. Because of that fact, amongst others.

Ramicek called for quiet, and then continued speaking. "I speak of House Marchenko. House Lord Gregori Marchenko contacted me directly, requesting an audience, which I granted. They border Zupanic and Claes territory, and were greatly worried by the StarCom invasion of our holdings. They wish to join, partly for mutual protection, but also because they see the value in what we are trying to achieve with the Union."

Lord Moafa Obamu stood, his dark ebony skin and vicious tattoos making him seem even more ferocious. "What is the meaning of this!" he demanded in his thick accent. "Lord Principal, you completely undercut my position."

"No slight was meant," Lord Principal Ramicek held his hands up. "Lord Mikhail knows me of old, and felt comfortable approaching me. I will propose a vote, that we entertain the suggestion and allow them to send a delegation for us all to hear. You will of course lead the arrangements and any negotiations, Lord Moafa."

Moafa narrowed his eyes, and then sat slowly.

"It seems sensible," said the sycophant Lord Brin Claes. Lord Luke looked at the man. He had lost more and more respect for Brin Claes. He was definitely a stooge for Ramicek, having virtually sold his political support to Ramicek in return for favouritism that Ramicek showed only very carefully and rarely. House Claes had once supported House Towers, but that political alliance had come to an end quite abruptly. "I propose we vote now on the inclusion."

"We need more information," Lord Luke shot to his feet. "A vote is precipitous at this point in time. Apologies Lord Brin, but that is a ridiculous suggestion." He sat back down, knowing only that he was risking a grilling from Ramicek Zupanic as to why he had openly opposed the plan. He was supposed to be working with House Zupanic, not against them, but Luke knew nothing could be further from the truth.

"Agreed," Lady Minister Monique Lapointe seconded him. "It would have ramifications for all our ministries," she added.

"Would we all agree at least to a vote to hear the delegation?" Lord Principal Ramicek asked. "With no commitment to accepting the proposal? We can all review the facts and make our cases afterwards." He received no objections, so the vote was called.

Lord Luke leaned forwards and hesitated over the 'nay' and 'abstention' holographic buttons in front of him. He was desperate to know what Lord Principal Ramicek was up to with this proposal. He had to know.

He hit the 'assent' button.

The votes came in. Lord Principal Ramicek grinned widely. "A unanimous vote," he said. "We will hear the delegation. This Council session is declared closed."

Lord Minister Luke Towers strode out of the Council Chamber, carefully avoiding all contact with anyone. He headed directly for the part of the complex that housed his own ministry, went to his personal office on the other side of the war-room, and closed the door.

He had barely sat down when the intercom bleeped. He depressed the holographic button on the display that popped up over his desk. "Yes?" he asked.

"You have a visitor, Lord Minister Luke," one of his ministers said. "A Miss Elaine Carrington."

"Show her in," Lord Minister Luke said, leaning back in his suspensor-chair. He straightened his Levitican Union uniform, and awaited her arrival.

An elderly woman entered the room, but every single ounce of her being radiated pure strength. She was nearly three centuries old, and had known his father, the late Erik Towers, for most of those centuries. She had faithfully served House Towers as their head of intelligence for decades. She was known as The Spider to those who both worked for her and against her.

"Elaine, please sit," he gestured at the chair opposite. "This is a very rare visit."

"Luke," she said, one of the few who would ever address him without his title. "We have had some new intel."

"It doesn't relate to House Marchenko, does it?" he asked.

"Luke? I'm not following."

"I'll tell you in a minute, but what do you have to tell me first?" he asked.

She grimaced. "I would not trust this to a message, or a comms," she said. "Sometimes the old method of delivery, mouth to ear, is best." Without any further preamble, she launched into her explanation of the information her network of spies had come across.

Luke Towers went colder and colder as he listened. Eventually, when she had finished, he said, "We must do something about this. I want you to go to the Blackheath System and tell my sister, immediately. We must capture the target before he is moved again."

"I agree," said Elaine Carrington. "But to strike into Zupanic space? You could cause a major incident, undermine the Union."

"Tell Sophia to contract her mercenaries to do it, using her own funds," Luke growled. "I know she will not object over this. They will give us deniability if they fail, but they also have the greatest chance of success."

"Very well," said Elaine. "Now then, Luke my boy, what was it about House Marchenko you want me to find out about?"

*

As he approached, the guards in the emerald green ceremonial uniforms, white-coloured breastplates shining in the light, saluted with open-hands to their white-plumed ceremonial helmets. The doors opened as he passed.

The relative peaceful calm of the corridor was shattered, as he emerged into the new Throne Room of Tahrir Citadel. Formerly a large eating hall, it had been completed renovated to suit its new purpose. A large dais at one end of the room held two thrones, upon which sat Lady Sophia Towers and her husband-to-be, Lord Micalek Zupanic. Rows and rows of suspensor-seats were arranged before them, with nobles and dignitaries present from all six Houses of the Levitican Union. They were talking amongst themselves in low voices, the susurration of multiple conversations combining into a great roar that assaulted his ears.

The roar quietened instantly as the herald raised the vox-caster to his lips. "Admiral James Gavain!" he announced in the thunderous tones of a god, the reverberations dying away as the assembled crowd fell silent. Lady Sophia and Lord Micalek, who had been sat patiently awaiting his arrival, both looked up from whatever thoughts they had been engaged in.

Admiral James Gavain walked down the central aisle, his gait steady and confident, and his face as impassive as ever. Inside, he was wondering at this unusual position. He was an ex-Praetorian Guard naval officer, a military man, who today had been waited upon by some of the richest and noblest people in the Levitican Union. Admittedly, his actions had ensured they still had a nation to call their own.

As he neared the dais of thrones, he saw that the front row of seats on his right had been given over to his command staff. All of them were assembled here today. General Andryukhin, ignorant of any protocol, raised a hand in a thumbs-up signal, grinning widely. It was nice to see him happy, for once, Gavain reflected of his old friend. Commodore Andersson sat there, a strange look on his face, one eye slightly teared. Andersson was much more than just an old friend, but he had also been Gavain's mentor since the days of the Red Imperium. The handsome Captain De Graaf was openly enjoying the spectacle, arms folded, looking relaxed and as if he was enjoying the show.

Gavain was uncomfortably aware of the holo-camera droids hovering in the air above and all around him, control crews set up near the dais, with more hand-held cameras for special shots. This would be appearing on holo-retinal vision news channels all across the Levitican Union, and beyond.

He saluted in the old Imperial style, and then bowed his head and upper body slightly.

Lady Sophia looked to her fiancé, and then stood slowly, gathering her long skirts around her, the expensive material flowing out. She looked like a queen, Gavain reflected. She was the Head of House for House Towers, and no-one could be in any doubt that she looked the part.

"Lords, ladies, gentlemen and gentlewomen," she began, "we are gathered here today to honour a hero of the Levitican War. Without Admiral James Gavain, whose strategic foresight and advice was invaluable to my brother the Lord Luke, and in fact formed the basis of our entire response to the StarCom Federation invasion, the Levitican Union would not be here today. Houses Claes, Galetti, Lapointe, Obamu, and Towers all suffered heavily under the Federation invasion, and we owe our thanks to the Admiral." She glanced at her husband-to-be Micalek Zupanic, and Gavain noted the odd exclusion of House Zupanic. It was factually accurate, to be sure, as Zupanic had not really been a subject of the StarCom invasion, but her husband merely smiled his devilish smile encouragingly.

"Admiral James Gavain was single-handedly responsible for saving the Blackheath System in direct military action," Lady Sophia Towers continued, and James began to cease to listen. He was excruciatingly embarrassed by the whole ceremony, and those of his command staff who knew him well had been merciless in the fun they had poked at him, but it was all a means to an end. House Towers and the Union would get their hero, and he would get his shipyards and starbase above the planet Tahrir. He wanted this over as soon as possible.

At some point during the speech, Lord Micalek Zupanic had stood, and he was now walking down the dais towards James Gavain. He held Lady Sophia Towers' staff of office in his hand.

"James Gavain, kneel," Lady Sophia said.

He knelt, moving gracefully onto one knee, knowing what to expect as he had been fully briefed beforehand. He lowered his head to the floor, after looking up at the form of Micalek Zupanic. Sophia's fiancé was one of the many sons of Lord Principal Ramicek, and he carried the strong family look, but he was also a very accomplished warrior and carried a brutal reputation. One of his many nicknames was The Butcher of Balthazar. He wondered again how truly happy Lady Sophia was, but in public at least, they appeared to be very happy in each other's company.

As Sophia spoke, Lord Micalek slowly moved the staff from one of Gavain's shoulders to the next. "One knights you Sir Admiral James Gavain, the first knight of the Levitican Union, ward of House Towers, protector of the Blackheath System, and a master of Tahrir with the freedom of the planet. Arise, Sir Admiral James Gavain."

As he came back to his feet, the Throne Room erupted in applause, suspensor seats whining as their occupants stood, a thunderous roar far in excess of the one before assaulting James Gavain.

General Ulrik Andryukhin stood to one side of the large master reception hall, staring out of the large wall-length window across the night-shrouded city of Tahrir, lost in thought. It was beautiful at night, with the scars of the recent war hidden by the embrace of the darkness.

Behind him, the hundred or so people invited to the reception after the ceremony chattered amongst themselves in small groups as they awaited the main meal to begin. He felt truly alone, even surrounded by all these people.

"Rik," he heard a familiar voice say gently. "Something interesting out there?"

Ulrik Andryukhin came back to the present, shaking his head and blinking. "No, James," he said sadly. In the reflection of the glass, he watched his friend James Gavain exchange a glance with Commodore Harley Andersson. Andersson touched him on the arm lightly, and then walked away to talk to someone else, leaving him and James alone.

Ulrik felt a flash of irritation. He had known of the relationship between Harley Andersson and James Gavain for years. James would probably have felt uncomfortable over the open display Harley had just made, if he knew his friend, and that irrationally annoyed Ulrik even more. They were lucky that they could behave in such a way and still be together, and he had to swallow his bitterness, reminding himself to be more mature about it. It just reminded him of his loss.

"You do not seem to be yourself," James said quietly. "The Ulrik I know was always the centre of the party."

Ulrik Andryukhin continued to stare into the glass of the window. Captain Lucas De Graaf was not far away from them, a glass of orange juice in one hand. He was completely teetotal nowadays, and never touched a drop of alcohol. The handsome man had three ladies around him, and was beginning to develop a bit of a reputation for the women in the mercenary outfit. Lady Sophia Towers was on the far side of the room, arm in arm with her fiancé Lord Micalek Zupanic. Everywhere he looked, he could see couples, flirting, attraction. He felt even more alone.

"It's just a mood, James, nothing more," Ulrik replied.

"We all miss Jules," Gavain said simply.

Ulrik was somewhat surprised. James always appeared to be ignorant of the emotions of people around him, and it had been Julia Kavanagh who had always said to him that James was cognisant of a lot more than he ever revealed. On a level deep down, Ulrik appreciated this, which was why they had formed such a strong group of friends in the past, before her death in the Levitican War.

"It . . . I will never forget," said Ulrik Andryukhin. In the Praetorian Guard of the old Empire, relationships were highly uncommon and even against regulations, but they had still happened. The one between Gavain and Andersson had been very informal and casual, but since the dissolution of the Guard and the Empire, they had become more and more overt about it. Ulrik and Jules Kavanagh had begun to share a single cabin, before she had been assigned to another ship, the same ship which had been utterly destroyed.

"None of us will," James Gavain said. "I miss her too, Ulrik."

"Silus Adare took her from me," said Ulrik Andryukhin. "I would give real money to know where he was."

"We might find him one day," James said quietly. "And when we do, we will not be returning him as a war-criminal to the courts of the Union, trust me. But until we do, I wanted to ask if you would be offended if I honoured Julia's memory. I am thinking of naming the new base we construct above Tahrir after her – Starbase Kavanagh."

Ulrik was quiet for a short moment. "That would be good, James."

James Gavain looked like he was going to say more, but then he simply nodded, slapped Andryukhin on the back, and walked away. He knew his friend was concerned about him, but the loss of his lover was something Ulrik Andryukhin had to deal with on his own.

*

Juan Ramirez entered the walkway's cafe in the downtown slum of the Cervantian city, limbs stiff. He was groggy, not having slept well. The enforcers did not like people sleeping rough in most of Biancia Polis One, but they did not police the slums to the extent they did elsewhere. He had found a quiet place to sleep rough behind a bonded warehouse, and for the last couple of nights had not been moved on.

The cafe was twenty-four hour, but even this early in the morning it was full of truckers and workers either between shifts or skiving off from work. He had to queue for the droid behind the counter to take his order. It was an old-fashioned way of serving food, and he was not really in a public facing mood today, but he needed a meal. He had a little money left, but it was dwindling rapidly.

He paid the Imperial quarter-shilling for his breakfast, and went to a booth to await its arrival. The booth was enclosed, so he had some privacy. The shiny surface of the table showed him how rough he looked.

He felt like crying.

The breakfast was served and he began to eat it hungrily. As he did, he reached out a hand blindly and activated the data-point built into the side of the table. A holographic display sprang into life before his eyes. He waved a data-waver over the terminal's scanner, his own personal details logging him straight into his mail account.

There were six new mails, four of them spam. One was from an interview he had attended last week, but such was his mood, he could not be bothered with it. It was probably just another rejection. He selected the other mail, a news article pulled up by one of his searches on the Vindicator Mercenary Corporation.

He read about the knighting of James Gavain. A secret borg, he would have loved to join them, and had even thought about applying for the Vindicator Mercenary Corporation, but he knew they tended to prefer ex-Praetorian Guard personnel. Another application he would never be able to be successful in, due to the competition. Despite the fact he owed his current circumstances to the mercenary outfit, his initial resentment had turned into passive interest and then active admiration of their exploits and contracts.

He finished his breakfast, putting the eating wand to one side. It was antiquated, and had kept misfiring as he tried to eat, causing him to slobber much of the meal. He wiped his face with a sonic cleanser, and then reached out a hand and depressed the icon for the second mail on the holographic display.

His eyes widened as he read.

"Yes!" he shouted out, causing the other people in the cafe to turn round and stare, some angrily.

He had been accepted as a navigations and scanners crewman on board a long-haul Cervantian cargo-freighter. There was no medical required, and he had to report for duty at any time within two days.

He remembered the interview. The female captain had seemed to be interested in him as more than just a possible employee, he remembered realising. It did not matter – he had employment. The SS *Yangtzee* Type-III cargo-freighter was due to leave Costa Bianca in three days time, on a long-haul multi-stop journey further out into the Mid-Sectors, into the Outer Sphere and on towards the Boundary. It would be the furthest he had ever travelled.

Happier than he had been in a long while, and actually whistling, he left the cafe with a bounce in his step, heading to the starport to report for duty today. No more sleeping on the streets for him.

*

Commodore Harley Andersson emerged from the turbolift onto one of the lower decks of Tahrir Base. Tahrir Base belonged solely to the mercenary company, constructed in secret and at great expense in the southern hemisphere of the planet Tahrir. It was built into the side of a snow-covered mountain, only a small proportion of it on the surface of a plateau cut into the side of the mountain range, the majority of it underground.

Commodore Andersson had left the Janus Shipyards, taking the majority of its equipment with him, and had journeyed to the Blackheath System to join James Gavain's mercenary outfit, which then had consisted of one ex-Praetorian battlecruiser, and some captured Cervantian ships. Andersson had greatly increased the size of the Vindicator Mercenary Corporation, joining his sometime lover and together forming a formidable mercenary unit.

Much of the equipment from the Janus Shipyards Praetorian base had been unloaded here, and now resided comfortably within Tahrir Base. More of it had been moved following the Levitican War, hidden in a number of caches across an uninhabited solar system used by the mercenaries as a training ground with House Lady Sophia's permission. The process of hiding much of the equipment in caches was still on-going, Admiral Gavain determined to spread risk by separately locating his company's resources and assets as much as possible.

Commodore Harley Andersson walked through the subterranean corridor of the base, on Level 11. Levels 10, 11 and 12 were reserved for the medical facilities of the VMC. The Vindicator Mercenary Corporation, under his guidance, had installed a fully-outfitted suite of medical bays, in-patient and out-patient wards, operating theatres, storage rooms, medical research labs and more on Level 10. It was an underground hospital. Levels 11 and 12 held much more than that; they held part of the future of the VMC.

He emerged into the control room, which overlooked the cavernous hall. The control room had a small number of medical operators on-duty, responsible for overseeing the largely automated systems within. Through the windows of the control room, he could see into the hall. It was a breath-taking sight.

The Accelerated Growth Biovats were stacked in rows, three AG-Vats on top of each other in orderly columns. Level 11 held twenty-five hundred AG-Vats, and each one was currently in operation.

Andersson descended on the stair-lift, and began to walk across the hall. It was quiet, although he could hear the voices from the people he was walking towards reverberating off the tanks which towered far above him.

He looked up, feeling almost paternal. The AG-Vats were nearing the end of their first cycle. It took just three months to cook up a new person, constituting them from molecular soup. Adults would emerge from the vats, covered in a special gel solution, already with their first cybernetic implants in place and with advanced knowledge of the world around them and varying levels of mature intelligence provided by educational programmes begun and continued throughout their growth.

They were using Praetorian Guard Imperial programming and bio-artificery. Some would become Marines, super-humans capable of great physical feats, whilst others would become front-line Naval crew, and yet more would become Auxiliary Support. Those judged most capable would be placed onto fast-track post-vat education programmes, to become junior officers.

Every three months, Tahrir Base could produce twenty-five hundred new mercenaries. In between two to four months from there, those twenty-five hundred mercenaries would join active operations. Tahrir Base had swung into full operation, desperate to replace the losses they had suffered during the Levitican War. Even with full operation, they still had to advertise for replacements on the open market through the Interstellar Merchants Guild.

Andersson approached the small knot of people clustered around one of the data-points at the end of a rank of vats. He saw James, tall and lean, hands on hips, staring up at the vats towering above him.

Next to him stood the Chief Medical Officer. Doctor Erin Presson. CMO of all medical facilities within the mercenary company, she was in charge of this facility in addition to her other responsibilities for all medical operations aboard the starships and the medical frigate they had captured during the Levitican War. She was a Praetorian herself, and had come with Commodore Andersson when they had abandoned the Janus Shipyards. He had served with her for decades, and had a great respect for her.

"Sir Admiral," Harley said, enjoying the grimace on his lover's face, "How is the inspection going?"

"Good, Commodore," Admiral Gavain replied, formal in front of other people. "And it's just Admiral."

Erin Presson turned to Andersson. "The first batches are due to be born in two weeks time, Commodore."

"How fast time passes," Harley commented. "I can't wait."

"We need the people," Gavain replied. "I am nearing the point where we have to start taking on new contracts."

"Do we need to?" asked Commodore Andersson. "We were exceptionally well-paid by the Union. We made billions of Imperial Crowns."

"Which are being drained by the repairs, the hiring of new crew, and the construction of Starbase Kavanagh," Admiral Gavain shot back. "We have a regular payment as well for the technology I sold to the Union, but that is not due to kick in for another year. We do have significant reserves, but we are a mercenary unit. We need to get back out in the field, Harley, and earn money."

"We're not at full strength."

"Some of our ships and ground forces are," said Gavain. "I am about to begin looking at new contracts. Do you want to review some with me, later?"

"Of course," Andersson said, happy at the suggestion of some time alone.

*

The five ships exited the warp, leaving hyper-space with a blinding flash of white light. Their forms were elongated, but snapped back into normal forms within a moment as they fully translated into real-space. They drifted forwards at a slow speed, the exact same velocity they had been making when they first entered the jump. They had safely materialised within the CD-891 System.

Captain Neill sat in the command seat of his bridge, on the tanker SS *Icelandic Pride*. The *Pride* was carrying a highly precious cargo, a vast tonnage of fuel for mass drive engines of starships, power generators for all manner of equipment, and many more purposes besides, the various grades broken down within a number of internal hull walls. It had been purpose-built for such transport, and within its hold, it carried enough fuel to meet the energy requirements of a small planet for a year, or a fleet running indefinitely.

Scans started automatically, searching for any other ships in the system. It was completely deserted, apart from them. Neill checked the holographic representation of the scan read-out, seeing the two cargo-freighters to either side of the small convoy, each carrying vital supplies for House Lindholm. Two House frigates were arranged fore and aft of the convoy, the Admiral-of-the-Fleets for House Lindholm now insisting that all strategically critical convoys of starships be protected by military escorts in response to the increase in piracy.

Captain Neill had read the reports. House Lindholm seemed to be suffering badly from the predations of a small number of pirate starships, rogues who called themselves the 'Pirates of the Cross'. They seemed to be targeting the small nation-state of Lindholm, newly seceded from the dissolved Red Imperium. There were all sorts of rumours as to why, but the popular theory was that the neighbouring nation-state of the Helvanna Dominion was behind the attacks, as a prelude to invasion.

"We're receiving the all-clear from the frigates," his comms operator said, bent over her console.

"Begin preparations for the second jump," Captain Neill said.

Their next jump would take them onto one of the busy trade routes, where they should be safer due to a higher traffic of starships. They had deliberately planned this route to minimise their stop-overs in uninhabited systems, where they were open to predation.

"Er, Captain .... there's some strange readings out there," the scanners officer suddenly said.

Out in the depths of space, the void rippled as a large starship suddenly revealed itself, chameleonic fields dropping. Emblazoned all across its hull were the symbols of the Christian cross and the skull mounted on its cross-piece. Completely stationary, the Interdictor was built upon classic Praetorian Guard lines, two nacelles for jumping extending out from the underbelly, a bulbous nose and boxy aft breaking its otherwise sleek lines. The special ship had activated its gravity well generator, a device which was designed to disrupt all warp-fields, preventing ships from jumping into hyper-space. The net was cast so wide, the convoy was trapped in the system.

It sat there, making no attempt to move within firing range, simply waiting.

The two armed frigates shielded up, glittering force fields sparkling as they accelerated away from the convoy towards the Interdictor. The convoy was ordered to pull back, heading for the extremes of the gravity well to try and reach a safe point to jump out-system.

The frigates had not pulled far away from the convoy when the dreadnought dropped its chameleonic fields above them. A dreadnought was a huge capital ship, the heaviest in existence, carrying unbelievable firepower, capable of engaging several battlecruisers at once and winning. The small frigates did not have a chance against the Pirate of the Cross super-capital ship.

Chapter III

Lady Wyn, wife to Lord Principal Ramicek Zupanic and the second most powerful person in the House of Zupanic, strode down the corridor, her personal honour guard flanking her to either side. She had married into the Zupanic household over a century ago, and with her husband they had created a formidable team, bringing stability following the excesses of her husband's insane father. She headed the shadowy intelligence services of House Zupanic, an arm of the House machinery that was feared more greatly than its military ever would have been. Mother to a large brood of sons and daughters, wife to the leader of the Levitican Union, and feared within and without Zupanic territory, she was not someone to be trifled with.

Tall, wearing a high-collared cloak in pre-Dissolution High Imperial fashion, her steely gaze swept the room as she entered it, taking in everything in a glance. She came to a stop, arm-length gloved hands on her hips, legs wide as she stared around her, the light catching the grey beginning to show in her raven black hair.

She could feel the thrum of the deck beneath her feet, the prison ship *LSS The Rock of Alcatraz* throbbing through hyper-space as if it were alive, or cognisant of its own fearsome reputation. *The Rock* was infamous for many reasons, its long service history within House Zupanic being marred with many bloody and terrible rumours.

She smelt the ozone in the air, coming from the force field before her. One of her bodyguards was currently deactivating it, the greenish ripple in the air dropping as they were permitted through into the first section of the high-security wing of the prison ship. She had to withstand another four such protective fields before she finally entered the high-security cell area.

"Xavier," she called out on entering the inner sanctum. "What progress?"

A handsome male turned, his deep brown eyes widening. He looked so innocent, Lady Wyn thought to herself, but as with so many of the Zupanic family, the exterior hid the monster within. "Mother," Xavier Zupanic said. "When did you board?"

"One boarded before the last jump," she said, voice cracking like a whip. It was rich, well-cultured, and spoke of the education which lent it the Imperial received pronunciation. "One will be leaving when *The Rock* next translates. One has come to see what progress you have made with your latest toy."

30

Xavier clapped his hands together childishly, beaming suddenly, excited to be showing his mother. Poor Xavier, she thought, a genius in so many ways, yet frighteningly cruel in the most unthinkingly childish way possible. His grandfather had bred true in him through Ramicek, that was for sure.

"Yes, lets," he said, taking his mother's hand and leading her through to the central hexagonal room. In the centre of the room was a stasis tank, a bio-vat full of a specially charged gel-like liquid that would hold its occupant immersed and sedated. Stasis tanks were usually used for medical treatments and surgery.

"What are the life-signs?" Xavier asked.

"Dormant, Lord Doctor Xavier, but healthy," an orderly replied.

"Leave us," Lady Wyn told the medics inside the room. She even dismissed her guards. "Show me," said Lady Wyn.

"I am rendering down his brain," Xavier almost slobbered in excitement. "The subject was not responding to the usual stimuli, these Faceless are obviously well-conditioned against such techniques. We've removed all its suicide triggers, so when it is brought out of hibernation, it can't self-terminate. There was some interesting technology there, I'm thinking –"

"Do we have it under our control?" Lady Wyn asked, interrupting to keep one of her younger sons on topic.

"Not yet, no, mother," Xavier pouted. He strode up to the stasis tank and stared in, almost lovingly. "The rendering is still on-going, I did say that."

"I know, Xav," she said.

"We have been able to extract some more information, however. This Faceless assassin was the one who took out King Ibbe Weiberg, and before that it assassinated the Praetorian High Command on Mars, did you know that?"

"The Praetorian High Command?" Lady Wyn breathed. "You have it all recorded?"

"As we delete the memory, I record it, so yes, of course, mother," Xavier actually sounded wounded.

"I will review that recording later, with great interest," said Lady Wyn. "Have we discovered its origins yet?"

"No, I still have a way to go," said Xavier. "We are trying to replace the wiped portions of its mind with re-programming, but again, it's highly resistant. I have never seen technology like it."

Lady Wyn strode forwards and stared through the tank glass. In the murky liquid, she could see the sleeping form of the cybernetic biomorph. It was able to change its form at will, and when it was at rest it had reverted to a black synth-suited figure - the material actually seemed to be a part of its morphing biology. They were the ultimate assassins, virtually undetectable. That House Towers had caught this one at all following the assassination of Lord Erik Towers was highly remarkable.

It was a sign of how successfully House Zupanic had fooled House Towers that they had surrendered the assassin who had killed their head of house with no hesitation.

*

Lord Micalek Zupanic stepped off the travellator-droid, onto the metacrete flooring of the launch-pad. He turned and extended a hand, aware that the holo-cameras were recording the scene as he assisted his wife-to-be in stepping down to the ground.

He was wearing the Levitican Union military uniform, primarily emerald green with white trim. They were the old colours of the House military for House Towers, but the Ministry of Military Defence had made them the Union's new colours. Lady Sophia was resplendent in an expensive souul fur cloak, the grey and white hide closed over her body and a hood pulled up over her head. He felt the cold late evening air whistle around his ears, military buzz-cut and flat-cap providing no protection from the winter weather approaching from the south of Tahrir.

"Thank you, my love," said Lady Sophia. She linked her arm into his as was their habit, and they began to walk across the starport, a close security detail around them, with enforcers preventing the holo-camera crews from following them any further.

"We're the new darlings of the media," said Lord Micalek. "It wasn't like this before our engagement was announced," he added.

"Nor for oneself," Lady Sophia replied.

They were forced to use the commercial Tahrcity Starport, as Lady Sophia's residence in the centre of the city had no personal landing pad, at least not one large enough to take a space shuttle and certainly not a space ship. Towers Manor was currently undergoing a major reconstruction to turn it into a palace suitable for a House Lady, following the destruction of House Towers' former palace, but it would be some time before it was ready. Until then, Lady Sophia and any noble guests were forced to use Tahrcity Starport.

Lady Sophia found that she did not mind in the least. Her time as head of house had come before it was expected, and even then, it was her brother Luke who should have been head of house.

Lord Micalek stopped before the noble barge, *LSS First Carriage*, which rose far above him and his Lady. Not only space capable but jump-capable, it was also the replacement for the *LSS First Ship*. The *First Ship* had been destroyed during the Levitican War, having been the personal conveyance of the House Towers lords and ladies for decades.

"Sophia," Micalek said gently, pulling her round and staring lovingly into her eyes, "I will have to leave you here."

Sophia stared back, careful to return the loving look. It was only half-contrived. She had been falling in love with the man she was forced into a political marriage with, at least until the truth had been revealed to her. Every time she looked at him, she wondered whether he was a part of the House Zupanic plots against her House; part of her wished him to be innocent, unknowing of the lengths his father had gone to, but another part of her knew how unlikely that was.

"It is a shame, Micalek," she lied. In truth, the strong mix of her emotions towards him made her relieved to be getting away. The horror of not knowing what he knew about the death of her father was extremely emotionally tiring.

"A shame?" he teased, gently pulling her into a hug. He had the typical Zupanic strength and size, combined with demonically handsome looks. "We will not be together for a whole month."

"When do you leave for the Zubrenica System?" she asked.

"The *Divine Right* is transporting my mother there, and then it's coming down to pick me up," he replied. "It should be only four days time."

"May the Emperor watch your steps," she said, quoting an old Red Imperium saying.

Micalek Zupanic laughed pleasantly. "That was a curse as well as blessing, under the Second Emperor," he pointed out. "If you did not have to leave, we could have those four days together."

"The people of one's House are suffering, Micalek," she replied. "One has delayed this tour of the worlds savaged by StarCom for too long."

"I thought you just couldn't wait to land in the arms of your mercenary admiral," he teased.

"Such jealousy? Hardly," she flirted, "One is not of interest to him, in any case."

"You do have an eye for the men, don't think I haven't noticed."

The playful and flirting tease was at once an amusing and hurtful reminder of that short space of time they had known each other before she had come to suspect Micalek's hand in her father's murder. "One must go. The noble barge is getting ready for lift-off."

"Farewell my lady. May the Emperor watch your steps," Micalek hugged her once more, then stepped back and saluted for the distant holo-cameras.

She bowed in return, then with not a word more, turned and began to walk up the red-carpeted boarding ramp.

At the top of the ramp she looked back over the launch-pad. Lord Micalek was walking away with his close security guard, heading back towards the travellator-droid and the crowd of media reporters. She watched him walk away, every move confident and strong.

All the while, in her peripheral vision and out of casual sight, was the head of intelligence for House Towers, Elaine Carrington.

Admiral James Gavain cancelled the holographic image on display in front of him, as the computer software controlling the door to his ready room aboard the *Vindicator* pinged him to tell him his visitors had arrived. <Enter,> he commanded it, over the datasphere.

He remained jacked into the ship's datasphere as his visitors entered. Lady Sophia he knew of course, but they had only limited information on the second visitor, an Elaine Carrington. He downloaded the data-file on her into his brain, absorbing what information they had in the blink of an eye.

His cybernetic implants made it easy for him to read the bio-signals of both. Lady Sophia was agitated, her heart-rate abnormally high, and he was detecting the same signs of stress he had in their previous conversations. Elaine Carrington, also known as The Spider by popular myth, was in contrast very calm and collected.

He stood and bowed to the Lady Sophia, as she said, "Sir Admiral, one does not believe you have met Elaine?"

"I know who you are," he said simply, gesturing to a chair. He had a cup of coffee on his desk, the old-fashioned cafettiere still warm. There were two empty cups, but both declined his pleasantry.

"So what do you know of me, Sir Admiral?" Elaine Carrington asked. Despite her centuries-old age, her voice was strong.

"What the Imperial archives hold on you, Pre-Dissolution," he replied with typical shortness.

She appeared to be as icy as he was. She merely tilted her head back, crossing her legs, and said, "Precious little, then, Sir. I have reviewed the file, recently. It is also inaccurate."

"It is of no consequence," said Gavain. "You are in the employ of Lady Sophia, much as I am from time to time."

"It is that we are here to discuss," Elaine Carrington said.

"Your employment?"

"Yours, Sir."

He leaned back in his chair slightly and said nothing, holding The Spider's gaze.

The silence continued overly long, until Lady Sophia broke into the contest of wills. "James," she said, her voice unusually low and now absent of its Imperial inflection. "How is the space station construction faring?" She had stood and had crossed to the small observation window in his ready room.

He stood with one last look at Ms. Carrington, joining her at the window. He stared out into space. The southern hemisphere of Tahrir obscured a large part of the view, but it was possible to see the first constructoships moving around what would become the housing for the main power generator. "Eventually it will be a combination shipyards and space station, and we will manufacture our own Praetorian-designed ships. Some we may even sell to the Union. We are constructing it to an Imperial standard template; it will be completely modular, so we can add sections when we wish to. But we have just begun, Lady Sophia," he said. "As you know. Is everything alright with you?"

"No," she shook her head, looking at him suddenly. He registered the pain in her eyes. Her heart rate had increased.

"What forces do you have at your immediate disposal?" Elaine Carrington interrupted.

"That is classified," he replied abruptly, turning away from Sophia to sit opposite the head of House Towers' intelligence services. Lady Sophia moved away from the window, but remained standing.

"I could probably find out," The Spider replied.

"Doubtful," Gavain said. "Even off-contract, we keep OpSec tight."

"Have you been looking for contracts again, James?" Lady Sophia asked, changing topics again, he noticed.

"Yes," he said. "As you are here, if you would like to co-sign." He held out a data-pad to her, mentally downloading the contract information onto the slate. "It is a contract for armed convoy, low-risk, but a decent pay-out, and it will allow me to test the performance of some of my newer crews. My three cargo-freighters and the two frigates will take on six runs for Hausenhof, allowing me to continue to foster our business relationship with them."

"They are suffering predations from pirates, most likely privateers from Korhonen or Cervantia, or both," said Elaine Carrington.

"That is correct," Admiral Gavain nodded.

"The three Houses have a truce, but it is unlikely to last long between any two of them," said Ms. Carrington.

"That is our assessment, as well," said Admiral Gavain.

"Of course," said Lady Sophia, passing her personal data-wafer over the pad. It registered the signature, and she handed it back.

Gavain frowned. He had expected more of a challenge from Lady Sophia. She had not even asked how much the contract was worth, or any further questions. This Elaine Carrington was more engaged than Lady Sophia. It was most unlike her. "What is the purpose of your visit?" he asked, bluntly.

"You are very straightforward, Sir Admiral," said Elaine Carrington. "It seems my profilers were correct, and the file I hold on you is accurate."

He did not rise to the bait, but looked at Lady Sophia. "You are agitated," he said simply. "And you mentioned employment. Are you here about a contract?"

Lady Sophia blinked once or twice. "One – I, need to ask you a favour," she said. "Well, a favour of you and the mercenaries. It is highly delicate, for reasons I'm sure you will appreciate."

"We are not the personal army of House Towers –" Gavain began.

"It is a favour for me, James," said Lady Sophia. "Please, hear us out. Elaine?"

Elaine Carrington merely reached into a sleeve, and withdrew a data-wafer. She placed it on the desk before Admiral Gavain.

As a precaution, Gavain allowed the ships virus-checker programmes unrestricted access to his neural pathways before he picked up the data-wafer. An implant on the palm of his hand opened, and he scanned the data within.

He kept the shock from his face as his cybernetic brain-enhancing cogitation implant read the data and translated it into his conscious, organic mind. He sat back, sipping his coffee, reviewing it slowly. His two visitors were perfectly quiet.

It was a summary of a contract against House Zupanic, a supposed ally to House Towers within the newly formed Levitican Union. There was a prison-ship, *The Rock of Alcatraz*, which was transporting a highly sensitive prisoner to an uninhabited system in Zupanic territory, a solar system that went by the name of Obrenovac. The Obrenovac System was used for some very limited mining operations, but apparently, House Zupanic had a small, secret military installation there.

He reviewed the plans of the installation, assessing them quickly, even as he continued to read the report. The contract was to recover the prisoner, who was apparently nothing other than a Faceless assassin. His current condition was unknown. He might be conscious or held in stasis, but intelligence indicated he was at least still alive. There were plans for *The Rock of Alcatraz*.

The contract would not be posted with the Mercenary Bonding Office of the Interstellar Merchants Guild. It would never be officially recorded anywhere. If they were captured, or their attempt to retake the prisoner was recorded and reported somehow, House Towers would not defend them. Without an official contract through the MBO, or a House-sanctioned letter of marque, they would be pirates in the eyes of Imperial Law.

"There are a number of questions," he said.

"We thought there might be," said Elaine Carrington, exchanging a glance with Lady Sophia.

"Why are you asking this of me? Why not use one of your own military units, or a snatch team from your intel services? Why an operation against House Zupanic, a member of the Union? I want the whole truth, or I will refuse – the risks in this are great."

"We will pay handsomely –"

"It is not about the pay," said Admiral Gavain. His steely grey eyes had gone ice-cold blue, a sure sign to anyone who knew him that he was deeply angry. "Something like this is not about the pay, my Lady. Explain to me."

"I'm sorry to ask, James. It's difficult to know where to begin –"

"Allow me," Elaine Carrington interrupted. She uncrossed her legs and stood. "There is a lot of information not contained within that wafer, and I would have thought less of you if you were not asking all these questions, Sir Admiral Gavain. Lady Sophia assures me you can know this, although, it is against my better judgement and my advice for it to be revealed to you. This cannot be written down, or recorded, or ever spoken of to anybody else. Do you understand?"

Admiral Gavain completely disconnected from the datasphere, un-jacking so his thoughts were once again completely his own. He felt that momentary disconcerted feeling, when he could no longer feel the presence of his crew, or the operations of the ship, as if they were mere extensions of his sub-conscious. After a moment he said, "Very well. Explain."

"We originally thought Lord Erik Towers was assassinated by the StarCom Federation, as a precursor to the invasion and the subsequent Levitican War. The Faceless assassin who committed the deed made a mistake in his escape, and despite killing many of the people in his way, was captured after being rendered unconscious."

"It is unheard of for a Faceless assassin to be captured," Gavain commented.

"But it was done," said Elaine Carrington. "Lord Erik was killed before he could announce that Lady Sophia was no longer to be heir to the house, and it would instead pass to her brother, Lord Luke. A week later, the Federation invaded, and amidst the war, all but a few noticed that House Zupanic were now in a position where they could potentially gain control of House Towers through a son or daughter produced through the marriage of Sophia and Lord Micalek."

"I and Luke postponed any decisions on the heirship, in the light of the invasion. After all, we almost did not have a landholding to pass on to any children of ours," said Lady Sophia.

"So how did the Faceless assassin end up in the care of House Zupanic?" asked Admiral Gavain.

"We passed him over," said Elaine Carrington. "It was Lady Sophia's decision, but I understand why it was made. At that point we had no real suspicions of House Zupanic's motives – the murder of Lord Erik looked like the StarCom Federation had committed it prior to the invasion. House Zupanic's Lady Wyn's interrogators are galaxy famous. StarCom invaded, Alwathbah was destroyed, the Union was falling apart. It was a difficult time."

"I remember," said Sir Admiral Gavain.

"We had some suspicions of House Zupanic's motives, but we thought they were limited to manoeuvring for power within the Levitican Union," said Carrington. "Then, post-invasion, my agents discovered that House Zupanic had secretly contacted StarCom, and offered to withdraw critical Zupanic ships from the Union's war-effort. It would have collapsed our resistance – your glorious plan, Admiral Gavain, would have failed if Lord Luke had not acted quickly in pushing the counter-attack."

"I see," said Admiral Gavain. He had wondered why Lord Luke had chosen the time he had to launch the counter-invasion. It had made little sense at the time, as personally Gavain had thought it too early. Now he could see why – he was pre-empting and forestalling a secret agreement between the invaders and House Zupanic.

"At the point when we realised just how extremely little we could trust House Zupanic's motives, it was too late. They already had the assassin they had contracted to eliminate Lord Erik," said Elaine Carrington. "The Faceless may have further information about the murder, and be proof should we ever need it to show the galaxy that House Zupanic were complicit in the assassination and not StarCom. We cannot have that assassin disappear into some Zupanic stronghold."

"I understand why you need to recover the Faceless," said Gavain. He looked directly at Lady Sophia. Now he knew why he had been picking up on such unhappiness about her whenever the marriage to Lord Micalek was mentioned. "Who in House Zupanic was complicit in the plot to assassinate your father?" he asked.

"We do not know," said Lady Sophia, "Another reason why we need the assassin back in our custody." She paused, and the pain was clear in her eyes once again. "Lord Ramicek and Lady Wyn definitely would have been behind it. We do not know if Lord Micalek was aware of the plot."

"It seems suspicious that when the bomb went off, Lord Micalek happened to have a personal force-field that protected both him and Lady Sophia. For the moment they need Sophia alive to ensure they have some claim to Towers territory, at least until the marriage is complete and there is a child to seal the bargain," said Elaine Carrington.

"I am sorry for you, Lady Sophia," said Gavain quietly.

Elaine Carrington continued. "We need that assassin snatched back, and quickly. We have no real House military, as all House militaries now serve the Levitican Union, only a small House Guard who are not equipped for a mission such as this. We could use one of my snatch-teams, as you called them, but that would be highly risky if we were detected. We need complete deniability. That is why Lady Sophia suggested you and your forces."

"We will pay out of my own personal money," said Lady Sophia. "Even House Towers' treasury is amalgamated within the Union."

"We would be pirates," said Admiral Gavain, "acting outside of Imperial Law. If we were captured, we would not have prisoner-of-war status, and could be executed immediately."

"We understand that," said Lady Sophia. "But much is at stake." She paused, and then asked, "You are the only person I can turn to. Can you do it?"

Admiral Gavain leaned back in his chair once again, taking the last sip of his coffee. He jacked back into the datasphere. In seconds he had accessed the information he required. His legendary strategic skills came to the fore.

"I believe so," he said, "but the risks are high."

"Any payment you wish," said Lady Sophia. "Money is no object here."

"The relevant part of my forces must jump immediately to be within the correct timescale. This will be no large-scale assault, but rather something much more subtle and unexpected. We will not be assaulting *The Rock of Alcatraz*, but the secret installation on Obrenovac X itself. *The Rock* will be too well-defended, and my losses would be too high. Something to minimise the risk of detection and identification is required."

"It would be suicide to assault Obrenovac X," said Elaine Carrington.

"Maybe not," said Gavain. "The Praetorians have better information than you on the facility – it was never secret to us, before the end of the Red Empire. Transfer the money, Lady Sophia. Leave the details to me. It will be done."

*

The figure walked down the dark corridor, augmented eyes easily countering the shadowed environment. A small honour guard of two agents walked behind him, their synth-skin suits jet black, making not a single noise as they escorted him to the end of the corridor. They wore white cloaks on their shoulders, each emblazoned with a particular symbol on their back.

The circular door irised open, and the figure walked through without even a hesitation in his steps. His guards stopped outside. He wore a long black cloak, hood pulled up over his head, and a face-mask that obscured his features. He was tall, but thin, and that was all that could be discerned about him. The only distinguishing features were the gold lines on the mask, delineating the eyes, the nose and the boxy mouth.

The holo-pit inside the Temple was as dark and shadowed as the corridor. It was a circular room, with a number of seats recessed into alcoves around a small dais. It was not particularly large, and the dais in the centre was emblazoned with a symbol. Very few people alive had ever seen the complex pictorial in its entirety.

The figure crossed the room to one of the nine seats, and sat down in one smooth motion. He did not even acknowledge the two other people in the room with him, but merely raised his head slightly into the air, and commanded, "Begin."

At his command, the holo-pit became active. There was a small delay, and then holographic representations began to appear. The people were in separate locations all across the galaxy, and at great expense, a continuous hyper-pulse communication was allowing them to link into this conference in real-time. They were all dressed identically to him, but had different colours highlighting their black face-masks. Six holographs shimmered into being, each one sat in one of the free alcoves.

"We nine of the Shadow Council are assembled," the figure said. As he spoke, his image appeared in the centre of the dais, to show that he had the floor and the right to speak.

"Hail the Master," each of the figures whispered.

The image of the Master whirled around, to face one of the holographic projections. This projection had blue lines on his black face-mask, as the only distinguishing feature. "Legate of the Fourth Circle," the Master addressed the figure. "Explain your efforts to recover our lost member."

His image whirled away, and the seated holographic figure of the Legate was whisked into the centre of the dais. "Council," the cloaked one said, "We have not yet been successful in locating the agent who was lost in the contract to eliminate Lord Erik, although we do have information. I have agents in place within House Towers and House Zupanic, at all levels, and we have not discovered where the assassin was transferred to. We know that the Lady Sophia handed the assassin over to House Zupanic, and that the assassin is still alive. He is currently in transportation on a prison-ship, to a location we have not been able to discern."

The blue-highlighted mask's figure whirled back to his designated seat, and a new image took his place. This projection had red lines on her face mask, and only the faint outline of her figure beneath the cloak gave her gender away.

"Legate of the Fourth Circle," the Legate of the Fifth Circle addressed, "The loss of my assassin is intolerable. We know he has not self-terminated. It is of the utmost importance that he is located and terminated immediately. What do you need to locate the assassin?"

The Fourth Circle Legate reappeared in the centre. "I need greater resources in the Levitican Union," he said simply.

The Master of the Shadow Council took the dais. "Legate of the Ninth Circle, answer the question. Can we provide greater resource?"

A shadowy figure with orange lines on his face-mask appeared. "We have another five hundred agents available in one month. We could release the batch to the Legate of the Fourth Circle early, although the final stages of their training would be incomplete."

The Master reappeared in the centre of the dais. "It will be done," he said. He revolved slowly, facing each Legate as he spoke. "Shadow Council, understand this. Only twice before in our centuries-long history have one of our Faceless assassins been captured. In both instances they self-terminated. In this instance it has not occurred. We must make every effort to procure his extermination. Collateral damage is acceptable, at any cost or level.

"We cannot be exposed. As soon as this prison-ship is identified, or we have other information, I want kill-teams to eradicate all trace and knowledge of our lost assassin. No information about the Faceless must survive."

Chapter IV

<Exit from hyper-space in three .... two .... one ..... we have translation.>

Lieutenant-Commander Jason Bramhall nodded unnecessarily, mentally calling up a holo-map of the system to be displayed in his minds-eye. <Passive scans,> he ordered. <What's out there?>

He waited a couple of seconds for the answer to come back. He had been a Lieutenant in Commodore Andersson's shipyards, and had joined the Vindicator Mercenary Corporation shortly before the Levitican War. He was trusted, and tipped for promotion, so when the VMC had captured six corvettes they had been formed together into a small support squadron and he had been put in operational command of all of them. He was highly pleased with the promotion, proud of his position, and determined to do his best for Admiral Gavain, Commodore Andersson, and the mercenary company.

<No ships detected at all,> the Sub-Lieutenant in charge of scanner operations informed him.

The *SS Adventurous* was an A-class ex-Praetorian corvette, the first ever class of ship manufactured by Martian Industries and as a model still in active service. Small and light, it was hyper-space capable and could land on a planet, making it perfect for covert operations, scouting, and a whole range of missions that the larger capital ships could not complete. There were typically sixty-five naval crew on board, and thirty Marines.

<Captain Markos has signalled us to commence the operation,> his communications Sub-Lieutenant said.

<Signal an affirmative,> he replied, knowing that the return signal would be sent back as a tight-beam data-squeal broadcast, difficult to detect by anything in system. They had jumped in as close as possible to the sun of the Obrenovac System, on the far side away from Obrenovac X and the secret Zupanic installation. <All hands, move to running silent.>

He glanced at Colonel Petra Raimes. She was fully suited up in her power armour, ready to lead the six squads of Marines into the assault. They knew each other from their days under Commodore Andersson in the Janus Shipyards, although he would not consider them to be friends as such. Technically, she was higher in rank than him, although aboard ship he had the final say on anything.

Most of the systems aboard the *Adventurous* corvette began to deactivate, running lights being extinguished and all stray emissions being dampened. The chameleonic field was activated, and as the corvette began its journey around the sun, it shimmered and disappeared from view, turning invisible.

It would take slightly less than two days for the *Adventurous* and the *Aggressive* to traverse the Obrenovac System to Obrenovac X. The *Remembrance* battlecruiser under Captain Danae Markos would follow behind, ready to provide heavy support if they were discovered and assist in their extraction. Discovery would be catastrophic – the whole point of the mission was to leave no indication as to their identity.

The mission to recover the Faceless assassin had begun.

*

The audience chamber spoke of the riches of the people who ruled the Compact. Two small thrones resided at the head of the audience chamber, not as big as the official thrones in the palace's Grand Hall. Star Marshal Ngu strode up to the empty thrones, and stood at parade-ground rest, straightening his uniform jacket slightly as he awaited the leaders of the Zhou-Zheng Compact to arrive for this audience.

Star Marshal Ngu was nearly a century and a half in years, but the rejuvenation treatments he took kept him looking young. He was not of any noble blood, but had risen from the rank-and-file, and his men and women loved him for it. He was as ruthless and vicious as any noble of either House Zhou or House Zheng, but he was absolutely devoted to the former Lord Zhou Ze, and by extension his new wife.

The audience chamber was empty apart from himself, a number of ceremonial guards, and the Solar High Chancellor Zhou Mao. Even though Mao was a member of the House of Zhou, Star Marshal Ngu did not trust him. They stared at each other inscrutably, neither displaying their mutual animosity. Zhou Mao was third in line to the throne, the son of Lord Zhou Ze, and also newly married to the former Lady Zheng Il-Sou's eldest daughter. There had been a rash of marriages between the two houses, binding them together very closely in the name of the Compact.

A door opened and a herald strode up to stand by the thrones. "All kneel for the Primarch and the Primarchess."

Even the guards went down to one knee and bended their heads as the Primarch Zhou Ze and Primarchess Zheng Il-Sou entered the audience chamber. They were both dressed in high-collared robes, panels on the collars depicting the new flag of the Zhou-Zheng Compact, the gold eight-pointed star of Zhou with the gold circle of Zheng in its centre, on a red, white and red tricoloured background.

They both ruled the Compact in concert. The Primarch Zhou and the Primarchess Zheng seated themselves upon the thrones, and after a long moment, the herald gave permission for all to rise. As the herald retreated, the hated Solar High Chancellor Zhou Mao crossed both hands into the opposite wide-cuffed sleeves, waiting for the audience to begin.

43

"Star Marshal Ngu, you requested this audience," said Primarch Zhou. "The court scribe will record it for history. Speak."

Primarch Zhou was an elderly man, his pointed beard half-grey with age. His wife was half his age, beautiful and radiant, and would inherit the sole rulership of the realm after Primarch Zhou's death – long may that be delayed.

"My Primarch and Primarchess," Star Marshal Ngu began, "I have come before you to make a request. To put it in context, may I have your kind permission to give you an update on the situation on the front?"

"We have reviewed it recently, but certainly you may," said Primarchess Zheng.

"Thank you, my lady Primarchess," Star Marshal Ngu bowed again. He nodded to the Solar High Chancellor, who used a control to bring up a small holo-map of a number of star systems, before Ngu and between him and the two rulers of the compact.

"This depicts Zhou-Zheng Compact territory," said Star Marshal Ngu. The map showed the forty-five star systems of the Compact. Nine of them were cross-hatched, to show that they were conquered territory. The Zhou-Zheng Compact was barely four or five months old, but already, their combined armies had launched into the hated borgite territories on their borders. They had completely subjugated a borgite House, and a month ago, they had launched an invasion of the borg House of Erdogan. The three systems they had taken from House Erdogan flashed red, but there were five systems deeper into Erdogan territory that flashed red and then the House Erdogan territory colour, a deep black purple.

"There are five warzones within Erdogan territory," Star Marshal Ngu began, "five solar systems we are currently engaged in, and if I may say, currently heavily committed to and bogged down within. In the Kyiv System, Odensa System and Chester System we are stalemated, with actions focusing on key planetary environments and the outcome still uncertain. In the Salmenko System we are slowly being pushed back, losing the battle. In the Hammerfall System we have made some small gains. This has been turned into a war of attrition - after our initial successes, House Erdogan appears to have adopted a strategy of holding us in place, not attempting to push us back but to grind our forces down."

"What do you attribute this strategy to?" Primarch Zhou asked. "Why do they pursue this course of action?"

"Their manufacturing base is bigger than ours," said Star Marshal Ngu simply. "They are on a war-footing, and in a small number of months, they will have new fleets and armies ready. They have instituted national draft. I believe they intend to hold us locked into these fronts, grind us down, and when we are weaker, they will push back in overwhelming force, and then subsequently invade our territory."

"Why not commit our reserve forces?" asked Primarchess Zheng.

"There is a significant proportion of the House Erdogan Army not yet committed," said Star Marshal Ngu. "I must keep our reserve ready to counter it when it is. At the moment, they are content just to reinforce or replace active units, which I will shortly have to do as our units become more battle-worn."

"What then is your strategy to counter Erdogan's apparent plan," Primarch Zhou asked, his slanted eyes narrowing.

"It is that I wish to speak of to you, Primarch and Primarchess. Firstly, we need to increase industrial capacity rapidly, with enforced labour if necessary. Secondly, I request permission to use our considerable monetary reserves to hire in mercenaries, to fight on the fronts in Kyiv and Odensa. Success there will allow me to roll across the front, conclude the theatres, and push on into the Erdogan heartland."

"Addressing the first request, where do you propose this enforced labour to come from?" asked Primarchess Zheng.

"House Erdogan slaves, my Lady Primarchess – military personnel taken from the PoW centres, and enforced selection from the civilian Erdogan population. Work camps can be established. Such a thing is against Imperial Law, but the Red Imperium no longer exists and both Emperors are long dead."

"This is a war against the borgite heresy," said Primarch Zhou, nodding slowly. "I approve of the idea of using the deviants to build our industry against them. What do you think, Il-Sou?" he asked.

She nodded. "I agree, Ze."

"Then let it be done. Solar High Chancellor, see to it immediately," the Primarch Zhou commanded. "And on your second point, Star Marshal?"

"I wish to hire mercenaries," said Star Marshal Ngu, "additional resource to tip the balance in the stalemated systems. The expenditure need not be for long, but we need a heavy influx of soldiers to tip the ground wars in both systems. I was thinking borg mercenaries – let us use their own kind against them. It would also give us a range of different tactical options to employ; my droids are being easily countered by the House Erdogan cyborg soldiers. We need to change tactics desperately."

"There is a delicious irony in this, also," Primarch Zhou Ze nodded. "It rails against my inclinations to use borg soldiery, but the more of them killed the better. Let it be done. Hire your mercenaries, Star Marshal, and pay them handsomely, but I expect to see results in very short order. It will be on your head."

"I understand, my Primarch."

*

The corvettes *Adventurous* and the *Aggressive* flew low over the surface of the planet Obrenovac X. The vicious sandstorms on the desert world were in full force, the atmosphere of the once-terraformed planet having been largely destroyed during the Pre-Imperium Drone Wars. Cities lay in ruins, their people long dead. The entire surface was ravaged, and the corvettes flew over the scenes of devastation, on their way to bring death once more to the Obrenovac System.

Being buffeted by the super strong sandstorm, the corvettes banked on the outskirts of a devastated city, and then started to come in to land. Shields were deactivated, and the hulls of the ships were being scored by the debris being carried in the sandstorm. As the *Adventurous* touched down, a large metallic container-tank was thrown against the hull, bouncing off with a tremendous clang and skittering away in the low-gravity.

<Colonel Raimes,> the voice of Lieutenant-Commander Bramhall came over the datasphere. <We're touched down. You have the green-light. Good luck, and good hunting.> The corvettes had ghosted in on the far side of the planet, away from the radar of the Zupanic military installation,

Colonel Petra Raimes sat in the command-variant of the *Rattlesnake* fast assault HAPC. The hover armoured personnel carrier was designed for stealthy insertions, trading armour for lightning speed and low profile to help evade detection.

<Thank you, Lieutenant-Commander,> she said. <We'll see you in one day's time, if all goes to schedule.> She closed down the private channel, and ordered the advance.

The carry-hold doors of the corvette opened, and she saw the devastating whirlwind of a sandstorm outside. The storm was rocketing past the open doors, and began to fill up against the right hand wall.

The *Rattlesnake* HAPC leapt forwards, going to full speed before it had even left the hangar. The other two HAPCs roared out after her. In the extremely low visibility it was impossible to see more than a couple of metres, and they stealthed, so she could not see the other three vehicles jetting out of the *Aggressive*.

She shook her head, wanting to laugh. Completely blind, they were on their way to assault an enemy installation. It was daring, and typical of Admiral Gavain to plan such a raid. She hoped her faith in his cunning was not going to be betrayed today.

*

Juan Ramirez coughed lightly, tired and wanting to go back to sleep. Someone was shaking him, and whispering at him to "wake up". He blinked once or twice, stretched, and remembered where he was. He smiled.

He rolled over in bed, looking up into the eyes of Captain Rosanne Diaz. "What is it?" he asked quietly, already knowing what she was about to say.

"You have to leave," she said, "it's getting close to the morning shift, and I don't want the crew to see you leaving my quarters."

"Aye, aye, sir," he said, swinging his legs out of the bed. He pulled his underwear on, enjoying the sight of the naked older woman. "Later," she laughed at him. "You have to go, now. Hurry, boy."

"Yes, ma'am," he said, saluting her mockingly as he shrugged his shirt on. "I don't think I can come back tonight, or tomorrow, the rest of the crew will be getting suspicious if I keep out of my bunk for too long."

"Good. I need the rest," she said, standing up and kissing him lightly on the mouth. She slapped him on the rear as he walked towards the door. "Tomorrow night, then."

"Tomorrow," he laughed, then nodded.

He left Captain Diaz's quarters, humming to himself as he walked along the deserted corridors of the SS *Yangtzee*. He passed only the occasional droid as he made his way down to the crew quarters. The cargo-freighter did not have many crew, and apart from the senior officers who had their own quarters, most people bunked together in one of the five sleeping quarters. Space was at a premium on the freighter.

He reflected on how good it was to be aboard the *Yangtzee*. As the navigations officer, he was on a decent wage packet, and it was building up his reserves of cash again. They had made a number of jumps, and were now outside Cervantian territory, travelling along one of the major trade routes towards the Boundary. He had been right though; Captain Diaz had offered him the job with more than just employment in mind.

He shrugged to himself; what did he care? He almost laughed to himself as he entered the crew barracks. The lights were off, and he took a moment to allow his vision to adjust in the darkness.

The sleeping quarters were almost empty. Two of the crew were sharing a bunk bed, but were fast asleep. The only other person in bunk at the moment was Second Cargo Mate Simeon Jimenez, chest rising and falling slowly.

He watched Simeon Jimenez for a moment, reflecting on how beautiful he looked asleep. He grinned, and then made his way to the bunk opposite.

"Juan," a voice whispered.

Juan stopped. Simeon Jimenez was awake after all. He turned around slowly. "You're awake?" he asked, reddening slightly in the darkness as he realised the stupidity of the question. He did not have to explain where he had been, as whether crew members went to sleep during their time off-duty was up to them, but he had been visiting Captain Rosanne Diaz with such regularity someone was going to get suspicious. He did not want to face any unwanted questions.

"Yeah," Simeon Jimenez whispered. He threw back the covers on his bunk bed gently. "Come here."

Juan's trepidation vanished, and he began to grin as he realised what was on offer. All thoughts of his liaison with Rosanne Diaz forgotten, he made his way over to Simeon's bunk.

*

The Rock of Alcatraz prison-ship had coasted in to achieve geosynchronous orbit with the planet Obrenovac X, precisely to schedule. Light shone out of its forward launch bay, and a shuttle-lander flew out, like a tongue extending from the maw of a monster.

It banked in space, and dived down towards the planet, heading for the thin atmosphere. Its nose barely glowed as it struck the upper regions of the planetary envelope, on a direct course for the whirling maelstrom of sand below and the installation hidden under the ruins of a giant city.

The Rock of Alcatraz conducted aggressive scans, searching all of space, alert for sign of any interlopers. They failed to detect the presence of the VMC starship *SS Remembrance*, the R-class battlecruiser stationary and hidden some distance away, protected by the very best of Praetorian Guard technology. If all went to plan, *The Rock* would never know they were there.

Colonel Petra Raimes stood in the control room of the installation. It was in reality a high-security prison, research station, and weaponry store. That House Zupanic chose to keep it secret from the rest of the Levitican Union she found interesting.

They had taken the installation successfully. They had left their *Rattlesnake* HAPCs out in the storm, traversed the last kilometres to the target on foot, and then infiltrated quietly during a swap-over in the guard. They had slaughtered the guard quickly, and then taken the security centre before the alarm could be raised. The senior staff had been killed in their sleep, the operators on duty taken completely by surprise.

Some of her squads had gone hunting through the medical research bays after the barracks were completely drenched in blood and death, whilst she personally had led the detachment to take the prison guards. The prisoners did not realise what was happening, as their overseers were despatched with precision.

They had the installation in their complete control within an hour of the initial assault, and had lain here waiting for another two hours, the *Rattlesnake* HAPCs being brought in under cover. They even faked patrols, so when the lander from *The Rock of Alcatraz* came in they would not suspect anything. The sandstorm not only made communications very difficult, but it meant that when the lander suddenly appeared in the skies above them, they had less than a minute to scramble to their positions.

<Here we go, people,> said Colonel Raimes on their battle-net, as the landing pad doors began to open.

The lander came in slowly, landing on the sand-covered ground. It rolled into the protective landing bay hangar, red lights flashing and casting long beams through the flying wind-whipped sand as the heavy blast doors began to close.

The lander's exit ramp was clanging to the metal floor, even as the doors banged shut with a final, thundering thump of metal.

Xavier Zupanic's body was wracked with a nervous shiver, and he giggled insanely, eyes twitching as the ramp of the shuttle hit the floor. He clapped his hands together, and said, "Come on, come on, let us get my little baby into his new home."

The armed guard, in power-armour suits, began to march down the ramp as a number of medical orderlies manipulated the hoverbed the stasis tank lay upon. A large mechanical arm attached to the hover bed had lifted the stasis tank containing the Faceless assassin onto the conveyance, assisted by special force field beams. The tank was kept restrained into place on the hover bed by even more force fields. The assassin floated peacefully within the tank, completely unconscious and utterly unaware of what was happening to him.

"Hurry, hurry, hurry," Xavier stamped his feet, "I want to play with my toy. You're taking too long!"

The hover bed floated out into the hangar floor. Xavier had now walked to the edge of the ramp, just behind it.

He was about to unnecessarily exhort them to greater efforts when the shooting started.

Colonel Petra Raimes strode up to the side of the hover bed. Praetorian power-armour was far superior to mere house military-made equipment, as was the training of her hand-picked assault squads, and they had cut through the enemy in under five seconds.

She strode up to the screaming man before her. The computer implanted inside her brain identified the man as Xavier Zupanic. She would review his file later, but for the moment, all she did was identify him, and blow part of his head away with her right shoulder-mounted laser.

<Squads three through six,> she commanded, <Take the rest of the lander. No prisoners. Squad one and two, secure the stasis tank.> She called her adjutant over, and asked the Corporal to use her boosted communications equipment to patch her through to Lieutenant-Commander Bramhall.

<Ghost One here,> he said.

<All is going well, Ghost One. We have achieved the primary objective. You may come and get us.>

<We'll be there in fifteen minutes, Ghost Two.>

The Colonel signed off without further comment. She ordered her adjutant to return the control room for the prison, and release the prisoners. They would make it look as if there had been a prison break-out. The story would not hold, as forensic examination and interrogation of any survivors following Zupanic reprisals would eventually reveal the truth, but their identities were secure and it would create more confusion.

She took a moment to stare into the stasis tank, curious despite herself. The Faceless assassin made her skin crawl within her armoured suit, the being even looking evil and dangerous when at rest. He twitched in his induced sleep, stirring the viscous gel-like waters of his tank.

Two hours later, the corvettes *Adventurous* and *Aggressive* broke the atmosphere of the planet Obrenovac X, and started to run silent as they made their escape. The mission had been a success, and they left without being detected by *The Rock of Alcatraz* prison-ship, on the other side of the sandstorm-wracked planet.

Captain Danae Markos checked her internal chronometer again, unable to hide her impatience through her body language from her crew. She was over two centuries old and very experienced, but she detested missions like this, where they had to wait for long periods of time. It was all a part of naval warfare however.

According to the mission time-line, the corvettes should have escaped hours ago, and already be running towards the point where they could safely jump out-system without detection. They had to maintain communications silence however, so there was no way of knowing.

Additional landers had launched from *The Rock of Alcatraz*, her captain showing impatience similar to hers. They had all tensed then. If something had gone wrong on the surface, and the corvettes had to escape under fire, this could get very nasty.

A lander reappeared above the swirling sandstorm's upper reaches, and once again Captain Danae Markos tensed in expectation.

Eventually, the *Remembrance's* communications officer said, <We have intercepted their communications, Captain. They have discovered the assault on the installation; they have not mentioned anything about us or the assault team. They're requesting additional assistance to contain escaped prisoners. They have recovered a Xavier Zupanic however, near-fatally wounded but still alive.>

<Damn,> said Captain Danae Markos. There were supposed to be no survivors. Hopefully he would not be able to identify his attackers, if he recovered. <No mention of the Faceless assassin?>

<They keep mentioning the absence of a stasis tank,> said her comms officer.

<That must be him, then. All hands, we're leaving this system. Helm, get us out of here.>

The *Remembrance* began to turn gently, coasting away from the planet. The prison-ship never suspected that the huge battlecruiser had ever been there.

Chapter V

Feldmarshall Horatio Grant winced as a gigantic tremor rang through the military base. "What was that?" he called out across the war-room.

"The western quadrant shields over the city have failed, sir!" an Oberleutnant working at one of the operations consoles shouted back. "An entire block has been destroyed under Compact guns!"

"Get those damn shields back up," Feldmarshall Grant said calmly to the General at his side.

"We're trying, sir," said General Zweigartner.

"Where's our own navy?" the Feldmarshall demanded. "Afterwards, I want to know how those Zhou-Zheng bastards slipped those destroyers in so close. And how the saboteur took out our power generators for the orbital guns. How long until secondary power sources are up and running?"

"Four minutes, sir."

"Fuck," he swore under his breath.

He could feel the entire building tremble again, a long, sustained shaking. He snapped his eyes to the real-time holo-map representation in the centre of the war-room, showing multiple turbolaser beams and torpedoes smashing into the city. At least they were not using weapons of mass destruction, but nevertheless, the death toll was going to be high.

"Compact troops are breaching the southern wall!" shouted out another Oberleutnant. "We have several hundred droid-troops in the city. I estimate two thousand will have breached within a minute. Heavy vehicles moving in with them, battlewalkers, SPOGs, and tanks."

"Shields coming back up! We have shields!"

"But the enemy are within the shield radius."

"At least the enemy destroyers can't target us," said Feldmarshall Grant to General Zweigartner. The holo-map image switched to show the scene above the planet. The enemy destroyers were already withdrawing back to safety, heading for the other side of the planet, and exchanging long-range fire with the squadron bearing down on them.

"The Compact forces in the city are negligible," said General Zweigartner. "Apologies for allowing this to happen on your visit, Feldmarshall, but –"

"It's alright, General, we are in a war and the enemy does do unexpected things some times," said Feldmarshall Grant. "I'll leave this in your capable hands. I'll be in your office whilst you finish this off."

"Yes, Feldmarshall."

Feldmarshall Grant returned the salute, and then marched stiffly up the stairs to the General's office. As the doors closed behind him he sighed heavily, removing the hexagonal cap from his head and throwing it on the desk. He helped himself to a glass of the General's real whiskey, and then sat down behind his desk. He called up a holo-map of the system.

The war theatre in the Kyiv System was brutal, and grinding both sides down. Morale was suffering, he knew, because of the longevity of the Erdogan nation's tactics, but ultimately his plan would prevail if they could hold onto this system and the others long enough for their new army to be manufactured and soldiers trained. It was in an attempt to boost morale that he had embarked on this tour of the front lines.

Kyiv was a small planetary system, with a weak sun. It held three inhabited planets amongst six inhabited moons, and one of those three was a super-planet seven times the size of Earth, named Kyiv Primus. Kyiv Secundus and its moons had fallen to the Zhou-Zheng Compact, but Kyiv Tertius was still in Erdogan control. Kyiv Quaternus and Kyiv Quinternus, both gas giants, were also in Erdogan control but their mining operations had been severely disrupted in the early stages of the Compact invasion, and were now no longer of any value whatsoever. The civilians had been evacuated from the gas giant stations and the mining and collection operations had completely ceased.

General Zweigartner, the theatre commander, had a relatively large number of naval starships in the system, but so did the enemy. Both sides were trying to protect the planets wholly in their control, whilst also maintaining a picket on their side of the planet Kyiv Primus. Other ships engaged in patrols, or ran silent and tried sneak attacks and raids on the other. All sorts of tactics were being employed, from false-jumps, to defensive patrols, to probe warfare. It was chaos in the Kyiv System; the Compact dared not launch a major naval offensive after their initial invasion had stalled, and Feldmarshall Grant's master-plan called for them to maintain a defensive position.

He zoomed the map in on Kyiv Primus. The large super-planet had three continents amongst numerous smaller islands. They held continent Eins, and a large part of continent Zwei, although Compact forces had completely taken continent Drei. Again, both sides had constructed massive defences on their sides of the planet, in addition to the defences that had already been in place. Mobile orbital gun platforms and power shield generators protected the ground forces from orbital bombardments whenever the naval picket lines shifted or there was a naval sally, and raids and sneak attacks were the most common form of warfare on the ground as well as in space.

The recent Compact sally was well co-ordinated, and had almost worked. A large Compact ground force had moved in on Kyiv Megapolis, the capital city which was still in Erdogan control, at the same time as the three destroyers had snuck in under stealth-conditions to launch their surprise attack. They had battered down the city's shields, but luckily only a small proportion of the Zhou-Zheng Compact droid army had managed to gain entrance. His cyborg defenders out-numbered them considerably.

Feldmarshall Grant leaned back in the chair, shaking his head and finishing the whiskey. He had hoped he could provide some insight to General Zweigartner, some tactical or strategic advice to swing the ground war in their favour. Unfortunately, he could see no magical answer. It would have to continue to be a brutal war of attrition.

He switched off the holo-map, and accessed his e-mail on a holo-screen display. There were a number of reports, but he automatically went to the military intelligence bulletins. There was one advisory note headed 'Mercenary Reinforcements for the Compact'. He selected it, and then read.

"Damn, really?" he slammed the empty glass down on the desk-top.

He re-read the report. It was confirmed. The Zhou-Zheng Compact had posted a number of contracts early this morning with the Mercenary Bonding Office of the Interstellar Merchants Guild. The MBO contracts were assessed as being high-value, guaranteed to attract some of the bigger mercenary outfits currently in operation across this part of the galaxy. Although limited information was available for obvious reasons, intelligence indicated that the Compact most likely intended for their new mercenaries to hit the front-lines. Start-dates for the contracts were fourteen days from now, or less. They were also accepting human or borg contractors, in an interesting twist. It was widely believed that the Compacts motives for the invasions were based partly on wishing to obtain Erdogan's vast industrial resources, but also extreme humanist racial hatred of the primarily cyborg nation.

He flagged the report and sent back a recorded holo-mail, demanding that he be kept informed as to which mercenary units were likely to accept the contracts. He needed information as to who was likely to apply, and what new forces were about to land on his front-lines.

*

<Admiral,> communications officer Lieutenant Forrest said to him across the datasphere.

Admiral James Gavain was sat on the bridge of the battlecruiser *SS Vindicator,* his flagship. He had been in a private discussion with Commander Saifa Al-Malli, his second in command of the ship. She was new, one of many ex-Praetorians hired on during one of their early recruitment drives on Parowa Czwarty, and he was still getting to know her in many ways. She had impressed him greatly during the Levitican War.

<What is it, Lieutenant?> he asked.

<We are being hailed from a ship that just jumped in from out-system. It is the Ambassador for House Lindholm.>

Admiral Gavain accessed the scanners, and located the ship of the Ambassador. An uplink from System Control told him that it was a private, scheduled flight. Most of the Ambassadors had withdrawn from the Blackheath System, heading to the Levitican Union's new seat of government. The unification of the six Houses of the Levitican Union had happened so quickly last year, that many houses saw little point in keeping full political presences amongst the individual houses. Externally, at least, the Union appeared to be politically stable. There were still embassies, but most were staffed by junior politico's, not full Solar Ambassadors.

<I will take it in my ready-room,> he commanded, standing up. <Commander Al-Malli has the bridge.>

He entered his ready room, the door closing behind him as he walked across to his desk. He passed the observation window on his way, seeing the construction of the new space station and shipyards underneath Tahrir. Commodore Andersson was doing well, and the construction was running ahead of schedule, but there was still some way to go until completion.

He sat at the desk and told Lieutenant Forrest to accept the transmission. A holographic image shimmered into existence before him, of a woman in the old Red Imperium standard dress for a Solar Ambassador.

He could not help himself. <Hail in the name of the *True* Emperor,> he said.

The Lindholm Ambassador laughed. It was quite a pleasing sound. <Sir Admiral Gavain,> she replied, <I am Ambassador Nyman, the special envoy to the Levitican Union for House Lindholm.>

<You are a long way from home, Ambassador,> he said. <You are supposed to be stationed in the embassy on Zubrenica XIX.>

<Indeed I am. I hope you realise that the message I convey to you in person is rated so important by my masters back home, that they felt it important enough for me to jump here especially.>

<I am the sole reason for you to be here?>

<Yes you are, Admiral.>

He blinked, once, slowly, whilst he thought. He accessed the latest intelligence on House Lindholm. It held eleven inhabited star systems, was primarily free-thinking in its attitude towards the cyborg/human question, and was currently a member of a mutual defence pact with two other houses. Rumours suggested that the new nation of Lindholm was about to form a more permanent alliance with the two neighbouring Houses.

They were close to the Helvanna Dominion, an exceptionally aggressive new nation formed out of the ashes of the Red Imperium. Led by a former General who had killed all of the previous house rulers, the Dominion and the former aggression of the StarCom Federation had been primary causes for the defence pact. Lindholm was also suffering excessive piracy, from a number of different possible pirate groups, but one particularly large and vicious outfit described as the Pirates of the Cross. The Pirates of the Cross seemed to consist of a number of ex-Praetorian Guard ships.

<Is it in relation to a contract?> he asked.

<It most certainly is, Sir Admiral,> said the Ambassador.

<A defensive or offensive contract against the Helvanna Dominion, or some form of contract against the Pirates of the Cross,> he said as a statement.

The Ambassador was good, she did not even react to his guesswork. <It may well be both,> she said. <The contract I have been sent to discuss with you does concern the Pirates of the Cross, but many amongst us think that the Helvanna Dominion may be behind the piracy, although we have no proof.>

<Explain the briefing concisely, Ambassador.>

<Very well, Sir Admiral. I'm transmitting a data summary to you now.>

He read the contract document, after it had been virus-checked, as the Ambassador continued to explain to him. <The Pirates of the Cross appear to consist of a large number of former Praetorian Guard ships. We need a force consisting of such similar ships in order to be able to defend against them; your mercenary company name was assessed as being the best unit this segment, Sir Admiral, which is why we have approached you directly. This contract is not being advertised on the board of the Bonding Office, although of course we will handle our transactions through the IMG.

<We are being hit all across our territory by these Pirates of the Cross. They are numerous and highly organised. They are causing severe disruption to trade and to our supply lines. They are also targeting House Rantanen and House Haugen-Berg. We fear the onslaught of the Helvanna Dominion, so regardless of whether they are behind these attacks or not, we need them stopped.

<Your secondary objectives should you chose to accept the contract, are to successfully defend the territory of House Lindholm from these pirates, and to discover whether they are operating independently or are actually privateers in the employ of another House. Your primary objective is to locate them, and eradicate them.>

Admiral Gavain had finished reading the contract. <It is certainly something we could do,> he said. <I find the terms interesting, but you are trying to buy us too cheaply.>

<This is very high-value!> the Ambassador interrupted.

Gavain smiled coldly, and the negotiations began.

Eventually the Ambassador sighed. <Very well, Sir Admiral Gavain. In return for a twenty-five million Imperial Crown bond from you, we will pay you an advance fee of fifty million Imperial Crowns once your ships are operational within Lindholm territory. We will pay you a further fifty million if piracy reduces in House Lindholm by thirty percent, and-or twenty million each for House Rantanen or Haugen-Berg. Upon discovering whether they are being backed or not, we will pay a further fifty million. We will allow you prize rights for ships captured, and partial salvage rights to fifty percent of total captures, in addition to ten million Imperial Crowns for every Pirates of the Cross ship destroyed or captured. We will pay four hundred million Imperial Crowns if you are successful in locating and utterly destroying the Pirates of the Cross organisation, such destruction to be identified as the elimination of a base or so severely handicapping the organisation they dissolve.>

<It is a done deal, Ambassador. Under the terms of our company charter, I must have more signatures on the contract, but I do not anticipate a problem there.>

<A pleasure doing business, Sir Admiral,> Ambassador Nyman actually bowed to him. <House Lindholm are very pleased to have you aboard and in our employ.>

<We will report in to your Admiral-of-the-Fleet Halvorssen in ten days time,> Admiral Gavain promised.

<Goodbye, Sir Admiral.>

<Emperors blessings,> he replied, and the communication was terminated.

He poured a coffee, smiling to himself now he was alone. He was very pleased with how that had gone. A new contract was well-overdue, and this seemed too good to pass up. Besides, there was another reason for accepting it.

On reviewing the intelligence she had released to him as the contract appendix, he had been given a holographic image of a T-class dreadnought. It could be any T-class ship, but there could not be that many T-class ex-Praetorian dreadnoughts in the Eastern Segment. It could quite easily be the *Thor's Hammer*, Silus Adare's ship. There was an old score to settle there, and in addition, the Levitican Union still had a heavy bounty on his head for the destruction of the planet Alwathbah.

Sipping from the coffee, he thought about the extensive ground forces he now owned. The Lindholm anti-piracy contract would employ only his naval ships. He resolved to find a separate contract, suitable only for his unattached Marine forces. He thought giving General Ulrik Andryukhin a contract of his own to complete may pull him out of his funk over Julia Kavanagh.

He dialled into the Mercenary Bonding Office, narrowed the selection, and read the results. The most high-value and acceptable risk contract was from the Zhou-Zheng Compact. They were virulently humanist, and very anti-borg, but then again so was Hausenhof and they had worked for them often enough. Business was business, he supposed.

He downloaded the contract, registered his interest, and was about to request that a long-range hyper-pulse contact be made through the HPCG station on Tahrir with Lady Sophia, when he was hailed by the scanners officer. Lady Sophia was currently on her tour of House Towers territory.

<Admiral,> Lieutenant Agrawal said, <The corvettes *Adventurous* and *Aggressive* have just jumped in system. No sign of the *Remembrance* yet, but the *Adventurous* reports that when the corvettes left the vicinity, the battlecruiser had still not engaged their target.>

Excellent, he thought. <Patch me through to Lieutenant-Commander Bramhall,> he commanded. If it was good news and they had indeed snatched the Faceless assassin, he would have a number of things to talk to Lady Sophia about.

*

Lord Minister Luke Towers, in his emerald green and white Levitican Union military dress uniform, was one of the last to arrive. He made his way to the head of the small crowd of people, his bodyguards falling back slightly. Public gatherings were still being avoided ever since the likelihood of assassination had been realised, under his orders. The Levitican Union government still resided in the reinforced military moon of Zubrenica XIX, after all, so they still adopted a cautious siege mentality.

He stood next to Lady Minister Monique Lapointe, at the end of the line of six ministers of the Levitican Union. Lord Ramicek glanced at him, no sign of rebuke for the tardiness on his face, but with no warmth of emotion either.

He looked up, staring at the gigantic orange-yellowy brown orb of the gas giant, Zubrenica Prime. The canopy of the landing pad had been opened, exposing the night sky on the moon. The atmosphere was held into the base by force fields that flickered peaceably in the still night air.

There was a rapidly growing dot in the distance, a ship outlined against the gas planet.

With all six government ministers in place, even with the entire moon locked down and security extremely high at all times, their bodyguards remained, ready for any sign of danger. The Faceless assassins were masters at assuming the shapes of anybody, and the enemies of the Union had used them before.

The dot had grown into a reasonably-size shuttle lander. On its underhull was emblazoned the symbol of House Marchenko, the house suggested as the seventh possible member of the Levitican Union. Luke still had not been able to discern any hidden plan in Lord Principal Ramicek's suggestion of their membership of the Union, but he was absolutely certain there would be one.

Luke thought to himself that perhaps it was time the Levitican Union Council changed its policy. The aggression of the StarCom Federation seemed to have abated. What use was a government where its leaders did not live amongst its people?

The shuttle had come in close to the force fields, slowing almost to stillness as it gently kissed the upper region of the protective envelope. It's hull glowed green as it began to slide through, the force fields opening to allow it egress to the enclosed landing pad. The energy fields formed a secure seal around the lander, swallowing it as it penetrated fully, to ensure that none of the oxygen escaped.

Landing repulsors firing gently, the lander touched down on the surface of the pad. Luke could feel the coldness radiating off from the shuttle, knowing that the force fields had retained the base's heat as well as its breathable atmosphere. The landing of the shuttle was so controlled that there was not the slightest back-draft from its touch-down, as with a series of metal clunks it came to rest on a number of extended landing struts.

He kept himself at military parade-ground stillness, awaiting the shuttles doors to open. Eventually they did with a small hiss of air, the landing ramp extending out as the double doors retracted.

A number of House Marchenko soldiers exited dressed in full power armour but with their helmets retracted into the collars of their suits. Weaponry was completely deactivated and inert. One carried a flag, a standard bearer. He flicked a switch to make it flutter as if there was a breeze, the infamous Marchenkan bear dancing in the pad. The canopy doors were already closing. The House soldiers of Marchenko were something else entirely, and perhaps not entirely human even by borgite standards.

A red carpet was rolled down the ramp by a number of servants.

Gregori Marchenko appeared inside the shuttle, emerging out into the false light, stepping thunderously down the ramp. He was every bit the monster in person that Lord Minister Luke had been led to believe.

House Marchenko were a vociferous borg nation, and went in for extreme and crude bodily modifications in much the same way that House Obamu's culture advocated tattoos. Gregori Marchenko was the epitome of such modification. His implants harkened back to a much more brutal and low-technology look, although in reality they were every bit as effective as modern cybernetic implants that were much more unobtrusive.

He was that heavy that he had two additional mechanical legs built, and they stalked independently to either side of his reinforced human legs. A heavy, fat man, his weight was not assisted by the black metallic crab-shell across his back, glittering with all manner of sensors and ports, and the brace of additional appendages fused into his extended rib-cage. In addition to his two human arms, four mechanical arms extended out two to either side, the upper pair rearing up over his shoulders in a grotesque parody of scorpion tails.

His face was half-metal, a red augmented eye constantly focusing and un-focusing. His head was hairless, and what could be seen of his flesh was puckered, sallow and unhealthy looking.

His wife the Lady Banuska Marchenko was no more visually pleasing, her augments making her unnaturally tall. Pincers on the end of two additional mechanical arms seemed to snap independently of her gait, adding a counter-balance to the heavy torso modifications she carried under the thin, almost translucent material of her dress.

House Marchenko's people were hardened borgites, and no un-augmented human dared live within their borders, even in Imperial times. It was in fact illegal to be un-augmented in that House's territory. The True Emperor and the False Emperor, who both favoured cyborg life, had viewed House Marchenko as one of their most loyal subjects. House Marchenko had actively fought against the Revolutionary Council.

Lord Minister Luke found the circus grotesques deeply uncomfortable. He shared to a lesser extent his late father's humanist viewpoint, and the people before him now outlined to him how alien and wrong cyborg mutation could become. His sister's mercenaries had implants that were much less obvious, it being impossible to tell physically that they were augmented – although sometimes their behaviour gave it away – and to them such outlandish modifications were extremely unnecessary.

He narrowed his eyes as he watched Lord Principal Ramicek walk towards the Marchenko nobles. House Zupanic was supposedly a humanist nation, although in truth many of Ramicek's children were augmented, including Lord Micalek who was due to marry Sophia. As ever with the man, Lord Luke wondered where Ramicek's true feelings on the age-old question lay.

Gregori and Banuska Marchenko were brought towards the line. "This is Lord Minister Brin Claes, of the Ministry of Justice," Lord Principal Ramicek introduced him. Claes bowed deeply, carefully disguising the disgust that Luke knew the old and extreme humanist would doubtless be concealing. Gregori Marchenko returned with an Imperial salute, his right-hand extendibles mirroring the breast-thumping greeting in an almost absurd parody.

What practical use do they have, Lord Minister Luke wondered. That Lord Brin had supported the possible introduction of House Marchenko to the Union just showed how much he had sold himself out to House Zupanic, to go against his own prejudices. Luke shared those prejudices to a much lesser degree, but he would never support House Marchenko joining the Levitican Union.

Gregori Marchenko was introduced to Lord Moafa Obamu next. The Machiavellian House Lord was a borg and a borgite, but his implants were impossible for the naked eye to see. He too bowed deeply, but this time Gregori Marchenko clumsily returned the bow.

Lady Minister Aria Galetti was a free-thinker, being neither borgite nor humanist in her leanings, although she was apparently augmented. She suffered from a genetic illness, which was countered only by a specific implant located in her abdomen. Without it, she would die, but some of the more extreme humanists would view even that life-saving implant as being unnatural. She had a genuine smile on her face as she greeted the House Lord.

Lady Monique Lapointe was a humanist, and she could not summon the smile, instead opting for a more political blank expression.

"And this," said Lord Principal Ramicek, "is Lord Minister Luke Towers, Minister for Military Defence."

"Your defence of the Levitican Union –" began Lady Banuska Marchenko, "- was admirable, Lord Minister," Gregori Marchenko growled, picking up where his wife had finished. Even his voice sounded artificial, there being a harsh electronic drawl to it. "We have been looking forward to meeting you."

Luke glanced at the Lady Banuska Marchenko. It was well known that the Marchenko's had taken the concept of the datasphere to an entirely new level. Whilst most cyborgs utilised datasphere technology as an information exchange, in some ways forming a hive-mind without sacrificing any of their individuality, the denizens of House Marchenko had no such freedom. Every Marchenkan was permanently connected to the hive-mind before birth, and had only a very limited sense of self. Even their noble house was connected into that consciousness, but with a greater degree of individuality. Lord Gregori Marchenko's father had created a nation of cybernetic slaves, with no more free will than any collection of drones.

Such arrangements of collective consciousness were politely referred to as collectives. In galaxy-wide slang the individuals, if they could be called such, were known as hivers. Many borgs the galaxy over found such collective borgism highly repellent.

"I have heard much about you," said Lord Minister Luke, as he rose from his bow. "I am sure we have much to discuss."

"Yes, we –" said Lady Banuska.

"- do," finished Lord Gregori Marchenko.

*

Lady Sophia disembarked from the small shuttle lander, Elaine Carrington at her side. She glanced up, noting the ripple effect of Tahrir Base's chameleonic field. Commodore Harley Andersson was just stepping down from a *Leopard* hover-jeep, looking at them as he did so.

"We should not have come," Elaine Carrington said, reproachfully but in a low tone of voice. A number of mercenary Marines were walking towards them. Her own bodyguard of four House Guardsmen stood behind her, loyal Towers operatives all.

"One had to see for one's self," she replied.

"I did not mean that," said Elaine Carrington. "Diverting from our scheduled tour to come back to the Blackheath System was too risky, following the snatching back of the assassin. Our unusual behaviour will provide the basis of suspicion to those who watch for such things."

"You are too paranoid," said Lady Sophia, before relenting. The Spider Carrington had always provided her, Luke and her father with excellent advice. "We have a cover story, a fault with the *First Carriage*."

"A flimsy cover story, the best I could manage on the short notice I had," Carrington replied, "and far too easy to see through. You should have followed my advice and not come back to Tahrir, Sophia."

Commodore Harley Andersson clapped his hands together against the cold as he stopped in front of them, effectively ending their conversation. "Lady Sophia, a pleasure to see you again. And Sarah," he said, referring to Elaine in one of her many disguises, this time as Lady Sophia's personal assistant. She looked two hundred years younger. "Admiral – sorry, Sir Admiral – Gavain is on his way down now. We have to perform a number of security checks first, do you mind?"

"This is a top-secret military base, one understands," Lady Sophia replied.

Andersson waved a marine forward. He or she, it was impossible to tell under the armour, used a special device which scanned and probed them. For a moment, Lady Sophia worried that it could see through Elaine's disguise, but even if it did, she knew it would not matter to anyone except Elaine. She was the co-owner of the Vindicator Mercenary Corporation, after all. She understood Elaine's need to keep her identity secret, but it would not be the end of her world.

"Perfect," said Andersson, but Lady Sophia thought she could see a momentary flicker of surprise on Andersson's face. "Come with me," he said, leading them back to the jeep.

Deep underground within the warrens of the mountain base, Lady Sophia felt her heart beat faster as she looked at the Faceless assassin who had killed her father, floating in the stasis tank.

"All life-signs are stable," said the Chief Medical Officer, Erin Presson. "It's just as well House Zupanic did not try to awaken him. They had missed a suicide implant – to be fair, so did I initially. When we do awaken this Faceless, I suggest we do it in a bomb-proof room, just in case."

"Are we at the point of awakening him?" asked Lady Sophia. She held a hand out to her assistant, Sarah, apparently for support to those watching. The Spider squeezed it once, to signify a yes.

"If you wish," said Commodore Harley Andersson. "The mind-scrubbing the Zupanics gave him is complete, and there's a fair amount of re-programming. We have the technology to do it whilst he is awake, however, so there is no harm. So Lieutenant-Commander Doctor Presson tells me."

"One would like to see him awake," said Lady Sophia. "One would like to talk to him."

"He won't tell you much," said Doctor Presson. "He's been mind-scrubbed. He won't recall anything further."

"There is a human need to look into his eyes," said Lady Sophia. "He might have been a tool, but he still killed one's father."

She saw Presson exchange a look with Andersson. She could see neither understood her need. There must have been some cyborg communication between them, because Presson suddenly said, "We will do it straight away. It will take one hour to bring the Faceless up." She turned away to begin the preparations.

"We also took a large amount of data during the snatch mission," said Commodore Harley Andersson. "Would you like to see it, Lady Sophia? It really is very interesting."

"Definitely," she replied.

"Sarah here will have to remain outside –"

"She comes with me, if it is all the same to you, Harley."

Harley Andersson hesitated. "Very well," he nodded.

He led them out of the secure medical unit, and into a side-office. It was a functional room, but it had been set up for them, with a number of suspensor-seats in front of a blank holographic display screen. It must be some kind of briefing room, or teaching room. Lady Sophia took one of the seats.

"We can re-programme the Faceless assassin to serve you, if you wish, Lady Sophia," said Commodore Harley Andersson suddenly. "James is within our datasphere now, and he's asked me to suggest it to you. There will be a cost, of course. I'm sorry, that's what he said to tell you."

One squeeze. "Please do it," said Lady Sophia. "Whatever it costs. Can you make him loyal only to me?"

"Given time, yes," Andersson nodded. Then he cleared his throat slightly, and activated the holo-screen. A moving image came up, showing scans that had been taken of the body of the Faceless, and memories from his brain.

"All of this comes from the House Zupanic data-files we took," he began. "So assume everything I speak of now, they also know. I doubt we have the only copy. We have absorbed the data already, however, and have learnt much.

"The cybernetic biomorph is of a greatly advanced technology. The Praetorian Guard were looking at something similar, for the next generation of marines for specific stealth missions, but the project was still in its infancy when the Red Imperium was destroyed. This is far in advance of what our own researchers had imagined.

"It's capabilities are astounding. It can change every part of itself, mimicking any human DNA down to a cellular level once it has absorbed the information. They are true chameleons, able to fool any type of scanning equipment that exists anywhere in the galaxy. When they take on the form of somebody else, they literally become that person, a simulant copy. Even some layers of their neural pathways alter, so they think and act like the person whose identity they have assumed. There are significant parts of the brain that do not change, however, and I believe this could lead us to develop some technology to identify them, assuming all Faceless are constructed the same as this one.

"Anyway, more on that later. Looking at the history of the Faceless is even more interesting. This one remembered his birth, in a bio-vat tank. We have only a couple of images –" these flashed up on the screen "- but it was placed to a foster family of some sort. We'll try and work out where that family lived from some of the images, the Zupanics had not progressed that far. It was put in the place of the family's real baby, which almost harkens back to the myth of changelings. A real cuckoo in the nest this one, because at a certain age it killed the family for some reason.

"Why whoever controls the Faceless programme them to do that, or place them with a family, I do not know. The next imagery from his memory shows some form of temple, although again we cannot place where. There are images of other Faceless, people training him. At one point he is called 'Ben' by his foster parents by the way. Then –"

Admiral James Gavain stepped up onto the *Leopard* hover-jeep, having left the large lander he had taken down to the surface. As the *Leopard* began to take him to the underground tunnels, he reviewed the scans taken when Lady Sophia and 'Sarah' had first arrived at the base.

He snorted ever so discretely, careful to keep his amusement away from the datasphere. He had thought as much. The life-signs and biological readings taken from 'Sarah' proved her to be no-one else other than Elaine Carrington, The Spider, Lady Sophia's head of intelligence. Their trip to the *Vindicator* had first aroused his curiosity and suspicion, as Elaine Carrington's bio-readings had been automatically taken as part of the warships security measures. His own intuition had led him to wonder where Elaine Carrington had been hiding. He had met Sarah a number of times before, but had no idea they were one and the same person.

How many other identities did Elaine Carrington have, he wondered. He would set Harley Andersson and Jonathan O'Connor onto the question, later.

Then he reviewed Lady Sophia's scans, an infinitesimally small part of his processing power automatically brushing lightly over the data. He read her bio-scans, and raised an eyebrow in an uncharacteristic sign of surprise.

"Harley," Lady Sophia interrupted. "What of my father? Who ordered the hit?"

"Ah," said Commodore Andersson. He stopped the image display. "The Zupanics were not very interested in this, as of course, they already knew. We have the data of the contract this Faceless was given. It quite clearly names Ramicek Zupanic as ordering the hit. Even though he was the ultimate customer, his instructions were for it to be made to look like the StarCom Federation had ordered the assassination."

"So we have the first hard, incontrovertible evidence?" she asked.

"Visual, text, and memory scans," said Commodore Andersson, "allowable in any Imperial Court of Justice under Imperial Law."

Admiral James Gavain walked into the briefing room, and strode straight up to Lady Sophia. He bowed, and then extended a hand immediately, palm up.

Lady Sophia looked surprised, but took his hand and allowed him to pull her to her feet. James was careful not to look at 'Sarah' once.

"What is this, James?" she asked.

"Congratulations," he said, simply. "As a borg grown in a bio-vat, I do not really understand this sort of family thing, but I believe it means something?"

Lady Sophia frowned, obviously utterly confused.

"What do you mean, James?" she asked. Harley had come forwards and put an arm around James's shoulders.

"James, you're supposed to let the woman tell you," he said, "apparently, tradition is they keep it to themselves for the first twelve weeks of the gestation period."

At those words, James registered the shock on Lady Sophia's face.

"You do not know, do you?" he asked.

Lady Sophia would, in other circumstances, have found the sudden awkwardness of the two powerful cyborg mercenary commanders almost hilarious. She was in no laughing mood at all however.

She had been given some water, and Elaine Carrington/Sarah/The Spider was stood protectively at her side. Lady Sophia was struggling to comprehend.

"I am pregnant?" she asked, her Imperial accent dropped completely.

"It is what the scans show," said Doctor Presson, nodding her head. "We can even tell you the father, if you wish."

Lady Sophia's heart stopped. She knew who it was, but had to ask anyway. "Who?" she asked, feeling her world crumble.

"Lord Micalek Zupanic," said Doctor Presson.

Lady Sophia closed her eyes, but could not withhold the tears. The father of her child was the son of the man who had ordered her father's death. Her child's grandfather had killed her child's other grandfather.

She would remember it later with guilt, but her first thought was of termination.

Chapter VI

Captain Rosanne Diaz was furious. As she stalked through the corridors of the *SS Yangtzee*, her second-in-command behind her, she was struggling with the feeling of betrayal.

Juan Ramirez, their new navigations officer and her regular bed-mate, had been caught in his sleeping quarters in an extremely compromising position with another member of the crew, Simeon Jimenez. That Juan was obviously bisexual meant absolutely nothing to her, the fact that she had obviously misunderstood the nature of his interest in her did. She had been coming to be very fond of the young man, almost at the point of suggesting they make it official.

Captain Rosanne Diaz reflected that she should have known better. Ship-board romances were not real, but casual sexual relationships on long voyages were very common. It was not just the personal level of betrayal she felt; there was another, much deeper and darker betrayal that as a humanist Cervantian she could not tolerate.

She strode into the sleeping quarters. She pushed her way through the crowd of people, the off-duty crew who had come here as soon as they had heard the news. Simeon Jimenez stood to one side, fear on his face as he looked at her. He obviously knew what he had been doing behind her back as well, she instantly thought.

The Chief Engineer, who also doubled as the chief surgeon and doctor, was bent over the gently shaking form of Juan Ramirez. Even as she watched, another tremor shook him. A small, elderly bio-medical scanner in his right hand spoke the truth.

"Is it for real?" she demanded.

The Chief Engineer looked up. "Yes," he said. "An implant in his body is malfunctioning. When he was .... with Simeon, it began to malfunction."

Rosanne Diaz stood there for a long time, fury raging across her face and her body language. "Storeroom three," she said "both of them. We're dropping them off at our next stop." She began to turn away, and then added over her shoulder, "if the dirty fucking metalhead gets a few knocks on the way, I won't ask questions."

As the door closed, she heard the first sounds of her humanist and very anti-borg crew beginning to lay into the prone form of Juan Ramirez.

Juan groaned. He was in pure agony.

He rolled over, and gasped for breath. It felt like an arm was broken, and he had certainly broken a couple of ribs. His entire world was a body of hurt, and it did not help that one of his cybernetic implants was still mis-firing. It was a form of torture, the shakes it threw through his body making the results of his vicious beating hurt even more.

He looked up in the half-darkness, seeing the frightened eyes of his former lover, Simeon Jimenez.

He raised a hand into the air, a tremble shaking it. "Help me," he whispered through cracked and bloody lips.

"Keep away from me, you fricking borg," Simeon hissed after a moment, his voice high. He stood up, spat in Juan's face, gave him a brutal kick to the stomach, and then an entirely new beating began in Juan's world of pain.

*

Admiral Gavain entered the briefing room aboard the *LSS Vindicator*, and as one the assembled command staff got to their feet. The briefing room was a converted mission control centre, designed more for tactical operations than a large conference room, so space was at a premium.

"Admiral in the room," said Commander Al-Malli, and they all saluted.

Gavain returned the salute. "Sit," he commanded, taking his position at the head of the circular table. A number of holo-projection units had been put in place, although only two were currently active. An expensive continuous hyper-pulse was allowing both Commodore Harley Andersson and Doctor Presson to attend via holo-image, when in reality they were light-years away in the Blackheath System. A similarly expensive interstellar communications link was permitting five of his ship's captains on the Hausenhof convoy contract to join the conference, from even further afield intergalatically.

The rest of Gavain's ships were located in the uninhabited planetary system named SD4-M2, a system they used regularly for training when off-contract precisely because it was away from the established trade-routes and virtually no ship apart from theirs ever visited, so the majority of his command staff were present in person having shuttled across.

"We have a lot to discuss," said Gavain, typically getting straight to the point. "Lieutenant-Commander Wybeck, the convoy contract is progressing according to plan?"

Ffion Wybeck commanded the SS *Apollo*, a captured Cervantian frigate, one of the few non-Praetorian ships in the mercenary company. She had the contract command, it being viewed as a very low-risk contract. The *Odyssey*, an O-class frigate, was the only other military ship on the contract, with the *Hannoverian, Deliverance* and *Featherlight* cargo-freighters – only the latter of which was unarmed – carrying thirty-five cargo-tanks of highly valuable interstellar freight for Hausenhof between them.

"We are on the second run of six, sir," Lieutenant-Commander Ffion Wybeck said. The holographic image of her was so real, it was as if she was sat there herself. Only the smallest time delay betrayed the fact she was not actually sat at the table. "We're heading towards the former front with Korhonen, and we've not had any contact with privateers or pirates or otherwise. Please be advised though, the political situation here is destabilising rapidly."

"It was never stable," Commodore Harley Andersson laughed.

"The Hausenhof nation continues with their rhetoric, blaming Cervantia particularly for the predations of the pirates against their shipping, and linking it to support from the StarCom Federation."

"The Federation did tacitly support Cervantia during their triple-way war," said Gavain.

"The Federation and Cervantia hotly denies it," said Lieutenant-Commander Wybeck, "but Hausenhof is reinforcing their front again. There has been a request for us to take on four separate runs to the Cervantian border, abandoning the schedule." She leaned forwards, and the data appeared in the centre of the table.

Whilst his officers debated the amendment to the contract, Gavain read the data carefully. It would add significantly to the risk of the contract, and he was concerned about the safety of his ships. Still, two of the cargo-freighters were Praetorian Guard designed, and carried their own weapon systems.

When he spoke, it called an end to the debate, and all fell silent. "Lieutenant-Commander Wybeck, I will inform Ambassador Grunehaube that we accept House Van Hausenhof's amendment to the contract, for the value given. However, I will make it conditional that if the truce between Hausenhof and Cervantia collapses and they return to war, it changes the nature of the risk. If that happens, we will have to revisit the terms of the contract, perhaps agree to cancel."

"Understood, Admiral," Wybeck nodded.

"I will contact you separately to confirm after this conference," said Admiral Gavain. "People, on to the next matter." He stood, carrying his coffee with him, and began to stalk around the table as he spoke.

"The time has come for us to move on. The Levitican War is over, and we need to start earning money. All ships are repaired, and thanks to our recruitment drive, we are back at an acceptable strength-level. Shortly, we create the first batch at our bio-vat facility, and we will begin to move into continuous production of our own Praetorian-grade replacements.

"The Kavanagh Shipyards are under construction. We will be in the position to begin building our own starships. Understand this, that whilst the ships manufactured will be used to enlarge the Vindicator Mercenary Corporation, we will also be selling them commercially to the Levitican Union. This is a new branch to our venture. Commodore Andersson has control of both projects, and will remain in Blackheath to oversee them.

"However, for the part you do not know. We have accepted a third, secret contract, to train an assassin for House Towers," he deliberately glossed over the detail, as to how they had come to have the Faceless assassin in the first place. He did see Lieutenant-Commander Bramhall grin widely, but luckily few of his command staff noticed. He would have a word with the young officer later. "As part of this contract, we are gaining access to, and developing our own, highly advanced cybernetic biomorphology technology. Doctor Presson, if you would."

Doctor Presson cleared her throat. As Chief Medical Officer, she was used to speaking at the regular command staff briefings, but she always became visibly nervous. "We believe that we can begin creating our own cybernetic biomorph Marines. Some here may have heard of Project Tango, which was originally a classified Imperial Praetorian project to develop a highly specialised elite strike-force, for special operations. We are in a position to resurrect Project Tango, and in less than two weeks we will begin growing our first biomorphic Marines."

There was silence around the table. "This is completely new technology," said Commodore Andersson, speaking for Presson. "The existence of the resurrected Project Tango is highly classified. We will not be advertising or speaking of the existence of the project, or its results. It is being funded by the contract for House Towers, although they will never know of its existence."

Admiral Gavain reflected that what they were doing, in generating and building upon new technology, would already be happening across all the disparate, seceded nations of the Red Imperium. How many were trying to create their own Weapons of Planetary Destruction, similar to the Tears of the Moon? How many others were building Praetorian-grade starships, besides the StarCom Federation? An arms race as deadly as the Imperial Civil War was taking place, and it was just as insidiously covert. He had no intention of being left behind. They needed to develop to maintain an edge, and the technology from the Faceless assassin may well give it to them.

"So, onto our next contracts," said Admiral Gavain, settling at the head of the table again. "Every ship and every person not tied into Tahrir Base, the Kavanagh Shipyards project, or the second Hausenhof convoy contract, is about to be fully engaged. We are taking on not one, but two, contracts. One is purely planetary-based, and one is purely naval-based. Ulrik?" He sat down.

Even out of his power armour and in field dress uniform, General Ulrik Andryukhin's heritage as a Praetorian Imperial Marine was obvious. Thick-set and muscular, the lighting strips overhead reflected from a head shorn of all hair, and a thick square goatee framed a straight-lined mouth. He managed to restrain himself for a least a short while from his normal expletive-lined refrain as he explained, details of the contract and a visual map of a solar system and planet appearing in the centre of the room.

"The contract is with the Zhou-Zheng Compact," he said simply. "They are currently engaged in a war with the nation of Erdogan, formerly House Erdogan in the days of the Red Imperium. Captain O'Connor will explain more about the background in a moment. The war is stalemated in a number of systems, and the Compact wish us to unlock it in the Kyiv System. They do not have the capability to fight effectively against borg soldiers and prevail, so they have hired us.

"We will jump shortly outside the system of Kyiv, at the following co-ordinates." They flashed up on the star-map. "Such a long journey into the system is required to maintain absolute secrecy, as we will be without escort, running silent into the system. We will have to evade Erdogan pickets and detection devices. The aim is to ensure that our arrival is not detected, to afford us maximum surprise when we begin our assault on land.

"The planet Kyiv Primus is currently contested by Compact and Erdogan forces, particularly on the continent Zwei. We will land in secret, behind Compact lines, on the continent of Drei, on the far-side of the planet away from Erdogan detection. There, we will rendezvous with the theatre commander, before embarking on a mission ourselves to strike at the heart of the Erdogan forces on-planet.

"Our full marine force of twenty-five thousand, barring those on the naval ships, will take part in this. The only ships we will have in support are our transporters, the *Monstrosity*, the *Marvellous*, and the *Titan of Stars*, as well as the medical frigate as we do not trust in the generosity of the Compact to look after our injured. We are including the medical frigate for free. I will have direct operational command of this contract, including that of the three ships. We may be able to call on orbital support from Compact naval ships if we are successful towards the end of the Primus operation, but we also know they are hiring us because they see us borgs as disposable.

"If we are successful, we may then transfer to Kyiv Tertius if we decide to take the optional contract extension. Kyiv Tertius is fully Erdogan-held, but do not underestimate the difficulties we are likely to encounter on Kyiv Primus. We will be landing in secrecy, operating over half an entire super-planetary distance, under Erdogan naval guns, deep in hostile territory, in the middle of a planetary war. Put simply, Jamie has properly buggered us up the arse with this one."

Everyone laughed as he sat down, and Gavain was heartened to see his friends taunting smile return. It had been long missed.

"The risks are high, but the pay-off is similarly high," said Admiral Gavain. "This is strategically stretching, but we have the capability to do it. We have thresholds for when we can declare the contract failed, but I do expect losses to be considerable. Let no-one be under any doubt – we will suffer, but we can also prevail. Jonathan?"

He let Captain Jonathan O'Connor, the Captain of the *Quintessential* star-carrier and also his intelligence officer, brief them all on the political situation and the background to the contract. When O'Connor had finished, Captain Enrique Delgado leaned forwards and spoke.

"Why are we taking this contract with the humanist Zhou-Zheng Compact?" he asked. The commander of the *Monstrosity* military super-transporter, and overall section chief for all the VMC's transportation fleet, was old even for a Praetorian. The Captain had been a long-time friend of Harley Andersson, and was one of the people Harley had brought with him from Janus. "The Compact hates borgs. They are just as likely to let us die, as to come and support us when or if we need it. We should be fighting for House Erdogan, not House Zhou or House Zheng."

"Erdogan is not offering high-value contracts," said James Gavain. "The Zhou-Zheng Compact is. If there are no other questions, you are jumping immediately after this conference is over." All marines were aboard their assigned super-transporters, ready to leave the SD4-M2 System and currently undergoing their own briefings on the contract. "The other contract we are taking is purely naval."

The holo-map changed, showing a star-map of the House Lindholm territory.

"All of the remaining starships, the corvettes, and the repair-ship, are to be engaged on this contract within House Lindholm. We are tracking down the Pirates of the Cross." Admiral James Gavain explained the background himself, but he saved the best for last.

"In one of the pirate attacks, black box recordings showed images of this starship." A number of people around the table looked shocked or grim as an image of a dreadnought flashed up on the holo-projector. "This T-class dreadnought may well be the *Thor's Hammer*, flagship of the notorious war-criminal Silus Adare. It has been recorded in at least one action against House Lindholm, although one of the primary starships is the *Vengeance*, under Captain Reichenburg. This will not be an easy contract either, people."

"If it is Adare, fucking kill him, Jamie," said Ulrik.

"If it is Adare, we claim the bounty first," said Admiral James Gavain. "For what he has done, the Levitican Union will pay us handsomely before they execute him."

"That would do me," said Ulrik, his face as black as a storm cloud. Openly, he said, "I should be coming with you."

<Later, Ulrik,> Admiral Gavain messaged him across the datasphere, <I promise we will talk later.>

<I'm furious with you,> said Ulrik. <Too damn right we will, Jamie. I should have the right to find Adare.>

Gavain hesitated. Although their conversation was private, and they had been friends for many years, there was such a thing as respect for rank. He decided now was not the time to pursue the matter however.

"We too leave immediately," he said. "People, this briefing is over. Within an hour, we shall all be heading our separate ways. The Vindicator Mercenary Corporation is back in action. May the Emperor watch your steps, and his blessings be on all of us."

The command staff repeated the saying, and the briefing was over.

*

"There you go, metalfreak," the cargo hand threw the rucksack at Juan Ramirez. He cried out in pain as it hit his still broken arm, which he had strapped into place himself with a piece of torn shirt. Luckily he had a light jacket, or he would have been naked from the waist-up. The rucksack with his worldly possessions hit the floor.

Juan Ramirez looked towards the small landing shuttle, blinking in the harsh eternal sunlight. He felt his legs give way under him, and he fell to one knee, and then collapsed onto his rear through sheer exhaustion with the pain.

"Where are we?" Simeon Jimenez demanded, of the cargo hand.

"A lovely little backwater planet called Farsight, in the Drenim System," the cargo hand replied.

"It looks like there's nothing here!" Simeon near-shouted, whirling around as he opened his arms wide.

"Shouldn't have pissed off the captain then, should you, Simeon," the cargo hand shouted back. "Good luck, mate."

"How am I supposed to get off this mud-ball?" Simeon howled.

"Good luck, mate. Fuck you, jack-head." The cargo hand slapped his hand on a panel, and the ramp up into the lander began to close.

Aware that he did not want to be near the shuttle as it took off, Juan Ramirez groggily pulled himself to his feet. In many ways, he was glad his incarceration aboard the *Yangtzee* had been brought to an end. Captain Diaz was literally abandoning them on a backwater planet in a backwater system, good to her word.

He staggered away from Simeon Jimenez, not wanting to talk to him or have anything more to do with him. His beating at the hands of his former sexual partner had hardened him somewhat. On one level he was glad the torture was over; on another, he felt the old despair. What was he supposed to do now?

He headed towards the terminal of what was laughingly called a starport. Two very bored enforcers watched him approach, taking in his state but evidently not in the least concerned.

The starport was more of a collection of large landing pads for small ships, not being designed to take anything larger than a tank-lander. There was little of value on this planet, he knew. The gravity was near-normal, but the heat was unbelievable. There were adverts for cancer-preventatives on the external walls of the terminal. Farsight suffered from eternal daylight on one half of its hemisphere, always facing the weak sun of the solar system.

There was a strong humidity to the air, and despite the area which had been cleared for the small and very down-at-heels city, he could still see the hundred metre high jungle canopy all around in every direction. Some parts of the city were actually built into the trees, at varying and different levels.

Diaz had apparently cleared him through customs and passport control, otherwise she would never have been allowed to ditch him here on Farsight. The droid checked his credentials, and he was waved through without much fuss.

His brain implant jacked into the local datasphere, which at least told him that as a borg he would not be out of place here. The information he downloaded informed him adequately of his plight.

Farsight was largely a chemo-agricultural planet, its teeming rainforests and jungles replete with all manner of natural herbs and materials for making drugs, both legal and illegal. It had a large black market, even according to its official records. It had a small side-industry in the exotic animals which were native to the world, in demand across the galaxy due to their unusual nature. There was nothing else remarkable about Farsight.

It was not the only inhabited planet in the Drenim System, a part of House Van Der Meer. There was a military moon, and another moon given over as a penal colony, both strictly off-limits. There was a small gas mining operation, and an extremely large commercial shipyards owned by Drax Naval Architects. He was stuck in the Mid-Sectors of the galaxy, near the Gulf of Medusa, with little civilisation for light-years around.

He felt like crying. He had some money, but that would soon disappear. He had not been on the *Yangtzee* long enough to make much. He would spend a significant proportion of it getting medical treatment from the local hospital, not having any medical insurance or being a native of the planet. It would be incredibly difficult getting a new berth from here, especially with no reference and a cancelled contract on his work history with the Interstellar Merchants Guild, and he did not have the money to book passage off-planet.

He collapsed against a wall on the walkway outside the terminal, staring at the rank of taxi-cabs, and tears rolled down his blood encrusted, dirt-stained cheeks.

*

James Gavain sat at his desk in his ready room aboard the *Vindicator*, knowing that they were due to make their jump shortly. His ships were just in the process of forming up, his command staff heading back to their ships after the briefing.

The maps for the Lindholm Contract floated above his desk. His plan was simple.

Whilst the *Vindicator* made its way to his initial reporting-in with this Admiral-of-the-Fleets Halvorssen, the rest of his ships would be heading to their start positions.

There were three major trade-routes through Lindholm territory. It would be impossible to cover all three, so he was maximising his chances of catching the Pirates of the Cross by concentrating on one route. The territory of House Lindholm was shaped like a kidney, one trade route actually running from its territory into the Helvanna Dominion, another one centrally across into House Rantanen, and a third curving down into House Haugen-Berg.

He would not worry about the Helvanna or Haugen-Berg trade-routes, but he was positioning his ships strategically to cover the Rantanen trade-route within House Lindholm territory, so that at least two of his ships could jump to any one of the designated targets along the pathway across the stars. It was a complicated dispersal pattern, made all the more difficult with the fact that the six target systems would constantly change. Organised into pairs, there would be at least one pair of ships that could be within one jump of any of the six target systems; hopefully they would each have two further jumps in their capacitors to conduct a limited pursuit if necessary.

The six target systems would constantly change, depending on the shipping logs booked in with the Interstellar Merchants Guild on behalf of House Lindholm. His six corvettes were key to the trap – with one in each of the six target systems, they would be able to jump out secretly if an attack occurred, and alert the ships which had to respond. The pirates tended to attack in out of the way systems which rarely had HPCG stations to signal for help, hence the need to have his corvettes spread out in an early-warning network.

Their initial objective was to respond to pirate incursions, perhaps scaring them off, but preferably engaging and capturing an enemy ship. The interdictor *Kinslayer* would be perfect for preventing a pirate ship from jumping out-system, but it would purely be a matter of luck if there was an incursion within its radial envelope. The *Kinslayer* was the only ship not in a pairing, as he was willing for it to use all three jumps to get to a target system. It could hopefully cover several target systems at once, but that would depend on the convoys in transit across the trade-routes.

It was always possible that the pirates would not hit a trade-route, deciding to attack a solar system being used for mining or other operations. It would purely be luck as to whether the system could get a distress signal out, and his ships were in the region to respond. He could not predict the unpredictable however, so he needed to obtain further intelligence on the Pirates of the Cross. The only way to get that was to capture one of their ships.

He had chosen the pairings of his own ships carefully. He had paired the *Vindicator* battlecruiser with the *Ubermacht* destroyer, so he would be in command, and the *Remembrance* with the *Universal* destroyer, so Captain Markos would be in charge. The *Carnivorous* battlecruiser was paired with Captain De Graaf's *Undefeatable*, the captain of the *Carnivorous* being currently untried as far as Gavain was concerned. He was very pleased with how De Graaf was doing following his recovery from alcohol abuse, and the man had gone considerably up in James's estimation.

O'Connor's *Quintessential* star-carrier was paired with the strikecruiser *Shadow*, as Captain O'Connor was an experienced commander. The *Revenging Angel* battlecruiser was paired with the strikecruiser *Snake-Eyes*, and the *Queen of Egypt* star-carrier with the *Solace*. The captains and commanders of all but the *Revenging Angel* were also relatively new to Gavain, although known to Andersson.

If he had a fusion-tanker, it would have been easier to cover the trade-routes. A starship could only make so many jumps before needing to recharge, and a fusion-tanker would allow them to hot-charge his ships for more jumps, extending their reach. It was dangerous and damaging to a starship to do it continuously, but for this sort of operation such an asset would have been advantageous.

He took a moment to reflect, leaving the plans. He was stressing and worrying. Once they were all out in the field, the safety of his assets would be very much up to the individual abilities of his theatre commanders. He had chosen as carefully as he could, but there was no denying it – the closeness, familiarity and reassurance he had felt when the mercenary company consisted of just the *Vindicator*, its crew and him was long gone. He had done the best he could, and now he would have to rely on the people he had chosen to command his growing fleet of ships.

Things had been so much simpler, once. He had changed, he knew. He was a mercenary through and through, focused on the bottom line. He had replaced loyalty to one man, the Emperor of the Red Imperium, with loyalty to money, himself and his people.

The plan was set, he had prepared as much as he could, and shortly it would be time to see if it would work.

<Admiral, there is a hyper-pulse message for you from Commodore Andersson,> the message came to him from Lieutenant Forrest. He ordered it to be played through to him.

"Harley," he said to the holographic image of his lover, as he appeared in front of him. "This is unexpected?"

"I'm using my own money," said Andersson. "I have precious little else to spend it on, and I wanted to talk to you."

In the Red Imperium, the Praetorian Guard had been created as the super-soldiers of the Emperor, and were not paid for their services having been born and bred for such service. The concept of money and having to make their own way in the galaxy had come as a shock to most of the dispossessed Praetorians. Many that Gavain knew were taking tentative steps into the world of consumerism, beginning to buy personal effects. The Praetorians were almost a race in themselves, and the changes were comparable to a culture shift. That culture shift was taking many different forms, he knew.

He himself hardly knew what to do with his own personal payments taken from the VMC. What money the Corporation earned he ploughed back into its assets and its people.

"Company money could have been used," said Gavain.

"This is personal, James," said Harley.

"I .... see," he said.

They had a five minute conversation, during which Harley expressed his love for James. At the end of the conversation, James was unsure, not knowing quite how to respond to his lover and his friend. Relationships had been outlawed in the Praetorians, and it was just one more culture change he had to get used to. The goodbye as the communication ended was awkward.

He found himself in the position of wondering when his casual acquaintanceship with Harley had changed into such deep feelings. He also wondered if he had the same level of feelings for Harley that Harley had for him. Probably not, he suspected. It was all out of his experience, and with Jules Kavanagh gone, he had no-one to confide in. He snorted to himself at the thought of discussing it with Ulrik Andryukhin, his other close friend. He thought of Lucas; Captain De Graaf had become a friend despite their shaky beginnings, perhaps he could talk to him? Commander Al-Malli was still new to him. Lady Sophia was a friend, but she had more than enough of her own concerns at the moment.

Despite his concerns about his position, he did not feel he could confide in Harley Andersson any more, the way he had used to. As their relationship had changed and become more serious, he also felt he had become more distant as he had become responsible for tens of thousands of people rather than just the *Vindicator*.

Of course he felt something for Harley Andersson, and indeed had a casual relationship with him even during the days of the Red Imperium. It had deepened he knew as they had been able to spend more time together, Harley crossing the galaxy to join him and the VMC, incidentally bringing a large portion of the ships currently forming part of the mercenary group. However, James wondered just how much he felt back.

He was surrounded by people, but he had never felt more alone.

He shook his head, deciding enough was enough. He was not doing himself any good, and such self-doubt was very uncharacteristic. Of course he felt deeply for Harley, but he did not know if it was love as Harley had just expressed to him. He would put it out of his mind for now, and concentrate on the contract and his people.

Still slightly worried, he stood and made his way to the bridge of the *Vindicator*, to be present for the first jump.

*

Lord Minister Luke sat in his office attached to the war-room from which he had directed the defence of the Levitican Union and commanded the entire Union military, nervous as to the upcoming meeting. When the door chimed and his personal assistant announced the arrival of his visitors, he brought all his training as a High General of the Towers military, pre-Union, and his position as a noble of a landed House to hide his discomfort as he stood to welcome the guests.

He bowed his head slightly, and then extended a hand in the traditional greeting. "House Lord Gregori Marchenko," he said, "welcome. Is House Lady Banuska not with you?"

"Lady Banuska is with Lady Minister Aria Galetti," the monstrosity that was House Lord Gregori Marchenko growled. "We welcome this opportunity to discuss matters of import, Lord Minister."

Luke paused, aware that through the hive mind collective, he was actually addressing the entirety of House Marchenko's collective intelligence. It was highly disconcerting to know that your words would become a matter of record to an entire hive mind. Doubtless they had some kind of security measures in place to keep some things secret?, he wondered. He knew that the Lord and Lady retained more of their own individuality than most Marchenkans, although that was not much.

Drinks were served and then the servants disappeared, as Gregori Marchenko awkwardly sat upon a suspensor-seat. It was not configured for his weight, and struggled to support him in the air for what in other circumstances would have been a humorous moment, before its computer automatically increased repulsion to bring Gregori back up to normal sitting height. His two mechanical legs splayed out unnaturally to either side as additional support, his over-shoulder mechanical arm extensions curling back into rest positions like a scorpion about to strike.

"I am glad of this opportunity you mentioned," said Lord Minister Luke, "I will admit, I have a number of questions for you."

"We are sure you do," said Lord Gregori. "Just as we are sure that you find our forms abhorrent. The animosity of your father towards borg life-forms was well-known, Emperor rest his soul in peace. We are curious and enquire; does this animosity reign as strong in his son as in him?"

Luke stared into the completely black orbs of Lord Gregori Marchenko. The human race had not discovered advanced intelligent alien life-forms in their spread across the cosmos, so we designed our own, he thought.

The truth was the best, he thought. Who knew what augmented implants Gregori possessed, to read things such as his heart-rate and body heat to detect lies.

"I do find you difficult to treat with," he nodded. "I have met borgs before, of course. But House Marchenko is a borg house to a very different level. Understanding your collective consciousness is outside of my realm of experience."

"We find a refreshing honesty in that reply," said Lord Gregori Marchenko, "and we will honour you with the same. We find unaugmented human life-forms completely alien, and we do not even consider the cyborgs throughout the galaxy as anything more than half of what we are. To be true borg, is to have union in the collective consciousness." Lord Gregori paused. "Lord Minister Brin Claes, whilst supporting our entrance to the Levitican Union, is very much a liar when it comes to our different natures, we find. We like your honesty, Lord Minister Luke, there is no need to pretend a star is a planet when it is not."

Lord Minister Luke resisted the urge to laugh at the comment about Lord Claes, but politically he avoided acknowledging it. "Which leads to perhaps the most pressing question of all about your request to join the Union," said Lord Minister Luke. "Why would what amounts to a separate race of people, joined together into one consciousness, collectively decide to join a Union consisting of many different houses with many different backgrounds. Some of us are borg, some are human, and we cover the range of opinions and prejudices from humanist to free-thinking to borgite. None of us are ever likely to join your collective mind, after all."

"An admirable question," Lord Gregori Marchenko replied. "On the question of Leviticans joining the House Marchenko collective hive mind, we would ask only as a condition of our admission that any serfs who wish to join our collective of their own free will are allowed to do so. We would establish missionaries on every planet to allow such a thing to happen."

"House Marchenko is known to enforce membership of the collective consciousness," said Lord Luke. "The concession I would seek in relation to that, is that you submit to all our laws. Enforced membership of the hive mind collective would be outlawed in the Union. You would have to change your own house culture, Lord Gregori. Is that acceptable?"

"We have agreed to that," Lord Gregori nodded. "You are not the only Lord to bring this to our attention. We acquiesce. We are confident that the opportunity of spreading the glory of the collective amongst the Union will outweigh those few born in Marchenko space that do not wish to join the collective."

Confident and cocky, aren't you, thought Lord Minister Luke. He found he had settled into the discussion, although the sight of the abnormal human before him still repelled him. "But, to come back to my point, on a wider note why would a collective hive mind wish to join a Union of 'free' minds?"

81

"We were not avoiding the question. We see many advantages to joining the Levitican Union, not least the fact that the Union has developed a reputation for tolerance of differing view-points not seen in many of the other new nations in the galaxy. We respect that tolerance, please be assured."

That does not answer my question at all, thought Luke. "That is true," he said, pressing the point. "So why else do you wish to join?"

"We were once a part of the Red Imperium," said House Gregori Marchenko. "We were won over by the First Emperor and loyally served him, as we did the second. We fought on the side of the second Emperor in the civil war, so technically we were at odds with some of the houses in the Levitican Union. But we are practical. The hive mind has applied much thought to this. The Red Imperium has fallen, and in the dissolution of the Empire and the wars that ignite all over the galaxy, we see a future where eventually we must fight for survival. We see the StarCom Federation still as the greatest threat to ourselves, but there are also others. You were successful in defeating them. We see the value in being part of a greater whole, by the very essence of what and who we are. We wish to lend our strength to a greater good, and see the Union as the best option we have. We are neighbouring Galetti, Zupanic and Lapointe territory, and are close to Towers. We have been a part of the Imperium for centuries, and are used to working in concert with forces not of our own nature, and we see the advantage in the striving for a common goal. We wish to have that sense of purpose again."

"I am beginning to understand," said Lord Minister Luke. "After all, the Levitican Union was born out of fear of the StarCom Federation, and a desire by our six houses, despite our differences, to survive following the fall of the Imperium. Are there any other reasons?"

"Yes," said Lord Gregori. "We spend a considerable time predicting the future based on extrapolations from the past. It is in human nature to build big empires, for them to break apart, and then to coalesce slowly again into bigger and bigger collectives, if you excuse the phrase. We see the Union as one of the greatest forces in the Eastern Segment, and wish to be a part of that from the outset. The prognosis for a successful future is good."

Lord Luke was almost bemused. Even the conversation was alien in its nature. "So what can you bring to the Union?" he asked.

"We have a stable economy," Lord Gregori replied promptly. "We bring access to a greater number of houses for the Union to trade with through existing arrangements and deals. We bring stability as a new member. We bring a strong military. We note the increasing predations of House Jorgensson, and the difficulties the Union is encountering with piracy. In particular, we can protect Union trade-routes and systems from piratical attacks with greater efficiency than you can currently achieve."

Luke nodded. "We are struggling with piracy, yes," he said, "as is much of the galaxy at the moment. It is a growing concern, and becomes more of an issue every week. House Jorgensson is another matter entirely, and is perhaps my greatest worry."

"House Jorgensson has always desired House Obama and House Towers territory. They now see you as weak after the war, and test your reactions. They may yet invade," said Lord Gregori.

"I would prefer them to join the Union, even though they are enemies of my own House," said Lord Luke. "We ... that is, the Union member houses, did initially ask them to join in the Charter of Leviticus, but they refused."

"That comment alone heartens us, as it shows that some members of the Union considered treating with people you viewed as enemies, for the greater advantage," said Lord Gregori. "It is that principle we wish to avail ourselves of, and to help in building a new, forward-looking nation."

"As Lord Minister for the Ministry of Defence, I find the possibilities in relation to defence very attractive," said Lord Luke, casting his eyes over the data displayed openly on the desk before him, relating to the military strengths of House Marchenko. "As a person, however, I am beginning to understand why you wish to join the Union, although I still harbour some doubts. I have no desire to see the Union diluted and weakened, in an attempt to make us stronger."

"We will reassure you in any way we can," said Lord Gregori.

"Just on a practical level, organising your integration into the Union would be time-consuming. We would have to find a role for you in a new ministry, so you would have a vote on the Council," said Lord Minister Luke.

"The Lord Principal has suggested a Ministry of Transformation and Integration, as a temporary post until the next elections in three and a half years time, to deal with both of those concerns," Lord Gregori Marchenko replied.

"What else has the Lord Principal promised you?" said Lord Minister Luke. "I do see from my notes that House Marchenko was always heavily reliant on Imperial resources for energy requirements and even natural food, your own territory not being particularly abundant in these types of resources."

"We do have such requirements, and our host units suffer," said the Lord Gregori Marchenko. "The Union has such things in abundance. We can see you realise that we have an immediate, earthly need for joining the Levitican Union as well as one of principle."

It is also probably your greatest reason, thought Lord Luke, your people are starving and you desperately need the resources we are selling throughout the Eastern Segment. I do not completely believe the thrust of your argument about 'greater good'. Aloud he said, "well, Lord Gregori, I shall consider my position in the Council vote on your membership, and continue to research the facts of the matter."

"We thank you, Lord Minister Luke. Can we count on your vote?"

"I have yet to consider," he smiled, standing to signify the meeting was over. Lord Gregori Marchenko clambered to his four feet, shook hands, and without a backward look left the office.

Lord Minister Luke exhaled heavily, and loosened his collar. He could still smell the cloying lubricant that Lord Gregori used on his heavy, unnatural implants filling the room. Sitting back down, he activated his personal messages console, and re-read the missive from the Lord Principal Ramicek Zupanic.

It was a note, asking him to support the entrance of House Marchenko in the name of Towers' pact with House Zupanic. There were reasons listed, but Luke found them difficult to swallow. He still suspected the motives of the Lord Principal, and he did not trust House Zupanic at all. There must be some hidden reason he had not discerned yet, but no matter how hard he researched the upcoming decision on their membership, he could not identify the plans that House Zupanic had.

He may yet be forced to vote in favour of their membership, despite his misgivings, to continue the illusion of House Towers compliance with the wishes of House Zupanic. If he was looking at the decision dispassionately, he could see any number of advantages in House Marchenko joining, putting aside his own personal feelings about their nature.

"Lord Principal," he whispered to himself, "what in the name of the dead, true Emperor are you up to?"

Chapter VII

Lord Micalek had landed at Zupanic Palace on the house capital planet of Zupanic, in the Dalcice System, a day before. He had attended to a number of matters that had been delayed too long before he finally sought out his mother. He had also spoken to some of the younger brothers and sisters, cousins, and more of the extremely large and many-branched Zupanic family tree.

He was fifth in line to the seat of the House, and as such he dreaded coming back to Zupanic Palace. He had gone to great lengths to spend as much of his adulthood as he could aboard naval starships or amongst the land armies. Technically his uncle and third in line to the throne, Vasily Zupanic, had been the head of the armed forces until the Union had brought all the House militaries together, but he was the more popular Zupanic family member as far as the lay military were concerned.

It was the fourth in line to inherit the throne after Lord Principal Ramicek, his elder sister Csarina, who had informed him where to find their mother. He should have guessed, he had realised afterwards, but at least going to track her down kept him out of the way of the rest of the family.

He entered the special medical suite quietly, waving away the sycophants and the House Guard still under his uncle's command. He entered the room silently. The only sound was the gentle hum of the specialist medical computers, and the broken snoring coming from another one of his brothers, Xavier, who was lying prone, sedated and unconscious in the angled suspensor bed. He would be dipped back into a healing gel-filled bio-vat tank in another hour or so, so the wall monitors said.

"Micci," said Lady Wyn quietly. "I knew you were back. I have been busy. Sorry."

"It is of no matter, mother," said Micalek. He moved to the bed, and placed a hand on her shoulder.

"Poor Xavier," said Lady Wyn. "Whoever did this must pay for it dearly."

"Whoever did this deserves a medal," said Lord Micalek Zupanic, walking around the bed and taking a suspensor-seat on the other side. His brother Xavier's body was half-destroyed. He had been lucky to survive. "The boy's insane. He's mental. If he died, the galaxy would be a safer place."

His mother looked up slowly. "That's probably true," she acknowledged. "But he is my son."

"What's the prognosis?" Micalek asked.

"He will recover, but slowly, and there will be many years of treatment," said Lady Wyn. "There is some brain damage, which is always more difficult to heal."

"It may result in an improvement."

"Enough, Micci."

Lord Micalek nodded once at his mother's command. "So how did this happen?" he asked. "Nobody seems to know?"

Lady Wyn looked around, and then withdrew a special device from her pocket. Micalek recognised it as a counter-measures device, to dampen and prevent any recording of their discussion.

"Micalek, it is time you knew the truth," Lady Wyn said. "You have always served the family's interests well, but your father and I kept you ignorant of our deeper plans in relation to House Towers."

"I knew there was something," he said, "in our family, there always is."

"Listen, child." He listened as his mother explained about the assassination of Lord Erik Towers, and how it was timed to happen between the announcement of his marriage and Lord Erik naming Lord Luke as his heir, precisely so that Micalek would become heir to the seat of House Towers after Sophia. It had been disguised as StarCom Federation retribution.

"So how are you going to make sure I gain the headship of house of Towers' territory?" asked Micalek, suspecting he knew the answer.

"We would have waited until you had your first heir by Sophia, and then she would have been assassinated like her father. Lord Luke will be disposed of shortly within the next month, to prevent him contesting the claim, and leaving no chance that he and Sophia can come up with some plan to alter the line of succession in House Towers."

Lord Micalek kept his face very carefully blank, but inside, he was a roiling explosion of emotion. His current engagement to Lady Sophia had never been anything else than a political marriage, an attempt by Lord Erik Towers to gain a superior place within the Levitican Union and gel House Zupanic's resources to his economic and military might, a power within the Union. Despite that, he had found himself growing closer and closer to Lady Sophia. They had been intimate for some time, and he spent many months since the announcement with her, getting to know her, and he thought falling in love with her. He believed she felt the same. That it was to be an arranged marriage meant little to either of them.

He had realised there was something wrong with her recently, she had changed. He wondered if she and her brother Luke knew of what had been plotted against them, and if they suspected him of complicity. "Why did you not tell me of this, mother?" he asked. If he had known, he might have been more careful of his emotions.

"We wished it to seem real to the Towers family," she replied. "And I saw how you two were acting together. If we had told you the truth of our plans, would that have ever happened?"

"You used me."

"Welcome to the realities of House politics, Micalek," his mother narrowed her eyes evilly. "You are under no illusions, do not play the innocent party to me. You have been married twice before. You are the Beast of Balthazar, and that was not done by someone weak-hearted."

"Another lie, put about by you and my father," he said. "And as for my previous marriages – you poisoned my last wife without my knowledge, because it no longer suited us."

"You did not cry then, Micalek. Do not cry over Sophia."

"I have no intentions of doing so," he said, but inside, he felt hollow. His heart was racing, feeling like it was breaking. There was something very different about Lady Sophia. To know that she was fated to die at the hands of Ramicek and Wyn Zupanic, his parents, would forever change his relationship with her. He desperately needed to get away from this room, and to think.

He did not make a move to stand up, knowing it would be too obvious, and besides which another point had occurred to him. "So what does this have to do with my brother?" he asked.

Lady Wyn explained about the Faceless assassin, how he had been captured as Micalek knew, and then transferred into Zupanic control. The fools in House Towers had given them back their hired assassin. She explained what Xavier had been trying to do, and how the facility had been struck by a commando raid, and that Xavier had almost died during the attack.

"We have no way of knowing who took the Faceless assassin back," she said. "But I suspect it was House Towers."

"Why?" he asked. "The Faceless are probably searching for him, it could just have easily been them."

"We have no way of knowing," said Lady Wyn, "but I find it interesting that shortly after the assassin was stolen from us, Lady Sophia diverted away from her scheduled tour of House Towers systems under the pretext of a very shaky cover story. I have had it checked out, and it is not true. She went back to the Blackheath System for some reason, and it is too coincidental that it happened after the strike on Obrenovac X. Do you think she suspects anything of our plans? Has she been acting any differently with you?" she finished.

"No," lied Micalek. She had been acting very differently with him, but he had put that down to the death of her father. "And as for suspecting 'our' plans, I had no idea of what you and father were up to, mother."

"We need to know what she is up to," said Lady Wyn. "What she knows. You need to go back to the Blackheath System, speak to Lady Sophia, and try to discover what they know. If they took the data we extracted from the assassin's mind at least some of our plans are revealed. We also need to recover that Faceless assassin, quickly. You can get closer than any of my agents can."

His first thought was that it would get him back to Lady Sophia and away from this palace of nightmares. How could he face her, knowing that her brother was about to be killed and she was only a couple of years away from also being assassinated by his family.

"Very well," he said, trying not to look annoyed. He needed time to think!

"We'll give you a full briefing on what to do and say," said Lady Wyn. She suddenly smiled, in itself a rarity from the witch. "I love you, son. Do your best for the House."

"I love you, mother," he lied. "I will."

*

It was said that one Praetorian Guard Marine was worth up to twenty House marines and soldiers. There had even been comparison tables published by the Red Imperium's Imperial Intelligence division, based on simulations and live-action data, ranking Imperial Marines against the armed forces of all the Houses in the colonised galaxy.

On the journey to the Kyiv System, General Ulrik Andryukhin had accessed this information out of interest. In comparison to House Erdogan's military, at least prior to the dissolution of the Empire, one of his Praetorians was reckoned to be worth twelve Erdoganites. This was largely because the nation of Erdogan had fairly advanced cyborg technology to place within their soldiers.

General Ulrik Andryukhin stood on the bridge of the military super-transporter *Monstrosity*. He had twenty-five thousand Marines jumping into the Kyiv System with him, which meant if the Imperial tables were correct, that they were equivalent to over a quarter of a million armed Erdoganites. He did know that the Erdoganites had a small number of ex-Praetorian Guard amongst their own forces, but whether any would be encountered on the planet Kyiv Primus was not certain.

The journey itself had taken almost two months in terms of transit-time, but in real-time it had been a little over ten days. A large proportion of the travel had been via stargate, the Blackheath Stargate catapulting them deeper into the Mid-Sectors and half-way around this section of the Eastern Segment.

Transit-time was the term used for the period of time which a starship spent travelling in hyper-space at faster-than-light speeds. A jump which in real-space could take little more than a couple of seconds or minutes, could be anything from a day to five or six weeks in hyper-space if a stargate had been used. Time flowed differently at faster-than-light speeds.

Captain Enrique Delgado, master of the *Monstrosity*, sat in the command chair behind where General Andryukhin stood. Somewhere in the ether the *Marvellous* super-transporter and the *Titan of Stars* were also travelling with them, carrying the twenty-five thousand Marines at fantastic speeds across the galaxy. Captain Delgado signalled the crew to prepare for hyper-space exit.

General Andryukhin braced himself, as the navigations officer called out across the datasphere, <Warp exit in three .... two ..... one .... we have translation!>

The *Monstrosity* shuddered slightly as it exited the jump, and Andryukhin felt a slight drag on his body. It felt like déjà vu, where half the brain caught up with the other half. He felt a small amount of nausea; it was not uncommon for people to be ill, even seasoned naval officers who had made hundreds of jumps getting just that one where they had to expel the contents of their stomachs after a bad jump. Andryukhin steeled himself, and the wave of sickness passed.

Common myth held that if a marine experienced nausea when they exited a jump, then their mission was going to go wrong in some way. He decided to keep his temporary feeling of sickness to himself.

<Structural integrity fields collapsing,> an operator reported.

<Jumping field deactivating, capacitors off-line,> another said.

<Scanners,> Captain Delgado commanded, <confirm location of other ships.>

<*Marvellous* and *Titan of Stars* have translated safely, sir, in expected positions. Formation has held.>

<Any immediate threats? Passive scans only, standard op,> Captain Delgado ordered.

<None in the vicinity,> the scanners officer reported. <It doesn't look as if we've been detected, either.>

<One minute thirty until we have weapons,> the tactical officer interrupted.

<Looks like we don't need them,> said Captain Delgado. <All ships, all hands, prepare to go to running silent. Helm, set course for the planet Kyiv Primus on the given approach vector.>

<Going to silent, Captain.>

<Vector locked in, sir.>

Andryukhin had been listening to the conversations on the bridge over the datasphere, even as he had been receiving the readiness reports from his own marine commanders. Every marine was ready and raring to go, although they would have to wait another couple of days whilst they made their way in-system. The M-class transporters could carry fifteen thousand Marines and their equipment at maximum, but he only had ten thousand in each, and the *Titan of Stars* could carry ten thousand, although it only had five thousand. It had been heavily modified in order to carry a multitude of Praetorian-grade equipment and soldiers. Eventually they would be at full-strength, he knew, and Tahrir Base would shortly be cranking out more and more new Praetorians for the mercenary group.

He brought his attention back to the mission. He desperately wanted to be with James Gavain, hunting down Silus Adare and paying him back for the death of his lover Julia Kavanagh. It was not to be, though, he had responsibilities. Sometimes he wished for the simpler life, when he had been a Major to Gavain's Commander, before the civil war. He acknowledged though that the simpler life had also meant accepting the atrocities of the tyranny that the False Emperor had brought to the Red Imperium.

Out in the depths of space, the three forms of the large transporter vessels shimmered as they began to run silent, chameleonic fields activating. They became invisible as they steamed forwards, main drive engines deactivating after their initial flaring to provide forward propulsion.

They were locked on to a course which would take them to the Zhou-Zheng Compact side of the planet Kyiv Primus, past numerous Erdogan pickets. The contract was now officially under way.

*

Juan Ramirez sat at the bar, drinking the last of the real alcohol lager. He had taken his time with drink. He did not have much money to spare, so he had been nursing it carefully. He had looked into the prices of interstellar travel away from this backwater mudball of Farsight, but it was not exactly a tourist destination, apart for the rich glory-seeking hunters who were after the local fauna.

Interstellar travel from here was far too expensive by far. He was stuck, without enough money, and he had no idea what he was going to do. The thought of living out the rest of his life here filled him with dread. Even if he managed to get some menial job to build up enough money to get off-planet, it would take him years to do it.

"Another please," he signalled the serving-droid. It whirred an affirmative, and dispensed a new glass of lager for him. At least the local beer was cheap, he reflected. The amount was automatically debited from his account through an implant in his right hand. At least here, far from Cervantia, he did not need to worry about hiding his borg nature. It was a small plus in an otherwise bleak situation.

The medical treatment had been expensive too, but he had paid for as much as he dared afford. His malfunctioning implant had been fixed, and a lot of the damage to his ribs and his broken arm. The surface bruises would fade in time, but he had at least been able to get some of the scabbed over wounds healed. He looked presentable, but he still moved like an invalid.

He stood up from the bar, taking his drink to a table by the open window. The air-conditioning in here was broken, so the ambient temperature had risen to unbearable levels. It was mid-day. Flies buzzed around him, but he did not care.

He looked out of the window, wiping sweat away from his forehead. The bar was near the top of an amazingly thick tree-trunk of a local agajuju tree, the sap of which also happened to produce a highly intoxicating and illegal drug known all over this part of the galaxy. All he could really see was a lot of trees, and bizarrely considering the heat, a lot of rain. It pattered on the roof, battering his hearing like the crew of the *Yangtzee* had battered him. It was approaching the monsoon season, which meant no work in the farms he was told.

"May I join you?" asked a voice.

He looked up. A middle-aged woman, insofar as he could tell, was stood there. She wore a spacers jacket, with a flash-patch bearing the legend 'Ymar Warriors'. Every House had its own zeroball team, and the Ymar Warriors were one of those that were admired and had fans all over the galaxy because of their successes. Since the fall of the Red Imperium, the intergalactic zeroball matches had all stopped. He wondered if they would ever start up again.

"Sure," he said, shrugging.

"You look like you've been in a fight," she said.

He frowned, angry despite himself. His characteristic charm had deserted him of late. "I paid good money for this treatment," he said, "how did you guess?"

"It's the way you walk. Are you trouble, mister?"

"It's Juan. Juan Ramirez. And no, I'm not. I was beaten up for being a borg, if you must know."

"Hey, I'm called Helenna. Helen Sirocco," she extended a hand. "I'm un-augmented, but I have no problems at all with borgs. I'm officially a free-thinker. I wish the galaxy could just learn to get along."

Juan snorted. "I'm from Cervantia. The bigotry there is unbelievable. I've learnt that the galaxy will never get along."

She laughed. There was a syrupy quality to it, a thickness to it that was a give-away to her fondness for a smoke of agajuju. "So young for one so cynical," she said. She was drinking an expensive brand of whiskey from the colour of it, completely neat, although nothing in this bar was expensive. "So why are you hanging out here?"

Juan sighed, and told her the whole story. He saw no reason not to. She interrupted with quiet questions sometimes, and he never even realised he was being quizzed. He went back to the *Featherlight*, his encounter with the Vindicator Mercenary Corporation and their seizure of the cargo-freighter he worked upon. He covered his extended stay on Costa Biancia, his joy at finding a berth on the *Yangtzee*. He even told her about his liaison with Captain Diaz and Simeon Jimenez, his malfunction, and his horrific beating.

"A sad story," she said at the end, "although not that uncommon in various guises, and decades old in some instances. The dissolution of the Red Empire did not stop the bigotry and this humanist-borgite hatred. You're not alone, kid."

He felt the tears well up again, unexpectedly. "It doesn't feel like it," he said, "I just have no idea of what to do."

"I have a suggestion for you," Helenna Sirocco said quietly.

Despite himself, hope lit his eyes. "What's that?" he asked.

"I come in here from time to time, knowing that spacers grounded on planets tend not to drift too far from the space-ports. If you can call that travesty out there a space-port. Anyway, I'm hiring crew. I don't need a navigator, sorry, but a scanners officer would be useful. You've done that, you said."

"Really?" his voice almost squeaked. He could hardly believe his luck. Then he suddenly realised, as his wits kicked in. "This is something illegal, isn't it?" he asked. "You're not advertising through the Interstellar Merchants Guild."

"Well, no I'm not, and I don't particularly like to use words like illegal," she laughed again. "Perhaps more in the greyer areas of the law. It's not as if the Empire is around anymore to enforce Imperial Law, and a broken law in one House territory is old history when you cross into another."

"What happened to your last scanners officer?"

"He earned enough money and wanted out. That being said, if we get caught doing what we do, the penalties can be stiff. I've done it for decades, even under the Red Imperium, but it's not a lifestyle for everybody. He did a couple of years, but now he wants to go straight. Good for him, I hold no grudges."

Juan Ramirez thought. He found himself liking this person. "Which ship, doing what?" he asked.

"It's called the *SS Nazareth*, although we have a couple of false identities, obviously. A lovely little cargo-freighter she is, specially outfitted with concealed weapons for when I need them. I've been around a while, and I'm connected to a number of different crime gangs, yakuzas and mafias across the Mid-Sectors and the Core. Even the odd House, believe it or not, and they're the worst criminals of the lot. We smuggle all sorts of things, depending on value. It could be weaponry, drugs, even just heisted cargo on its way to a fence. Sometimes we take people, smuggling them out of certain situations – but never slavery. I have no brook with slavery."

"Slavery?" Juan queried.

"It still exists out towards the Boundary and the Frontier," she replied. "You don't get it in the Core, the Mid-Sectors or the Outer Sphere, not really. Not in this section of the galaxy, anyway, but it still exists, kiddo."

"And you need a scanners officer?" Juan repeated.

"I'm having to do it myself at the moment, so yes. Having a scanners officer who can double as a navigations officer would help, should anything happen to my navs operator too," said Helenna Sirocco. "What do you say, kid? It might be your best way off-planet. Do it for a while, see if you like it. The risks are there sometimes, but then the money's damn good."

He thought, but he did not really have an alternative. It would get him off the planet, which would be good, and it was probably the only chance he was going to get. Besides which, he was no angel. "Yeah, sure," he said.

*

There was a blinding flash of light, and the *Vindicator* battlecruiser appeared in the Tonsberg System, elongated beyond all possible tolerances for a construction made of metal. As it fully materialised, translating back into real-space, the optical illusion cancelled out and the ship snapped back to its normal parameters.

The Tonsberg System had once been the capital system of House Lindholm, pre-Imperium. Half the populated planets had been destroyed in the Drone Wars, and although they had been rebuilt, much of Tonsberg was famous for its memorials and museums to that dark time. The Lindholm capital had been moved to the Frederickstad System, a number of jumps away. Tonsberg still had great value to House Lindholm as a commercial and industrial power-house, but it was on a tour trail famous the galaxy over, and made almost as much revenue out of tourism as it did its various locally-based businesses.

93

The Identity Friend or Foe signal was broadcast, and the automatic defences within the Lindholm-owned star system deactivated, the ships in-system standing down from alert. The *Vindicator* was expected.

A battlecruiser coasted out to within communications range from the stationary squadron of ships, the legend *LhSS Emperor's Fist* emblazoned across its prow and flanks. The two battlecruisers could not be more different, the strong lines of the Mars-manufactured Praetorian battlecruiser distinct from the Lindholm ship's configuration.

The *Vindicator* was larger, with more weapons ports and highly advanced technology. It had a slightly bulbous prow, a thick main body with a series of three domes along its spine, a boxy, bulky rear that housed the main drive engines and two large nacelles running the length of body at forty-five degree angles from the main superstructure.

The *LhSS Emperor's Fist* was long, with an extended rectangular spine, and a bulbous main body slightly reminiscent of the ancient blimps. Two curved wings spread around the bulbous central body, jutting forwards beyond even the spine. It was a distinctive Nihima Corporation design, bought by many houses from the Core right out to the Frontier.

Despite their identical classification as battlecruisers, because the *Vindicator* had been a Praetorian Guard ship of the Emperor Himself, it was many decades in advance of the otherwise ultra-modern Lindholm ship, and could quite comfortably engage three or four of the Predator III-class starships.

Admiral Gavain sat in the spare flag chair at the centre of the bridge on the *Vindicator*, to the left of Commander Al-Malli's captains chair. The command section of the bridge was railed off from the remainder of the control centre, pits running either side of a long walkway extending down the cavernous room. Within the railing, around which the most important control stations were located, there was an expansive gap of clear deck. It was within this deck that a holographic avatar image of a man wearing an Admiral's uniform of House Lindholm's navy appeared.

"Admiral-of-the-Fleet Halvorssen," Admiral Gavain did not stand, remaining seated.

Jakub Halvorssen was on his feet, legs wide, arms crossed behind his back. He cut an imposing figure, and looked every inch the man he was – the commander of the naval forces of House Lindholm. "Sir Admiral Gavain," he greeted him. "Velkomen."

"We are here to inform you that we are moving into position," said Admiral Gavain. "In less than one day, my forces will be in place."

"Do you intend to share those positions with me, Admiral?" Halvorssen asked. He had a strong Eastern Mid-Sectors twang to his accent.

"No," Gavain shook his head. "Operational Security."

Halvorssen did not look impressed. "If you insist. Just ensure that you are effective in carrying out the contract, Admiral. I expect to see results quickly. The first payment will be released to you, as promised." He manipulated something near his right hand, perhaps a console of some sort, but it was not part of the holographic image.

"We will perform to our best," said Gavain. "Do you have any further information for me, Admiral?"

"It's your job to find me the information," said Admiral Halvorssen. "I want to know where these Pirates of the Cross are hiding, I want them stopped, and I want to know if the Helvanna Dominion is behind their piracy."

"Best not to jump to conclusions," Gavain said. He certainly had no intentions of doing so. "What is the situation with the Dominion?"

"It is deteriorating," Halvorssen looked concerned. "They are building up along their borders, at staging grounds that can reach into our space. I feel war is inevitable. I cannot have these Pirates of the Cross operating in my rear, whilst trying to defend against the Dominion, Sir Admiral."

"We will be incommunicado for large periods of time," said Gavain. "We will transmit a special code, so your forces can identify mine and vice versa, and prevent any blue-on-blue incidents."

"Good thinking, if you are going covert," said Admiral Halvorssen. He hesitated, and then said, "I believe Ambassador Nyman's informed you of the defence pact we have with House Rantanen and Hausen-Berg?"

"Yes," Gavain nodded, taciturnly.

"The defence pact is about to become something more, Sir Admiral. In less than an hour's time, we formalise a new treaty amongst our houses. We are forming a new nation - it seems to be the thing to do, these days."

"Fear of StarCom brought the Levitican Union together," Gavain shrugged. "The OutWorlds Alliance, Republic of Varrental, and many more have all been born of such a need. What shall the new nation be called?"

"The Aalborg Alliance, after the name of the system where it was created," said Admiral Halvorssen. "We follow in the fashion set by your Levitican Union."

"It is not my Levitican Union," said Gavain. "We are mercenaries, and hold no allegiance to any state or person except the one True Emperor, may his bones rest in peace."

"So you say," Admiral Halvorssen looked unconvinced.

"What do your simulations say of success against the Dominion?" asked Gavain, already having directed his own intelligence chief to conduct such hypothetical analysis. His own data suggested the Aalborg Alliance of the three Houses would be hard-pressed to succeed long-term against the Dominion.

"That is a matter for me," said Admiral-of-the-Fleets Halvorssen. "Our success factor increases dramatically without the Pirates of the Cross disrupting our economy and our trade routes. Do your job, Gavain, and do it very, very well. It is of vital importance to our war-effort, whenever this war with the Helvanna Dominion begins, that the Pirates of the Cross are stopped."

"Understood," Gavain nodded his head once again. "Gavain out."

*

With a blinding flash of light, the *LSS Divine Right* appeared in the Blackheath System, flowing through the terminus point of its jump with practiced ease. Defensive forces identified it almost immediately, and stood down, even though the arrival was unannounced.

Shortly after it achieved orbital geosynchronicity with the planet Tahrir, a message was beamed down to the planetary surface, recorded by the appropriate data-core, encrypted, and sent back out into space, blasting at unimaginable speeds through the unreal hyper-space, propelled by the hyper-pulse communications generator at the centre of Tahrcity.

Lord Micalek was in the Blackheath System, and he wanted Lady Sophia home. He had something urgent to discuss with her.

*

Lord Minister Luke entered the council chamber after their brief recess, pale white, a deeply distressed look upon his face.

"Lord Minister Luke," Lord Principal Ramicek Zupanic said from the head of the circular table, "you look concerned. Is there some kind of issue?" The tall, thin, lithe man sat in a chair that completely dwarfed him, even with his fashionable high-collared cloak in place, it being a throne especially designed for whoever held the title of Lord Principal.

"Forgive me a moment, Lord Principal," said Luke, and began to walk across the room stiffly. His eyes were locked on Lady Minister Monique Lapointe. He approached the relatively young woman, unsure how to break the news.

The rest of the council fell silent, turning to look at him, ignoring their advisors.

"What is it, Luke?" asked Lady Minister Monique.

He knelt down by her side, deactivated the voice-mic at her part of the table, and whispered something. The whispering continued for some time, and the entire council could see the look on Lady Minister Monique's face. It went from disbelief, to shock, to horror. She stood, said something to a junior member of the House, and left the room.

Lord Minister Luke resumed his place at the table.

"Lord Minister Luke? What is .....?" Lord Principal Ramicek queried.

"Another pirate attack has occurred – unfortunately, it was deep in the Lapointe System. We are still awaiting full details, but from the sounds of it, House Lady Elouise Lapointe has either been killed or taken prisoner." Elouise Lapointe was Monique Lapointe's mother, and head of the House.

The entire council began murmuring. The various attendants, recorders and junior ministers who waited in the recesses broke their usual silence, causing Lord Principal Ramicek to lift the heavy metal ball in his right hand and bang it against the disc-shaped base for silence.

As the heavy metal tones rang away, he said, "Lord Minister Luke, how is this possible? Pirate attacks have always been in House Zupanic, Claes or Galetti space, not Lapointe."

"It is confirmed as pirate," said Lord Luke. He was very careful to keep his suspicions from his face. He wondered whether Lord Principal Ramicek was behind this, dressing the attack up to look like a pirate incursion. "The Rose Pirates, so-called after their distinctive signature and symbology, are positively identified. Some of the ships used are identical to those in our other territories."

"How do you intend to counter this?" Lord Minister Brin Claes asked.

"If anything, this lends even more importance to tapping the military resources of House Marchenko," said Lady Minister Aria Galetti.

"I *will* have order in this council," said Lord Principal Ramicek coolly. "Luke, please answer the question."

He glanced at Lady Aria. "House Marchenko is one possible solution," he said, "mercenaries are another. Increasing military production and diverting additional resources is yet a third. I have distributed a paper on this, following my presentation to the council a number of sessions ago, but we have not yet reached agreement on it."

He sat back down, reflecting that he was becoming more political with his answers. He had become more seasoned in the position as the months went by. He had always felt his sister would have been better placed for a Ministry position, rather than him, but he was finding the job easier as time passed. The Levitican War had certainly been a baptism of fire.

"We will debate this at the start of the next session," said Lord Principal Ramicek, "and we will not leave or move onto another topic until we have agreement this time, Lord Minister Luke, I promise."

For what that is worth, thought Lord Luke, although it was a better outcome than he wanted. Ramicek seemed shocked over the news, but the man was as brilliant an actor as he was a manipulative schemer. "Thank you, Lord Principal."

"Yes, Lord Brin?" Ramicek asked, responding to the request to speak which had appeared on the display in front of him.

"We were going to vote on the entry of House Marchenko to the Levitican Union," said Lord Brin Claes of the Ministry of Justice, "What do we do? We can't continue the council votes without Lady Minister Monique Lapointe or a duly authorised replacement representative, according to the Charter of Leviticus."

Lord Principal Ramicek hesitated, obviously torn about what to do, and was literally saved from answering by the approach of one of the junior ministers from Lady Lapointe's Ministry of Economic Affairs and Trade. He read the data-slate in front of him, then nodded to himself and raised his head.

"Lords and Lady of the Council," he said, "we will adjourn again for a further half-hour. Lady Minister Monique sends her regards, and says she will rejoin to complete the voting session before taking a leave of absence to see to necessary House business. We are adjourned."

He slammed the ball on its dais once, and the heavy tone rang out like the final toll at the end of days.

Lord Minister Luke had resumed his place at the table, glancing across at Lady Minister Monique Lapointe. She was composed, but nothing could hide the deep redness around her eyes. He reflected that much of the old guard was disappearing; her mother Elouise had been a strong ally and friend to his father Lord Erik, the ties between Houses Lapointe and Towers going back years.

He had spent the unexpected adjournment explaining to everyone what had happened when the Rose Pirates had struck. It looked like sheer fortuitousness on the part of the Rose Pirates, that they happened to have jumped into a system where Elouise Lapointe's ship was laid-up, recharging. It had been an uninhabited system, off the trade-routes, and the pirates were obviously using it to pass through Levitican space. Their vectors showed them to be moving in a direction to take them into Galetti space. Luke had already determined that it was a possibility they were coming out of House Jorgensson territory, and if that was true, they were crossing Lapointe space to stage their attacks. He would have to station patrols across the systems in Lapointe.

He also viewed it as a possibility that the Rose Pirates' accidental happening upon the Lapointe House Lady's vessel was no accident at all. It could be a carefully disguised assassination attempt, if the pirates were linked in to a House, be it either House Jorgensson or House Zupanic. He was sensible enough to realise that however much he viewed Ramicek Zupanic with deep suspicion, he could not be behind every incident in the galaxy.

The debate over the joining of House Marchenko to the Union was lacklustre, with neither the supportive or obstructive being particularly vehement in their points. All felt the shadow that had been cast over the decision.

Luke argued against to a small degree, although he also agreed with some of the positive points. Brin Claes and Ramicek Zupanic were heavily in favour, the former most likely taking the latter's lead, as he always did. Not for the first time, Luke wondered what hold Ramicek had over Lord Brin. Lord Moafa Obamu was arguing deeply against, on the basis of many of the concerns that Luke held over the collective House. There was a distinct humanist flavour to his arguments however.

Lady Minister Lapointe and Lady Galetti were relatively silent. Aria Galetti was a free-thinker and a very intelligent woman, and she was playing her cards close to her chest on this one. Lady Monique Lapointe had been deeply against, but all of a sudden what few things she said were in favour of House Marchenko. Perhaps she was thinking that if Marchenko's military and resources were part of the Union, then the Union would be better defended and her mother would be alive. She was pale, and very, very distant from the whole proceeding.

"Lords and Ladies," said Lord Principal Ramicek eventually, "we must vote. I must also declare this to be an open vote, with no anonymity, considering the import of what we are deciding. As per the Charter, on a vote of an additional House joining the Levitican Union, there can also be no abstentions. Do all agree?" There was no dissent. "Then let us vote, council. Will House Marchenko join the Union?"

Lord Principal Ramicek leaned forward, and pressed the 'aye' button. A holographic counter in the centre of the room displayed his vote and his name.

Lord Minister Brin Claes was next. He voted 'aye'. The vote then went to Lord Minister Moafa Obamu, who voted 'nay'.

At two-to-one, Lord Minister Luke hesitated on his turn. He had been lobbied by Lord Principal Ramicek, who had reminded him of the pact between their houses. Luke should vote with House Zupanic, but inside, he felt tempted to vote 'no' purely on the basis of how much he distrusted Ramicek. However, he knew he had to keep up the pretence, and he also was far from convinced it would actually be calamitous to the Union to include them. He voted 'aye'. One more vote for yes, and the majority would rule.

Lady Minister Monique was next. She hesitated, and looked as if she were about to faint, but she pressed the 'aye' button.

A look of shock and then resignation passed the face of Lady Aria Galetti. In that moment, Luke realised she was going to vote 'no', but now the motion was effectively carried. Keeping her composure, she voted 'aye'.

"We have five votes for yes, one vote for no, and the motion is carried," Lord Principal Ramicek Zupanic banged the metal ball again. "Let the records show that as of today, on the terms proposed and agreed, the Council of the Levitican Union has approved the membership of House Marchenko."

Chapter VIII

The planet Kyiv Primus was a super-planet, seven times the size of earth, but for all its greater size it was remarkably similar in colour at least. Swirls of white cloud combined with the deep blueness of the oceans and the greens and browns of the three large landmasses, giving it a rich but above all overly familiar colouring. The poles were even capped with a frosty white.

Due to the slow rotation of Kyiv Primus, the Zhou-Zheng Compact side of the planet was currently dark, facing away from the small and weak sun. The rotation meant that for nearly three whole Imperial Standard days, the planet was either shrouded in night-time or lit by day-time. A whole local planetary day took five and half Imperial Standard days to complete. Only the proximity of Primus to the sun allowed it to have anything approaching a predominately temperate climate.

Kyiv Primus had a lower than normal gravity, at two-thirds Standard. Oxygen levels had been brought up to suitable for human life by the minimal terra-forming required several centuries ago, the meteorological system comparable to Earths. For all that, the vicious flora and fauna of the highly dangerous and predatory eco-system also served to make the planet as alien as possible.

The *Monstrosity*, *Marvellous*, and *Titan of Stars* dropped their chameleonic fields safely in the shadow of the planet, having pre-warned the Zhou-Zheng Compact ships of their presence. Silent in the depths of space, they began the operation to drop off their Marine cargo, Vindicator Mercenary Corporation landers shuttling an entirely new army of tens of thousands of ex-Praetorian Guard Imperial Marines into the war.

The stream of Freiderich and Heinerich-class landers were all adaptable, multi-purpose vehicles capable of carrying any mixture of troops, vehicles and weaponry. Starfighters and starbombers carried by the *Monstrosity* and the *Marvellous* provided a roving screen of escorts down through the planetary atmosphere, to the designated landing zone. The LZ had been chosen to be far enough around the curvature of the planet that with the proper approaches by the landing craft, the Erdoganite land army and the naval forces on their side of the planet would be unable to detect their insertion into the theatre.

The entire operation to land would take the highly-trained, elite marines less than fifty minutes to accomplish. Twenty-five thousand soldiers and their equipment would have landed on the planet with House Erdogan forces unaware of their arrival.

One of the Freiderich-class landers detached from the stream of craft, heading in a slightly different direction. Escorted by a flight of five starfighters, it punched through the atmosphere of Kyiv Primus, clouds scattering away from their insertion point.

Their flight-path was highly secret, but known to the Zhou-Zheng Compact. They flew down on a sharp, almost vertical descent towards the centre of the continent of Drei, a cold, southerly land-mass. They levelled out, approaching the vast military complex that was barely more than a month old.

The military complex was Base Command, a large stronghold where the Compact controlled its drone armies and the entire land operations for the Kyiv Primus theatre. It had been constructed rapidly by their engineers in the first few days of the battle coming to Kyiv Primus.

General Ulrik Andryukhin was coming to pay his respects.

The ramp had extended out even before the lander had touched down, General Ulrik Andryukhin stepping off and landing lightly ten metres down, his power-armour suit aided legs flexing and taking the fall easily. The X-visored helmet on his suit was fully attached to the suit, his body physically melded into the armour to the extent where it had become another skin. The suit itself was new, a set of highly-prized rare experimental armour salvaged from their last major contract.

His adjutant, Sergeant Calaman, landed barely a nanosecond behind him, the rest of his command squad falling after her in tight order. He noted that their precision was second to none. They were the best people he had, and as he was a fighting general in the best traditions of the Praetorian Guard, they were also effectively his honour guard.

Expected as he was, there was an honour guard from the Zhou-Zheng Compact to meet him. His skin crawled as he looked at them. Every single one of the sixty soldiers arranged in ranks of thirty either side was a drone. They were fighting robots with very limited artificial intelligence, the horrors of the Drone Wars having taught the human race more than enough about allowing them to be sentient.

They walked across the landing strip of Base Command briskly, the drone soldiers falling into place and bracketing them to either side.

"Do you remember Kentax, Sergeant?" he vocalised aloud, so the drones could hear.

"Yes, General," said Sergeant Naomi Calaman.

"We cut a hundred thousand frickers like these tin-pots to shreds in less than a day," he remarked loudly.

He could hear the amusement in her voice. "That we did, General."

He watched, but not one of the drones reacted. He did not really expect them to, but he knew that they were probably being listened to by their operators, and the remark would have annoyed their human controllers considerably.

As they approached a large building as unremarkable and functional as all the rest, Ulrik used the enhancements in his suit and his biological implants to quickly scan and identify the drone nearest to him, pulling up a data-file over the datasphere to provide him with the advanced tactical information the Praetorian Guard had maintained on the model. He absorbed and knew it all in less than a blink of an eye.

The Nihima Corporation made Model Ninjua-4 walked alongside him, humanoid in form but heavily armoured. An expensive model, it was capable of independent operations as well as being group-controlled, and was one of the best drone soldiers on the market. It was designed for operating alongside human soldiers, humanist House armies that utilised drones typically also having large flesh-and-blood contingents to their forces, operating in concert with the drones. Heavily armoured, it was easily the size of him in all his genetically super-enhanced glory.

Drones or droids were typically controlled by human operators, either locally by human soldiers fighting alongside them, a group-controller based many kilometres behind the battle-front, a gigantic land-based control vehicle, from a control-ship in orbit, or more often from a combination of all. The multiple redundancy was there in case the controlling battle-net was hacked. In addition, advanced units like the Ninjua-4 could operate intelligently and independently in case all controlling communications were broken, or in deep communications isolation following pre-determined orders.

Battle-droids and drones came in all guises, shapes and configurations. Outside, Andryukhin had seen droid-tanks, massive dronewalkers and even hovering droidcopters. Some 'soldier' units had tracks, or hovered above ground, and could be as small as a hand or larger than a tank.

Still, however, cyborg armies tended to have the edge. There was no replacement for a human/machine hybrid, in General Andryukhin's biased opinion, and it had been proven many times over. It was certainly what the Zhou-Zheng Compact were discovering in their planetary battles against the borg Erdoganites. The True and the False Emperor of the Red Imperium had used cyborgs and drones together, but both had kept the borgs for their elite unit, the Praetorian Guard, because of their superiority.

A door opened, and Andryukhin and his squad were admitted into a luxurious office. A darkened window covered one entire wall, and Andryukhin suspected that behind it lay the central war-room of the Compact. They were not going to be permitted into every secret and plan the Zhou-Zheng Compact had, obviously.

He strode forward, mentally commanding his helmet to part and retract into the collar of his power-armour. He gave an Imperial salute, one gauntleted fist banging with a ring off his chest-plate. He would not lower himself to offer a hand to shake, as James Gavain had been trying to teach him.

"General Ulrik Andryukhin, reporting for duty and contract commencement," he said levelly.

The man wearing the Compact's Star Marshal uniform looked young for the position, but he was something of a tactical and strategic genius according to his data-file. It was affording him little in this theatre, however. Behind the man two life-size holographic representations of Zhou Ze and Zheng Il-Sou rotated gently, either side of the Zhou-Zheng Compact flag. His devotion to the House of Zhou was legendary.

"I am Star Marshal Ngu Soo Su," he said. "Your arrival is on-schedule. This is good."

"I'm not staying long," said General Andryukhin. "The contract said to present myself, which I have done. We have our mission to complete. Have there been any tactical changes since your last update?"

Star Marshal Ngu sat down, his face inscrutable but the weariness suddenly appearing in the set of his shoulders. "Yes, there has," he said, handing over a data-chip. Ulrik took it and downloaded the information contained within, assimilating the full data much faster than Ngu could ever explain it to him.

"Two days ago, we were pushed back by a major Erdoganite offensive on the continent of Zwei. We have almost lost the continent, now holding what is effectively little more than a beachhead to the south of the central, equatorial land-mass. We are under sustained attack, and may lose our foothold in the next day or two. If that happens, the war on Kyiv Primus will have turned very much in Erdogan favour. Their tactics seem to consist of holding us in abeyance; they will not cross the ocean to fight us here in Drei, but they will further tie down my forces, and we will lose all hope of ending this stalemate in the Kyiv System."

"I agree," said Ulrik. "If you lose the southern salient, it will be difficult to turn the war around. However, they will not be expecting the Vindicator Mercenary Corporation."

"I am very much hoping that you will prove to be the hammer that cracks the battle for this planet, smashing the stalemate in our favour."

"Have our initial orders changed in light of this development?" General Andryukhin asked.

"No," said Star Marshal Ngu, "although you must now understand that getting reinforcements to you will be much more difficult. You are still tasked with the primary objective of taking Kyiv Megapolis, the capital city on Zwei, and the secondary objective of disrupting Erdogan operations to such an extent that my regular forces can overwhelm them on continent Zwei."

Ulrik nodded. Their contract was to break the stalemate, and specifically, to enable Compact forces to take the planet of Kyiv Primus. The key to that was the continent Zwei. The Erdogan forces on Eins, whilst being numerous, were of lesser strategic concern. The bulk of the Erdogan land army was on continent Zwei. Break Zwei, and Eins would fall easily.

A large proportion of the Compact land army was trapped in the shrinking salient on the southern coast of Zwei. Whilst there were reinforcements and significant operations on Drei, the Compact needed to evacuate its forces on Zwei or lose them, if they could not turn the battle around in the next couple of days.

"What is your plan, General Andryukhin."

He was prepared for this. "As stated in our contract, in order for us to maintain operational security, that will remain confidential, Star Marshal."

Star Marshal Ngu did not look impressed. "Very well. You have three days to make an impact on this theatre, or I estimate I will lose the salient. In thirty hours time, I will have to decide whether to commence a controlled evacuation of the continent Zwei. Before then, General."

"Understood, Star Marshal."

"Also understand this, mercenary. I have staked a large part of my reputation on the premise of bringing in *borg* mercenaries to fight our war for us. I have come here to this planet to oversee how well you perform against the enemy personally. The Primarch Zhou is allowing me considerable lee-way with the proposal to utilise borgs against borgs, but failure is not an option. Primarchess Zheng will have my head if it fails. If I lose my head, you will lose more than your payment."

Andryukhin almost responded violently, but restrained himself. He activated his helmet, the armour enclosing his head safely. His external voice-mic activated. "We will not fail," he said aloud, and privately he thought, we will not be threatened by you either. "I will take my leave, Star Marshal."

Back aboard the Freiderich lander, flying rapidly towards the designated Landing Zone for his invasion force, General Andryukhin sat in a private seat, at the rear of the small cockpit for the lander. A holographic map rotated gently in front of him, playing over and over again the detailed plans he had made for the assault onto the continent of Zwei.

His forces were always intended to operate independently of the Zhou-Zheng Compact, with the likelihood of planetary, air or space support always factored out of his overall plans. The reversed situation on the continent had little to no impact on his plans; in fact, it would make taking the capital city that little bit easier.

The first stage of the operation consisted of his forces setting up and arranging themselves in the Landing Zone, in the appropriate launch waves. The second stage consisted of an underwater approach, to take them up on the eastern coast of the continent. The third stage was the beginning of operations overland on Zwei, the slow consolidation of his forces which would have scattered during the second stage approach. The fourth stage was the assault on Kyiv Megapolis itself, all the while ostensibly under the guns of the Erdoganite navy. He had ways to counter that superior fire-power, however.

He grinned fiercely to himself. He was bred for war, cooked up out of molecular soup for the sole purpose of conducting such violent operations. Following the loss of Julia Kavanagh, he definitely needed something to distract himself with, and it felt really good to be out doing what he was best at.

He was going to enjoy this, he knew.

*

Lieutenant-Commander Jason Bramhall was nearing forty-eight hours of being awake. His augmentation allowed this easily; he could run for almost a week with little or no sleep before feeling any detrimental effects. It was the same for all Praetorians, a result of careful genetic manipulation and purpose-built implants.

His A-class *Adventurous* corvette was on silent running, hiding in the fringes of the Saana System. Saana was un-colonised and within House Lindholm territory, but it was on the major trade-route that Admiral Gavain had elected to defend. It did however boast a large commercial space-station, a deep-space astronomical observation array, and a small military starbase. Being on a busy trade-route, there were ships jumping in and out-system regularly.

The *Adventurous* and the five other A-class corvettes of the Vindicator Mercenary Corporation were strung out, covering six planetary systems as part of the early warning system. When on silent running, a space craft extinguished all its distinctive running lights and powered down all of its systems, utilising only passive scanning equipment and dampening what few traces of its existence it would emit. Chameleonic fields effectively turned it invisible even to the naked eye, blending its physical form into the blackness of space.

There was a tendency for spacers on such vessels to talk in quietened tones, if indeed they talked at all. Jason Bramhall was perfectly suited for such missions, loving the quiet, coupled with the dangerous tension and the tingling of the nerves. Jacked into the datasphere, what few electronic communications were sent pseudo-telepathically between his crew were imbued with that tension.

He sipped quietly from his juice, sat in the command chair of the small bridge of the *Adventurous*. The vessel only had sixty-five naval crew members, the small vessel economical in every operation. On the bridge his second in command also served as tactical officer. The other bridge crew consisted of a helmsman, a navigations and scanners officer, and a communications operator. Contrast the five bridge crew with the near hundred that would serve on a battlecruiser or dreadnought, and it would give a sense of the scale of the corvette compared to such behemoths.

<Lieutenant-Commander, we're picking up increased comms traffic,> said his comms officer. <It sounds like they're getting worried.>

Lieutenant-Commander Jason Bramhall felt his internal systems, half of them on hibernation, jump automatically to full alert at the same time as the ship itself parodied his own internal workings. In many senses when jacked into a datasphere, the ship was little more than an extension of his own body and that of his crews. <Details, Sub-Lieutenant?>

<Just a moment, sir .....> he waited a number of seconds as Sub-Lieutenant Helios worked. This far out from the space station, starbase and astronomical array, they were not able to detect incoming jump signatures. They got around the issue by hacking into the commercial and military communications network, to get the warning they were in the process of receiving. <Confirmed, sir, incoming jump signatures, and there's no ships scheduled for translation at this time. Three to five ships, sir.>

<They must be assuming they are hostile,> said Lt-Cdr Bramhall.

<Yes, sir, the starbase is launching their frigate.>

Bramhall shook his head. House Lindholm had three frigates assigned permanently to the system, and one of them was always in dock. At a time when they knew they could become a target for increased pirate activity, to have one ship always indisposed was not sound thinking. Besides that there were currently three convoys, one of them armed with a further escort of an ancient light cruiser and a frigate, and a number of civilian ships unassigned to convoys passing through to various destinations. The system was busy with traffic, and it could not be accidental that if the incoming ships were hostile, they had chosen this moment to strike.

<Orders, sir?> his helmsman asked.

<We will keep position until we have an ident,> he said. <All hands, hold to running silent.>

The next few minutes went by slowly. All of a sudden there was a flare of light, easily visible on the highly magnified visible scanners, and as it faded the forms of four starships were revealed. At this range they could only conduct visual identification, but it was enough.

<Pirates of the Cross,> said Sub-Lieutenant Helios. <Ident confirmed. One dreadnought, two strikecruisers, and one interdictor>.

The trap was sprung. <All hands, prepare for immediate jump,> Lieutenant-Commander Bramhall ordered. They would jump out-system to another, utilise the local HPCG station, and warn all available Vindicator Mercenary Corporation ships to jump in to the Saana System.

*

In the main personnel cabin of the *King Cobra* HAPC, General Ulrik Andryukhin breathed shallowly. His bodily system was mostly on shut-down, gaining some rest whilst he awaited completion of the six hour journey.

The mission clock was ticking, but he had no other option but to wait.

Through the very localised datasphere, he could see a picture in his minds-eye of what lay ahead of the *King Cobra*. A startled fish smacked against the forward visualiser camera, gone in an eye-blink, caught unawares by the speed and the chameleonic field the *King Cobra* was generating.

The *King Cobra* was moving deep underwater, having crossed most of the ocean towards the eastern seaboard of the continent Zwei. His ten man squad was supplemented by the driver and a gunner on the roof from another unit.

They had lost contact with all other units some hours ago. Even communications were now banned, utter silence being imposed for the multiple point insertion onto the continent. An aerial drop-off had been viewed as too risky, so he had chosen an amphibious approach.

His very best soldiers were in the vanguard of the approach. They would land on the eastern coast, and make their way inland, disposing of patrols wherever possible to clear the way for the heavier units that would only be an hour behind them. The enemy would eventually become aware of their approach, but they would have no idea of the size or strength of the force speeding towards them overland.

The *King Cobra* was beginning to rise in the water.

Andryukhin released the combat drugs into his system, rapidly gaining full alertness. <We're on, you fuckers,> he said, to wake up his squad. <Look to it.>

The rest of his squad were instantly awake and suddenly moving, checking their weaponry and the status of their suits. <Three minutes until land-fall, General,> the driver said.

<Acknowledged,> Andryukhin replied, his own suit and weaponry checks completed. He forced himself to remain still as he waited. He had a full battalion hitting the eastern coast of continent Zwei as the vanguard, which would operate in small squad units supported by one HAPC. Behind them were coming the second wave, a full brigade of heavier vehicles and a large contingent of assault troopers, another two battalions and a master battalion.

The *King Cobra* began to emerge from the water, climbing up onto the beach. As it coasted gently out of the water, creating the minimum disturbance, it would have created a strange sight. With full chameleonic shields, it was not possible to see the vehicle at all, but the effects as it rose out of the water would have been visible. Luckily it was still night-time, there was no-one to see, and a quick scan of the surroundings proved that there were no electronic detection devices to monitor their approach.

Praetorian technology was the best. Only ten minutes into the drive overland, the driver suddenly slowed down. <Potential hostiles ahead,> he reported. <One vehicle, General.>

<Disembark,> Andryukhin ordered. <Assess, and if hostile, engage according to the RoE. *King Cobra* to be ready to support.>

The *King Cobra* went from its carefully calculated advance speed to dead-stop almost immediately, disembarkation ramp already open. General Andryukhin led the way out, the unit fanning out around him as they passed the *Cobra*, falling into a standard Praetorian assault pattern. One Marine would always be covering another's blind spots with overlapping fields of fire.

They were already in deep undergrowth. Even at night, it was hot, the rainforest they were within currently dry. Eventually, moving silently despite the treacherous conditions underfoot, Andryukhin ordered a halt. He had spotted the potential targets.

It was an Erdoganite patrol. The House soldiers had stopped, obviously skiving off their duties. It was incredibly poor discipline, and not one Praetorian would ever dare emulate it. The fighting was thousands of kilometres to the south, however, and they felt able to be lax. The vehicle was a light MM24 hovertruck, designed either for cargo transport or for carrying troops, but despite a quad-autolaser gun mounted on the roof, they were hardly a threat. The quad-lasers were not even being manned.

<Ten targets,> said Andryukhin. <Assigning targets now. On mark, eliminate in person. No projectile weapons.> Targets were selected and assigned quickly.

<Mark,> he said, even as his power-armoured legs were propelling him forwards.

He crossed the fifteen metres to his target in less than a second, aided by the suit and his super-enhanced muscles, going from a prone position to full assault at a speed a non-augmented could never match. His power-claw activated, the tines snapping brutally around the head of his target. He carried on, rolling and half-tearing, half-cutting the head away from his target.

He rolled to his feet, the decapitated head bouncing away. His target had never even seen him coming. A total of two seconds and it was all over; he had checked, and his unit had completely eliminated the enemy. Such was the efficiency of the Praetorian Marines.

<Well done,> he said, <Dispose of the bodies, booby-trap the truck. One minute. Let's keep to schedule and get moving again.>

Andryukhin knelt down to the ground, and used a device to fire a one-off signal module deep into the ground. As the bulk of his forces followed on, they could trip the devices to show them the path to follow.

*

Admiral Gavain sat calmly within the flag chair on the bridge of the *Vindicator*. He had returned to the bridge an hour ago, knowing that the three-day transit time of the jump was nearly over.

They had received the HPCG communication from Lieutenant-Commander Bramhall, informing them of the pirate attack on the Saana System. Full details of all civilian and House Lindholm military ships in-system had been provided, their known locations, as much information as was needed for them to be effective when they landed in the battle-zone. They were coming in at a reasonably far distance away from the battle-zone, for several reasons.

First, the interdictor may now be active. If it was, the gravity well it generated would prevent any ships from jumping out, but would also disrupt and potentially destroy any ships jumping in. Second, the pirates would have a short period of time to detect their pending arrival, and he wanted to ensure that his ships could have full shields before they engaged. Third, the *Queen of Egypt* star-carrier and the *Solace* strikecruiser were able to make a double-jump to the Saana System, and he ordered them to respond as well as his own *Vindicator* and the *Ubermacht* destroyer, and he did not want them jumping in at the same co-ordinates in case there was a catastrophic mis-jump. Fourth, if any of the civilian ships were scattering and evading the enemy, they could stray into his jump-point and cause a catastrophe if he were not careful.

It was only a shame that his own interdictor, the *Kinslayer*, could not make it to the Saana System, and then they would have been able to trap the enemy. He had to hope their own interdictor was fully active, and they would be trapped by their own tactics.

Although they had been in hyper-space for nearly three days, when they exited the terminus point of the jump, only five minutes would have elapsed in real-space within the Saana System. The pirate attack would still only be just beginning.

<Exit from hyperspace in three .... two .... one ... we have exit.>

It was absolute chaos in the Saana System. There were twenty-eight civilian ships, and those still able to were scattering, convoy discipline completely broken. A number had already been disabled by the Pirates of the Cross. The interdictor was firing at long-range, using its weaponry to pick off some of the more distant ships, whilst the dreadnought was moving in on the small military starbase, simultaneously firing on it and the frigate frantically trying to undock, along with the two frigates surrounding it. The heavy ship was more than capable of taking on those odds.

The strikecruisers, an L-class and an S-class, were busy ravaging the civilian ships, launching multiple marine strikepods at as many as they could reach. They were also engaging the out-classed convoy defenders, primarily targeting the ancient light cruiser, ignoring the other Lindholm frigate for the moment.

The *Vindicator* and the *Ubermacht* destroyer translated into the system.

<Commander Huyton,> Admiral Gavain commanded calmly, <long-range supporting fire on the strikecruisers, three-quarter speed. *Vindicator* to advance, target the strikecruisers. Ignore the dreadnought for now.> He did not want to engage the dreadnought until his star-carrier and strikecruiser had jumped in.

He watched the scanners carefully through the datasphere, waiting to see how the enemy reacted. The interdictor still had its gravitational generators fully active, so the Pirates of the Cross were intending to remain and fight. He would have done as well; even with the Lindholm ships in-system, the dreadnought alone could engage the *Vindicator* and the *Ubermacht*. The fight was almost equal – for the moment.

<Shields going up,> Commander Al-Malli informed him. <I want idents on those ships, data-tac.>

<The K-class is identified through its modifications – it's the *Kingdom*, sir.> Lieutenant Woolfe said. <We're taking heavy electronic assaults, battle-grade viruses, fire-walls are successfully resisting. These have been further developed since Imperial days, sir.>

Admiral Gavain reviewed the data on the *Kingdom*, and its last known commander. It had been involved in the Battle for Mars that had ended the Red Imperium, but it had been grievously damaged. It was fully repaired now however, and it had disappeared shortly after its refit at the Janus Shipyards, its commander apparently not being impressed with the Dissolution Order.

He looked at the T-class dreadnought, wondering which ship it was. Was it Silus Adare? he thought.

<Commander, the dreadnought is breaking off and coming about!> scanners officer Lieutenant Agrawal suddenly announced.

<They are activating IFF signatures,> Lieutenant Woolfe said.

<Show me,> Gavain demanded, breaking in on the battle-net. He usually left Commander Al-Malli to command the ship whilst he focused on the wider strategic plan, but this he had to know.

<Taking fire from the *Kingdom*!>

<*Ubermacht* opening full batteries on the L-class.>

<Idents showing now, Admiral,> said Lieutenant Woolfe, data-squealing the information directly into his brain over the datasphere.

Gavain was legendary for his impassive reactions and cool persona, but he saw Commander Al-Malli look at him in surprise as he inhaled sharply in shock. The L-class was the *Linebacker*, the S-class strikecruiser the *Serpent*, both old Imperial Eighth Fleet ships which had defected very early on from the StarCom Federation with Captain Dolf Reichenburg. It was not that which surprised him.

The T-class dreadnought was the *Thor's Hammer*, the ship of Rear-Admiral Silus Adare.

<Incoming hail for you, Admiral,> communications specialist Forrest said, <It's Adare.>

<Accept it,> ordered Gavain.

Silus Adare grinned and his eyes widened as the holographic image of Admiral James Gavain appeared before him. He was sat in the command chair of the *Thor's Hammer*, wearing his old Praetorian uniform. The emblem of the False Emperor had been placed back on his breast.

<James Gavain,> he said, relishing the name, <What are you doing here, my friend?>

<I am no friend of yours, Adare.>

<Come now. You would not even be alive it were not for me. If I had not betrayed the StarCom Federation, you would have died in the Blackheath System.>

<You are wanted for the war crime of the destruction of the planet Alwathbah,> said Admiral Gavain. <Surrender now, Silus.>

Silus Adare laughed. <Surrender? I was about to demand yours.>

<Not a chance. When did you join the Pirates of the Cross? Are you working for Reichenburg?>

Adare felt a flash of irritation. <That is my concern.>

<Admiral,> his scanners officer broke in, <ships translating in.>

<Reinforcements, Gavain? Are we too much for you?>

<Surrender, Silus.>

<Never,> Adare said, cutting the comms link.

Adare assessed the situation. The star-carrier *Queen of Egypt* and the *Solace* strikecruiser had just jumped in. The star-carrier was already launching fighters and bombers. The odds had just changed.

He was tempted to stay and fight, but there was a bigger picture to consider.

<Order the *Kingdom* to deactivate the gravity well generators,> he said quietly. <All ships, jump out-system, full retreat.>

<The strikecruisers are turning back, Admiral!>

<All ships, target the *Thor's Hammer*,> he commanded, <Strafe the strikecruisers, but engaging the *Hammer* is the ultimate objective. Captain Thurman, use your fighters and bombers to disable the *Kingdom*, I want it taken. Marines to board from the *Solace*, Captain Marrion.>

He received a number of confirmations of his orders.

In a *Great White* super-bomber, Marine First Lieutenant Abraham Salvador acknowledged the orders from the Captain Louise Thurman of the *Queen of Egypt*. The *Great White* super-bomber was the largest aerospace vehicle the Praetorians had ever developed, and besides a formidable arsenal, carried a single-fire torpedo-launcher with a payload of ten torpedoes. The *Great White* was a nightmare for any capital ship.

Jacked into the datasphere, his wing of three super-bombers were protected by an escort of seven *Tigershark* starfighters. They were advancing rapidly on their given target, the *Kingdom* interdictor. The *Thor's Hammer* was about to become a danger to them, the strikecruisers still being too distant. The *Kingdom* had launched its small complement of fighters to protect itself, but it was not enough.

As the *Queen of Egypt* and the *Solace* began to fire on the *Kingdom* interdictor, First Lieutenant Salvador zeroed in on the skull and cross emblem emblazoned on the rear hull of the *Kingdom*. It was attempting to turn, its gravity well generators deactivating.

<Fire,> he ordered. The *Great White*'s opened up, adding their torpedoes to the salvoes being fired from the *Solace* and *Queen of Egypt*. <Fast reload, I want three launches before we pass.>

He watched as the rear shields of the *Kingdom* almost failed, his torpedo being the last to hit.

Captain Louise Thurman gave the order for the *Queen of Egypt* to adjust its heading at an angle away from the *Kingdom*, protecting the strikecruiser *Solace* from the heavy weaponry of the *Thor's Hammer*. The dreadnought was beginning to pound her star-carrier, and she was only thankful that it had not turned to bring its formidable broadside to bear on her.

The enemy strikecruisers, under heavy fire from the *Vindicator* and long-range assault from the *Ubermacht*, were about to enter the fray.

<Well done, Lieutenant Salvador,> she congratulated the pilot directly over the datasphere, watching the *Kingdom's* rear shields completely fail. <Captain Marrion, launch Marines, please. All wings, protect the strikepods. When they land, switch targets to the dreadnought.>

<Aye, sir,> Captain Peter Marrion acknowledged the more senior captain's orders. <Marines, you have a green light.>

The *Solace* carried three hundred Marines, and the moment he gave the order, the strikepods carrying all of them launched at the rear of the *Kingdom* interdictor. He watched their progress carefully, wincing as one, then two, and then a third of the strikepods were blown away by the fierce incoming fire from the *Thor's Hammer*, which had diverted its fearsome forward fusillade to try and prevent the boarding action. It was of little use, the majority of the strikepods striking home on the *Kingdom*.

<Marines aboard the hostile,> his mission control specialist reported.

<Divert fire to the *Thor's Hammer*,> Captain Marrion ordered.

<All enemy ships are dropping their shields!> the call came, <capacitors charging for jump!>

<Marrion,> Gavain suddenly opened up a communications channel to him from the *Vindicator*, <switch fire back to the *Kingdom*. Do not let it jump with our troops aboard. The Pirates of the Cross might be abandoning their marines, but we are doing no such thing.>

<Aye, aye, Admiral.>

First Lieutenant Salvador found himself ducking involuntarily as a massive MAC projectile whirred less than an arm's length underneath the *Great White* super-bomber.

<Great evade,> he congratulated the pilot. <Torpedo away.>

A torpedo was launched, glittering as it rapidly crossed the distance to the *Thor's Hammer*. It had dropped its shields, in preparation for a jump, and he punched the air as he watched the torpedo slam deep into its prow. It penetrated several decks and then detonated, the small nuclear explosion tearing the nose apart.

His jubilation evaporated as heavy quad-laser fire stitched heavily through the *Great White*. Its engines were destroyed, and it began to burn.

114

<Eject, eject, eject!> he roared at his crew. The cockpit canopy blew away and he was thrown into space, seconds before the super-bomber detonated.

<*Thor's Hammer* is jumping!> his scanners officer called out. <It's gone! *Linesman* jumping in five seconds ...>

Admiral Gavain remained outwardly calm, but he was annoyed that Silus Adare had escaped. <All ships, target the jump capacitor nacelles for the *Kingdom*. Do not, repeat do not, let that ship jump.>

Commander Saifa Al-Malli turned the *Vindicator*, bringing starboard weaponry to bear on the *Kingdom*. She had held the fire of the starboard batteries, not wanting to endanger the Marines aboard the *Kingdom* interdictor, but Admiral Gavain had given the order. Even as the *Vindicator* battlecruiser fired staggered broadsides in a continuous assault on the enemy strikecruiser, the entire starboard weaponry opened up on the *Kingdom*, targeting its port nacelle.

The nacelle was destroyed within three seconds, blowing apart. The *Kingdom* was not going anywhere.

Gavain saw that all the shields on the *Kingdom* had now failed. <Launch Marines at the interdictor,> he ordered Al-Malli. <I want that ship taken quickly.>

<Major Adeoye,> Commander Al-Malli said, <Launch strikepods at the *Kingdom*.>

Gavain watched Adeoye's Marines streak away in their fast-moving strikepods, punching into the hull of the *Kingdom* even as the enemy *Serpent* strikecruiser jumped out-system.

<Track their jump headings,> said Admiral Gavain. He was tempted to order a pursuit, but there were too many places they could have gone, and he did not have enough ships to pursue the Pirates of the Cross effectively. Nevertheless, the information of where they went may come in useful.

Major Adeoye strode onto the bridge of the *Kingdom*, encased in his power-armour suit. He stabbed his energised sword into the side of the pirate marine, who had been waiting at the hole their breach onto the bridge had caused. He brought the massive autolaser shotgun mounted on his left arm around, and shot the marine several times at close range.

The rest of his squad were entering, tearing into the enemy on the bridge. Even as he fired his shoulder-mounted heavy duty lasercannon at near point blank range into another ex-Praetorian pirate marine, he saw two of his squad trigger their heavy chemical flamers into the pits of the bridge, crew shrieking in horrendous agony as they were consumed by the washes of orange flame.

The captain of the *Kingdom* was standing, firing a hand-laser at Major Adeoye. He brought his autolaser shotgun up and blew the man's shoulder and half his face away.

He felt a tremendous impact from behind, warning systems alerting him that he had suffered major damage. As he staggered forwards, his rear armour partially shredded, a series of automatic cannon rounds sheared into his back and blew his left arm away, shattering the shoulder blade. Emergency drugs were pumped into his system, and he rolled as he fell, turning round and firing the lasercannon at the enemy who had struck him from behind.

His shot hit just as his adjutant saved him, swiping a power-sword through the neck of the Pirate of the Cross marine and decapitating the attacker.

Adeoye sank back to the floor, waiting for the pain to recede as his power-suit worked its magic on his system. By the time he stood back up, getting gingerly to his feet, the battle for the bridge was mostly over.

<Bridge secured, Admiral Gavain,> he said across the datasphere. <We have the *Kingdom*.>

<Status?> Commander Saifa Al-Malli said.

<Sixty-two fatalities, one hundred and twenty-one wounded,> he said. They had suffered heavy losses, but then they had been fighting ex-Praetorian Guard, just like themselves. Only the superior numbers of both the *Vindicator* and the *Solace* Marines had enabled the success of the mission.

<Check the data-core,> Admiral Gavain ordered tersely.

He gave the order to his adjutant, the Corporal breaking off from dispatching a barely alive bridge crew member to access the computer control station down in the port bridge pit. He looked up.

<Sorry, Major,> the Corporal reported. <They've wiped the entire data-core. All the information has been purged.>

<Damn it,> Major Adeoye swore.

Admiral Gavain gave the order for a systematic cleansing of the civilian ships to take place. There were enemy Pirate Marines aboard a number of the civilian ships, having been abandoned by their masters. He received the news from Major Adeoye.

They had successfully defended the system and a large percentage of the civilians. The mission was a success from that point of view. The capture of the *Kingdom* was also a bonus, partly for the ten million Imperial Crowns they had just earned, but also because he intended to claim it as a prize right.

It was also a failure. They needed information in order to track the Pirates of the Cross down. He was also disappointed to have come so close to Silus Adare, and to have lost the chance to kill or capture him.

At least he knew for sure that Adare was part of the Pirates of the Cross. Their feud was far from over.

Chapter IX

There had been a number of engagements as they had advanced across the continent Zwei, but there had been no casualties whatsoever. They were a number of hours into the advance, and were nearing Kyiv Megapolis, the Erdogan-held capital city. General Andryukhin knew that the main ground force was less than thirty minutes behind them now, advancing under chameleonic covers.

They would now be directly under the guns of the starships that Erdogan had in orbit, as well as the satellite network. He had no doubt that by now, the Erdoganites would know that something was happening out here, that their patrols were going missing on a particular vector approaching the capital city of the world.

The rainforest had given way to a mountainous, rocky region. They had climbed to a higher altitude, and had begun advancing along the edge of a wide glacial valley that would eventually lead to the desert that Kyiv Megapolis had been built upon. Daylight would soon be approaching, and the attack on the city was scheduled for one hour from now.

He was hunkered down on the lip of the valley edge. It was not particularly deep at this point, and he could see the plains in the distance. He was more concerned at what lay below them.

There was a full company of House Erdogan soldiers, a hundred borgs and their locally House-produced Erd-5 HAPCs, with their sponson-mounted tri-lasers to either side. They were parked around a battery of six Self-Propelled Orbital Guns, expensive Markhov Industries Mkh-23 *Longbows*, in addition to four Erd-9 main battle tanks which had just rolled up. The SPOGs had their massive cannon raised into the air, and were circled around an Mkh-14 *Umbrella* mobile shield generator. Their commander had dismounted, and was talking to the captain of the infantry and the commander of the orbital battery.

Andryukhin had waited nearly ten minutes for another one of his squads to divert to his position, to support the attack. He could not leave such a strong force in his rear. The other squad was laid up on the other side of the valley.

With his personal chameleonic field fully active, he began to lead his squad down the alley. The passive datasphere told him that the squad opposite was doing the same. As he began the careful descent down into the valley towards the enemy, he kept a careful eye on the positions of the four team members who were deeply infiltrated into the enemy camp.

They were fully camouflaged, invisible to the naked eye, moving stealthily amongst the soldiers and their vehicles. They had placed various charges on some of them, the explosives also stealthed to prevent their detection. It was a delicate operation, and high-risk. The entire assault was going to be difficult, but this was what they trained for, every day of every week.

It was imperative that they completed the assault quickly, with the maximum of efficiency, to prevent the enemy starships and satellites above detecting them. They had large area-effect chameleonic generators, which would disguise their actions once they were fully deployed. They had to set up the four receiving posts in a circle around the enemy to create the shroud to allow the attack to be launched.

He almost mis-stepped on his way down the sharp decline of the valley side, having to spread his arms for balance to stop from making a noise. His heart almost stopped, and it was an automatic reaction to snap his head up, to see if the rock he sent bouncing down the valley side was spotted by the Erdoganites. They were so self-absorbed, they did not even notice it. They were completely relaxed. So far, he had not been impressed with their self-discipline or alertness.

He continued down, watching the progress of his marines. The four infiltrators were still planting charges, the soldier carrying the chameleonic field generator had it positioned and it was ready to be remotely activated, and two of the four receiving posts were already in place. He had split his squad up, each man or woman operating individually, and had assigned each a number of targets to eliminate. It should be over in seconds, twenty marines against a sizeable Erdogan force.

They had been trying to silently hack the enemy comm-channels, but for some reason had not been able to. They had to try passive attacks, without full efficiency, as an aggressive hack would most likely have been noticed and possibly traced.

An Erdogan trooper who was sat atop the curved bullet-like front bonnet of a *Longbow* SPOG suddenly shouted a warning, pointing directly at one of Andryukhin's infiltrated Marines.

There was a pregnant pause, and time seemed to slow down. In that split second, Andryukhin realised they had been discovered. Even with the naval ships and satellites above them, and their area-effect chameleonic field not yet ready to be activated, he had to give the order. They had been discovered.

<We've been fucking discovered. Stealth not an issue. All squads, attack!> he roared across the datasphere, the entire speech taking less than the speed of thought to communicate.

The Erdoganites had already reacted, his infiltrated Marine taking close-range fire. He was firing back, but under the fast borg-enhanced reflexes of the Erdogan soldiers, he was already heavily wounded.

Andryukhin sped up, abandoning stealth and running down the rest of the valley. The multi-missile launcher mounted around his helmet like a collar roared into life, high-explosive missiles streaking out even as he targeted the enemy soldiers around his discovered infiltrator with heavy-duty rotary cannon. He saved the injured Marine's life, cutting down several of the enemy in that first second, including the one alert bastard that had blown the operation.

Behind him the *King Cobra* HAPC roared over the lip of the valley, still stealthed as the twin las-cannon mount on its roof opened fire in concert with the under-slung lasmachine gun, spitting tracers down at the camp over his squad's heads in between thick powerful lances of fire.

The charges detonated, several of the vehicles blowing up into the air. Every one of the tanks blew apart spectacularly, although there was one that was only slightly damaged, coasting sideways on its repulsors and crushing four Erdoganites to death as it crashed to the ground.

Still firing his rotary cannon, Andryukhin congratulated Sergeant Calaman as, higher up on the valley incline, she had taken out the three commanders with her long-range sniper-lasrifle. She was shifting aim rapidly, the lasrifle firing almost like a rotary cannon as she quickly shot, killed, shot, killed, shot, killed, taking out two to three of the enemy every second.

On the other side of the valley, a *Cobra* HAPC came flying over the edge, firing its two under-slung lasmachine guns. Between it and the *King Cobra,* and with the help of Andryukhin's multi-missile launcher, they destroyed the last remaining and damaged Erd-9 repulsortank. It blew apart spectacularly.

Andryukhin was now amongst the enemy, leaping up and slamming his power-claw into the sponson mount of an Erd-5 HAPC. With a screeching of metal he ripped the tri-laser away, a Marine barely a second behind him casually plunging the nozzle of his chemo-flamer into the hole.

To the background of tortured screaming, Andryukhin jumped up onto the bullet-shaped front of one of the SPOGs, turning to spray the enemy with his rotary cannon, protecting the fallen infiltrator.

Less than ten seconds later, it was all over. Every enemy target was down, and although he had taken two heavily wounded, there were no fatalities.

<Fucking well done,> he congratulated his team, still standing on the SPOG and casting a fearsome figure as he rotated his upper body from side to side, surveying the scene of destruction. <Now get that chameleonic field up and running, those eagle-eyes are watching us. All of you, activate your personal cham-fields. Once the area-effect's up, spike the SPOGs so they can't be used. Sergeant Calaman, you're in charge, see to it.>

He jumped down from the front bonnet of the *Longbow*. <See to him,> he ordered two of his Marines, pointing the claw tines at the fallen infiltrator. The man's single-strip visored helmet had been shorn in two, and half his head was missing. There were still life-signs, despite the numerous injuries, his power-suit sealing up the wounds and pumping powerful sedatives into his system now that the immediate battle was over.

Angrily, General Andryukhin crossed over to the now stationary *King Cobra* HAPC, charging up the ramp. He passed the small medical station, sitting at the comms post in the cramped interior. He manipulated the controls, checking first on the progress of the main body of his force. They were still advancing to schedule.

He cursed. They had been detected by a destroyer in orbit. It probably would not fire just yet, but they had to get out of the area now.

General Gerhard Zweigartner, theatre-commander for the Kyiv System, strode into the war-room deep within the military fort near the centre of Kyiv Megapolis. The Megapolis was built on a plain at the foot of the glacial mountains and valleys to the east. A slowly rotating holographic image of the sprawling mega-city showed that the shields were currently down. With the Zhou-Zheng Compact almost thrown off the continent Zwei, far away from the new front-line and with aerospace superiority, there was no need for them to be active.

As he reviewed the data being relayed to him and his command staff, he briefly considered raising the shields, but decided that was an over-reaction.

"So what is the situation?" he demanded of his second-in-command, a holographic image of Oberst Konstantin Leder. The rank was equivalent to a Praetorian Colonel, but the Erdogan Combined Armed Forces had no naval ranks. The Oberst had operational command of all Zweigartner's naval forces in-system. Oberst Leder was aboard the destroyer currently in geosynchronous orbit directly above Kyiv Megapolis.

"We captured these images four minutes ago," Oberst Leder said. A holographic display showed Zweigartner an image of a power-suited Marine, stood atop one of his *Longbow* Self-Propelled Orbital Guns, directing the enemy forces.

"This is less than three hundred and fifty klicks away," said Zweigartner. "Who are they?"

"My analysts identify the suits as Praetorian in manufacture," Oberst Leder's image replied.

Zweigartner thought quickly. Before he had left the Kyiv System, Feldmarshall Horatio Grant had warned him of the intel stating that the Compact had hired mercenaries, but unable to identify which unit. Was this the work of those mercenaries? he wondered.

"General, Oberst," one of his operatives interrupted, "we have received the odd report of similar such attacks on the continent. We assumed they were Z-Z stragglers, rogue units falling across our patrols. We have also lost contact with a much larger number of patrols, although they only have to check-in every couple of hours. This is the map." The operative manipulated the holo-projector.

Zweigartner gasped. "Why did you not call me to the war-room before!" he raged. The operative paled.

It was obvious from looking at the map. All the way from the east coast, almost up to Kyiv Megapolis, there were a number of isolated dots where missing patrols or the occasional 'rogue' or insurgent attack had been recorded. It did form a pattern when looked at in the whole, a number of pathways running directly towards Kyiv Megapolis.

"I've seen this before," said Oberst Leder quietly.

"So have I," said General Zweigartner. The last time he had seen this had been in the days of the Red Imperium, nearly four decades ago, when House Erdogan had fallen out of favour with the True Emperor and he had sent his Praetorians to teach them a lesson. That had been during a sanctioned House War with House Zhou, as well. "These are standard Praetorian Guard tactics."

"The Megapolis is in danger," Oberst Leder pointed out.

"I agree." Zweigartner thought fast, pulling up maps and data through his datasphere connection. He began to issue orders rapidly.

<People, listen up. I want these units to withdraw from the southern Zhou-Zhou engagement immediately, and make their way by lander back to the city. Raise the city shields, now! Oberst Leder, I want your two destroyers covering the approaches to Kyiv Megapolis, be wary in case there is a naval attack. Be ready to launch fighters and bombers. Everybody, I want Kyiv Megapolis on high alert, an assault may be imminent!>

He hoped he was not over-reacting, but his experience in the sanctioned House War had taught him many things about the Praetorian Guard. One thing he had learnt was there could never truly be too much caution where they were concerned.

*

<We have translated, Admiral,> said Commander Zehra Sahin.

Rear-Admiral Silus Adare nodded his acknowledgement, shifting in the flag chair slightly. <All is as it should be?> he asked.

<No threats detected, sir. The only ships in-system are ours.>

Silus Adare accessed the scanner logs, reading the IFF's of the ships within range. It instantly told him which ships were currently out on raiding missions. He also spotted the V-class *Vengeance*, Captain Dolf Reichenburg's ship.

Ranks were largely pointless and meaningless out here, but the Praetorians who rested in this system tended to keep the ranks they had left service with at the point of the Dissolution Order. For the purposes of discipline, Adare insisted his own crew and people adhered to the chain of command, but outside the ship with their allies of circumstance, it was not properly recognised. Admiral Silus Adare stroked his black, square goatee, as he demanded, <Get me a comms to Dolf, now.>

<Aye, aye, sir,> the comms lieutenant said.

Silus Adare leaned back in his chair, glancing to one side. Marine Lieutenant-Colonel Iyan Lamans stood there, legs wide, hands clasped in the small of his back. He returned the look. <Yes, Admiral?>

<You need to start training,> said Silus Adare. <Practice a boarding action on V-class battlecruisers.>

<You're thinking of Gavain's *Vindicator*, or Reichenburg' *Vengeance*?> Lamans grinned evilly.

Silus laughed on their private channel. <Perhaps I'm thinking of both,> he replied.

Lieutenant-Colonel Lamans and Commander Sahin had defected from the StarCom Federation with him, assisting his massacre of the loyalist crew in the middle of a battlefield. He did not necessarily trust them, but he would not be where he was now without their assistance. The T-class *Thor's Hammer* dreadnought had been captured by their combined treachery. It was as much a home to him now as anywhere else in the colonised galaxy. He was attached to the powerful ship as much as someone like he could be, particularly with the sort of psychotic tendencies his Red Imperium-era psych-profile recorded.

<Communication established, Admiral,> Commander Sahin interrupted.

Adare activated the link, an image of Captain Dolf Reichenburg appearing before him.

"You're early, Silus," Captain Reichenburg said. "And there's fresh damage to your ship, too much. What's happened?"

"It's a pleasure to see you too, Dolfy-boy," said Silus, knowing that phrase annoyed Reichenburg immensely.

"Silus. Transmit your black box recording, now."

<Send it,> Silus ordered Commander Sahin. "It's coming across now, Dolfy-boy."

He waited for Reichenburg to review the transmitted, decoded, scrubbed and virus-checked data, which for a cyborg and a battlecruisers data-core was a task completed in a couple of seconds.

"This so-called Sir Admiral James Gavain and his mercenaries," said Captain Reichenburg coldly. "You seem to know him?"

"Indeed I do," Adare said, continuing to explain the circumstances in which they had met.

"It was foolish to reveal yourself and the identities of the ships, it gave away vital intelligence," Reichenburg continued. The fact that he disliked Adare was obvious to all watching the exchange. "That was hubris or pride on your part, I do not know which, but it was unforgiveable. Do not do it again."

"Yes, sir," said Adare, stressing the last word to make it a mockery. "We do have a more pressing problem, though. Gavain has obviously been hired to combat us, at least in the Lindholm operating theatre. He is formidable."

"I understand," said Reichenburg. "But for now, you are to leave this vendetta. I will find you another mission to complete. Repair the damage to your ship, and await further instruction. Reichenburg out."

The image disappeared. Silus Adare sneered openly. "Emperor curse your bones," he snarled.

*

Doctor Erin Presson stood in the classroom, watching the "new-born" post-Praetorians hard at work. They had been released from their accelerated growth bio-vats, and after undergoing a lengthy medical assessment, had shortly been plunged straight into their post-emergence education. Before even reaching adulthood in the bio-vats, which was approximately three to four weeks of gestation, they had already received a full education and knew the basics of whichever military specialism they had been programmed for – the programming achieved both by implant and genetics.

She nodded to the bio-artificer nurse, their "vat-mother" for the remaining three weeks of real-world orientation, and left the classroom. A short journey up one floor, and minutes later she was entering the cavernous AG bio-vat hall of Level 11.

She walked across it, staring around at the bio-vats. They were full again, another two thousand and five hundred post-Praetorian super-soldiers in production. The babies were already at the equivalent physical age of a teenager. She smiled, feeling almost maternal.

She paused at the end of one row, staring at their contents with interest. These contained an altogether different type of soldier, an experiment based on their new-found knowledge gained through analysis of the Faceless, both their own analysis and that of House Zupanic. The Faceless they were growing were mixed with Praetorian technology, and would become a brand new type of infiltrator spy-soldier, an elite class not known in the days of the Red Imperium.

They were trialling with fifty of them, and she was prepared for failures to occur. It was always the way with a new experiment. She had agreed to it only when James Gavain had indicated that he would not dispose of any rejects, and that they would continue to sustain and nurture them into old age, even if the entire batch failed. That was on the provision they had a suitable quality of life. Failures were otherwise rare, but did occur, and in the old days the False Emperor had them disposed of.

In two month's time they would know whether the experiment had been successful.

She carried on, crossing into the room where the Faceless captive was being held. He was completely compliant, re-programmed to be obedient to Lady Sophia, as Gavain had ordered. She strode up to the Doctor she had left in charge.

"What is the situation?" she asked.

The Doctor started, as he had been that intent on observing the Faceless assassin. He passed her a data-pad. "The subject is ready," he said, "all tests completed and confirmed."

Erin Presson nodded, and then jacked into the datasphere.

<Commodore Andersson?> she called, opening up a private channel. He was already jacked in, and responded within a nano-second.

<Yes, Doctor?> he asked. There was a slight tinge of pre-occupation to the comms, his emotion of mild annoyance leaking through the connection slightly. She was interrupting something, but he had responded.

<The Faceless assassin is ready to be handed back to Lady Sophia. Re-programming is confirmed as complete. He is hers.>

<Excellent news, Doctor. Lady Sophia is due in-system shortly, I will inform her as soon as she arrives. Prepare him for transport. With a guard, just in case.>

<Yes, Commodore.>

Commodore Harley Andersson returned to his re-examination of the data. Sat in his own private office above-ground on Tahrir Base, he had discovered something truly remarkable.

He had been performing several actions at once, jacked in to the data-core of Tahrir Base. He had been examining the latest intelligence from Jamie Gavain's encounter on the Lindholm contract, cross-referencing it with all other known data. He had been reviewing the performance statistics of the base operations, and also managing the various personnel requests. He had been designing a new training programme. He had been reviewing the construction plans for Base Kavanagh, and talking to one of the design supervisors. All of it was simultaneous, but he had stopped all of the actions as soon as the red flag had been raised in the data-core.

The cross-referencing of intelligence on the Pirates of the Cross attack in the Saana System with the intelligence database he and Captain O'Connor maintained had turned up something that required all of his processing power to verify and review.

He checked again and again, but there was no denying it.

They had received an update from the Levitican Military, Lady Sophia ensuring that they received even the classified files. The full details of the attack which had resulted in the death of Lady Elouise Lapointe had been provided, including black box recordings recently salvaged, scrubbed and analysed from some of the ships involved.

The data received from Admiral Gavain's interdiction in the Saana System included a full analysis of all four Pirates of the Cross ships. They had captured the *Kingdom*, but all of its data had been wiped, so there were no leads there. However, as part of the routine scans conducted during any battle, the computers had recorded a distinctive battle-field repair to the L-class *Linebacker* strikecruiser, a patching on the starboard nacelle that had obviously been conducted in the field and not in a proper starbase.

Out of the ships that had struck and killed Elouise Lapointe, all of which had been ex-Praetorian Guard, there was one L-class strikecruiser bearing exactly the same patching. There was no doubt from the separate data scans that it was the L-class *Linebacker* that had participated in the killing of Lady Elouise Lapointe.

Further, there had also been a K-class interdictor involved, which could or could not have been the *Kingdom*, and a T-class dreadnought which could or could not have been the *Thor's Hammer*. The ships which had hit the convoy Lady Lapointe had been travelling within did not broadcast IFF signatures, and as such, those two in particular could have been any K-class or T-class ex-Praetorian ship. Neither class was particularly common however, and the presence of the L-class *Linebacker*, which was now confirmed, made it highly likely that the ships Gavain encountered in the Saana System under the name of 'Pirates of the Cross' were the same ships that had struck the Levitican Union under the name of the 'Rose Pirates'.

Andersson stood up and ordered a synthesised coffee, thinking all the while and continuing to conduct his analysis through the datasphere. There was a significant problem with the identification. The Lady Elouise Lapointe's ship had been destroyed in the JC-3993 system, an uninhabited system technically within the territory of the Levitican Union. Due to timings, the *Linebacker* could only have been in the JC-3993 system in Levitican space, and then the Saana System in Lindholm space, by use of stargate or fusion-tanker. The difficulty was that there were no stargates that would allow the pirate ship to utilise them. Pirates tended to avoid them, precisely because they wished to avoid identification.

So, Commodore Andersson thought, the facts are that the Pirates of the Cross and the Rose Pirates are the same organisation or allied in some way. They are attacking both Lindholm territory, and Levitican Union territory. They have access to resources and some star-spanning capability we have not identified yet.

He cross-referenced the information he had so far with even more, held within the data-core of Tahrir Base, and discovered a further uncomfortable truth. As part of the Kyiv Contract, the Zhou-Zheng Compact had provided them with a vast amount of intelligence on House Erdogan dispositions.

House Erdogan were also suffering heavily under piracy attacks. These pirates identified themselves as the Crown Pirates, although Erdogan appeared to be more efficient at dealing with them so far. Again, they were ex-Praetorian Guard. One of the ships recorded as hitting a particular Erdogan system, the data stolen by Zhou-Zheng Compact intelligence, could also actually be the L-class *Linebacker*. There were similar possible matches between the other ships.

There were other piracy incidents all across the Eastern Segment involving ex-Praetorian Guard ships. It was not surprising, as the Dissolution Order had suddenly left a large number of highly trained elite soldiers with no home, no command structure, and no purpose in life. They had to survive somehow. A vast number that had not joined a particular house or nation, or become mercenaries, or simply vanished, had turned to piracy.

More information was needed. The Pirates of the Cross, the Rose Pirates, and the Crown Pirates were interlinked. The Levitican Union thought House Jorgensson were supporting the Rose Pirates, House Lindholm and the new Aalborg Alliance thought that the Helvanna Dominion were using the Pirates of the Cross as privateers, and Erdogan thought that the Compact were employing the Crown Pirates. Elsewhere in the Eastern Segment, Hausenhof, Cervantia and Korhonen all thought they were suffering Praetorian Guard piracy sponsored by each other, and Amiens was similarly suspected of sponsoring piracy in their area.

The truth appeared to be that there was a link between all these piracy organisations.

It was only a small part of the picture, Andersson knew, but it was significant information and would be of value to Gavain in the Lindholm Contract. House Lindholm was paying them for any information related to the origination of the Pirates of the Cross. He himself needed much more data, as at the moment it was all circumstantial.

He requested a HPCG communication through the Tahrcity station, knowing that Gavain had to be informed immediately.

*

Juan Ramirez hefted the automatic shotgun strapped around his shoulder, adjusting it to a more comfortable position.

He had carried weaponry before, knives and shivs, and an energised power-blade that he had owned for about a year, but the only projectile weapon he had ever touched had been a handlas that one of his own friends had once obtained. A combat auto-shotgun was a completely different prospect, and although he did his best to look like he knew what he was doing, he kept checking the safety to make sure it was engaged.

He was now back to doing navigations, rather than scanners, as quite worryingly the previous navigations officer had met with an unfortunate 'mishap'. The accident had occurred shortly after he had been hired, which only made him wonder how ruthless Helenna Sirocco could be.

They had left the Drenim System, and he had plotted in a course to another system for a legitimate pick-up. Captain Helenna Sirocco had informed him that this was just a cover, however, to explain their journey. They had travelled out of Van Der Meer space, heading back towards the Eastern Segment, officially destined for the major system of Ghannia, carrying vital medical supplies and synthesisers needed to combat the plague which had broken out in the small house territory. The house was near Amiens territory, threatened by that new nation in the never-ending cycle of wars following the destruction of the Red Imperium, and they were even being paid by their customer House to use a stargate to get there quickly.

Upon exiting their stargate-assisted jump, they had however made a small diversion here, to the uninhabited KQ-3407 System. The *Nazareth* had flight clearances to travel to Ghannia all the way from Drenim, but their flight-path did not include KQ-3407, or a small, uninhabited moon within that system.

The Type-III cargo-freighter had launched its cargo-lifter, a gigantic crab-like shuttle towards the surface of the moon. The moon had low gravity, but a breathable atmosphere, and their pilot had skilfully manoeuvred it over the cargo-tank pod that rested in a grassy clearing on the planetary surface. The mechanical arms had engaged, and the cargo-tank bonded at a molecular level with the lifter. When they blasted off, they would lock the type-III cargo-tank into one of the spare holding docks on *Nazareth*, and then the smuggler ship would continue on its way to Ghannia.

They would be dropping off more than just medical supplies at Ghannia. They were delivering weapon-grade fabricators, guns and explosives to a crime gang in operation there, so Captain Sirocco had informed Ramirez.

Juan stood on the edge of the exit ramp from the cargo-lifter. It was that high in the air when it was straddling a cargo-tank, that it extended for a lengthier walk than normal to the surface. He wore an oxygenator mask despite the breathable atmosphere – there were pockets of lethal gas which drifted across the moon's surface and could strike without warning. The moon was not inhabitable for that reason.

Captain Helenna Sirocco stood before him. He had mixed feelings towards the new crew he travelled with, many of them being less than desirable characters, but he liked the captain. He was careful enough not to take that any further though, his experiences on the *Yangtzee* teaching him to be more careful who he slept with. As a youth he had run with one of the small juvenile gangs of his home-city, but had been lucky enough never to get into major trouble with the enforcers or he would not have been able to qualify as an interstellar-trained navigator.

A small group of people had approached them, seven in total, all of them carrying weaponry. The first thing Juan Ramirez had noted was that they all bore the same tattoo, a snake curling around an eagle that looked suspiciously like the Red Eagle, the letters S and M in the background and woven into the pattern.

For the first time, he realised that Helenna Sirocco also bore the same tattoo, as she showed it to the man who seemed to be leading the group. He accessed the data-files in his brain, and identified them as the Salchuzura Mara. For the first time, he truly began to regret what he had put himself into. The Salchuzura Mara were famous across the Mid-Sectors and even the Core, one of the strongest and most notorious crime gangs.

"Juan, come forwards," Helenna Sirocco motioned him over.

Extremely nervously he approached the group. From where he had been stood, he could not hear most of their conversation.

The man stood before them was very heavily tattooed, and he had the cold hard eyes of a murderer. Juan felt a chill as the person bored a stare as piercing as a laser at him. "Yes, Helen?" he asked.

"Who is this kid?" the tattooed man asked. He had a heavy Mid-Sectors accent.

"The new navigator I mentioned," said Sirocco coldly. She appeared not to like the man before her, despite the fact they were obviously in the same gang. Juan was still amazed to know that she was in the Salchuzura Mara.

"And he can be trusted?"

"As much as any on my crew," said Sirocco. "His story checked out."

"So not much," the man replied, rattlesnake-fast. "As ever, your responsibility Helenna."

"No one crosses me," said Helenna Sirocco. "Juan, calculate the flight-path on this. How long after we've made the drop on Ghannia?" She passed across a data-wafer to him.

"Borg," sneered the man, as he held the wafer over his open palm-up right hand, a cone of light extending from the implant as he accessed the data.

"Stow it, Calto," Sirocco snapped.

Juan Ramirez put all of his processing power into calculating the flight-path. He felt some surprise at the location.

The Eastern Segment was so-called because it followed a galactically eastern vector out from Earth. It stretched from its narrowest point outside the Sol System, in a widening cone through a portion of the Core into the Mid-Sectors up to the line accepted as the boundary with the Outer Sphere.

Right in the middle of the Mid-Sectors region of the Eastern Segment was a large area of uncolonised space called the Gulf of Medusa. The Medusan Gulf was a region sparsely populated with star systems, full of all sorts of astronomical dangers and hindrances to jumping, and completely uncolonised for two reasons. The sporadic star systems had naturally few inhabitable planetary bodies, and those that either did or had been terraformed centuries ago had been destroyed during the worst excesses of the Drone Wars. The entire Gulf of Medusa was therefore a large region of space where there was no civilisation whatsoever. Due to the difficulties of traversing it, there were no trade-routes across it. It would be dangerous to try and traverse it, as any ship encountering difficulties would have little chance of rescue.

The Medusan Gulf touched many of the new Post-Imperial nations and Houses. House Amiens, Van Hausenhof, Zupanic, Marchenko, Lindholm, Zheng, and many more all bracketed it.

The designated journey would have them flying from the Ghannia System near Amiens rapidly expanding borders, into the Gulf of Medusa. They had a rendezvous a small way in, although he was not given the details of whom just when, and then afterwards they had to continue on deeper into the Gulf to an unremarkable system far away from any civilisation or assistance, getting closer to the centre of the very Gulf itself.

"Nine point six Standard days in real-time," Juan Ramirez said, "with one month, eight days and eleven hours of transit-time."

"There you go," said Helenna, "ten days."

"I will inform our contact," said the intergalactic gang-member known as Calto.

"You do that. We'd better get on our way." Helenna Sirocco clicked her fingers and gestured back into the lander.

Chapter X

General Andryukhin stood outside the grounded *King Cobra* HAPC. The Kyiv Primus long night-time was about to come to an end, the first streaks of pink dawn touching the horizon in the vector they had approached from. Even if dawn had broken properly, he would create no shadow, the chameleonic field hiding him completely from the naked and augmented eye.

The three members of his squad appeared at the lip of the crater, announcing their presence over the datasphere. <Get aboard,> he motioned. They had returned from their sortie, placing the bombs as close to the glittering shields as they could.

He took one last look at the glittering haze of the dome-like shield protectively covering the vast Kyiv Megapolis. The Erdogan forces were alert, and had activated their full city defences. Star Marshal Ngu had contacted him to say that the Erdogan were diverting tens of thousands of troops away from their front in the southern regions of the continent, but Andryukhin knew it would be too little, too late. The Erdoganites only had their – not inconsiderable – defences presently in the city to block his pending assault.

There were actually three shields he had to penetrate. The first outer shield covered the entire city, the secondary middle shield designed more to protect if the first failed. Then the central part of the city was protected by a third and final shield, in case the other two fell.

He entered the *King Cobra*, hunkering down. He checked the status of his forces; the thousands following after his vanguard were now in place, ready to begin the assault, and the landers, starfighters and bombers had left the continent Drei a half hour ago. As of yet they would still be undetected by the Erdoganite forces.

Standard Praetorian tactics consisted of concentrating their usually smaller but more capable force against the weak points of the enemy. Today was going to be no exception.

All bombs were now in place. He had his thousand pathfinders within the blast zone, and his second force in place. They would assault in three waves, each barely minutes after the other.

<All units,> he announced, <Radiation shields. Prepare for detonation in ten seconds. We are go.>

General Zweigartner was exceptionally tense, trying not to pace and failing miserably as he kept a close eye on everything that was happening within the war-room. Deep in the centre of Kyiv Megapolis, it was the nerve centre for the entire defence of Kyiv Primus, and yet he had a suspected Praetorian Guard assault about to take place.

His eyes tracked to the large-scale holo-map showing the disposition of his naval forces. Oberst Leder had ensured that both his destroyers were now positioned directly above the city, with a flanking guard of three frigates in case there was a co-ordinated naval attack.

All three layers of shields were raised within the city, yet another holographic representation showing the roughly circular layout of the megapolis and the three domes that protected its outer, middle and inner regions. He had a sizeable force within the Megapolis, a mix of fresh troops newly landed, veteran units assigned to guard the city, and a greater proportion than he liked that had been rotated from the southerly front with the Zhou-Zheng Compact.

There was already a renewed push by Compact forces occurring on the southern edge of the continent. His enforced diversion of a large part of the Erdoganite army, rushing them back to defend the Megapolis, had given them the chance they needed to halt their orderly and slow withdrawal. They were already in danger of reversing their decline.

He clenched his fists, hoping he was not overreacting. Feldmarshall Grant's intelligence had been precise however; the Compact had hired mercenaries, and there was every chance that they were ex-Praetorian Guard, and they were even now camped outside his city.

Then, finally, the long tense wait was over.

<Multiple detonations, General!>

<Show me!>

The primary holographic interface, a massive display hanging over the war-room, switched to a live feed from one of the orbiting destroyers. It was zeroed in on the Megapolis, and particularly on the eastern approach.

Zweigartner saw the tell-tale mushroom clouds of high-yield, focused nuclear bombs rising above his city, and his jaw dropped.

<How many?> he demanded.

<Twelve nuclear bombs ->

< - rad counters are registering significant fall-out ->

<Outer shields failing, shields failing! We're losing sectors east-two, east-three, east-four, east-five ->

<Bring those shields back up now!> General Zweigartner roared.

<Impossible, General, the feedback has fried them. It will be at least fifteen minutes before we have re-ignition.>

<Oberst,> General Zweigartner addressed the orbiting naval officer, <Prepare for suppressive fire all along the eastern city sectors. The moment something moves out there that shouldn't - flatten the area. All civilians are evacuated out of the limits into the middle sectors, you have free-fire.>

<Aye, General. We have no target, yet, though. If your range-finders spot anything, feed them through to us.>

<No range-finding. As soon as we have contact, fire. Wide-area effect!>

General Ulrik Andryukhin felt the buffeting of the tremendous shock-wave washing over them, making the reinforced *King Cobra* HAPC rock sickeningly even for a marine as it struggling in the blast. It had been dangerous to site so close to the detonation area, but it was a calculated risk.

The ground was still rumbling, and there was a horrible sick feeling to the air registered by his suit, as he jacked back into the datasphere. Modern electronics could withstand the electro-magnetic blast, partly because of their organic nature, but even so as a precaution they had all jacked out of the datasphere and shut it down to prevent any nasty feed-back.

<Forward units, advance into ground-zero,> he ordered. <We must be at the secondary wall within two minutes, according to mission clock.>

As a series of affirmatives came back to him, the chameleonic shielded HAPC rose into the air, and began to scoot across the scorched plains into the outer limits of the city. Within seconds they had crossed the line where the shields had previously been energised, and were moving on to the second shield wall.

<SPOG units,> he signalled, <You have fire clearance. Spot and move, keep it fresh.>

Major Smythe was the Vindicator Mercenary Corporation marine who was in command of the artillery detachments for this operation. They had been snuck into forward advance positions, and had been laid-up awaiting the detonation of the nuclear bombs.

Artillery was his specialism, although like all marines he kept himself updated on all forms of warfare. He loved the orbital artillery most of all, and like most things, the old Praetorian Guard had some of the best.

A large number of his vehicles consisted of *Black Mamba* Self-Propelled Orbital Guns, special variants that also doubled as electronic counter measure vehicles. They each packed a double turbolaser generator, that could punch up through most planetary atmospheres and hit objects in orbit.

He himself was sat in a *Constrictor* SPOG-TL, a ground-to-space torpedo launcher. The single rack on its back, with the tube carefully aligned, could fire a torpedo up towards a capital ship and cause tremendous damage.

They were camouflaged, as were all units on this assault, but for the orbital artillery the chameleonic fields were even more important. Their only way to survive against naval starships was to fire and then move rapidly to a new position, sniping almost in a deadly game of cat-and-mouse.

<All units,> he called, <You have targets, we are go. Fire!>

Aboard the *ESS Guillotine*, Oberst Leder had left his command chair and was stood around the tactical stations, observing their operations personally rather than across the Erdogan battle-net. They were scanning the city limits on the planetary surface below intensely, alert for the first sign of any movement, ready to commence firing.

That was the reason why he saw, rather than being notified on the sphere, that there was heavy incoming ground-to-orbit anti-ship fire. One minute it was quiet on the surface, and the next it had exploded into action.

<Raise shields!> he demanded. With no confirmed threat to his ships until that second, they had been on yellow alert only. They had not expected to take surface fire!

<Triangulate and fire back!> he roared, even as the ship shook violently under multiple laser hits. They cored into the underhull of his beloved ship, smashing into his batteries with precision. Seconds later the torpedoes struck, a spread of ten exploding all along the hull almost simultaneously. He was actually lifted off his feet, and for a sickening moment he found himself floating in the air – they had knocked out their entire ship-wide anti-gravity generators.

Cursing, his magnetic boots activated and he clamped himself back down to the deck.

<We took out two targets,> his tactical officer reported, <but the majority of the hostiles had already moved.>

<We won't have aft shields for one minute, we've suffered too much damage.>

<All ships, increase orbital height!> he demanded. <General Zweigartner, our ability to provide suppressive ground fire is significantly reduced. Sorry, sir.>

General Zweigartner slammed a fist into the console before him. It was about to get worse.

<General!> a scanners officer called out, <We're picking up ghost images out on the eastern seaboard – possibly landers coming in!>

The *King Cobra* skidded to a halt, turning rapidly to present its rear hatch to the drop-zone. It had banged open and Andryukhin had his feet on the ground before it had stopped its short drift.

<General, Lander Two and Lander Six have been detected by the enemy, we think,> a message came over.

<Unavoidable,> he said, <Keep me informed. The second shield wall will be breached by the time they arrive.>

His squad followed him to the energised, hissing shield wall. He knew the enemy forces would be on full alert by now, but even automated defence systems had been knocked out by the nuclear blast. In any event, his advance pioneer forces had made it to the second line of defence completely without detection.

His secondary force was already moving up behind, and was less than a half-minute away. His ground-to-orbit artillery units were beginning to take damage, but the efficiency of the enemy ships had been greatly reduced. As they had advanced through the city limits, a number of *Porcupine* mobile shield generators had glided into their concealed positions, ready to create a safe corridor for the advancing waves of landers carrying the bulk of his forces to safety cross the outer city. The landers would also drop his huge *Legate* land command vehicles as they advanced, to further defend his troops from the fearsome firepower above their heads.

Once they got through the second shield wall, however, he would not need to worry about defence; he would be using the enemy's defences against themselves.

He watched as the *Hedgehog* shield borers set up against the energising dome wall of the enemy shield. The second layer of shields would lead them into the populated area, and whilst he would try to minimise innocent casualties, in any city war it was unavoidable.

The *Hedgehog* shield-borers extended their massive arms, the special coding on his visor allowing him to watch the machinery at work through their stealth fields as they decoded the shield frequencies. They began to penetrate into the shields, and in a matter of seconds, they had begun to open up corridors throughout the protective shielding.

Much as a starship could temporarily open holes in its own shielding to allow it to fire its weaponry, so the *Hedgehogs* opened up breaches in the enemy defences. Once they had penetrated, they could widen those breaches rapidly, enough to allow even landers to fly through.

<Mount up,> he called to his squad, grabbing hold of the rungs on the exterior of the *King Cobra*. They would be carried into battle externally now, ready to drop off and engage when they had to.

<We have total penetration,> he announced to all his units, <we're through the second shield wall.>

General Zweigartner wanted to howl his frustration, but knew he could not. He had to think of his men. His normally calm exterior was melting under the ingenuous assault the enemy had conducted against him.

His naval starships dared not get too close, and were engaged in sniping fire with the chameleonically protected forward units of the enemy. There could be no hope of overwhelming suppressive fire from orbit, despite their stellar superiority.

The eastern segment of his first shield wall had been blown apart by nucleonics. His second shield wall, he had just been informed, had been massively breached in multiple places, but again, the warning had come too late.

As of a couple of minutes ago, large enemy forces had begun to heavily engage his *within* the second shield wall. They had already taken at least a third of the eastern interior, and were advancing rapidly to the third and final shield defence.

His analysts were predicting that there were at least between five and eight thousand of the enemy out there, although it was impossible to tell as they were advancing under heavy chameleonic fields. His own Erdoganite units were mounting a defence, and although they were scoring some severe hits, they were falling back under the superior technology and capability of the enemy.

Then, he had been told that multiple landers were unshielding within the city limits, as they began to cross the still energised second shield wall through the massive breaches. From orbit his stellar naval ships could not fire down because of the angle of the breaches, but when he had ordered what little support they could provide to target the landers, they had bounced off the *enemy* mobile shield generators that had somehow been snuck into the battle-zone without Erdogan forces detecting their presence.

The landers were numerous, and supported by starfighters and starbombers that were now wreaking havoc in the eastern air-space. His analysts had revised upwards the estimate of enemy numbers into the tens of thousands.

He dare not drop the second shield wall, which was in itself protecting the enemy, in case there were more of them waiting outside for him to make that call. Even as he watched, reported enemy contact showed that they had passed the half-way point to the third and final shield wall.

Superior enemy numbers were punching a hole to the heart of the city, and it seemed there was little he could do to stop them. In less than ten minutes, the safety of Kyiv Primus and the nerve centre of the Erdoganite resistance against the Compact had been completely compromised.

Marine Captain Zuo Li-Chan ordered the pilot of her *Executioner* super-heavy assault battlewalker to plough forwards. The shields around the *Executioner* flared as they contacted the building, weakened by numerous shots from the twin-cannon MAC mounted on the right arm of the humanoid war machine.

The building tore itself apart as the vehicle crashed through, emerging on the other side of the street. Captain Zuo rotated the massive torso of the vehicle, bringing its formidable weaponry to bear on the rear of the enemy machine.

The smoking twin-barrels of the Magnetic Acceleration Cannon on the right arm fired at almost point-blank range, the two heavy projectiles slamming into the back of the squat AH-7 Medium Combat *Goblin*, its own shields flaring and then failing as it took further fire from the *Executioner's* shoulder mounted plasmacannon and the six chest-mounted lasercannons.

Captain Zuo was already drawing back the mighty power sword mounted on the left arm as her pilot ran the *Executioner* towards the *Goblin*. Its construction made it ungainly at turning, and even as it tried to traverse around with a complicated shuffle of feet, the energised blade sheared deep into the back of the battlewalker. It punctured through to the cockpit, crisping the people inside as Captain Zuo swept it backwards and forth, cutting through armour as if it were paper.

The *Executioner* pushed away, the *Goblin* falling forwards. As it fell, the Vindicator Mercenary Corporation marines that had been pinned down by its vicious fire ran past, their *Cobra* vehicle emerging into the open to pick them up and carry them on into the fight.

Seconds later the *Cobra* shook and rolled as a heavy foot kicked out from around the corner, an AH-6 *Atlas* Heavy Combat battlewalker entering the fray. It carried a super-heavy MAC cannon, and the Vindicator Mercenaries ran from the *Cobra* as it fired at point blank range.

Captain Zuo swung her battlewalker around, receiving a feed from 1st Lieutenant Chaveux, who had been in the process of mounting the HAPC when it had been struck by the enemy. Around the corner from which the *Atlas* was emerging, were another two *Goblin* battlewalkers and an *Aztec Warrior*. The *Executioner* was good, but it was now heavily outgunned.

Urgently, she called for assistance.

Marine Sergeant Drapier crept along the top of the building, gaining a new vantage point. The skyscraper was tall, and he had an unimpeded view of much of the battlezone that the city was descending into.

His squad were all operating individually, as they had been assigned to sniper duties for this particular battle. He carried a powerful sniper variant las-rifle, keyed into the display on his suit, amplifying his senses through the scope mounted on its long barrel.

He crouched down on the roof, so high up he could watch even the starfighters wheel and whirl around in their frantic battle. The datasphere was alive with targets, and units calling in for assistance.

Fancying a difficult shot, he acknowledged the call of a starfighter pilot, a Marine 2nd Lieutenant O'Neil. He zeroed in on the starfighter's location, seeing that it was being dogged as it swung around, through, over and under buildings by an enemy Erdoganite starfighter.

Lining up the shot, compensating for speed, objects, distance to target, and wind velocity, Marine Sergeant Drapier fired.

The super-hot laser bolt zipped through the air, covering the two kilometres to its target. With a snap, it smashed through the canopy of the enemy dogfighter, cleanly blowing the head of the pilot away.

The starfighter began to go out of control, but Drapier was already aiming and firing at another target. He would remain stationary for another minute before moving again, and in that time he could potentially take out between sixty and eighty targets.

2nd Lieutenant O'Neill received confirmation that the sniper shot had struck home, and even as the enemy starfighter was crashing into the skyscraper, he was whirling his *Mantaray* fighter/bomber around the building. He had an urgent call from Captain Zuo to respond to.

He shot his starfighter around a corner, coming up on Captain Zuo's position, jinking it at high-speed down a small alleyway, rising up and over a walkway-bridge, and then releasing the bomb-bay hatches, firing missiles as the *Mantaray* streaked down the street beyond.

As he roared over the enemy battlewalkers, munitions dropping and turning the street to scrap, he snapped his head to the left, seeing Captain Zuo's battlewalker striding forwards and firing at point blank range into the enemy *Atlas*, still staggering forwards from the explosion.

As the *Executioner* pumped heavy fire into the enemy *Atlas*, and the *Mantaray* shot by overhead, 1st Lieutenant Chaveux could feel the heat from the series of massive explosions that had wrecked the street beyond.

Signalling two of his men forwards, they jumped up at the form of a *Goblin* battlewalker that was staggering out of the inferno the *Mantaray* had left in its wake. He clambered up to the cockpit, using his powerclaw to open the burnt canopy. He was dropping away even as his two team-mates were using their chemical flamers to gut the inside of the walker.

As he hit the floor, he turned to watch the *Atlas* machine falling back, the *Executioner* striding over it, slamming a heavy foot down onto one arm, the MAC cannons firing at point-blank range to liquidise the crew inside. The ground actually shook with the twin impact of the fearsome artillery weapons.

General Ulrik Andryukhin fired his rotary cannon straight into the air as he clambered onto the back of a grounded civilian hovercar. The enemy starfighter lost its wing, cartwheeling out of control and smashing into the side of one of the tall skyscraper blocks, exploding with a blossoming of fire, metal, and metacrete.

<Target down, protect our fucking air corridor better, no more get through,> he demanded.

As the affirmatives came back, he was reviewing the situation. They had carved out a huge tract of the city, marking their territory right up to the inner, third shield. The dropship landers had brought the majority of his force through, and now they were under the secondary shield, protected from the destroyers up in space who in any case were struggling against his anti-orbital defences, which were firing and moving rapidly.

This was the riskiest part of the operation. He had nearly twenty-two thousand of his twenty-five thousand strong force within the city, an amazing feat in such a short period of time. They were protected only by that second shield, which had not dropped yet, using the enemy's defences against them.

<Get those *Hedgehog*s in place now,> he demanded, <I want that third shield penetrated!>

<One minute, sir,> a Captain replied.

He jumped down from the hovercar. <Elements of the third defence penetration force, prepare for move in one minute. We must bring this to an end.>

He ignored the affirmatives, concentrating instead on the master tactical displays within his mind's eye. The enemy were fighting back, but his force was more than strong enough to resist.

<Remote drones are reporting that the third shield wall is being penetrated, General – they've opened up holes in the third wall!>

General Zweigartner felt the horror strike through him, and for a moment he could not say anything. Then he snapped, <All defence forces, defend against the enemy incursion ->

<It's too late, sir, they're coming through!>

<Defend!> he snapped, calling up the display to look at the units that were stationed against the third wall breaches. Even as he watched, the blue tags denoting his own forces were snapping out, as red tags flew through the breach. He saw some of the enemy being eliminated, but it was not enough – their presence and fighting ability was overwhelming.

He paled. He realised they were zeroing in on the headquarters he was stood in. The entire Erdogan defence of the system was controlled from this room, which was essentially a converted upper floor of a hotel block.

"All staff, evacuate the war-room now!" he shouted, a second before a massive bang shook the building.

General Andryukhin finished applying the anti-grav jetpack to his back, magnetically sealing it in place, even as he looked up at the tall building where the Erdoganite headquarters was located. <Well done, Lieutenant O'Neill,> he congratulated as the *Mantaray* zoomed away from the burning hole it had created in the hotel's upper floors. <Insertion squads ... jump!>

He mentally triggered the anti-grav jetpack, and he was flying upwards into the air at tremendous speeds. In the space of a few seconds he had curved, flying through the fire of the burning building like an avenging angel, the jetpack unlocking as he strode through into the upper floor, firing at all targets. Several squads had followed him, and in an eye-blink the Praetorian Marines were inside the Erdoganite headquarters.

General Zweigartner was crossing to the emergency escape lift at the back of the war-room, still too far away when the wall on the far side of the headquarters exploded.

He was pulling his las-pistol from its holster, turning around and firing with all of a cyborg soldier's enhanced reflexes, his flight abandoned. Inside he knew it was over.

General Andryukhin strode into the room, his enhanced sight picking out the enemy and identifying them. His primary target, General Zweigartner, was spotted in a nano-second.

He activated his power-claw, running forwards with reinforced and suit-powered legs, crossing the distance even as las-pistol shots singed his armour with little effect. The tines of the claw snipped, and General Gerhard Zweigartner's head burst like a melon.

Shortly it was all over. Sergeant Calaman strode up to him, saluting with the Imperial salute, before saying, <Headquarters secure, sir. We have their central operations hacked, their datasphere battle-net in our control.>

<Send the false orders to the Erdoganite forces,> Andryukhin ordered. <Signal the Zhou-Zheng Star Marshal Ngu, tell him now is the time for the counter-strike.> He switched channels. <We have the primary target,> he informed his forces, <move onto the next stage of the plan. Take the city from the inside, out.>

It was then that he finally smiled within his helmet. By the Emperor, it felt good to be in the field again.

*

Feldmarshall Horatio Grant shook his head as he re-read the report again, sat within the private ready room of the starship that was conveying him on the tour of the House Erdogan front-lines.

The disaster which had occurred on Kyiv Primus in the space of a couple of hours yesterday was unbelievable, but a testament to the superiority of the mercenaries the Zhou-Zheng Compact had hired.

Erdogan Intelligence had managed to piece together what had happened. Vindicator Mercenary Corporation mercenaries had struck in force unexpectedly against the capital, targeting the military headquarters where the entire defence of the planet was being directed from. General Zweigartner was presumed dead.

The capital had fallen, and with the penetration of the Erdoganite datasphere, false orders had been disseminated to all his forces in theatre. The Zhou-Zheng Compact forces had completely and utterly crushed a large proportion of the in-theatre military, and had even today moved onto the last remaining continent. It was unlikely that the continent would hold, so all of Kyiv Primus would fall.

He knew there was little way of getting the message to his forces on the continent of Eins, but he had to try. He recorded an urgent message for all his forces to evacuate the planet, and head to the planet Kyiv Tertius. It was still in Erdogan control, but defence would be difficult with the battle-net so heavily compromised.

The Kyiv System was going to fall, he knew.

He cursed the Vindicator Mercenary Corporation. How could they work with the humanist bastards that are the Zhou-Zheng Compact, he wondered. The more devious part of him wondered if they could be bribed to turn, but he doubted it considering their reputation. Nevertheless he directed Erdogan Intelligence to try.

A massive blow to their war-effort had just been delivered.

Sighing, he turned his attention to the next report on his list. It was a missive covering the pirates plaguing the war-effort, disrupting their build-up of reserve forces far behind the battle-lines. A link to the Zhou-Zheng Compact had not been discovered yet, but surely it was only a matter of time until it was.

Chapter XI

Birds twittered peacefully in the small trees planted along the east garden of Towers Manor, singing songs to each other as the hotter and closer of the two suns began to rise high into the sky, warming the planet Tahrir and announcing the start of planetary summer. Lady Sophia Towers knelt gently, the five Labrador puppies running around her outstretched hands playfully. Despite herself, in that brief moment she had forgotten everything and was smiling.

Then she caught sight of the House Guards, four of them patrolling quietly on the walls of Towers Manor, and the smile faded. Two of them were House Towers' military, and two of them were House Zupanic. Lord Micalek was waiting here for her return, and the thought of seeing him both excited her and brought her dread.

She straightened, asking one of her attendants to restrain the puppies, and set off for the east entrance into the Manor. She touched a hand to her right ear, and the secret miniature speaking device that was hidden behind on the bone of her skull.

"Can you hear me?" The Spider Elaine Carrington asked. *"Use the finger-pads to confirm."*

Lady Sophia was wearing two elbow-length gloves, and disguised within the finger-tips of the left hand were special contact pads. If she pressed her thumb against her index finger, it would mean 'yes', whilst if she pressed the thumb against her middle finger it would mean 'no'. A press on the pinkie finger would signify that she felt she was in danger. She was also wearing contact lenses, to allow The Spider to observe what was happening in the room.

She pressed her index finger to signify an affirmative, and serenely walked into the Manor house, the new capital of House Towers' territory, in the country some way beyond the limits of Tahrcity. She crossed through the familiar family home with ease, ignoring the House Guards of Towers and Zupanic, and hesitated only momentarily before entering one of the many drawing rooms. Mentally steeling herself, she activated the door and it slid aside.

Lord Micalek Zupanic, dark, handsome, and devilish, stood with his back to her, staring out of the window at the southern garden. He turned quickly as she entered.

"Lady Sophia," he smiled, and instantly she saw that the smile was obviously forced. He had never been so easy to read before. "It is very, very good to see you."

As the doors shut, giving them complete privacy, she moved to hug him. She forced her own fake smile, and as ever, her heart felt broken. How long before her pregnancy began to show, she wondered? "One is overjoyed to see you again," she said, "especially when it was unexpected."

"Ah well," Lord Micalek frowned. "I heard the question there, Sophia. Come, sit, we must talk urgently."

"Be careful, there may be a trap here", said the voice of The Spider.

As she sat in one of two large-backed, ornate chairs in the window, sun shining onto her right side, she crossed her legs and thumbed a 'yes, I agree'.

"This is all very mysterious, Micalek," said Lady Sophia.

"When I went back to Zupanica, a lot was revealed to me," he said. "I am very sorry, Lady Sophia, but I bring you some terrible news. Please understand, I was not aware of this until my mother revealed it to me. I did not know."

"Careful, Sophia."

"You are worrying one, Micalek. What is this about?"

"There is no easy way to say this. My mother and father conspired and plotted to assassinate your father, and make it look like it was the StarCom Federation. I am so, so, so sorry. I swear upon the eyes of the Emperor, I did not know at the time."

Lady Sophia felt the shock of hearing the admission, and opened her mouth in an involuntary gesture, even as Elaine Carrington was saying *"Be wary – this admission may not be what it seems – do not reveal what we know about it under any circumstances"*. The warning helped to quash the sudden hope she felt, that the man she loved had not been involved in the murder of her father, but she had to play this so carefully.

"One – I, I just do not ...." she stammered.

"You must act like you do not believe it!"

".... this can't be true," she said. "What are you telling me?"

"I will explain," he said, and began to outline the entire story, much as The Spider and House Towers' spies had discovered it to be. Despite herself, in hearing the story, she began to cry, and at one point Micalek went to console her. She moved away in her seat, and as she looked at him, the pain in his eyes was obvious to see. He was either an excellent actor, or she was being too hopeful in believing his innocence. She just did not know what to believe.

"My Lady," he said kneeling, "please believe me, I did not know about the plot."

"Accuse him gently, test him to see if it is true."

"How can one believe this?" said Lady Sophia. "That you did not know that Lord Principal Ramicek and Lady Wyn plotted to kill my father is .... difficult to believe."

"I understand you can only take my word for it, Lady Sophia. But there is more. I do now know that the plan is to ultimately kill you, once you and I have a child. Lord Luke is also in imminent danger, they are plotting to target him. The plan ultimately is for me to become the sole ruler of House Towers, its territory and land placed in the domain of House Zupanic."

"Do not reveal the pregnancy – too dangerous. I will deal with the threat to your brother."

"This is pure evil," said Lady Sophia.

"This is Imperial politics," Lord Micalek corrected. He began to reach for her from his seat, but stopped as she flinched openly. "I have no intentions of letting it happen, my love. Please believe me. If I intended to go along with the plan, I would not be betraying my family now."

"And why are you betraying your family?"

"Because I love you," he said.

The words stabbed a knife as sure as an assassin's blade through her heart. She so desperately wanted to believe him. She looked shocked once again.

"I have made my choice, Lady Sophia. I could side with my family, join the plan, and watch them murder the woman I love. Or, I could turn against the family that has lied to me, has used me, has constantly plotted and is so devious it cannot be trusted. The family that killed my last wife – something I am not letting happen again! What I feel for you goes far beyond anything I could feel for the monsters and deviants I call family."

"Nice words," the scorn in Elaine Carrington's voice was harsh.

"I love you too, Micalek," said Lady Sophia, and there she was not lying. "I will need time to think about all of this."

"I know, and I will wait as long as it takes."

"Thank you."

"I know that there is a strong likelihood you already knew all of this, though not my innocence of the plan. My mother suspects that you have stolen back the Faceless assassin, that you have him or it in your power. The Faceless assassin was stolen from a secret military base last month. Lady Wyn suspects you were behind it. Do you have the assassin?"

"Aha! Deny that we have the assassin! This is what it's all about. They know we likely know, so they have taken a risk of 'revealing' the plan to discover if we have the assassin! It's a trap!"

No, it's not, thought Lady Sophia.

"One knew about the plan," said Lady Sophia, even as Elaine Carrington began howling, "One's brother also knows. We knew of Lord Principal Ramicek's duplicity, and no, we were not sure of your involvement in it."

"You must have been tortured by the knowledge. I can see why you did not ask me though, and why you have never challenged me about it. All I can say is that I am yours, Lady Sophia. I have chosen you and House Towers over House Zupanic's *current* rulers."

"Current rulers?" she frowned, picking up on the stressing of the word.

"I know that even if you have the Faceless assassin, you won't tell me. I have to earn your trust, but I will wait, for as long as it takes. But I ask that if you do have the Faceless, you use it to eliminate my father, Lord Principal Ramicek. And my mother, Lady Wyn, my uncle Vasily and my sister Csarina. With me ruling House Zupanic, you will never face a threat from my House again. Further, I will sign a document in secret, confirming that 'should' I ever come into the position of leadership of House Zupanic, I will name any first-born child we have as my successor – and that if anything ever happens to you or your brother Luke, I will never have a claim on House Towers territory. Just so you know that I am not interested in your holding. I genuinely am not. It is you I want."

Lady Sophia found this hard to believe. She was struggling to comprehend.

"Don't confirm we have the Faceless – at least listen to me there! Don't do the deal!"

"One wants the document as proof of your intentions," said Lady Sophia.

"Too close to an admission, Sophia!"

"Of course, my love," said Lord Micalek, nodding. "And when it comes to my proposal on the joke I call a family? The assassin? Our future?"

"This is not right!"

"Excuse me a moment," said Lady Sophia. She pulled off her gloves, and gently placed them on a small hovering table at her side. The earpiece and then the contact lenses followed, all items dying and losing power as they lost contact with her skin.

"This has not been a private conversation then," said Lord Micalek, paling.

"No, of course not," said Lady Sophia. "One has already admitted to knowing the duplicity of your family. One does love you, Micci, but one needs to know you are loyal to one and one only, as your wife. This is your only chance. My vengeance will be terrible if you betray me, is that understood?"

"I understand and swear I will not –"

147

"Prepare the document. Then come to me later, tonight, for one has missed you. Note that one has chosen you over her own advisors."

"And of my family?" Lord Micalek asked. "I need to know that my betrayal of them will culminate in the removal of the threats to both you and me."

"And your ascendancy to the head of house of House Zupanic," Lady Sophia pointed out. "One will not confirm that one has the Faceless assassin, but one does have the capability to ensure it occurs. It will happen. That is a promise."

"You seek vengeance and security as much as I," said Lord Micalek, understanding dawning on him.

"Oh yes," and more, Lady Sophia thought, thinking of the child in her belly. "Whilst you prepare and sign the secret document, also write down all intelligence on the activities of House Zupanic. One wants to know particularly how they wish to kill one's brother Luke, how to prevent it; the movements of Ramicek, Wyn, Vasily and Csarina; and what the Lord Principal is up to with his plan to introduce House Marchenko to the Levitican Union. That concerns one greatly."

"So, my family will be removed?"

"They will," Lady Sophia said. "Now, go do as one says, husband, and we shall see each other tonight."

That night, Elaine Carrington sat in her special office within Towers Manor. She was no longer fuming over the lack of respect and caution Lady Sophia had shown. Ultimately, both Sophia and Luke thought that she was no more than their advisor and servant – it was the role she had chosen centuries ago, and happily kept. The only person who knew otherwise was dead, and that was the safest way of keeping a secret.

Lady Sophia and Lord Micalek were in their own quarters, enjoying a quiet night. The Spider did not have it under observation, Lady Sophia proving to be quite good at preventing her attempts to spy. She was probably using more technology from her pet mercenaries.

Being cut out of the loop was annoying, but Elaine Carrington was not someone to hold onto a grudge. The day had been rather surprising in a number of ways, not least because she was suddenly re-assessing her judgement of Lady Sophia. Familiarity had led her into the old trap of missing how much someone could change whilst you watched.

Lady Sophia had always been a driven person, capable of great things. Her business acumen was without question, holding her own private fortune gained under her own abilities without the support of the fantastically wealthy Towers family coffers. Politically she was also very astute, and in advance of her brother Luke, although he was adapting well to the Levitican Union.

No, one of Lady Sophia's defining qualities had always been her kindness, a morality that Elaine Carrington had found rare and endearing. However, many things had changed, and today she had displayed vindictiveness and a ruthlessness Elaine had not suspected existed.

She had challenged Lady Sophia on what she had been thinking of on reaching the pact with Lord Micalek, a man she did not trust and could not be trusted. Lady Sophia had replied that although she loved him, if he double-crossed her, there would be a fifth name added to the murder-list. Until then Micalek would be useful as a window into House Zupanic, a super-agent, regardless of her feelings.

The sheer calculating brutality amazed her – and being the woman she was, The Spider admired it. Imperial politics was brutal, but in the post-dissolution, post-Imperial time they lived in, how else was anyone to survive?

She sent the order to have the Faceless assassin dispatched immediately to eliminate his first target in the Zupanic family. Lady Sophia had even got a plan for the order in which they were to be removed.

Then Elaine had reviewed the data Lord Micalek had just provided. Lord Luke was to be assassinated by the Faceless organisation, not on Leviticus, but when a tour of duty was proposed in House Marchenko territory. He would be killed in transit. With the knowledge of how it was to be carried out, she could prevent it. If indeed the information was true – she would formulate a back-up plan for that eventuality. The first true test of Micalek's information would unfortunately put Lord Luke in danger, but this was the type of high-stakes game they were playing.

As to the inclusion of House Marchenko in the Levitican Union, sponsored by Lord Principal Ramicek, there was not much information. There was some possible link to Lady Wynn, of all people, who had suggested and proposed it, but whatever the plan there was Lord Micalek did not know. Or claimed not to. All he knew was that Lady Wynn had claimed she first suggested it to Ramicek, but no more than that.

There were some minor reports on the other manoeuvrings of House Zupanic, mostly internal to them. The Spider read, logged, and databased them out of interest.

She then moved on to a slightly more interesting subject, informed by two reports. The first was Lord Micalek, who seemed to indicate that his mother knew more about the pirates plaguing the Levitican Union than she let on, but there was no real detail.

The second report was slightly more interesting, and Sir Admiral James Gavain had permitted his Commodore Andersson to release it to her, through Lady Sophia. In carrying out a contract for the new Aalborg Alliance, and House Lindholm, they had uncovered a startling fact. The pirates plaguing many nations throughout the Eastern Segment appeared to have a link, and were in fact one and the same organisation.

It had also been proven through the presence of the war-criminal, Admiral Silus Adare, and the *Thor's Hammer*. They were seeking more substantiation of the conclusion, but the link through several ships had been proven. It was a shocking position to be in. Lady Sophia was currently debating what to do about the situation – rather than make any overt moves within the Union, she had suggested to Elaine that they make clandestine contact with a number of states throughout the Eastern Segment currently being afflicted. Elaine would do so, warning that the information had to be currently checked.

"May you live in interesting times," Elaine Carrington muttered the old curse. She could feel in her bones that there was something big going on, which had yet to reveal itself, but it would have monumental repercussions.

As if the fall of the Red Imperium had not already been enough.

*

Juan Ramirez sat on the small control bridge of the *Nazareth* freighter, somewhat tense but knowing that there was little he could do about his situation. He was signed on with Captain Sirocco, and was now working for the Salchuzura Mara, one of the most dangerous criminal gangs in the Core and Mid-Sectors, if not further away.

The *Nazareth* had jumped to their rendezvous point after the delivery to Ghannia, the destination being a long month away and this forsaken, deserted system right on the edge of the Medusan Gulf. There had been a ship waiting for them, another cargo-freighter called the *Breath of Damascus*.

Captain Helenna Sirocco had received a visit from the Captain of the *Breath*, a short, evil-looking man who also carried the holographic tattoos of the Salchuzura Mara. His halitosis was a sad comment on the name of his ship, Juan had reflected at the time. He had remained on the bridge whilst the two Captains talked, and four of the cargo-containers were transferred from the *Breath of Damascus* to the *Nazareth*.

The last cargo-container was just coming in to be berthed into its secure holding pod, when the private Captain's ready room doors opened and the two Captains exited. Sirocco bade the short man good-bye, and then went and sat at the Captain's chair.

"Right you lot," she said, "as soon as he has left the ship, and that container is docked, we're jumping to the next rendezvous point. Our cargo is more than just highly illegal, and no, I won't tell you what it is. If we're stopped by anybody other than I expect, we attack, understood?"

There was a series of affirmatives, and Juan joined it, masking his unease.

She stood up, and passed Juan a data-slate. "Prepare for jump to these co-ordinates," she ordered, turning back to return to her chair.

Juan Ramirez read the data-slate heading and co-ordinate data, which also as usual carried the timeframe in realspace that the journey had to be completed within. Jacked directly into the datasphere, the figures were automatically translated into the navigations computer. In his mind's eye he saw a three-dimensional representation of their target zone, and actually hesitated in confusion.

"Erm – Captain Sirocco?" he said.

"I know," she replied.

"But there's nothing there. The target destination takes us into deepspace in the Medusan Gulf. No systems, no planets, nothing." Even though the Gulf of Medusa was a large region of uninhabited space, there were still occasionally some systems, uninhabitable or destroyed as a testament to the horrors of the Droid Wars as they were. It was possible to cross the Medusan Gulf, but it was highly dangerous. This destination took them deep into the nothingness of space. "In order to make the jump within the timeframe, there is no way of doing it without terminus being at no reserve capacity on our jump capacitors. We will be stranded there."

"We won't. Calculate the shortest journey time now, crewman."

Deeply concerned, he did as ordered, and came up with the answer. "We can do it in nine jumps," he said, "but there is no margin for error." The last two jumps would take them into deepspace, they would no longer be jumping from system to system, and there would be no return.

"Load the flight plan, Ramirez. The Captain of the *Breath* has left, the ship is secure," said Captain Sirocco. "All hands, prepare for jump in two minutes."

*

With a flash of light and an unnatural elongation of its size, the Zhou-Zheng Compact capital ship exited hyperspace and jumped into the Kyiv System. The ship was brand new, fresh out of the shipyards around the planet Shanwei, and one of a kind.

It was built in the new style of the Zhou-Zheng Compact, effectively a long, bulky X-shaped structure, four wings at perfect right-angles to each over jutting out and curving into fins as they reached the engines at the rear. Heavily armed and armoured, it was the size of a dreadnought class, but was also built for luxury as well as war. It was the personal conveyance of the Primarch and the Primarchess, and was named the *ZCSS Hei'an Zhuan*, or in Imperial Standard, the *Epic of Darkness*.

It coasted in towards Kyiv Primus, a number of the Compact starships falling in around it as it neared the planet. The ships of the Vindicator Mercenary Corporation remained in their orbits, but sent an electronic salute.

A shuttle rose up from the surface of Kyiv Primus, speeding across the void, carrying Star Marshal Ngu Soo Su to the rendezvous with his rulers.

The youthful Star Marshal Ngu marched into the audience chamber, the hated and un-trusted Solar High Chancellor Zhou Mao at his side. Despite his devotion to the House of Zhou, and by extension now the House of Zheng, the Star Marshal would never find the reserve necessary to trust the deceitful Mao. He had heard that only a few days ago, a number of businessmen had been summarily executed, taking the blame for another one of Mao's failed plans. The Primarch and Primarchess had ordered the executions, believing their advisor's version of events. If the man had any honour, Ngu reflected, he would have committed suicide out of shame by now.

Jackbooted feet stamping on the marble floor, which had a pure gold representation of the eight-pointed star and circle of the Compact worked into its stone, Star Marshal Ngu came to a halt. He immediately fell to one knee, head bowed, the Solar High Chancellor following his example a split second later.

"Rise," said Primarch Zhou Ze, his voice aged and cracked but still commanding nonetheless.

Star Marshal Ngu regained his feet and assumed a parade-ground rest, whilst the Solar High Chancellor quickly crabbed across the floor to take his position on the right side of the Primarch, hands folding inside the outsized sleeves of his customary long robe. His simple clothing was a stark contrast to the ostentatious and rich clothing of the Primarch and Primarchess, with their high collared and expensive robes, heavy jewellery and crowns of pure gold, diamond, jade, onyx and ruby.

"Star Marshal," Primarchess Zheng Il-Sou spoke, her feminine and beautiful voice strong and commanding, despite her youth being even greater than Ngu's one hundred and fifty years, "you are to be congratulated beyond measure on the success within the Kyiv System. Your audacious plan to hire borgite, ex-Praetorian mercenaries has paid handsome dividends, and reminded all the Compact of your strategic brilliance. Is all of the Kyiv System now under Zhou-Zheng Compact control?"

Of course, Ngu knew that both his rulers knew it was, but he nodded and said, "the last of the Erdoganite forces were destroyed or taken prisoner two days ago, my Primarch and Primarchess. The Kyiv System is fully under Compact rule. We have captured significant amounts of Erdogan hardware and military systems, largely due to the breaking of their military battle-net within the system and falsified orders rendering the Erdogan forces effectively useless. The victory in Kyiv is one of the most outstanding in the Compact's history."

The fact the Compact was little more than a year old did not take away from his statement, he felt. It was an amazing victory, and even StarCom News Media was reporting it as such throughout the colonised galaxy. They gave great credit to the Vindicator Mercenary Corporation, but within the Compact, the state news media glossed over this to point out that the reason of their hiring had been the genius of Star Marshal Ngu, and gave him the honours for the victory. Compact media would never glorify borgs, whether they were in the employ of the state or not. This was a humanist war against the borgite menace, after all.

"Then step forward, Star Marshal Ngu," Primarch Zhou Ze beckoned.

Hiding his puzzlement, Star Marshal Ngu stepped towards the dais upon which the two thrones rested. As he neared, Primarchess Zheng actually stood, something that very rarely happened in official audiences. A hovering droid-box opened, and within lay a medal.

"Kneel, Ngu Soo Su," Primarch Zhou commanded.

He went to one knee, and bowed his head. Primarchess Zheng lifted the medal out of the box, and gently placed the chain over his head. "We award you the Medal of the Star and Circle Sun, the first award of its kind, given for outstanding service to the state and to humanity. This is to be the new highest honour in the Compact, and history will record it was first awarded to you. Congratulations, Ngu Soo Su."

"Well done, Soo Su," said Primarch Zhou, addressing him by his personal name for the first time Ngu could ever remember.

Standing up, he returned to his place in the centre of the chamber, but then bowed again. "I am at a loss for words. I am highly honoured by your generosity." He could not resist glancing at Solar High Chancellor Zhou, whose mask was very carefully kept in place, but at the look he saw the smallest hint of a tightening around the eyes. He took a small amount of pleasure in his old adversary seeing him be so successful.

"So explain to us, Star Marshal," said Primarch Zhou, "What effect does this have on the grander plans and the war of extermination against Erdogan?"

"A significant effect – this pushes back the front line significantly. I am moving our reserve forces into this system to hold it, and the primary assault force in Kyiv can now jump into either the Odensa System or the Chester System, and end the stalemates there. I intend to strike galactic west west south, and take Odensa with overwhelming force. Meanwhile, I would like to offer the mercenaries another contract – to move into the Chester System. With your permission, of course."

"It is granted, is it not?" Primarch Zhou looked at his wife.

"It certainly is," Primarchess Zheng nodded.

"Then that is the plan I will follow. We are still being pushed back in the Salmenko System, but if we take Odensa and Chester quickly, the loss there will be of no importance. I would like to hire another borg mercenary company – these are ex-Praetorian Guard as well, a fairly large mercenary undertaking calling themselves The Red Legion, under a General Marcus Zander. I will send them into Salmenko. I would commit some of my reserve forces to Salmenko and reinforce Hammerfall, and then move the majority of our forces deeper into Erdogan territory, hitting at their industrial base. Their planned war of attrition will fail, and we will cripple their manufacturing ability, eliminating their new armies and fleets before they are completed or ready."

"Success is in sight then, and the deadlock is broken," commented Primarchess Zheng.

"It is, Primarchess. Further, we now have access to a large Erdogan population in the Kyiv System. The work camps in our home systems can be strengthened dramatically, and some limited transportation of prisoners off-planet will begin immediately. We will gut Kyiv of Erdoganite pestilence in a much better way – I intend to set up work camps primarily in the Kyiv System to deal with the borg population. The first is already under construction, near Kyiv Primus' capital city, Kyiv Megapolis, and will be ready in two days time."

"You intend to turn Kyiv Primus into a death world?" asked Solar High Chancellor Zhou. "We originally set up the work camps to support our military build-up. We have no such military manufacturing base here in Kyiv, nor does one exist. Are we not better transporting the majority of the borg population off-planet and back into the Compact heartland?"

"But this will become a manufacturing base," said Star Marshal Ngu. "I need a forward operating base if we are to strike further into Erdogan territory, and the militarisation of the Kyiv System will provide that support. The work camps will be set up here."

"Your objections are noted, Solar High Chancellor," said Primarch Zhou quietly, "but we will follow the Star Marshal's plan. Ensure that our enforcers arrive on planet, to oversee the induction of the population into the work camps."

"They are already on their way, Primarch," said Star Marshal Ngu, bowing. "I have already taken care of it."

"The death rates in the work camps back home are quite high," said the Solar High Chancellor. "What are your projections for the death rates here in Kyiv?"

"Ten to fifteen million a month, with an induction rate of thirty to fifty million a month," replied Star Marshal Ngu. "In one year, this system will be our strongest new manufacturing base, Erdogan will no longer exist, and we can continue the fight against other borgite nations."

"Let it be so," Primarch Zhou nodded.

Chapter XII

The Wassenaar System was the last stop-over for the convoy, before it made a long double-jump to the Sanchezza System. Both were within Hausenhof space, although the latter was right on the border with the Cervantia and a former Cervantian colony captured in the last war post-Dissolution.

Wassenaar had a weak sun, and although inhabited, it was sparsely populated. It was used mainly for farming and mining, and had something of a tourist industry due to its beautiful, isolated worlds. There were some ships in system, but all of them were staying away from the designated jump point for the military convoy routes.

There were two Hausenhof military frigates in-system at all times, guarding the jump point, as well as a number of gunboats and corvettes. A military starbase was under construction, a large fixed structure to complement the twelve gun platforms already peppered around the fringes of the jump point.

Lieutenant-Commander Ffion Wybeck knew all this from the mission briefing that their Hausenhof employer, through Ambassador Grunehaube, had given them. This convoy run was their last, and she was in overall command of the convoy.

They were transporting weaponry to the front, military ground vehicles and supplies for the expected war with Cervantia. It was looking more and more likely to happen any day now. Hausenhof was convinced that the piracy they were suffering, from a group known as the Swan Pirates, was entirely sponsored by Cervantia.

Wybeck herself commanded the *SS Apollo*, a Hunter-class frigate and one of the few non-Praetorian Guard starships in the VMC, although it had been significantly upgraded with Praetorian technology. The O-class *SS Odyssey* Praetorian frigate was also present, under Lieutenant-Commander Lancaster, although she was the more senior in terms of rank by length of service to the mercenary company.

They were escorting a military convoy, which in addition to the Hausenhof ships also consisted of three fully-laden VMC ships, the *Hannoverian* and *Deliverance* heavily armed cargo-freighters, and a modified *SS Featherlight*, a captured Cervantian Marbella-class cargo-freighter. There were another three Hausenhof cargo-freighters, all similarly loaded, and two military transporters.

Lieutenant-Commander Wybeck was sat on the bridge of her ship, mostly observing her crew and reviewing the miscellaneous daily and sometimes hourly reports that a military ship operating to Praetorian standard conducted.

Jacked into the datasphere, the *Apollo* felt like an extension of her skin, every mind of every crewman except that third on shift break jacked in and connected to her. There was a fair amount of chatter, and part of her observed it even as she constantly monitored the life-signs of her ship.

All of a sudden, the peace was shattered.

<Lieutenant-Commander, we're picking up jump signatures ..... two ..... no, three sources.>

<Where?> she demanded, and in reply the holographic viewer in front of her chair instantly switched to a three dimensional space map of the surrounding region. The jump signatures were coming in within the designated jump point.

<Hausenhof military has nothing planned to come in,> said her second-in-command.

<All hands, battle stations, move to red alert,> Wybeck said calmly. <Communications, signal the convoy, prepare for hostile incursion.> She considering ordering her two frigates to activate their chameleonic fields, but there was no point – the enemy were jumping in so close it would be impossible for them to be effective. The only advantage to such a close jump was that the enemy would be unshielded for at least one minute, and unlikely to be able to fire back for the first twenty to thirty seconds after translation.

She was thinking quickly. <How long until the unknowns translate?> she demanded.

<Between fifty and fifty-five seconds,> scanners replied. <Estimate them to be cruiser sized.>

<Get Hausenhof military in on this now, we are possibly out-matched,> she said. She mentally recorded her orders, and directed for them to be communicated to Hausenhof military.

Real space was torn asunder, and the first two ships came in, followed a few seconds later by the third. All three were of Praetorian design, and proudly wore a stylised swan with widened wings on their noses.

<Searching for positive identification, Swan Pirate symbology confirmed, one L-class strike cruiser, one S-class strike cruiser, and one U-class destroyer.>

The destroyer was a phenomenal piece of hardware, but designed more for long-range engagement, and it had come in far too close. Wybeck made the snap decision that it must be intended for use against the longer range gun platforms and the half-built but operational starbase, whilst the two strike cruisers were to attack the convoy. Or perhaps it was their bad luck that they had jumped in so close, but she doubted it. It had been intentional. One thing these pirates never seemed short of was intelligence.

<All ships, target the S-class,> she demanded. <I want it knocked out of the fight!>

<Firing.>

<I want identification on those ships now!>

All she could hope was that the enemy were not expecting their convoy to have heavily armoured praetorian cargo-freighters, as well as her frigates.

Empty, deep black space had become a vast torrent of multi-coloured lethality, created by a vast quantity of fire. The enemy had come in at a point so that they were facing the convoy sideways on the starboard side, the convoy arranged in a standard double-row of three freighters a line. By coming sideways they would have full broadsides available as soon as the effects of leaving hyperspace had been reduced, and they were back up to operating power.

The *Hannoverian* and the *Deliverance* unleashed a broadside of their own, followed by the lighter fire from the *Featherlight*. The frigates had come up and round whilst the enemy were jumping in, and were at a higher angle but also had their broadsides presented. They changed heading to try and put the target ship, the unidentified S-class, between them and the other two ships.

The S-class ship shuddered as it came under the heavy fire, shields un-energised and essentially defenceless – for the moment. Fire exploded all along its hull, one torpedo smashing directly through the Swan symbol on top of the nose and exploding violently inside, blowing out the underhull with its venom.

<Twenty seconds until they are ready to fire,> said her data-tac officer. <I'm bombarding them with viruses, but they are resisting, their fire-walls are upgraded.>

<Hausenhof gun platforms and starbase are targeting the destroyer, they are ignoring your request, Lieutenant-Commander.>

<Where are their two frigates?> Wybeck demanded.

<Coming in, but on a heading for the destroyer.>

Bastards, she thought to herself. <Take out the S-class before the enemy are operational,> she demanded. <Destroyed or immobilised, I care not which!>

Coming around, the *Apollo* was the one that scored the knock-out shot. It had changed vector and was accelerating quickly towards the rear of the S-class strike-cruiser. A spread of three torpedoes slammed in quick succession into the boxy engine decks, stripping them away, followed quickly by a head MAC round which hammered through the remaining decks and exposed the engine core. Turbolasers spiked like a rain of fire into the exposed section, laser cannon crews switching targets and stitching up the hull as they realised the enemy was opened up.

<All power has died on the S-class, it is dead in the water!> her data-tac officer shouted across the datasphere. The datasphere rocked with the noise of the crew celebrating.

<Five seconds until the L-class is able to fire and re-shield,> came the warning, <fifteen until it is moving.>

<We have a virus in the destroyer! It's been purged but we pulled information!>

<Ident on the ships. *Scimitar, Labyrinth and Unassailable*.>

<All ships to switch fire to the *Labyrinth*,> Wybeck ordered, even as she pulled up the history they held on those three ships.

<All ships confirm orders.>

<Hausenhof frigates opening fire on destroyer, as expected.>

<Destroyer is fully operational. Firing long range on gun platforms, ignoring convoy. It has only sustained minimal damage.>

<Ships launching from the *Scimitar*! Heading for the convoy. Most probably Marines!>

Wybeck responded, <Determine and track their headings, prepare to launch our own Marines to defend if they are targeting Hausenhof convoy ships.> The Hausenhof convoy ships did not have their own Marine complements to defend them, or those that did were inferior House military, and not up to facing off against Praetorian Imperial Marines.

<*Labyrinth* is firing ..... they're targeting us!>

Wybeck felt the ship rock as it came under fire, not so much physically but through her neural link on the datasphere. They had probably identified that the orders for the defence forces were coming from her ship.

Their shields were holding, but now was the point where the fight became much more equal and dangerous. Even just one strike cruiser could successfully hold off and defeat two frigates.

*

The woman walked up to the hotel reception desk, and the automated droid behind it acknowledged her presence by lighting up.

"Good afternoon," the droid said, "welcome to the Third Hotel Savrecik, which is part of the highly successful interstellar Hotel Group of Venus Leisure, with luxurious emperor-class hotels in place all across the colonised Galaxy. How may I be of assistance to you today?"

"I have just arrived in the Dalcice System on extended business," the woman replied. "A reservation was made for me for one Standard month."

"Certainly, it would be pleasure to help you," said the emotionless droid. "If you are a Zupanic national or a Levitican Union national please present your identity holo-lith, or if you have travelled from outside the Levitican Union please present your interstellar passport and your Union visa to engage in business activities."

"Here you go," said the woman, handing over her passport and work visa.

There was a moment or two, and then the reception droid said, "It all seems to be in order. You have been booked into room 12105, on the hundred and twenty first floor. Please follow the guide-droid to your room. Should you need any assistance activate the guide-droid, which will deactivate automatically when not required, privacy being assured by Venus Leisure. Please enjoy your stay."

"Thanks," said the woman, as a guide-droid hovered up and began to move slowly away. She tapped her floating droid-case, and it followed her into the lift elevator.

A couple of minutes later she was locking the door to room 12105.

"Do you require any assistance at this time?" the guide-droid asked.

"No, thank you," said the woman.

"Re-activate me if your require any assistance," said the guide-droid, floating over to the desk at one part of the expansive hotel room, and settling into a docking pod. All its lights went out.

Acting normally, the woman sent her droid-case over to the large emperor-sized bed, and then went to the guide-droid. She waved her hand over it, an implant automatically checking that it was truly deactivated and there was no chance of spying.

Satisfied, she went back to her droid-case and opened it. The holographic image of clothes disappeared, revealing the workstation concealed within. She activated the electronic counter-measures device within, and then stepped back.

The cybernetic biomorph dropped its disguise, the features of the woman blurring and the skull definition disappearing, eyes becoming black orbs to match the jet black skin. The clothing disappeared, morphing back into the body of the creature.

This was a Faceless assassin, and more importantly, it was the Faceless assassin that belonged to Lady Sophia. It could not remember any form of life or existence apart from waking up in a military facility somewhere in House Towers territory.

It physically shrank its size so it could use the workstation on its bed more easily.

<Identify> said the computer within the workstation.

<Codename : Black. Passcode : Four-Four-Four-One-Omega-Alpha-Four-Three-Nine>

<Confirmed. Welcome, Agent Black.>

<I am in location in the Dalcice System, on Zupanica, within the capital city of Savrecik, under the false identity provided. First stage complete. Confirm my next orders.>

The orders were dumped directly into the assassin's brain. The mission briefing was simple. If a certain event occurred, he was to automatically proceed in the assassination of Vasily Zupanic and Csarina Zupanic. Both could be despatched together or independently, but both were resident on Zupanic and there would be opportunities to eliminate them together. It mattered not what the method of assassination was, or whether it was public or privately accomplished. It was to be a clean operation, witnesses were allowed. Self-termination was mandatory if it was captured.

The trigger event was interesting, the assassin thought. He was only to commence the assassination operation if it was announced in state media or the StarCom News Media that Lord Luke was going on a military tour of duty around the Levitican Union.

*

Admiral James Gavain sat in his ready room aboard the battlecruiser *Vindicator*, drinking slowly from his cup of real coffee as he thought, one elbow resting on the desk as he stared out of the observation window at the starscape behind him.

Since his engagement with the Pirates of the Cross, they had struck once at the newly formed Aalborg Alliance and House Lindholm, his ships arriving too late to stop it. Admiral-of-the-Fleets Halvorssen had not been best pleased. There had been numerous piracy attacks elsewhere in the galaxy however, and Commodore Andersson had successfully linked them.

It was typical then, that whilst his patience was wearing thin on this contract waiting for the Pirates of the Cross to attack, that another pirate group somehow connected to them had attacked his ships on the Hausenhof Convoy Contract.

He had just finished re-reading Lieutenant-Commander Wybeck's report. It had contained both good and bad news.

The good news was that they had successfully identified the three Swan Pirate ships. This had in turn allowed them to link at least one to the Rose Pirates, and another to the Pirates of the Cross attacks. It was all more evidence. They had information on all three ship's defensive abilities, captains, and more. Andersson and O'Connor would be trawling for information, any clues that would lead them to the root of this pirate conspiracy.

They had also captured the S-class *Scimitar*, which was fantastic news, although the cost in terms of Marines had been excessively high. It was there that the positives ended, as once again, the pirates had completed wiped all databases. There were however prisoners to be sent back to Tahrir base for interrogation. The *Labyrinth* and the destroyer *Unassailable* had done considerable damage to the system defences, but the convoy had managed to escape relatively unharmed despite also being boarded by the enemy. The convoy had eventually jumped into its target system, so the Hausenhof Convoy Contract was now complete.

Before leaving the system, unfortunately, the pirates had inflicted an incredible amount of damage on the *Apollo*, Wybeck's ship. It was so badly affected it was not able to jump, and nearly eighty percent of its crew had been killed in the battering it had taken. The ship was not space-worthy any more.

With a heavy heart, Gavain made his decision. He completed the orders telling Wybeck to take command of the captured *Scimitar*, and utterly destroy the *Apollo*. Even though it had been a captured Cervantian ship, he was not going to leave any Vindicator Mercenary Corporation starship abandoned in space.

He also signed the orders promoting Wybeck to full Commander, and granting her permanent command of the *Scimitar*. Despite losing her own ship the *Apollo*, it had been in exceptionally difficult circumstances, and she had acquitted herself bravely, and saved the rest of her command from heavy damage. He judged it to be a good performance.

The contract in Hausenhof was at an end. Wybeck and the ships had to return to the Blackheath System, undergo repairs at the nearly completed starbase, and then the *Scimitar* and the *Odyssey* could jump out to join the Lindholm contract against the Pirates of the Cross.

A message had come from General Andryukhin. The contract there had ended successfully, with some brilliant news coverage throughout the galaxy. A number of contract offers had already been made from a number of other Houses, but Andryukhin was reporting that he had been approached directly by Star Marshal Ngu to undertake another contract for the Zhou-Zheng Compact, an invasion of the Chester System. It was high-value, but carried the same high-risk. Andryukhin made it clear he did not like working for the humanists, but would accept the contract if James thought it worthwhile.

James Gavain weighed up the other offers against the Compact contract, and then composed his message to Andryukhin to sign the contract. He electronically signed his version and sent it with the communication, so that as another Director, Ulrik could sign his copy and the contract would be binding.

James was then briefly distracted by an intelligence report from Harley Andersson. Both he and O'Connor regularly provided intelligence reports on all activity within the galaxy, to keep Gavain informed. This one was of interest, as apparently the StarCom Federation had suffered a severe setback. Someone had stolen their Tears of the Moon technology, the same technology that had led to the destruction of the planet Alwathbah, and concerningly, that person was now offering the information discretely to numerous bidders. The person or persons, whoever they were, had also stolen a significantly large number of InterStellar Hyperspace Missiles equipped with the Tears of the Moon warheads from the Solar System, right under the nose of the StarCom Federation military, and were selling the missiles individually to any interested party. Even the Levitican Union had been approached.

Gavain actually shuddered at the thought of missiles capable of crossing intergalactic distances, and delivering payloads strong enough to destroy a planet utterly. It was horrific.

In other news, Andersson reported that the Kavanagh Shipyards, although not yet fully completed, was partially operational. The training of the first batch of borgs was going well, and in less than a month he would have his second batch 'hatching'. This included the fifty super-marines based on Faceless biomorph technology.

James Gavain then moved on to his next task. Lady Sophia had acted on the intelligence his mercenary company had given to her on the pirates, and a likely conspiracy or link between the various groups in the Eastern Segment. She informed him that she had instructed The Spider to approach a number of the affected governments, with a view to forming a temporary alliance to deal with it. She was doing it as House Towers, and not as a member of the Levitican Union, which he found very interesting and understandable considering the politics concerned.

Thinking about it, James Gavain realised he had an opportunity here. Should Lady Sophia be successful in communicating with the various intelligence agencies of the affected houses, he might be able to wrangle a super contract and payment out of all of them for tracking the pirates down and eliminating them. It would make the considerable payment from House Lindholm and the newly formed Aalborg Alliance pale in comparison.

He considered carefully. Lady Sophia would probably jump at his suggestion to pay the VMC with Levitican Union funds to eliminate the pirate groups. Ambassador Grunehaube was the logical choice for him to contact in Hausenhof. Unfortunately he would need a contact in House Erdogan, so he decided he would ask Andryukhin if he had spoken to anybody in their military, at least someone that he had not killed. It might ease some of Andryukhin's discomfort about working for the Compact, and Gavain could see no reason why he could not take a contract with Erdogan to eliminate pirates at the same time as working for the Compact, providing it was kept secret. He had no contact with House Van Der Meer, who were suffering attacks from the Pirates of the Sextant, and who also suspected that Amiens were sponsoring it. He could task Andersson with making the contact.

His future course decided, he sat back and smiled, pleased with himself. He had changed so much since Imperial days, when he had felt lost following the civil war against the False Emperor. He was now a mercenary, and he was finding it easier and easier to think like one, spotting opportunities in everything.

Then the smile faded ever so slightly. Was this life and what he had become enough for him, he wondered. He had been a man of duty, loyalty, the best of the best in a field he had not chosen but had been specifically bred for – and after becoming a traitor on the grounds of morality and principle, he had turned into a man motivated by doing the best for the survivors of the civil war, and the best way he had found of doing that was chasing the bottom line.

Was chasing the bottom line truly the best way? Or had he lost sight of his reasons for becoming a mercenary, and being the mercenary was now his reason for existence?

*

"We have translation in three .... two ..... one ..... warp exit!" Juan Ramirez announced.

As the *Nazareth* translated from hyperspace, he felt the usual sense of disorientation before his senses came back to him fully. It was a smoother transition than normal, and he wondered if that was because he was so concerned about what awaited them here, his emotions and sense were heightened and so he resisted the normal pull of the translation.

The tension in the air of the small bridge and its seven crew was palpable.

"I'm detecting nothing on scanners, Captain," said the scanners operator. The fear in her voice made Juan's heart beat faster. "We're in deep space, and there's nothing out here."

"Wait," was all Captain Sirocco said. "Comms, begin broadcasting the identification signal I gave you."

Juan tensed even more. They had jumped with no recharge in the jump capacitors to this spot, the target destination they had been given. It was deep space in the vast emptiness of the Gulf of Medusa, with no solar system, planets or stars nearby. There was no way to recharge the jump capacitor. Without recharge, they could never jump out, and would face a slow, painful death as the ship's power slowly failed.

He had secretly patched into the comms system using his borg implants, finding the security codes ridiculously easy to crack. His former, somewhat nefarious gangster past had probably helped there. He listened to the communications signal as it was sent out on an open, all-sphere broadcast wave, decoding it and getting nothing but a simple codeword – 'Rosicrux' – and a short sequence of numbers afterwards.

"All hands," Captain Sirocco addressed the entire crew on the internal speakers, "await my orders. We have arrived at the destination."

"Captain! Spatial disturbance detected, three-sixty, thirty-two, two hundred K!"

"Show me," Helenna Sirocco ordered. She had never lost her cool or calm.

The holographic viewer in front of the viewscreen sprang into life, visual sensors focusing on the area where the disturbance had been detected, so two hundred thousand kilometres ahead of them. Space was rippling as a massive chameleonic field was being disrupted and lowered, a field that operated on a size and scale Juan had never dreamt it could ever operate on.

Revealed, in the middle of deep space, was a large space station. It was of a construction that Juan had never seen in his life. It looked alien, and did not seem to fit any Imperial or House standard construction, although it was emblazoned with the Red Eagle of the Imperium so it obviously dated from the time of the Emperors.

One end was shaped as a large shell, a circular ball rotating within a series of circular rings. Power crackled from the ball to the rings visibly. A long, thick corridor connected it to a shell, a bulky boxy body with two round halves that were more Imperial in design. Another long, thick corridor let out in the other direction, away from various empty docking pylons and weapons blisters, to what looked like the portal of a stargate. All but one of the starship berths was empty, a fusion-tanker docked in place.

"We're receiving a hail, Captain," said the communications crewman.

"Connect me in private," Captain Sirocco ordered.

Juan watched as a special secrecy field snapped into place around her chair, allowing Sirocco to receive and discuss the communication in private. He did not worry – the hack he had placed into the communications station would allow him to retrieve and listen to a recording of the communication later.

Eventually the field snapped back down, and Captain Sirocco pressed the holo-panel button in front of her that allowed her to address the crew. "All hands, we were going to recharge at this Deepspace Station, but the plan has changed. We're using the stargate here to jump directly to another location, where we will recharge and carry out the final delivery of our cargo. Prepare for the best sight in your lives, my people."

She deactivated the internal address system. "Helm, to the stargate; Navigation, allow the Deepspace Station to patch into our nav system. We're going through that stargate."

"Aye, sir," said Juan in time with the helmsman, as he set about his orders.

Much later, Juan sat in his own room. As a senior member of bridge crew, he was allowed his own room, although calling the three metre square box a room was perhaps overly generous. He had retracted the showerhead and called down the bed, and now lay anxiously with his back against the wall, aware that the *Nazareth* cargo-freighter was currently speeding through hyperspace, propelled by the massive force of the stargate to their final destination.

On the small shelf opposite him, some of his holo-liths displaying models of the Vindicator Mercenary Corporation ships were on display. Even his favourite distraction of immersing himself in their mythology was no comfort tonight.

He had seen the co-ordinates this so-called Deepspace Station had downloaded into the ships system, and checked them. Once again it was taking them into the depths of nothingness, but in many ways this area of deepspace was even worse. It was surrounded by numerous black holes, and only certain angles would get them past the massive and dangerous void. They were going further than he had ever heard of any ship ever going, even during the Droid Wars when the few and sparse colonies within the Gulf had been utterly destroyed.

Shaking his head against the growing discomfort of what he had landed himself into this time in the tragedy he called his life, he opened his palm-reader and read the data-chip he had ejected from the navigations console before leaving his night shift. The data-chip had recorded the communication that Sirocco had engaged in with the Deepspace Station.

The image of a big, heavy, muscular man had appeared in Juan's mind's eye, and there was a strange, complicated symbol on the flag behind his command chair. He spoke first.

Man: This is Commander Decay, of Deepspace Fourteen. You are Captain Helenna Sirocco, of the Nazareth?

Sirocco : Yes, sir, I am Captain Sirocco.

DeShay : Do you have the cargo, Captain Sirocco?

Sirocco : All the missiles and warheads, sir. We're ready to transfer them, but our rendezvous ship is not here?

DeShay : No, there has been a problem. The ship was intercepted on its course here, and detained. There will be no rendezvous or transfer. Dolf Reichenburg himself has ordered that you use the stargate here to carry on the delivery, through Deepspace Six, right to Dark Heart.

Sirocco : Yes, sir, of course I can do that – but we have a problem. We've already broken protocol and carried the mission on past one handover, it's unprecedented to carry on to past a second handover in the journey. The bigger problem is that whilst I am cleared for Dark Heart, all of the rest of my crew are not. Not even my Salchuzura Mara comrades know of Dark Heart – ha, as far as I know.

DeShay : Reichenburg is aware of this. When you return from Dark Heart, you will head to System XJ-1201, where you will be met and boarded. Your crew will be terminated, and you will be given a replacement.

Sirocco : This delivery is that important?

DeShay : Do not question your orders, or ask for more information than you are permitted to have.

Sirocco : Understood, sir. I was not questioning the orders. My crew have operational permission to see Dark Heart, but then will be killed and replaced when we head to XJ-1201. I understand.

DeShay : Good. Make way to the stargate, and jump. Load the nav-comp. We are ready for you.

Sirocco : Yes, sir. In the name of Rosicrux.

DeShay : In the name of Rosicrux.

Juan reviewed the recording several times, but every time he did, it sent shivers down his spine. Whatever Dark Heart was, and whatever Rosicrux was, he and the entire crew were to be killed because of them.

*

Lord Minister Luke had sat very quietly through a very boring representation by Lord Minister Brin Claes, the Zupanic puppet, who was proposing an amend on a very unimportant aspect of Levitican Union law. He wondered idly if Lord Principal Ramicek put these discussions and debates into the agenda as a way of either satisfying Lord Claes' ego, or to give them all some relief from the more serious debates they had to consider.

He glanced to the side, trying not to make the look obvious. There had been a number of discussions in the Council recently in relation to House Marchenko, and they had resulted in some changes.

The five Ministries of the Levitican Union had been joined by a sixth, the Ministry of Transformation and Integration. It was a bit of a nothing ministry in Luke's opinion, although some of his fellow Lord Ministers had pointed out to him the need for such a thing. The Levitican Union was still coming together, and a lot of ministries were struggling with ensuring that all of their proposed changes were taking place. It was a ministry of project managers, thought Luke dismissively.

The figure at his side was the new Lady Minister, Lady Eranisch Marchenko. She was one of the several hundred daughters and sons of the massive Marchenko noble family, ranked about ninety-fifth born, so Lord Luke Towers was informed.

She was immense, of the same size as Gregori Marchenko, her father. The collective borgite woman showed very little feminity. With a face like granite, half metal and whirring servos and sensors, no less than six legs to support her immense bulk, a lower half built like an insect and an additional set of mechanical arms ending in a laser-scribe on one and a claw on the other, it had taken some getting used to her presence.

Lord Luke Towers was also uncomfortably aware that she had a direct connection back to Gregori Marchenko and the Marchenkan hive mind. It transpired that the collective mind of the Marchenkans was not always joined at all times; the millions of workers, if they were in a distant system or out of range of the central consciousness, always had a House Marchenko family member present who would provide a temporary central node for the collective consciousness, until such point as they could reconnect to the central hive mind.

Lady Eranisch Marchenko was the central consciousness for the Marchenkan citizens now in the temporary Levitican Union capital of Zubrenica XIX. Everything she learnt and heard was reported back to the central hive mind – and by extension, the rest of the Marchenkan race – by HPCG on a regular basis.

Lord Luke forced himself to pay attention as the votes were cast on Lord Claes' proposal. He had already made his mind up on the issue. The vote was carried by five affirmations, one negative, and one abstention.

"And now, before we end the day's session," said Lord Principal Ramicek, "We enter any other business. I ask the Council if there is anything unscheduled that they wish to discuss?"

Lord Minister Luke leaned forward and pressed his button, marginally ahead of Lady Minister Monique Lapointe and Lord Minister Brin Claes.

"Lord Minister Luke Towers?" Ramicek asked.

"I will keep it brief, as we are all tired," said Lord Luke, getting to his feet. "I wish to request funding from the Council for a special project, which is not currently within our budget. We are suffering increasingly heavy piratical attacks throughout the Levitican Union, despite the increased military presence offered by the reinforcements given to the Union military by House Marchenko. We are too large, now at a staggering eighty-two inhabited systems, to cover all our trade routes and uninhabited systems with sufficient defence. A new strategy is required.

"I believe there may be an alternative answer – tracking the pirates back to their base of operations. The mercenary unit Vindicator Mercenary Corporation, which as all here will remember, the Levitican Union owes its very existence to, believes it may be able to source the base of the pirates. They do not have a location yet, but think they may be able to track them down, as well as providing a much needed boost to our defensive forces at this terrible time. Faced with the need to reinforce our border with House Jorgensson, I find this the most attractive option in dealing with the ravages of the Rose Pirates."

He sat back down. His sister had asked him to do this, and he had done his best.

"Does the Vindicator Mercenary Corporation have intelligence they believe could lead to the base of the pirates?" asked Lord Principal Ramicek, eyes narrowing.

"They have not shared that with me," said Lord Luke. It was technically the truth, but he knew of the intelligence that House Towers was keeping from the rest of the Union, gained by the VMC, speaking of the link between all the pirate organisations in the Eastern Segment.

Lady Monique Lapointe stood. "How much is Sir Admiral James Gavain asking for?" she asked.

Lord Luke stood and told them. He could see Lady Lapointe doing some quick calculations.

"Is this acceptable from a budgetary point of view?" Ramicek asked.

"Yes," was the reply, "we can do it, but there will be some projects which have to be deferred a number of years. Those we will need to select and vote upon."

"Very well," said Lord Principal Ramicek. "Does anyone else have any points on this subject they wish to make? No? Let us vote, then."

The votes came through as six in favour, one abstention.

"Motion carried, give the VMC their payment," Lord Principal Ramicek nodded at Lord Luke. "Lady Lapointe, in the next council session, you will present a list of the projects that have to be deferred as a result of this decision. Now, I believe you had something you wished to discuss?"

"It was in relation to ongoing piracy, and I believe Lord Minister Luke pre-empted my question with his proposal." Lady Lapointe nodded to Luke, and sat down. Luke was not quite sure why, but he saw something in her eyes then. She was not the person he once knew, as he supposed was only natural considering the loss of her mother to the pirates, but he was feeling that there was something else that darkened her soul of late.

"Withdrawn, then," said Lord Principal Ramicek. "Lord Brin Claes. You had something you wished to propose?"

"Yes," said Lord Brin, standing. "There is something, and it relates to the piracy as well, and the ongoing effect it is having. The piracy affects all our ministries, but it is also beginning to affect our people, and I believe the morale of our military is becoming lower and lower because of it, as I am sure Lord Luke would agree. I propose therefore that we take the unusual step of sending a Lord Minister out on tour of the military, rather than one of his ministers - but the Lord can still attend council sessions by HPCG. I believe Lord Luke should go on a tour of the military stationed around the Levitican Union."

Here it comes, thought Lord Luke, keeping his face carefully neutral. They get me out of the Council, so they can have me assassinated. Ramicek, you use your puppet Brin to set up my murder, now? How much of your plan does Brin Claes know?

"This is a brilliant idea," said Lord Principal Ramicek. "What sort of timetable and destinations would such a journey cover?"

"We have a plan," said Lady Eranisch Marchenko, standing with a terrible whining of mechanical limbs. She transmitted it to all the Lord and Lady Ministers, and Luke read it with interest. The first part of the journey would take him out of Zupanic space and into Marchenko. He ignored the rest – he was supposed to be assassinated on that leg of the journey, he knew. If the information from Lord Micalek was correct.

"Let us vote," said Lord Principal Ramicek.

The vote came out as seven in favour, Lord Luke agreeing. The die was well and truly cast.

He stood. "I will prepare a statement for the media tonight, and transmit it first thing tomorrow morning," he said.

Chapter XIII

Major Alexey of the Zupanic House Guard stepped smartly out into the harsh sunlight of the planet Zupanica, crossing the primary courtyard of Zupanic Palace quietly. As he approached behind the assembled squad, he shook his head.

He had no less than six full squads of House Guard protecting today's convoy, and they would be riding in a combination of repulsorcycles, airtrucks and hover-jeeps, all around the central droidcar carrying Vasily and Csarina Zupanic, the third and fourth in line to the throne of House Zupanic. A further fourteen squads were spread out across the route, in various stationary positions. There were another four companies ready to come out on short notice aboard thrustcopters if there was an issue, and a company of fightercraft ready to scramble. The public had largely been cleared from the convoy route by an army of local enforcer policemen.

It might seem excessive for a simple media-aimed visit by two high-ranking nobles of the Zupanic family, but the horrors of the Imperium had taught them to be careful, not the least the Dissolution of the Empire and the numerous Faceless assassins that seemed to target the lords and ladies of the various seceding Houses. The Levitican Union had suffered assassinations. It remained a fact that any House Lord or Lady was a potential target – and within House Zupanic, he reflected, the greatest threat to any noble family member was the rest of his or her noble family.

"I can't be bothered with this," said one trooper to the colleague at her side.

"It's far too hot even by Zupanica standards for this," her comrade agreed.

"Attention!" the squad sergeant called out, spotting his commander approaching.

"Lax," the Major shouted out, the entire squad stiffening to attention. They wore armour, but it was a poor shadow of that worn by the former Praetorian Guard. "Get in position now, the Lord and Lady are due in three minutes. You two," he called out at the two troopers who he had overheard. They froze and looked at his scarred face in terror.

He read their name badges. "Grgic and Peric," he said, "for your lack of enthusiasm, you're on the repulsorcycles either side of the droidcar. Anyone targets the Lord and Lady, you're getting shot with them, okay?"

"Yes, sir," said the female Grgic quickly, faster on the uptake than her comrade.

Major Alexey mounted his hover-jeep, which was at the very rear of the convoy so he could observe his squads as they covered the protection of the two nobles. He watched Grgic and Peric mount the two free repulsorcycles, watching them lift slightly off the air as they gunned them up for action alongside the flanks of the nobles' droidcar.

Vasily Zupanic and Csarina Zupanic were carried down the grand steps into Zupanic Palace by a hovering droid-platform, the robot skimming quickly over the ground with protective force-fields in place as they crossed the open ground.

The old Vasily Zupanic, brother to Ramicek, stood by the door as his niece Csarina was allowed to enter the droidcar first. Once the door had cycled shut, Major Alexey spoke into his command mike, "Convoy, we have go, repeat, we have go. Let's do this, people."

In a well practiced motion, the entire convoy of a phenomenal number of vehicles rose high up into the air. The lead vehicles turned, heading towards a rectangular exit-hole opening in a very small north-facing section of the glittering shields that surrounded Zupanic Palace. The entire palace was protected by a force field more commonly found protecting cities, the paranoia of the Zupanic family extending even to such a simple device.

Major Alexey watched the first vehicles passing through, relaxed for the moment. He was not expecting any trouble today, House Intelligence under Lady Wyn had not given him any indication to think there would be any, but his job was to stay alert.

Even as he was thinking that, the droidcar began to pass through the hole in the shield dome's wall.

With a snap, the shield shut quickly, neatly tearing the droidcar and two repulsorcycles in half.

Major Alexey gasped. The energy field had closed in an eye-blink, neatly shearing through the three vehicles trying to pass through it. Half of his protective convoy was on the other side of the shield-wall. Half of the droidcar was falling to the ground before his eyes, burning up, the bodies of Vasily and Zupanic exactly vaporised by the closing thickness of the energy wall. Troopers Grcic and Peric had also died, their bodies atomised by the viciousness of the closing protective energy field, bits of their cycles falling with the two halves of the droidcar either side of the Palace wall.

A few seconds later, Major Alexey began screaming into his radio as his wits returned.

The Faceless assassin in the employ of House Towers, Agent Black, nodded to itself. He had penetrated Zupanic Palace easily, inserting himself yesterday. He had taken the shape and form of a servant who was off-shift until tonight, using the body of the servant to gain access to the lower floors of the Palace.

It had been simple enough to disguise himself as a trooper, and get into the shield wall control room. He had inserted his remote-control bypass into the shield wall computers, and then returned to the upper floors of the Palace as the servant.

He stood up, carefully bypassing the dead body of the servant at his feet. It had been necessary to kill the identity of the first person he stole, as he had spent more than twenty-four hours pretending to be the person. Earlier yesterday morning, Lord Luke Towers had broadcast his Union-wide message on the state media, confirming his was going on a tour of duty of the Levitican Union military. That had been the trigger telling Agent Black to carry out the assassination.

The assassin held his wrist up to his face. An implant emerged out of the wrist, an implant he had taken from the droid-case he had used in the hotel room.

<Codename : Black. Passcode : Four-Four-Four-One-Omega-Alpha-Four-Three-Nine>

<Confirmed. Yes, Agent Black?>

<Targets Vasily and Csarina successfully eliminated. New orders required.>

<New mission. Proceed immediately to the moon Zubrenica XIX. The new target is Lord Principal Ramicek Zupanic. Take up position to strike and await the trigger event. You must be in a position to escape the assassination, but if in danger of capture, immediate self-termination is required. Any form of assassination is acceptable, but there must be no collateral damage to any non-targets. The area is highly secure and has high-profile non-targets that must not be harmed. Immediately after assassination you must hide on location on Zubrenica XIX to await next target arrival in-system. A long term cover is therefore advisable. Downloading mission details, maps and information now.>

<What is the trigger event?>

<You are only to proceed with the mission if there is an attempted or successful assassination of Lord Luke Towers, reported through the state media or StarCom News Media. Confirm understanding.>

<Understood.>

Now, how to get up to the moon, he thought to himself.

*

The figure entered the holo-pit nestled deep within the Temple of Shadow carefully, every step measured as he crossed the complex pictorial symbol woven into the central floor of the chamber. The black mask he wore was delineated with gold lines, marking him out as the Master of the First Circle of the Shadow Council. The two agents in black synth-skin, with their white cloaks over their shoulders, who had accompanied him to the chamber bowed and then retreated, the door cycling shut behind them.

There were nine alcoves within the circular holo-pit chamber, and there were figures already in four of them. They all wore black robes, the same as the Master, their black face-masks lined with different colours to denote the command of the different Circles they were responsible for.

He assumed his seat in the alcove, and leaned back. "Begin," he commanded simply.

Holographic representations appeared in the four empty seats, linked in seamlessly from their various locations across the colonised galaxy by a continuous hyper-pulse communication. Once they had coalesced into being, another image appeared in the centre of the room, an exact replica of the Master, showing he had the right to speak.

"Acknowledge me!" he demanded angrily.

"Hail the Master," each of the figures whispered, and it was possible to detect the fear at this unusual start.

The image of the Master whirled viciously to face the Legate of the Fifth Circle, who was actually present in the room this time. "Legate," he growled, "Explain yourself, immediately. A Faceless assassin has been used in the terminations of Vasily Zupanic and Csarina Zupanic."

The woman who wore the red-lined mask of the Fifth Circle kept her cool as her image was magnified and whirled into the centre of the room as she spoke, replacing the Master. "Shadow Council," she said, "the Faceless assassin that eliminated Vasily and Csarina Zupanic is not in my control. My only possible conjecture is that it is the assassin we lost." She stood, bowed, and turned to the Master. "If you wish my head, I will remove it myself for this failure."

Her image disappeared, and the Master re-appeared in the centre of the circular room. "That is not necessary .... at this time." The room seemed to grow colder than it already was. "Legate of the Fourth Circle, have you located our missing member of the Fifth?"

A figure with blue lines on his black face mask appeared. "We have not located any trace. House Zupanic suspects that House Towers stole the assassin from their custody, but they have no conclusive evidence. The Lady Wyn attempts to discover if they are to blame, but they have no evidence as yet. We of the Fourth Circle are paying close attention to the House Zupanic's attempts to discover who took the assassin from them. I also have agents within House Towers, but there has been no indication yet that they are involved."

"Intolerable," the Master hissed. "Legate of the Third Circle, your conclusion?"

A figure with white lines on his face mask was whisked into the centre of the room. "If we are to engage in conjecture, the political situation in the Levitican Union would seem to indicate a reasonable chance of approximately seventy percent that House Towers stole back the assassin, and are now using the agent of the Fifth Circle to prosecute a vendetta against House Zupanic, having determined some if not all of the truth behind the Zupanic family plan to acquire Towers territory and total control of the Levitican Union."

The red-lines mask re-appeared in the centre of the room. "House Zupanic has approached us to assassinate Lord Luke Towers. The Legate of the Third Circle has given permission for this."

The Legate of the Third Circle appeared back in the centre. "I did indeed. House Towers and House Zupanic have turned murderous in their intent towards one another, an escalation in the political situation there that was not foreseen. The situation is in danger of destabilising the Levitican Union even further than the introduction of House Marchenko and the Rose Pirate attacks."

The Master took the centre of the room. "The likely location of the assassin is, today, Zupanica, in the Dalcice System. He cannot be allowed to leave that system. Legate of Second Circle, are your talents required for this?"

A figure with silver on her face mask appeared in the centre of the holo-pit. She was not present in the room. "I would advise against it, Master. Whilst there is no doubt we could swamp the Dalcice System, it would risk much, as well as by necessity requiring the elimination of the entire system. The government of the Levitican Union is based there, the collateral damage is unacceptable at this time. An action by the Fifth or Sixth Circle may be more in order."

The red-lines masked woman took the centre of the holo-pit. "I can have assassins of the Fifth Circle in place within twelve hours. We are not used to counter-assassin work, however."

"No-one is, this has never been an issue before!" snapped the Master.

A figure with dark purple on his face mask enlarged and took the centre of the room. He had a nasty, sibilant, broken quality to his voice. "My agents could be in the system in force in three days time, to nine days for full effective coverage. It would help if we knew the lost assassin's next move," he said pointedly, looking at the Legate of the Fourth Circle.

"If it is a vendetta against House Zupanic, being orchestrated by House Towers, it is ninety-three per cent likely the next target will be in the Dalcice System," the Legate of the Third Circle said. "Therefore the assassin will remain in system."

The Master appeared for the final time in the centre of the room. "Then here is what we do," he commanded. "Agents of the Fifth Circle will be in place today. Agents of the Sixth Circle are to be present within the time period specified. When our lost assassin strikes next, he will be pursued and terminated with extreme prejudice. Agents of the Fourth Circle will assist insertion in all instances. Even if it reveals our presence, it will be achieved at all costs."

*

General Ulrik Andryukhin was in his own personal office aboard the SS *Monstrosity*, the M-class super-transporter in orbit around Kyiv Primus. He sat reviewing the details for their planned assault into the Chester System.

He was deeply uncomfortable about working for the Zhou-Zheng Compact. Their money was fantastic, they were easily the highest paid contractors in the entire Segment at the moment. Yet Ulrik could not shake the feeling that all was not as it should be. Money was not everything, and that seemed to be something that his friend Jamie Gavain was missing.

The Compact were waging an almost genocidal war against borgs. It was the worst aspects of the humanist bigotry at its most extreme. Admittedly, Ulrik knew that before they had risen up against the False Emperor, even in the days of the True Emperor, there had been borgite bigotry against the unaugmented. He had been aware of that and even participated in it, so his own soul was not clean. At least he had been one of the many who had risen up against the False Emperor, however. Who was left to take arms against the humanist bigotry of the Zhou-Zheng Compact, apart from nations like Erdogan?

General Ulrik Andryukhin strongly felt they were fighting for the wrong side, and had said as much in his last hyper-pulse comm with Jamie. His old friend had replied that they were mercenaries, and the wrong side was the side that did not pay them. That was their new reality.

Maybe it was the unfair loss of Jules Kavanagh, a relationship that in itself would never have been allowed in the old Imperial days, but Ulrik know looked at everything differently and wondered if they were doing the right thing. He was bred for war, like all the Praetorians, and what was a weapon if not for using. The only difference now was that they did it for themselves in the name of money, and not the Red Imperium of Mars in the name of the Emperor. There had to be a line though; they were borgs, admittedly very advanced examples of that species, and the Zhou-Zheng Compact were prosecuting a war of hatred against all of his kind. And he was fighting for them – where was the right in that?

Captain Enrique Delgado, commander of the SS *Monstrosity*, interrupted his thoughts. <General Andryukhin, the new Zhou-Zheng Compact liaison has arrived aboard ship, and will be with you presently. She has requested to see you immediately.>

<Understood, Captain. Allow her into my office as soon as she arrives on the bridge.>

<Aye, sir.>

Andryukhin concentrated on his plans, until the door to his office opened and the woman entered. He jacked out of the datasphere, all the plans and holo-maps vanishing from his consciousness, as the woman strode confidently up to his desk. She wore the Z-Z Compact uniform, and looked fairly attractive. Ulrik smiled despite himself.

"General Ulrik Andryukhin," he saluted in the Imperial way.

She bowed, hands pressed together in the House Zheng or House Zhou way, he did not know which. "General, I am Da Wei Sao Su Ani, your new military liaison for the Chester System contract."

Andryukhin knew that 'Da Wei' was a Compact rank roughly equivalent to a Praetorian Lieutenant-Commander. "Sit," he said tersely. "We never needed a frikking liaison for the Kyiv System contract, so why we require one for the Chester System contract is a mystery to me."

She sat, crossing her beautiful legs wonderfully, Andryukhin could not help noticing. "Ah, well, General, this contract is somewhat different. A lot of strings had to be pulled to get me assigned to you. You see – well, are we alone? We're not being overheard?"

"No, of course we're not," said General Andryukhin. "But aboard this ship, strategic secrecy is never a problem. We're all ready to go on Star Marshal Ngu's command, to jump into the Chester System."

"I know," said the Da Wei Sao. "I am genuinely a Da Wei within the Zhou-Zheng Compact military, House of Zhou. I worked my way up through the ranks. But I am also an agent for Erdogan."

Andryukhin heard those last words. Within a nano-second he had jacked back into the datasphere, and warned Captain Delgado to have a number of marines posted outside his door, ready to enter immediately. His situation was compromised, there was an enemy spy in the room.

Aware he could do nothing if she was carrying a bomb, that he was a dead man – although he wondered how in all the names of the Emperors she had managed to get through their security checks and scans – he said simply, "Come again, miss Sao?"

"I am a secret agent for Erdogan. I have not always been, I used to work for Imperial Intelligence. But the end of the Empire brought an end to my greater employment for the Emperor, so to speak. I found a new employer who paid just as well in House Erdogan."

"I'm fucking pleased for you. You understand of course that I'm now shitting bricks wondering what you're doing in my office?"

"General, I'll keep it brief, as we have to discuss my cover story and all the things Star Marshal Ngu wanted me to convey to you. But I do work for House Erdogan, and we have come here to offer you a counter-proposal. We understand that you will never break your contract with the Zhou-Zheng Compact for Chester, but we are prepared to offer you your next contract, in excess of the one with the star-and-circle dragons."

"Keep talking."

"We know you are jumping into the Chester System, to 'surprise' Erdogan forces. We feel however, that we could come to an arrangement. We wish to contract you after the contract expires, to directly strike a blow against the Zhou-Zheng Compact. We are already in the process of secretly withdrawing from the Chester System, and when your forces land General, we can put up enough of a resistance with sacrifice units to make it look believable, but we will withdraw from the system immediately so you can end your contract with Zhou and Zheng."

"You would sacrifice an entire System just for that?"

"We have a bigger prize we wish you to help us take," she said. "Much bigger. Agree to the proposed contract from Erdogan, and we could reverse the direction this war has taken. And undo much of the damage you Vindicator Mercenaries have done to us borg."

"So, in return for another contract with Erdogan, you will allow us to easily complete this contract to take the Chester System?" said Andryukhin. "Because you believe it will allow you to win the war?"

"No, I did not say that," said the double agent. "But it would allow us to reverse a great deal of what the Compact have achieved recently, thanks to you."

"What is the nature of the contract?" Andryukhin asked.

She began to explain. He listened in sheer disbelief, then slowly, he began to see the sense in it as she explained the wider reasoning for it.

"Very well," he said, "I am a co-Director, and could sign this un-bonded contract, but I have to run something like this past James Gavain, you understand?" This contract would never appear on the Interstellar Merchant Guild's Mercenary Bonding Office records, that was for sure.

"Of course," she nodded.

Then a further thought occurred to him. Gavain had asked him if he could find someone within the Erdogan military to contract with against the pirates. Hating himself for displaying the same opportunism that Gavain did, Andryukhin raised the point with Da Wei Sao, if that was even her real name.

"All I can do is ask my superiors. I certainly will. I am scheduled to talk to my handler within two hours, and the message will reach Erdogan Feldmarshall Grant within the day. It would be his decision on whether Erdogan agrees to another contract, but everyone knows Erdogan is suffering badly under the pirates. Many think it is Zhou-Zheng Compact sponsored, but I have never found any proof. That was my primary mission, until you landed in Kyiv, you know."

Andryukhin laughed, a twinkle in his eye. "Glad to have distracted you, my lady."

She smiled, genuinely he thought. "That you have, General, that you have. However, there is one thing we would also like you to be aware of."

"And what is that?"

"Have you heard of the deathcamps that Zhou-Zheng is building on Kyiv Primus?"

"Deathcamps?"

"The Compact is sending millions of borg to their deaths on Kyiv Primus, right here, right now," said the agent Sao, very simply and very quietly.

*

Lord Micalek and Lady Sophia were walking through the Towers Manor west gardens, the Tahrir summer now fully upon this section of the planet.

"One still misses Alwathbah," said Lady Sophia wistfully, speaking of the planet that had once been the capital of the Towers territory, before the Tears of the Moon had utterly destroyed it. "It was cold much of the time, but so beautiful. The mountains around Tiananmen stood like jewels in the crown of House Towers."

Lord Micalek nodded, enjoying the feel of her arm through his. "Alwathbah was a beautiful planet by all accounts. It is just as well that the StarCom Federation are still paying reparations for its destruction." He paused, stopping walking, and Lady Sophia turned to him. "But we have to think about now, Sophia. Your brother Lord Luke is in mortal danger."

"We know. One has passed on the information you have provided, we will be able to protect him. He will not be killed."

"My mother is using the Faceless again," said Lord Micalek. "Even when you are protected, the Faceless always find a way through. That is why both Emperors used them so much, and why they are so feared."

"We have some advantages," said Lady Sophia, shrugging. "We know where the assassination is to take place, although not how. We have the technology now to find the Faceless, thanks to one's mercenaries. One is paying them a considerable amount to protect one's brother."

"You have engaged the VMC to protect your brother? But how can those mercenaries –"

"Enough, do not ask," said Lady Sophia. There was a warning in her tone that warned Micalek that he still had to earn her trust.

"Yes, Sophia," Micalek bowed his head. "But it has started now, has it not. My uncle and my sister were killed a day ago."

"They were, yes," said Lady Sophia. "One is upholding her end of the bargain, husband."

"You are indeed. Who in my family is next? My mother or my father?"

"Please, do not ask," Lady Sophia shook her head.

"We have to start trusting each other, Sophia. Is this your captured Faceless assassin you are using? It has all the hallmarks of a Faceless assassination operation."

"One cannot confirm or deny."

"Sophia!" Micalek felt frustrated. He shook his head, looking at the ground, before he looked back up at her eyes.

"Ok, Micci," said Sophia. "It is fairly obvious by now. Yes, of course one is using the Faceless assassin. There is no point in denying it now."

"Yes," he nodded. "I must speak to my mother shortly by HPCG. You understand that I must pretend to still be loyal to House Zupanic. The communication will be secured this end, you will not be able to hear what I say, but if you did, it would sound like I was double-crossing you? I am not going to tell her about your possession of the Faceless, or certain other things, but I must give her something or she will suspect."

"One understands," said Lady Sophia. "This is a dangerous game we are playing. Towers and Zupanic are now moving against one another, and in the process, we are going to disrupt the Levitican Union. Hopefully not too much. But the threat to my House must be dealt with – my House comes before me and my brother, never doubt that."

Lord Micalek had already been in a long discussion with his mother, Lady Wyn, by hyper-pulse communications generator before she brought up the subject of House Towers. He was in what used to be a StarCom building in Tahrcity, but following the war was now operated by Levitican Union personnel. Despite this the entire live communication across the stars was coded in House Zupanic ciphers, scrambled so none could eavesdrop.

"I am still not receiving satisfactory intelligence from you regarding the operations of House Towers," said Lady Wyn. "I take it they were behind the deaths of Vasily and Csarina?"

This was such a dangerous game he was playing, Lord Micalek thought to himself before he answered. "Yes, mother, they were."

"Who is the next target? Me or your father?"

"I do not know. I did ask but did not receive a response."

"It matters little, my son, I am prepared," said Lady Wyn, coldly. "More importantly, is House Towers using the captured Faceless assassin?"

Lord Micalek hesitated, and then gave his answer.

Chapter XIV

Captain Lucas De Graaf sat in his command seat aboard the *SS Undefeatable* destroyer, reflecting on the likelihood of yet another boring day awaiting action. This contract with House Lindholm and the new Aalborg Alliance was possibly one of the worst he had engaged in since starting the VMC business venture with James, Ulrik and Jules Kavanagh last year. There was so little that happened during it; they were constantly waiting for the pirates to make the first move. He was used to offensive action, not this picket duty.

He chuckled to himself lightly, sipping from a cup of synthesised herbal tea. There was a time, especially immediately after Dissolution, when he had not wanted any more military action in his life at all. He had descended into alcoholism, and it had been James Gavain who had saved him, he strongly thought. He owed that man much.

This contract was not going particularly well he thought. The occasional briefing from Gavain to the rest of the fleet indicated that he was working on a plan to make it more offensive, but it would take time. Until then, they had to wait for the Pirates of the Cross to attack. It was highly vexing, the VMC starships strung out along the convoy routes, waiting for them to reappear.

All of a sudden the communications lieutenant called out, <We're receiving a Code Red hyper-pulse comms, it's from the *SS Arduous*,> she said.

Despite himself, Captain De Graaf felt the hope rise in his heart. <Play it,> he ordered.

A moment later an image of Lieutenant Vickers, the woman in charge of the A-class corvette *SS Arduous*, suddenly appeared as a holographic representation in the middle of the command deck of the bridge.

"This is Lieutenant Vickers to all VMC pickets. We have just jumped out of the Storvorde System." Lucas De Graaf accessed the datasphere, reading quickly that the Storvorde System was not colonised, but was a significant military base for House Lindholm, with a large starbase and shipyards, and on the major convoy route they were protecting. "Four Pirates of the Cross starships jumped in approximately two minutes ago in real-time, transmitting their jump positions with this message. We have a positive identification on the V-Class *Vengeance*, the ship of Dolf Reichenburg, which has jumped in close to the starbase with an unidentified C-Class battlecruiser. There are two destroyers, a U-Class and a P-Class, which must have jumped into the system undetected at a point prior to the assault – they were using cham-fields, and suddenly opened fired as the battlecruisers were jumping in-system. At the point we left the battlecruisers were launching approximately six hundred Marines at the starbase. Vickers out."

De Graaf reviewed the data. The pirates had chosen the best possible time to attack; there were no convoys in the system, so there were no additional military ships to deal with, only four defensive Lindholm frigates. The starbase, although heavily armoured, was caught by surprise with shields down, and the destroyers had done significant damage, targeting their shield generators first. The starbase was being boarded; in a very short period of time the Pirates of the Cross would have the starbase. They would probably target the defenceless shipyards next. There were no less than three convoys due to jump into the system between one and two hours time from now, and De Graaf could only assume that they intended to take them unawares. The blow to the Aarlborg Alliance military effort would be significant.

His navigations lieutenant was feeding him data already, without being requested to do so. The Storvorde System was only one jump away for his ship and the *Carnivorous*, so they would be the first on the scene. It was a double-jump for the *Quintessential* star-carrier under Captain O'Connor and the strikecruiser *Shadow*, and a risky triple-jump for Admiral Gavain and the *Ubermacht* destroyer. De Graaf's two ships would arrive within three minutes in real-time, O'Connor's four minutes after that, and if he decided to take the triple-jump, Gavain a further six minutes on.

De Graaf grinned. There was a strong chance they could eventually outnumber the enemy. Captain Reichenburg may have committed an error.

<All hands, prepare for jump,> Captain De Graaf ordered, <Tell Captain Zane McDonnagh to jump to these co-ordinates in-system, this is our plan of attack,> he transmitted the details across the datasphere with the speed of thought.

<All systems ready, Captain.>

<Jump!>

Captain Dolf Reichenburg sat impassively in his command chair, observing the success of the battle so far. His Marines were in on the starbase, the initial wave by shuttle suffering heavy damage from the defending frigates, but then the strikepods had landed the majority of his force. They were already shutting down some of the unshielded starbase's weaponry systems, their primary mission objective.

One of the defensive frigates was torn apart, destroyed by his weaponry. A second was unshielded and rolling out of control, a fifth of its hull missing. The remaining two defensive frigates, although putting up a fight, would not last much longer.

<Hostile three shields are failing,> his tactical officer announced.

<Order the *Cathedral* to switch targets, *Vengeance* to join, eliminate it,> Reichenburg ordered, spotting that because of its position the third frigate would be caught between their broadsides. It would be destroyed with the heavy fire of the battlecruisers at this close range. <The *Paralysis* and *Untouchable* destroyers are to continue to concentrate fire on the starbase.>

<Our shields are nearing fifty percent> his tactical officer said. <The *Cathedral* is managing sixty percent. At current rate of fire from the starbase, we will lose shields in three minutes>

<Not acceptable,> said Reichenburg, <Tell the Major in charge of the Marines he has two minutes to silence the starbase weaponry systems. Destroyers to switch targets to weaponry batteries.>

<Aye, sir.>

All was going to his master plan, he thought. With the starbase neutralised, he could put the shipyards to the torch, severely hampering the Aarlborg Alliance war preparations against the Helvanna Dominion. The three convoys due in within the next two hours would be caught completely unawares, and they would end up taking a large amount of booty from this operation, as well as striking a wounding blow on their target nation, the Alliance, and particularly House Lindholm.

<Incoming jump signatures!> scanners suddenly announced.

<What?> Reichenburg was alarmed. <Where?>

The holo-map showed him. There were only two, but they were of a large size. Their positioning was perfect, too perfect to be a coincidence. One was coming in quite close to their sphere of operations, whilst another was further out, but both had the starbase between their arrival points and the two destroyers. The destroyers would have to change angle significantly to be able to target the new arrivals, and there was no realistic way Reichenburg could order that.

He narrowed his eyes. He guessed the ship further out would be a destroyer, a long-range killer, whilst the one jumping closer in would be a heavier ship, a battlecruiser or even a dreadnought.

<This warzone just got hotter,> he informed his crew, <prepare for new hostiles.>

De Graaf gripped the edges of his seat as his destroyer translated into the system. In the space of a second, he took in the lay of the battlefield. There was only one frigate left operational, and scanners were telling him that the starbase was infected with pirate Marines.

<Turn the *Undefeatable*, full broadside on the *Vengeance*. Tell McDonnagh that when the shields are down, he is to launch all his Marines at the battlecruiser. We ignore the starbase for now, it will have to suffer.>

<Aye, aye, sir.>

<We're taking heavy fire from the *Undefeatable*, sir, shields at thirty ...... twenty percent,>

<The *Carnivorous* battlecruiser is taking heavy fire, they are targeting us.>

Reichenburg was furious. <I want as much damage on that *Carnivorous* as possible before its shields kick in,> he growled across the datasphere, his fury transmitting to everyone on the battle-net.

<Our shields are gone!>

Captain Zane McDonnagh, the untried and untested commander of the battlecruiser *Carnivorous* as far as the senior officers of the VMC were concerned, felt honoured to be in the leading part of the battle-plan.

<We're taking significant fire from both battlecruisers.>

<Shields due in fifteen seconds.>

<Starbase batteries have ceased to fire on enemy destroyers. The batteries this side are targeting the *Vengeance*, they must see what we are doing.>

<Fourth defensive frigate is targeting the *Vengeance*.>

<We have identified the second battlecruiser as the *Cathedral*.>

<Data viruses are having no effect, we are not breaking through their firewalls.>

<The *Vengeance* has lost shields! Lost shields!>

Captain McDonnagh let out an undignified and dirty laugh, which made his crew smile and he knew they loved already. <Launch Marines,> he ordered. <All strikepods, take the *Vengeance*!>

<Shields gone, shields gone.>

<Captain Reichenburg, they are launching strikepods, five seconds until we are boarded!>

Reichenburg felt a stab of fear through his heart, but immediately silenced it with combat drugs. <How many Marines do we have on board?> he asked.

<One hundred.>

<How many coming in?>

<Full complement, four hundred.>

Not exactly brilliant odds, thought Reichenburg.

<Captain De Graaf, incoming jump signatures!>

<Show me,> he demanded.

He examined the holo-map, keeping one part of his mind focussed on the battle. Although the starbase weaponry was falling more and more silent with every second that based as the Pirate Marines rampaged through it internally, his destroyer was doing phenomenal damage to the *Vengeance*. Marines were already being launched on the *Vengeance,* and even as he watched them go in and examined the holo-map, he simultaneously ordered that fire be switched towards the enemy battlecruiser *Cathedral*.

There was no telling if they were VMC ships coming in, or Pirate ships, but they were due to translate into the system within forty seconds. The odds were that they were VMC, as the timing matched the potential arrival of Captain O'Connor.

<We have been fully boarded, Captain Reichenburg. Three hundred and sixty of the enemy Marines survived our defensive fire.>

<All hands, repel boarders,> Reichenburg ordered.

He turned his attention to the incoming jump signatures. He was not expecting any further Pirates of the Cross ships, so he could only assume these were VMC ships or Aarlborg Alliance starships.

Space tore open as the VMC ships entered the Storvorde System. Captain O'Connor in the *Quintessential* had brought his Q-class star-carrier in at a distance from the starbase, but incredibly close to the known position of the two destroyers. They had not moved, and he smiled.

<Launch all starfighters and bombers immediately, priority targets are the destroyers,> he demanded. They would be particularly susceptible to his vast quantity of small spacecraft. <Once their shields are down, prepare to launch Marines, I will advise target.>

<We are being hailed by the *Untouchable*.>

Even as O'Connor acknowledged the incoming message, he saw that the *Shadow* S-class strikecruiser had jumped in at such a position that it would very shortly be able to assist the *Carnivorous* in its current ongoing firefight against a ship being identified as the *Cathedral*.

Strikepods peppered the skin of the de-shielded *Vengeance*, so O'Connor knew that the battle was going well and Marines would be aboard the lead ship of Reichenburg.

<Jonathan>, said Lucas De Graaf through the communications, <Perfect timing and positioning.>

<I took a guess at what you would do, coming in first, sir,> Captain O'Connor replied.

<Excellent guesswork. We're trying to take the *Vengeance* by boarding action, I want the *Shadow* to assist. What you decide to do with your enemy destroyers up there is up to you. The starbase is virtually knocked out, overrun with the enemy, but if we see off these capital ships we can deal with that afterwards.>

<Understood, sir.>

Sir Admiral James Gavain kept his face characteristically impassive as he surveyed the battle scene, his *Vindicator* battlecruiser and the *Ubermacht* destroyer coming in at a safe distance away from the battlezone. It was the only way, unfortunately, as he knew that most likely two pickets would already be in-system and it would be too dangerous to attempt a close jump without knowing where exactly those ships would be.

What he saw was very pleasing however.

The starbase was completely overrun with enemy Marines, and none of his mercenary Marines had yet targeted the Alliance headquarters. Instead De Graaf had very sensibly focused his attention on the *Vengeance*, a high-value target. It was dead in the water, and scans showed that his Marines were aboard it and in control.

Of the *Cathedral* there was no sign, but there was a fading jump signature. The *Shadow* and the *Carnivorous* had been chasing something, presumably the enemy battlecruiser which had escaped. Further afield, one destroyer had escaped, but another, a P-class identified as the *Paralysis*, was under heavy fire and had also been boarded. Gavain ordered the *Vindicator* to move to assist, he wanted his own Marines under Major Adeoye aboard that ship.

He then told his communications officer to put him in contact with Captain De Graaf.

<Sir,> Lucas De Graaf saluted, <We have the *Vengeance*, and Captain Dolf Reichenburg has been captured, injured but alive. It is in our control. Two enemy ships have escaped, but the destroyer *Paralysis* will be ours in two minutes or so. We need to consider the starbase and the Pirate Marines trapped there.>

<I understand, Lucas,> said Admiral Gavain wryly. <It appears you have left me very little to do.> He hesitated, then nodded and added, <Very well done.>

*

The special operations room was one of five situated just off the main bridge on the *Vindicator* battlecruiser, and all of them were highly multi-functional. It could operate as a simple conference room, a reception room for special guests, or as a war-room in protracted campaigns.

The room designated 'SOR-C' was currently a hive of activity. A number of crew within the tactical and data-tactical divisions from three starships – the *Vindicator*, the *Undefeatable* and the *Quintessential* – were working together, pouring over the new intelligence they had gained yesterday from the successful defence of the Storvorde System, and the capture of both the *Vengeance*, the *Paralysis*, and a large number of crewmen.

Admiral James Gavain entered the special operations room. All of the crewman stopped, saluted him on his entrance, and then immediately carried on working.

Gavain walked through a number of holographic images, crossing directly to the central workstations in the middle of the room. Captain Jonathan O'Connor stood up from his suspensor chair, Captain Lucas De Graaf already in a standing position behind him as they discussed something.

Across the datasphere, James Gavain said, <Gentlemen, I only have a short period of time. I am expecting the Admiral-of-the-Fleets for the Aarlborg Alliance to jump in-system shortly. Give me an update, I need to decide what we are sharing with them.>

<Yes, sir,> said Captain O'Connor, his excitement and intelligence coming across clearly on the datasphere. His eyes were alight with the challenge <We're going through the data as fast as we can. The *Paralysis* mainframe, data-core, datasphere, and secondary and tertiary redundancy systems were all completely wiped and scrubbed. The attack on the *Vengeance* left them only a short period of time to do the same thing – they have been successful in obscuring a large amount of data, but they only achieved a partial wipe, and we are recovering data forensically piece by piece.>

<In addition to that,> said Captain De Graaf, <we've been engaged in a number of preliminary interrogations of senior and junior staff, including Reichenburg. None are breaking, their internal implant protection systems are too advanced to be penetrated easily, but we have picked up some information from these interrogations as well.>

Gavain knew that those interrogations, should they continue to be unsuccessful, would eventually move into more physical means, rather than mental and cybernetic investigations. Torture was a better word for what was coming, as a last resort. It was distasteful, but used correctly may yield the results he required. The Praetorians had always used such tactics on the Houses they had policed in the name of the Emperor, and some skills were not easily forgotten.

<I understand the sources,> Gavain said, <what of the results? Do we have a location on the enemy base of operations?>

O'Connor traded a glance with De Graaf, his excitement fading slightly. <Unfortunately not, Admiral. We do know it is somewhere in the Gulf of Medusa however; the *Vengeance* has been travelling in and out of the Gulf of Medusa. We have some images of at least two different deepspace stations, with stargates built into them. At least we know how the enemy are travelling from one end of the Eastern Segment to the other so fast – they have access to secret stargates within the Gulf of Medusa that we never knew existed.>

<Deepspace stations?> Gavain questioned.

<Highly secret bases of operations,> De Graaf commented. <They were used by the Red Imperium sparingly, or so we thought. They are located in the depths of space, away from any solar system, are highly shielded and chameleonically camouflaged, and virtually impossible to locate unless you have their exact location.>

<How secret were these installations? Even in the days of the Imperium, I do not recall any mention of them in the Gulf of Medusa, or coming across them before,> said Gavain.

<Obviously a high classification of secrecy,> said O'Connor. <It's not like the Janus Shipyards. There may well be an entire network of deepspace stations with this stargate technology that we were not aware of. In fact, by looking at a map of pirate attacks, it suggests that there are many more than just the two in the images we've found.>

<All connecting to a pirate base somewhere?> said Gavain.

<We can't even begin to hypothesize where such a base would be, if it even exists,> said O'Connor. <It may just be that they are using this network of deepspace stations. The Gulf of Medusa does contain some barren solar systems, or destroyed systems, but they are few and far between – most of it is just empty space.>

<Keep trying,> said Gavain, hiding his disappointment behind his usual impassive face. <Anything else?>

<We have a number of known locations for the *Vengeance*, but most of its travel history has been completely wiped,> said O'Connor. <We have some information on pirate ships – we can now definitely identify at least nine, but we have images of many more. We have nearly two hundred names of senior staff identified, all former Praetorian Guard. This is a large organisation of pirates. They also are not just purely Praetorian Guard – we've discovered that some of their support network consists of civilian ships, although perhaps those on the wrong side of the law; smugglers, gangsters, those sorts of people. We have some of those civilian ships identified.>

<Download the list to me,> said Gavain. <I understand my fifty super-soldier spies are almost ready for field deployment. Perhaps if we penetrate and take over one of those civilian ships, we can find the pirate base of operations or get more information on them.>

<We do have a name for the overall organisation though,> said De Graaf. <All the pirates, with their various names, are linked together. They call themselves the Rosicrux. There are numerous references to Rosicrux; 'In the name of Rosicrux', 'The Rosicrux Operation', 'The Rosicrux Conspiracy', and so on.>

Gavain digested this information. They carried on into some of the minutiae of the detail of the investigations and interrogations, before Commander Al-Malli addressed him from her command seat on the bridge.

<Admiral Gavain?>

<Yes, Commander?>

<We have an incoming ship, we suspect it is the *AASS Emperor's Fist* and Admiral-of-the-Fleets Halvorssen. We're on alert just in case. There is also an incoming HPCG communication from General Andryukhin, a continuous hyper-pulse, live-feed.>

<Understood.> Gavain thought quickly. <I will take Ulrik's message in my ready room. When the *Emperor's Fist* arrives ask Halvorssen if he would like to come aboard for a briefing and discussion.> He disconnected from the internal communication. <Gentlemen, carry on. You have another day or two, but I intend to be jumping out of this system shortly, depending on how my conversation goes with Admiral-of-the-Fleets Halvorssen.>

<James?> Lucas De Graaf asked, the questioning tone there.

<Later, Lucas. Good work, both of you, pass on my congratulations to the team.>

With that, Admiral Gavain left the operations room, heading back to his private office.

Gavain was still lowering himself into the ready room's seat as the holographic image of General Andryukhin appeared on the other side of his desk. Ulrik was standing, he wore his power-armour, and the look on his face was dark and furious. The image was not helped by a slightly bad connection, the holographic representation of his friend flickering and spluttering.

"Rik," said James Gavain, despite himself somewhat concerned, but hiding his wariness at the obvious murderous mood of his head of Marines, "this is unexpected. I was not expecting a live comms. Are you still in the Kyiv System?"

"Yes, Jamie, I am," said Ulrik Andryukhin. "We have a severe problem, mate, a fucking bad one."

"Explain," said Gavain curtly, all seriousness.

Ulrik explained quickly and simply about the Erdogan double agent, and that they had been approached to take on another contract directly for Erdogan after they had jumped into the Chester System.

At one point James interrupted to say, "It is a great concern that they know we are due to jump into Chester. The surprise element is gone, it increases our risk mightily. They will be prepared for you."

Ulrik Andryukhin explained that Erdogan had offered to put up a token resistance to make it look convincing, but withdraw completely from the Chester System. At first Gavain could not understand why they would do that, but as Andryukhin explained the Erdogan plan, and the contract they wished the VMC to take for them, he saw the logic in it. It was a diabolical blind and bluff on a vast scale, the Erdogan Feldmarshall had the genius of the devil.

"I also took the opportunity to pass on your message about Erdogan potentially paying us to track down the pirates plaguing them," said Andryukhin. "My little double agent Sou has come back very quickly, they have agreed that they will take it." He said how much the Erdogans were willing to pay.

James' eyes lit up. "That is fantastic," he said. "Let her know we will sign the pirate contract immediately. I will send you a contract with my signature, and we will register it with the Mercenary Bonding Office to make it official."

"And what of their proposed contract immediately after we take the Chester System?" Andryukhin asked.

"It would severely harm the relationship we have built with the Zhou-Zheng Compact –" James began.

"Fuck the relationship with the Compact," Andryukhin ground out.

James blinked, but otherwise showed no emotion. "We have worked hard for this, and are getting good media coverage and a high pay-out. Contracting with Erdogan against the pirates is one thing, especially now it looks likely that none of the nations suspected of sponsoring the various pirate groups are actually doing that, so we are not going against the Compact at all. But to deliberately complete the Chester System contract knowing it is part of an Erdogan ploy and trap obeys the letter of our deal, but not the spirit. To then take the Erdogan contract and strike against the Compact puts us in direct conflict with them, and I do not think that is advisable at this time."

"Jamie!" Ulrik snapped, smashing his fist into an object that was not being transmitted by the holoprojectors. "We should never have started working for the fucking Compact in the first place!"

"What makes you say that, Rik?" James asked quietly. His eyes had narrowed, a warning to any who knew him.

"I'm sending you some pics and recordings," Ulrik was more than furious, and James was surprised to see that underneath the palpable anger was a great deal of discomfort and pain. "The agent told me of the deathcamps the Compact operates. They have set one up on Kyiv – we, James, you and I have enabled them to do this! They are killing millions and millions of borgs, just like us. It is murder – more than murder, its fucking genocide! They work them to death, keep them in bad conditions, and then kill them before they bring the next load of unfortunates in. Kyiv has been turned into a fucking deathworld! *And we helped them do it!*"

"General," said James Gavain firmly, "contain yourself." He had already reviewed the entire download, and it shocked him to the core. It was horrendous. Ulrik had obviously somehow gained access to the new deathcamp built just outside the Kyiv Primus capital of Kyiv Megapolis, and had recorded the data through his own suit sensors.

There were many images that would play on James Gavain's mind later. He saw men, women and children, borgites all, being kept in terrible, cramped conditions. Many were already showing signs of malnutrition. They were recording working on numerous projects, with human Compact overseers in enforcer uniforms brutalising them into doing so. A large building was seen, with tired people being lead inside. A small drone had been released into the building by Andryukhin, and it had been trapped inside the furnace room, its feed only dying when the gigantic oven had fully burnt the borgs, their flesh and implants all, into ash, and the heat had overwhelmed and destroyed the drone.

"No, James, not this time!" Ulrik snapped. "We are doing the wrong thing. We should not even go into Chester, we should re-invade Kyiv now and shut that deathcamp down!"

"We will not break a contract we have already signed, Rik," Gavain shook his head. "Our word is our bond, we would be debarred from the MBO or at least excluded from certain contracts, and our customers would not be able to trust us."

"This is bigger than a contract and money, James!" Ulrik roared. "How can you be so fucking blind?"

"General, your language –"

"No, James. You need to hear this. I cannot believe you have just seen what I sent you, and you are talking to me about contracts and money. Some terrible things happened in the name of both the True Emperor and the False Emperor, and the traitorous usurper's actions were just like the Compacts, but against the unaugmented and not the borg. We, you and I, and many thousands of others in the Praetorian Guard turned against the False Emperor, seeing that the horrors he was inflicting on the unaugmented were not right. They were morally wrong. I am a borgite, I believe in the supremacy of the borg race, but even I did not agree with what the False Emperor was doing to the unaugmented humans. You agreed with me, though you're a free-thinker. You found it abhorrent. This is no different, and even worse, it is borgs, our own, being killed in the name of pure hatred." Ulrik was snarling now. "How can you even sit there and talk to me of money and contracts! There are bigger things in this galaxy to think of."

James Gavain was speechless. He felt the sting of the accusation, and realised that it only stung because of the element of truth. "Ulrik, we are mercenaries, we made the choice to do this, we have to stick to the contract –"

"We should fuck the invasion of the Chester System off, and do something about this here and now!"

"No, General, I expressly order you to complete the Chester System contract."

"Jamie! Think, man! *This is not right!*"

"We must stick to our word. We are mercenaries, and we need to preserve our reputation and earn the money –"

"Jamie – we became mercenaries because we were bred for war and there was little else in the galaxy we could do, apart from join a House or one of the new seceded nations, or become pirates, or become dispossessed and splinter. But sometimes we have to be something more than just money-soldiers! What has happened to you, man? Where are your morals, your principles, you've completely lost your way! You are not the man I knew at all if you can even contemplate allowing this travesty in the Compact to continue, and for us to support the abusers makes us no better than them!"

Gavain finally snapped. In a cold, dark, dangerous voice, he said, "General Ulrik Andryukhin, you are my friend, but you are going too far. You will follow my orders and respect the chain of command. You will complete the Chester Contract, we will honour our promises. Leave me to think on the Compact and whether we accept any more contracts from them, but ultimately, it is my decision. We will end this conversation now, I will communicate with you later today with further orders on what to tell the Erdogan double agent."

"Jamie –"

"Admiral," James Gavain ground out.

"Admiral –"

"No, General. You have my orders, await my message later today on how to play this politically with Erdogan. There is much to consider – not least that if we appear to refuse their contract, they could significantly damage us in the Chester System, knowing we are coming. I need time to think. And General Andryukhin?"

"Yes, Admiral?" he made the title sound like a swearword.

"Never, ever speak to me this way again. I shall trust you to follow my orders, but Emperor help you if you even think of disobeying me. This conversation is over."

With that, absolutely furious and extremely hurt in equal measures, Gavain ended the hyperpulse communication.

<Admiral,> Commander Al-Malli contacted him directly, having detected the closing of the feed, <Admiral-Of-The-Fleets Halvorssen is now aboard the ship, and is coming up to the bridge. Shall I allow him into your ready room?>

Gavain took a deep breath, standing to go and make himself a coffee. <Yes, Commander, show him straight in,> he said, even though he truly wanted some time to his own, to think. The argument with his friend had unsettled him deeply.

He accessed the pictures and video recording again, feeling the horror strike at his stomach and his heart twist and bleed as he watched the terrible pictures and recording in his mind's eye. It was truly disgusting, abhorrent, inhuman, what the Compact was doing to their conquered borg populace.

He kept thinking of the harsh criticism Ulrik had given him, but also wondered whether or not his friend had the truth and the right of it. Had he changed that much, had he lost his way so much in the pursuit of the mercenary lifestyle and success that his morals had suffered as a consequence. He had been wondering whether there was something more he should be doing than this, and it now it turned out that one of his decisions made in the pursuit of money had inadvertently made him an accomplice in mass murder and genocide. In that respect he was no better than Silus Adare.

Admiral-Of-The-Fleets Jakub Halvorssen was elated at the success in the Storvorde System, and told the mercenary Sir Admiral Gavain this as he sat sipping his cup of real coffee in the former Praetorian Guard's ready room.

He did note that there was something different about the mercenary Admiral today. He was famously calm, cool and inscrutably hard to read, an outwardly emotionless person. Yet despite the tremendously good news he was imparting, and Halvorssen's own elation at finally having a success story against the pirates to tell, Admiral Gavain appeared somewhat sullen, tired and concerned.

They had discussed some of the intelligence in detail, and Halvorssen had confidence that Gavain was sharing a great deal with him, and was hiding nothing in that regard.

"Which brings me onto a somewhat delicate point," said Admiral-Of-The-Fleets Halvorssen. "Are you aware that House Towers of the Levitican Union has contacted us directly, regarding the pirate attacks they are suffering?"

"Yes, I was aware Lady Sophia had done so," said Admiral Gavain.

"It appears that there truly is a link between the apparently separate pirate groups afflicting the Eastern Segment, this Rosicrux conspiracy. There is mention of a super-contract, a contract offered to your outfit from all the nations being attacked by the Rosicrux. Are you behind this?"

"I have suggested it, yes," Admiral Gavain nodded once.

"Well, from my point of view, we have already contracted you to do this."

"I am aware of that."

"We will not be offering you more money, Admiral Gavain. With the greatest of respect, you are being too greedy in expecting us to sign another contract for more money for you to do something we have already agreed upon." Halvorssen noticed the uncharacteristic flinch at his use of the word 'greedy'.

"I see," said Admiral Gavain quietly.

"If you can assure me however, that you will pursue this Rosicrux conspiracy to its end and terminate it, we have no real objections to you also working for other houses to the same end, and politically, my masters are quite keen to build alliances elsewhere in the Segment and this is seen as a chance to do so. So please, go ahead and co-operate, but we will not pay you more."

"Very well," said Admiral Gavain. Halvorssen had been expecting more of a protest from Gavain, but then the mercenary continued, "We have taken significant damage to some of my ships. We need to repair. With your permission, I would ask that you release us from our duties within Aarlborg Alliance space. In order to pursue the pirates, it would be better for me to get my ships repaired, and then prepare to proceed into Medusan Gulf space when we have knowledge of where to jump to. Staying here in House Lindholm territory will not achieve the greater objective."

They had a bit of a discussion on that point, Halvorssen even raising a concern that without VMC ships in his territory how did he know that Gavain was concentrating on the pirates? Gavain had replied that they were not in an exclusive contract, so he could run several contracts at once, and it was at his discretion what forces he devoted to chasing the pirates anyway. He also assured Halvorssen that he had a personal reason in wishing to chase down the war-criminal Silus Adare, and he also had a greater desire to see the ex-Praetorian Guard Rosicrux conspirators eliminated.

Eventually, Halvorssen agreed, and their discussion was at an end.

Gavain had spent most of the rest of the day in his ready room, alone, something which even the new Commander Saifa Al-Malli had learnt was a sign that he was deeply troubled by something. His friend Lucas De Graaf attempted to speak to him about it, but Gavain was not willing to talk. Even O'Connor made an attempt, and despite his warming to the man, James could not bring himself to discuss what was bothering him.

The truth was that his argument with Andryukhin had greatly disturbed him. He had been thinking to himself that there had to be something more than being a mercenary, and now, in the worse way possible, it had been highlighted to him that his mercenary manner and pursuit had contributed inadvertently to the deaths of millions of borgs.

They were working with other humanist nations, such as Hausenhof, and some of those houses within the Levitican Union. Humanist by definition meant anti-borg. What was happening in the Zhou-Zheng Compact was a step beyond the normal humanist viewpoint, an extreme form of anti-cyborg racism on a par with the actions of the Old American colonists, the dictator Hitler, the tyrant Ascici, the monstrosities of the Droid Wars, Perepolous, or the actions of the False Emperor.

He had taken most of the day to decide what to do, and although he still had much more thinking about himself and the direction he wished to take the VMC in, his mind was made up on what had to be done.

He recorded a message for General Ulrik Andryukhin, which within it contained an apology for losing his temper, understanding his friend's feelings and just how bad the situation was. It was a very open, heart to heart admission of Gavain's own feelings, his worries and concerns.

Gavain had specific instructions on how to reply to the Erdogans regarding their offer to withdraw with token resistance from Chester, and on their suggested assault contract against the Zhou-Zheng Compact.

But the message also contained the order – proceed with the Chester Contract.

*

General Ulrik Andryukhin sat in his private office aboard the super-transporter *Monstrosity*, reviewing the recorded message that had just arrived from his friend and commanding officer.

He allowed the holographic image of James Gavain to remain as it was at the end, with his head slightly down and eyes looking at the desk in his ready room of the *Vindicator*, an unimaginable number of light-years away at the other end of the Eastern Segment.

He had been dreading the message coming, and despite his vicious temper, he had regretted the way he had spoken to his old comrade, knowing at the same time that he was right. He had no doubt in his mind of that.

He did however have his orders.

Whether he agreed with them wholly or not, they had to be followed. His training in the Praetorian Guard, his own personal nature, his very gene-code, his loyalty, told him to obey. It was true, he had once turned traitor to the False Emperor, but he would not do that to James Gavain.

<Captain Delgado,> Andryukhin addressed the commander of the *Monstrosity*, and the operational squadron commander for the *Marvellous* and the *Titan of Stars*.

<Yes, General?>

<We have our orders from the Admiral. We have clearance from the Zhou-Zheng Compact. We are not to delay any longer – prepare for the jump to the Chester System. We must leave within one hour.>

<Aye, General.>

<And send the liaison Da Wei Sao to my office.>

<Yes, General.>

General Ulrik Andryukhin leaned back. He had his orders on the message and arrangements to make with the Da Wei double-agent, and they would be carried out too.

*

Admiral Silus Adare sat in the flag chair of the immensely large and monstrous T-class dreadnought *Thor's Hammer*, the ship having just jumped back into Dark Heart. He was returning, fresh from a particularly successful raid on House Van Der Meer space.

The *Cathedral* and the *Untouchable* starships were waiting for his return, and both captains hailed him immediately. He instructed his communications officer to take both calls, and he listened to them in concert. The capture of Dolf Reichenburg and the loss of the *Vengeance* was terrible news on one level, but also he had never particularly liked or cared for the person who had been chosen to lead the Rosicrux operation. To be truthful, the psychotic Admiral had very little liking of anybody, he was just not capable of that emotion.

<Admiral Adare,> Commander Zehra Sahin suddenly said, <We are receiving another hail. It is from the Rosicrux Solar Administrator.>

<In the ready room,> he commanded, uncrossing his legs and standing. Tall, broad, and heavily built, he was constructed more like one of the Marines than a naval officer. With his jet black hair and dark goatee beard, he cut an imposing figure as he crossed the extremely large bridge, the ready room doors closing behind him.

He stood in front of the desk, crossing his arms, commanding the communication to start with the simple word, <Activate.>

An image of the Solar Administrator appeared before him. The woman was cloaked in white, but the hood was down so he could not even properly see her face, and the colour of the cloak was faded. He had only spoken to the Solar Administrator a couple of times before, the figure usually dealing direct with Reichenburg as the commander of the Rosicrux pirates. He held no fear, but he knew a lesser person would have done. Solar Administrator was an old, Red Imperium title for someone who managed a solar system.

"Admiral Silus Adare," the woman spoke, her voice light but dangerous.

199

"Solar Administrator," said Adare, saluting smartly and crisply in the Imperial manner.

"You are doubtless aware of what has happened to the *Vengeance*, the *Paralysis*, and Captain Dolf Reichenburg?"

"I have just been informed, yes, sir."

"We have received intelligence that the *Vengeance* information systems were not completely wiped. We do not know what information the Vindicator Mercenary Corporation has been able to retrieve from the *Vengeance*, but we must assume and prepare for the worst. Conflict with the VMC is most likely unavoidable, and potentially our operation in the new Aarlborg Alliance may be compromised."

Silus Adare could not help but smile. He was going to go head-to-head with his old adversary, James Gavain again, he could feel it in his hot blood. "This is not a desirable situation," he said in a cheerful voice.

"No," the Solar Administrator agreed. "Silus Adare, I am here to confirm that you are now the leader of the pirates operating out of Dark Heart in the name of the Rosicrux. Do you accept this honour?"

Silus Adare could not contain his pleasure. He was to be put in charge of the entire operation, replacing Dolf Reichenburg. These were good days indeed.

"Yes, I certainly accept, sir," he said.

"Excellent. Your orders are to continue the various operations in the different nations to the best of your ability, and to prepare Dark Heart for defence in case it has been compromised."

"I will, sir," he said.

Chapter XV

Juan Ramirez licked his lips nervously, knowing that the exit time was fast approaching. It was incredibly difficult for him, maintaining his outer demeanour as if he did not know that he and the entire crew were eventually to be eliminated, once they had left the Gulf of Medusa and arrived at System XJ-1201.

He had resolved that he had to escape the ship somehow, but did not know how or when he would be able to abscond. He had debated telling the rest of the crew of their peril, but knew it was a hopeless and pointless thing to do. The danger of them not believing him, and betraying him to Captain Helenna Sirocco, was far too great.

The *Nazareth* had jumped from Deepspace Fourteen to another deepspace station, Deepspace Six. The stargate had thrown them a tremendous distance further into the Gulf of Medusa, getting even closer to the centre. Deepspace Six's stargate had activated, and catapulted the cargo-freighter even further into the Gulf, and now they were barely seconds away from exiting into this place called 'Dark Heart'.

"Exit in three .... two .... one .... we have translation," the call echoed around the small bridge.

Despite himself, Ramirez felt his heart leap into his mouth, nervous as he felt the familiar pull as the ship translated from the warp of hyper space into real space. He was also more than a little curious as to what Dark Heart was.

The forward viewer and the holographic display at the front of the bridge showed that they had once again ended up in a vast region of deepspace. This area of deepspace was not empty, however.

There were a number of vessels in this region of space. He knew from his infatuation with the VMC and his early childhood memories of the Red Imperium that the majority of the warships here were ex-Praetorian Guard, although there were also some non-military support ships of various descriptions. It was a veritable war-fleet.

They were transmitting their IFF codes, and the information scrolled into his brain from his connection to the datasphere. With an even greater shock, one of the names stood out. The *Thor's Hammer* T-class dreadnought was here, the ship of the war-criminal Silus Adare.

"We are being challenged," said the comms crewman.

"Reply with this verification code," said Helenna Sirocco, passing it to the comms crewman.

A few moments later the reply came back, "They have accepted our code, and are giving us permission to advance."

Advance into what, thought Juan Ramirez. There were a number of ships out here, but beyond that not much else. No sooner had he finished the thought, before everything changed before his eyes.

Space just blurred. There was no other way to describe it. One moment he was looking at nothing but emptiness with a number of warships and civilian fleets filling the void, and the next, the entire region seemed to ripple.

It soon became obvious that a number of vast, gigantic chameleonic fields had been in activation, and they had suddenly been dropped. Ramirez actually felt his jaw drop as the truth of the Dark Heart artificial solar system became revealed to him.

The chameleonic fields had been hiding three rogue planets, celestial bodies that were not attached to any solar system. Each of them was heavily industrialised, and armed and armoured. Only one had a viable atmosphere, one had a poisonous cloud covering a large proportion of it, and another had no atmosphere at all, but it was possible to see that each and every planet had been heavily developed. The planet with no atmosphere had a number of huge meteorite rings around it, and there were local mining ships shifting through them like ticks on an animal. It was technically impossible for the planets to be there, rotating slowly to provide gravity, but large constructs showed how the planets had been stopped and kept in position, their endless eternal drift brought to an end. The technology used to achieve such a thing was amazingly in advance of anything Ramirez had ever heard of.

There was a stargate a safe distance away from the three planets, which were held so close together there were actually long stretching space-lift corridors between them. The space-lifts went between the planets and starbases and spacestations to various stationary space platforms, which then linked to a ground-based platform which permanently moved on rails which went the entire circumference of each planet.

In addition to the stargate, there were another two large military starbases, bristling with weaponry, and one huge shipyards of a size Ramirez could only have imagined previously. There were numerous gun platforms, smaller stationary objects which existed for the sole purpose of providing defence. A mining base nestled above the rings of the third atmosphereless planet. There was also a large commercial space station, long and elongated and of a phenomenal size. Of even more amazement were the two huge constructs, made of metal and round and essentially artificial planetoids in all but name.

This Dark Heart was an artificial system, Ramirez realised, designed and created for Emperor knew what reason. The power of the chameleonic fields hiding it was immense. There were a far greater number of starships, intra-stellar craft and smaller ships in system than it had first appeared.

Who would create such a thing, and why would it be hidden so deep into the Gulf of Medusa, beyond civilisation and colonised space, Ramirez wondered.

The rest of the crew on the bridge were also in shock, with the exception of Helenna Sirocco, who only Ramirez knew had seen it before. "Crew," she said, amusement in her voice, "If you have quite had enough of the staring, we have a cargo to deliver. Helm, head to the first planet, Dark Heart Alpha."

Ramirez read the new data that Helenna Sirocco was loading into the computer systems of the *Nazareth*. It was a fairly large amount of data on this artificial system, and gave the names of Dark Heart Alpha to the rogue planet with atmosphere, Dark Heart Beta to the poisonous rogue planet and Dark Heart Gamma to the atmosphereless rogue planet. The two smaller artificial planets had the names of Dark Heart Delta and Dark Heart Epsilon. It transpired that the two Deepspace Stations they had used to travel to the system were all part of no less than eighteen such constructions, all of which formed a vast interstellar network known as The Web, their stargates linking the edges of colonised space to this secret, artificial system deep in the Gulf of Medusa.

As they drifted on through the assembled fleet of war-ships and civilian ships, Ramirez truly felt like he was entering the den of the lion.

The crab-like cargo lifter touched down on the surface of Dark Heart Alpha, landing gently on a large starport facility nestled at the edges of a gigantic city. Ramirez had found the journey down to the planetary surface as interesting and terrifying as the rest of his experience so far in the system, watching as the lifter flew over uncountable acres of farmed land, a number of gigantic cities and all manner of strange buildings and unknown villages, some of which were obviously inhabited and others which were not.

The cargo-container the lifter carried was lowered down the small gap to the floor, even as the small and cramped crew compartment behind the cockpit was opened up to the natural air of the rogue planet. The cargo-container was carried between the six grabbing arms of the lifter, and it thunked onto the metacrete with an audible grind of metal.

Captain Helenna Sirocco led the exit from the cargo lifter, stepping out into the cool air. Juan Ramirez and another two crew hands followed, their job being to open up the cargo container. He saw a convoy of flatbed hovertrucks were awaiting them.

There was no sun, so the entire planet was lit by artificial light, making it look evil and dark from a distance. Amazingly, there was a huge artificial construct in the air, a blimp of some sort which provided the kind of light a sun would project. There were many of these solar blimps scattered all over the planet, moving like a shoal of fish together, providing a fake day and night to the surface.

Basking in the heat the powerful solar blimps provided, combined with the rails of gigantic heaters like old-fashioned lamp-posts rising into the air, Ramirez was sweating already. They left the ramp of the lifter, and the pilot retracted it.

With a series of magnetic and metallic clumps, the lifter disengaged itself from the cargo-container. With a blast of repulsors it lifted back off into the air again, Sirocco, Ramirez and the other two crew hands a safe distance away, and then as it rose higher, thrusters kicked in and the lifter powered away to get the second of the four cargo-containers from the *Nazareth*.

A droidcar and a military hoverjeep were speeding over the starport metacrete towards them. They came to a halt a few metres away, and doors on both opened.

Ramirez felt the shock, more at the second figure than the first. The first figure was female judging from the way the white robe she wore hung on her, a complicated symbol woven into the cloth of the all-in-one piece of clothing. A hood was high over her head, keeping her face in shadow, but it was possible to see a gleaming white face-mask of some description which would have hid her features anyway.

It was the second figure that worried Ramirez more. Tall, heavy, built like a Marine, he personified evil. He wore a Praetorian Guard's red-and-black naval uniform and cap, but again the symbols woven into it were complex and different, with no sign of the Red Eagle. His goatee beard and jet black buzz-cut hair gave away his identity more than anything to Ramirez, who had always been a fan of the Vindicator Mercenary Company, and knew their history and the story of the destruction of Alwathbah like it was a childhood fable.

The man was none other than the war-criminal Silus Adare.

"Captain Helenna Sirocco, I am Admiral Silus Adare," he introduced himself without preamble. "Captain Reichenburg has been captured or killed, so I am now in charge of the military here. You know the Solar Administrator already I am told."

Captain Sirocco saluted. "Aye, sir," she said, "that I do."

"I'm here to see the cargo," he said. "You are bringing it all down?"

"Yes, Admiral," said Sirocco. "Four Tears of the Moon warheads, and four InterStellar Hyperspace Missiles, delivered as promised."

"Excellent," Adare smiled, an evil glint in his eye.

Juan Ramirez could not believe it. This was turning into an unbelievable day. He had taken part, unknowing admittedly, in providing four missiles capable of crossing interstellar distances, equipped with lethal planet-killer warheads, to a war-criminal whose very crime was being the first person in the colonised galaxy to ever have used the planet destroying technology.

A number of droids were marching towards them, walkers that were capable of lifting and unloading the ISHMs and their lethal, planet shattering warheads.

"Crew," said Sirocco, turning back, "open up the cargo-containers for our employers."

As he worked, Juan Ramirez reflected on his options. He still did not know how he was going to escape the *Nazareth*, but at least now he truly had a destination to aim for when and if he did escape. He could run to the famous Admiral James Gavain, tell him about the war-criminal he so desperately wanted, and hopefully find safety under the protection of the VMC.

*

Gavain felt the pull of the exit from hyperspace, and although not on the bridge but in his ready room, he was jacked into the datasphere and caught the announcement from the helmsman Lieutenant Vries that they had translated into the uninhabited system of KD-7832.

<All hands, we have a temporary stop-over whilst we recharge the jump capacitors> the newly promoted Commander Erica Georgia announced.

Commander Georgia had been his third-in-command, but with the *Vengeance* now captured, Gavain had decided that it was time to promote Saifa Al-Malli to Captain and give her the command of the ship. The battlecruiser and the *Paralysis* destroyer had been partially repaired to the point where they could at least jump into and out of solar systems.

There would have to be a re-organisation in the command structure aboard his own ship, of course, and a larger change in the ranks throughout the entire VMC. Luckily the recruiting station on the planet Tahrir was swamped with applications from Praetorians throughout the galaxy, both in person and by HPCG. There were many more applications than he could ever possibly need or require, so gaining extra crew would not be an issue, even if he did not take into account the two new batches of Marines and naval crew that Erin Presson had produced.

The entire fleet of ships had rendezvoused at an earlier jump, and Admiral Gavain stood to stare out of his observation window at the ones he could see. It felt good to have his naval force assembled back as one again.

They were returning to the Levitican Union, heading for House Towers' territory in the Blackheath System. The Kavanagh Shipyards would be used to repair the damage to his ships. Hopefully by the time the repairs were complete, they would have more solid intelligence on the location of the Rosicrux. He had until then to think of his next move. Hopefully with the intelligence agencies of several Houses active on the issue, it would not continue to be a problem.

At the moment the only thing he could think of doing was beginning a sweep of the Gulf of Medusa, in the hope that the pirates were based at one of the abandoned solar systems. It was a reasonable guess that they were quite deep into the Gulf, hence the reason for the Deepspace Stations with their stargates, but finding them would be exceptionally difficult.

If Reichenburg and the prisoners had not broken by the time they returned to the Blackheath System, he decided, he would sanction the start of a more intensive interrogation. There was little realistic alternative.

He thought briefly once again of Andryukhin's accusations that he had lost his morals and his principles. Perhaps he had, in his pursuit of the mercenary ideal, and surely enough he had turned the Vindicator Mercenary Corporation into a highly successful organisation. He had the germ of an idea however, and it was beginning to grow.

There was something worthwhile he could do, and he had explained this to Ulrik in his message. Hopefully his friend had seen the sense of the idea, and saw it as a possibility. The idea still needed more work, and Gavain would try to work on it, find a way to make it a reality. He would talk to Lady Sophia, he decided, see what she thought. Much would also depend on her, as well as finding the Rosicrux conspirators, wherever they were.

He sipped at his coffee, staring off into the stars, but his mind was even further afield than the starscape he observed.

*

The military transporter had jumped into the Zubrenica System a number of hours ago, arriving at the designated jump zone and transmitting the correct clearance codes. It made its way past the vast number of heavy asteroid fields, heading further in-system.

Following the loss of the Leviticus System, the Levitican Union Council had relocated temporarily here, to the Zubrenica System and a moon in orbit around the large gas giant planet, Zubrenica Prime. It was a heavily industrialised and militarised system, and the Levitican Union Armed Forces had a heavy presence here.

The military transporter was a Meridian Military Industries MMI-24-MT Rider Class model, and it was transferring thousands of Levitican Union Armed Forces troopers to Zubrenica XIX. The soldiers protecting the Council of the Levitican Union were regularly swapped out and changed in the thousands almost on a weekly basis, there being sixty thousand stationed on the tiny heavily armed moon at any one time.

The military transporter had taken up a stationary position around the moon, and numerous lander shuttles had begun dropping towards the surface, ready to begin the transfer.

The trooper walked into the barracks room, selecting an empty bunk that had only barely minutes before been vacated by one of the soldiers transferring out. He straightened the Levitican Union Armed Forces uniform, disposing himself of the two droidcases he was carrying, stowing them in the special locker.

Explaining to his friends that he needed to go and get some refreshment, feeling a little ill after the space journey, he ignored their jeers and taunts as he left the barracks room for the empty restroom cubicles.

Checking he was alone, the trooper looked in the holographic mirror that had snapped into being at his approach, satisfied the disguise was still intact.

He raised his wrist, and the implant emerged from the back of his hand.

<This is Agent Black. Confirmation that I have arrived at Zubrenica XIX, and am on-site.>

The House Towers Faceless assassin then allowed the implant to meld back, hidden safely in his body. At the first opportunity he had to leave this disguise, knowing it would cause ructions within the military as they realised a trooper had disappeared in unexplained circumstances. Absences were rare on Zubrenica XIX, primarily because there was no way for the troopers to get off the moon except in a military transporter, and the entire moon itself was an armed base.

Agent Black intended to take up a new disguise in the diplomatic corps, the civilian workers that housed the ministries that the various House Lords and Ladies oversaw. It was the only way to get close to his target, Lord Principal Ramicek.

He would assess the best way to eliminate the Lord Principal, and from there await the trigger signal of a successful or failed attempt on the life of Lord Luke Towers.

Juan Ramirez sat at the navigations console on the bridge of the *Nazareth*, anxiously waiting for the drugs to take effect. It had taken him some while to research and find the correct mixture, but he believed he had done so, and he had synthesised the drugs in secret using a specially adapted food synthesiser. In the journey back from the Dark Heart System and across the Gulf of Medusa, he had been an exceptionally busy person.

They had left the Gulf of Medusa, jumping back into what was defined as colonised space. They had entered a small system, in the Mid-Sectors, called Longshot. The Longshot System was inhabited, and belonged to the very small House Lemans. The House had a terrible reputation for policing its own territory, and that was doubtless part of the reason that the *Nazareth* under Sirocco had chosen to exit the Gulf here. Lemans was well known for its tolerance of all forms of illicit and illegal activities, and the Salchuzura Mara were very much the strongest supporters of the corrupt and inefficient House. If Korhonen, the largest and most aggressive house nearby, had not been so preoccupied with Cervantia and Hausenhof, the House of Lemans would most likely have been swallowed by their aggression following the end of the Red Imperium.

Ramirez knew the other reason they had jumped into the Longshot System, the first inhabited system they had reached since officially leaving the Medusan Gulf. The Longshot System was only seven jumps away from hitting unclaimed space and the solar system XJ-1201, where he and the rest of the crew were due to be killed by the Salchuzura Mara for their sudden knowledge about the Dark Heart System.

They were only half an hour away from jumping out of Longshot. They had not fully recharged, managing just enough for one and a quarter jumps, but were just waiting for their slot to use the designated out-system jump point. They would then lay up in the next system, fully recharge, and jump away from their 'official' flight plan with House Lemans. And to their deaths, he knew.

He did not have much longer. Despite himself, he was beginning to panic. This was his only decent chance, and he had prepared for it the entirety of the way back to civilised space.

All of a sudden, his stomach heaved. He paled quickly, and it heaved again. A third time, and he had managed to drench the entire navigations console with his stomach contents in a spectacularly violent explosion.

"Ramirez!" Captain Sirocco snapped. "What in the name of the Emperor?"

The rest of the crew were reacting. One, a woman who he was sure had some attraction towards him, came to help him. He guessed that attraction had vanished now; aware of it as always, he had determined after the experience which led him to being on the *Nazareth* in the first place never to mix pleasure with his job again.

"I – I'm sorry, Captain, I must – I – " he broke off to violently throw up again. The female crewmember trying to help him backed away in audible disgust.

"Get off my bridge," said Captain Sirocco. "Go to your bunk and get over this. Use the medic station if you must. Have you loaded the nav co-ordinates?"

"I – I – y – yes, Capt –" he broke off to throw up again.

"Off my Emperor-forsaken bridge!" Sirocco roared.

Staggering through the corridors of the ship, Juan Ramirez had returned to his room, but not for long. He had taken a dermal hypojector from the medic station, and apart from collecting the small bag of items he just did not want to leave behind, had stopped only to infuse his blood-stream with the antidote to the poison he had created.

He was still feeling very badly ill, but at least the vomiting had stopped. He had been through far greater pain however, and it had served the function of getting him off the bridge when his duty was to remain there. Before a jump, the navigations officer always had to be on duty.

He checked his internal chronometer as he continued on through the narrow corridors of the *Nazareth*. He also used his secret back-door hack into the datasphere, especially shielded to guard his jacking in being registered by any of the other borgs on the ship, to check how close they were to jumping. The *Nazareth* had moved to the jump point. They were just awaiting clearance from System Command to jump, the backwash from the previous ship jumping out-system still dissipating. The permission was likely to come shortly, in no more than a few minutes.

Panicking, knowing how much he had riding on this, he made it to the emergency escape pod.

There were no crew about, and he did not have long. He felt like he was going to vomit again as he waited, and then finally, through his secret access to the datasphere, he was informed that the permission to jump was given.

Unjacking, he knew that Captain Helenna Sirocco would be giving the command to jump. He held his hand over the emergency open panel, trying to still his stomach, knowing that any second now the jump initiation capacitors would be unleashing their field of energy. The warp accelerators would kick in barely a minute afterwards, and the ship would jump.

He felt the thrumming in the deck change beneath his feet. The jump initiation capacitors had activated.

He forced himself to wait thirty seconds longer, knowing that if he did this too soon, he would never escape.

Finally he slammed his hand on the switch, the circular door opening before him. He threw his bag into the escape hatch. He reached up, using the handrail to pull himself up and through the circular entrance, even as it was still cycling open.

He dropped through into the inside of the emergency escape pod, slamming the door shut behind him. At its opening, he knew that warnings would be going off on the bridge, but now it would be too late to stop the jump.

He strapped himself into one of the eight restraint chambers on the inside of the escape pod, jacking into the pod's immediate datasphere. It would not launch until the restraint chamber was fully activated, but on slapping the quick engage button, within two seconds he was secured.

<Launch!> he mentally ordered the pod.

With all safety indicators engaged, the escape pod fired its detonation charges.

It was all too much for the weakened and ill Juan Ramirez. Despite the restraint chamber and the safety mechanisms it incorporated, he lost consciousness.

The escape pod was propelled into the firing chamber from its rest position, magnetic acceleration coils charging in a nano-second and propelling it like the round of a MAC cannon out of the hull of the *Nazareth*.

It shot away into space, propelling at an incredibly high velocity. The whole point of escape pods was that they gained a rapid distance from their host ship in the shortest period of time possible, and this one was no exception.

It flew through space, propelled by the magnetic acceleration coils, and only gained more speed as its own engines ignited. They blew into operation, and the escape pod rocketed away from the *Nazareth*.

With a blurring and flashing of pure white light, the *Nazareth* warp accelerators ignited the jump field around it, and the ship translated into hyperspace, beginning its faster-than-light jump out of the system.

"What the hell happened there!" demanded Captain Helenna Sirocco.

"It looks as if we fired an escape pod just before we jumped, Captain," said one of her crew.

"I know that, I'm asking why?"

"We don't know," her crewman said.

Helenna Sirocco frowned. This was not right. It was too coincidental, something like that this happening after they had broken Rosicrux protocol and been to the Dark Heart System. Escape pods did not just fire themselves.

Her eyes fell on the empty navigations console.

"I want all crew to report in now," she said, "No exceptions. Find out who was in that escape pod." Intuition was leading her to suspect she already knew who was in it.

Whilst she waited for the confirmation, she went to the barely cleaned navigations station, sitting down in the holographic port. She keyed in certain information, to pull up the answer she wanted. They had a four day jump in transit time, but would have to recharge in their next system. They could jump back to the Longshot System after the recharge, which would take approximately nine hours in realtime due to the strength of the sun they were heading for.

Effectively, whoever had deserted her ship, had a nine hour lead on them before she could return to Longshot. That was nine hours to get clear, she might be able to catch them. It was imperative in the name of Rosicrux that the deserter was caught. It was too coincidental that they had been to Dark Heart and no someone had gone absent without leave.

Eventually the report came back, "the only person not signing in is Juan Ramirez, Captain. I've sent a crewhand to his room, and he is not there."

"Search the ship, make sure," said Sirocco, outwardly maintaining her calm, but inwardly knowing that she was now in really deep trouble. She had to get Ramirez back before he left the Longshot System.

Juan Ramirez opened his eyes slowly, and then as memory came flooding back, they snapped open.

He was staring at a ceiling.

"Lieutenant-Commander, he's awake," he heard someone saying.

"I'm coming," said a distant voice.

Juan sat upright, only to feel a hand suddenly pressed on his shoulder. He was in a small medical bay of some sort, and a person wearing an Imperial School of Medica badge on her House Lemans military uniform was stood in front of him. He had been on a suspensor bed.

"What –" he began.

"Be careful," said the doctor, who looked far too old to even be working for the House Lemans military. His weight if not his advanced age made him an unfit military specimen. "You've been unconscious for some time. Let me check you over."

He submitted to the examination by the doctor, who was using a medical multi-scanner tool which was strapped securely to his arm. At one point, Juan said, "What happened? Where am I?"

A door had opened behind him as he spoke, and a female voice said, "You are aboard the House Lemans frigate *LeSS Bearhide,*" said the woman. "I am Lieutenant-Commander Bonnet, and I would very much like to know what in the name of the Emperor is going on?"

The medical multi-scanner de-powered. "You're fine," said the doctor, "You've had a nasty stomach virus, brought on by ingested pharmaceuticals, but apart from that no ill effects. Some badly healed bones you need to get seen, mind you. You'll live." With that the doctor stepped back, and left them alone in the room.

Juan Ramirez focused on the Lieutenant-Commander Bonnet, as she said, "My question stands, man. Give me some information. I'm trying to decide whether I need to pass you over to the enforcers, let you go, or give you to the Salchuzura Mara. Which is it?"

Juan Ramirez walked through the starport terminal, nervously awaiting the announcement.

He had lied through his teeth to the Lieutenant-Commander, explaining that he had fallen out badly with the captain of the ship. He explained it away as relationship trouble. She had threatened to abandon him in a deserted solar system, so he said, and as a result he had taken the opportunity to escape while he could.

He saw that the Lieutenant-Commander Bonnet was very doubtful of his story, but she had confided in him that she did not like the Salchuzura Mara and their control on the House she served, so she would send him in a shuttle back to Longshot IV. She obviously suspected the *Nazareth* was connected to the Mara, and had no love for them. There he could do what he wanted, Bonnet had said.

Ramirez had counted down the time anxiously. He knew that in nine hours time, the *Nazareth* could jump back to the Longshot System. With his knowledge of the Rosicrux and the Dark Heart System, there was no way Captain Sirocco would not pursue him. He was now well and truly on the run for his life.

It had taken a little over four hours for the shuttle from the *Bearhide* to get him to the planet Longshot IV. Thankfully it had landed in the main starport, and he had wasted little time in a hurried thanks to the crew of the shuttle before hastily making his way into the starport.

The Salchuzura Mara strode around openly in House Lemans territory, gang tattoos openly on show, and with great fear in his heart he forced himself to steadily walk past them. Sirocco might work for the Rosicrux in truth, but she also was a member of the interstellar criminal gang and obviously using them for her own ends, and he could not take any chances.

He spent some time examining the starport departures board, cross-referencing it with the cost of flights and also mentally checking his bank account now he was connected to the local datasphere. He did have more money in his account, but not a huge amount. There were enough Imperial Crowns to get him far away out of this system.

He selected a civilian passenger transporter, not luxurious by any means but relatively cheap and going a long distance, far out of House Lemans territory. It was heading to the Isdalsto System, in House Jorgensson territory. He did not have the money to get Levitican Union territory and the VMC from there, so if the worst came to the worst he would have to steal it. He saw little other option. It was the closest he could get with the funds he had.

He had paid the fare to get aboard the Isdalsto System-bound passenger transporter, a budget flight which nonetheless cost a fortune, as all interstellar travel did. The human ticket agent demanded a bribe, which she blatantly and openly told him was all going to the Salchuzura Mara. They owned the starport.

Juan stepped into a private communications booth. There was one thing he was going to try, before he boarded the passenger transporter. He cycled through the options on the holographic display before him, choosing the low cost timed holo-mail option. It would be transmitted in a communications bundle as part of the hourly StarCom-operated hyperpulse communications despatch.

He addressed it to James Gavain in the Blackheath System, and copied it to the infamous VMC recruiting office in Tahrcity. He could not encode it, so had to be careful what he said.

"All passengers, the boarding gates to the shuttle for the passenger liner *Stellar Swan* are now open. Please proceed with all haste to the boarding gates, they will shut in thirty minutes." The message repeated another two times before it was replaced with another.

Juan Ramirez sent the electronic mail, and then left the communications booth, heading for his escape off this planet and out of the system.

Chapter XVI

Captain Helenna Sirocco sat in the starport of Longshot IV, dreading the meeting that was about to take place. She had contacted some of her Salchuzura Mara friends, introducing her distant clan credentials and getting their assistance to track down the missing Juan Ramirez. The information she received back was not good.

She was not one given over to nervousness, but she was now. The local clan chief for the branch of the Salchuzura Mara that controlled this sector of space was actually on-planet, and he wanted to see her. She knew of his reputation, and knew that like her, he was also aware of the Rosicrux and worked for them as well as the ferocious criminal gang that provided their cover.

In the private booth of the public house bar, which could be locked and screen-shielded for privacy, she sipped from a strong alcoholic whiskey drink as she waited.

The clan chief slipped in quietly, startling her with his presence. He waved a hand, and the screen-shield came up, responding to his cybernetic implant.

"Ranger Captain Sirocco," he said, using her Mara title. His voice was throaty, and slightly mechanical, the sign of a bad implant when he had obviously been too junior to afford a proper voice box replacement.

"Clan Chief Zimenis," Helenna swallowed. She gave the secret Mara sign, both hands crossed over her chest in a parody of the Imperial Red Eagle, head bowed.

"Explain yourself."

"Juan Ramirez was a member of my crew," she said, "he escaped. It seems he was captured, or retrieved, by a House Lemans military frigate. None of the Mara here knew of his import to me and the Rosicrux. He was transferred to this starport, and I know little more than that. He must be found before he escapes."

"It is too late," said the Clan Chief. "He has escaped. He bought a ticket to Isdalsto in House Jorgensson territory, and holo-camera footage shows him boarding the shuttle. He is aboard a passenger liner which left the Longshot System little more than three hours ago."

"In the name of the Emperor and Rosicrux," Sirocco swore. She thought quickly. "There is no way that I can alter my journey. I have orders to proceed to ... a system, and make a rendezvous."

"I know, your crew is to be killed," said Clan Chief Zimenis. "That is also how I know that Juan Ramirez is of such importance. He was to be killed too, because he has apparently seen more of the Rosicrux than our friends in that organisation are prepared to tolerate."

"What is your clearance?" asked Captain Sirocco.

"Higher than yours," said the Clan Chief. "I was in contact with our masters in the Rosicrux. The orders are that you are to proceed to System XJ-1201, and dispose of the rest of your crew. Try not to lose any more. I will use my position in the Salchuzura Mara to send our own people after this Juan Ramirez. That he has seen the secret base of operations is not acceptable, Sirocco."

"Am I to be punished?" she asked.

"The Rosicrux does not act like that. You are a valued member, despite your failure here. Ensure you complete the rest of your mission, Sirocco. Leave Juan Ramirez to me."

"Can you catch him in time?" she asked.

Here the Clan Chief laughed. "Oh yes," he said. "The passenger transporter follows a pre-designated route, which terminates at Isdalsto. We recovered a communication he sent, so we know he intends to go there, and will not disembark elsewhere. The Salchuzura Mara does not have a strong presence in House Jorgensson, but they will intercept and kill him as he leaves the transporter."

*

Lord Luke Towers sat in the lander, his honour guard around him. He was taking a heavier guard with him than would be expected, but there was a specific reason for that. He looked through the observation portal behind him, seeing the form of the LSS *Knightsword*, his own personal dreadnought capital ship, receding even further into the distance.

His tour of the Levitican Union military had begun. It was to be highly publicised, a propaganda piece designed to increase morale amongst the soldiers his Ministry was responsible for. It was to counter the bad news being caused by the possible upcoming war with House Jorgensson, and the continuing ravages of the Rose Pirates.

Whilst on tour, he was being connected through to the thrice-weekly Council meetings by HPCG continuous link. He found it even more tiring than actually being present in the Council Chamber room.

The tour so far had consisted of a short journey up through Zupanic space, to this, the last system before they crossed into House Marchenko territory. The plan was for him to visit the Marchenkan capital, then cross down into Lapointe and Galetti territory, into Claes, and then back through Towers and Obamu before returning to the Levitican Union.

In truth, he knew the Zupanic family did not intend for him to ever leave this system. There was a military base here in the Caussus System, but they were landing in the civilian starport before going on a long tour of the city, and ending up in the vast military complex where his speech would be made.

He did not know how or where, but the information from Lord Micalek was that he was to be assassinated here on this planet.

Caussus Tenth was a dark world, distant from the Caussus sun. Overly cold, Lord Minister Luke Towers felt the harsh wind hit him as he disembarked from the military lander, walking down the ramp with his honour guard all around him. Five starfighters flew overhead, rocketing by for the holo-cameras as their supersonic boom echoed around the starport.

Luminous globes hung in the air, lights carried by hovering drones. It was very dark, it being Caussus Tenth's equivalent of night-time. The harsh world had naturally occurring poisonous rain, and the protective rain-shields were deployed above the city. The night sky was dark, but it was possible to see the clouds gathering. On the horizon, lightning cracked down, and some fifteen seconds or so later there rumble of the thunder hit.

What a depressing planet I could be ending my existence on, thought Lord Luke.

The civilian starport had four large battlewalkers standing on its metacrete, in a diamond pattern around the ten-vehicle convoy that would take him through the city. As he touched his first boot on the planetary surface, all four turned and saluted him, before their heavy upper bodies rolled back to face forwards.

Lord Minister Luke Towers knew that his own trusted military guards were scanning the vehicles before he boarded them. Each was clear, and indeed, where vehicles from his own dreadnought that had been brought in especially before he landed. The security checks were immense. No-one who was not one of his own trusted crew was even coming near him today.

As he sat in his conveyance, he thought hopelessly to himself that even that would not stop a Faceless assassin. They could have penetrated his crew before he even left Zubrenica. The Faceless were nearly unstoppable, and although they did sometimes fail to hit their targets, they rarely failed.

The first battlewalker stepped forwards, and the convoy began to move.

Simultaneously, every single luminous globe in the air above him exploded.

Tremendous blasts of fire slammed down towards the ground, fiery explosions killing many of the innocent bystanders and camera crews recording his visit. The lander was washed in fire, as was the entire convoy. Only the specially reinforced shielding of his armoured car prevented the explosions from biting through the car and killing him.

"I'm taking off!" roared the Lieutenant in charge of his car. As it began to rise, Lord Luke felt powerless, unable to prevent the attack upon him or take any part in it. He knew many people had just died because of his presence. The sheer lethality of it was unbelievable.

Yet there was more to come. It was as well the driver had lifted the car high into the air, following a pre-planned and practiced escape route, because the sudden darkness that had hit the starport was shattered by a heavy blast.

Lord Luke's eyes opened wide in that split-second before the blast, however. Where he had supposed to sit was not where he was actually sitting, having assuming a different position on entrance and closure of the car doors. A special bullet, propelled by a field-penetrating laser shot of unbelievable power, had just ploughed through the aircar. It had taken three of his guards out as it powered through the shielding that had been strong enough to withstand multiple explosions, hammered through the armour of the car, and passed back out the other side.

In the next second, the entire landing pad of the starport detonated. The heavy battlewalkers disappeared in the outrageously violent flame, the detonation strong enough to do them severe damage. Other cars in the convoy did not survive, being burnt to cinders in an eye-blink.

"*Knightsword*, emergency evac required, under attack," Lord Luke's driver demanded, taking the car even higher into the air. With supersonic booms, the starfighters appeared again, slowing down to a holding position around the car, keeping level with it and protecting it with their own skin.

An hour later, his trip to the planet Caussus Tenth abandoned, Lord Luke reflected that it was just as well they had been prepared for anything. If he had walked onto the planet without foreknowledge of a potential assassination attempt, he would now be dead. As it was, all their careful preparations had come dangerously close to not saving him.

The murderous ability of the assassin scared him. To completely destroy an entire section of a starport, at the cost of hundreds of innocent lives, made him incredibly angry.

Even worse, he never even saw the Faceless assassin that had fired the shot at him, and the assassin was never found.

*

Admiral Silus Adare was, despite himself, enjoying his new-found position as the leader of the Rosicrux gangs of pirates. He had a larger fleet of ships than he had ever imagined he would be in control of, even in the days of the Red Imperium of Mars, and to be working for something he saw as vital to the future of the galaxy made him feel fulfilled with purpose once again.

The ferociously powerful T-class dreadnought *Thor's Hammer*, the largest ship of its kind in the galaxy, had remained for some time in the Dark Heart System. There was much that Adare had to organise, so he had temporarily taken him and his ship away from field duty whilst he worked on the plans the Rosicrux had for him and his new command of 'pirates'.

<Admiral,> Commander Zehra Sahin, his second-in-command, contacted him through the datasphere. <The Solar Administrator has boarded, and is on her way to the bridge.>

<Allow her access to my ready room on arrival, I am ready Commander.>

<Aye, sir.>

Admiral Silus Adare continued with his work, awaiting the arrival of the Solar Administrator. When the door to his ready room opened, the Solar Administrator entered with her usual gliding gait. Behind her stood the power-armoured figure of Adare's commander of Marines, Lieutenant-Colonel Iyan Lamans.

<Iyan, you are dismissed,> Adare said, standing as the Solar Administrator glided towards him. The vast Lieutenant-Colonel saluted and retreated, even as Adare said, "Solar Administrator. What brings you to my humble abode?"

"We have a problem," said the Solar Administrator. She stopped speaking, her white face-mask under the hooded robe focusing on the strange construction and the figure trapped within it in the corner of the ready room. "What is that, Admiral Adare?"

Adare grinned. He walked over to the construction. It was similar to a bio-vat tank, but the gel within it was completely the wrong colour. The figure within it twitched and turned, obviously in some form of everlasting pain.

"This is Special Agent Caterina La Rue," he said, "formerly of the StarCom Central Intelligence Department. Don't worry, she can't hear us. She was assigned to watch over me when the StarCom Federation had blackmailed me into working for them. A distasteful woman, all told, the bane of my life. I keep her as a pet, and a reminder to me and others that I am never, ever, to be crossed." As he had spoken, his voice had grown harsher and more vindictive, but suddenly it cleared again as he returned to his desk. "But we are not here to speak of my pet. You said there was something urgent to discuss?"

"Indeed there is," said the Solar Administrator. It was impossible to tell what she thought of Adare's 'pet' behind the white face-mask. "We have a significant problem. The Captain of the *Nazareth*, the ship that delivered the missiles and warheads to us, has lost one of her crew." The Solar Administrator went on to explain the circumstances and the situation.

"The crew were not cleared to see the Dark Heart System, but I and Reichenburg felt at the time it was more important to get the weaponry systems here. This may now turn out to be an error."

Adare thought quickly, his full attention on the issue. "I will need to know their flight-plan, what they most likely saw," he said. "But you indicated that the Salchuzura Mara will intercept and capture this Juan Ramirez at the Isdalsto System? We may not be completely compromised."

"Juan Ramirez intends to make his way to the Vindicator Mercenary Corporation," said the Solar Administrator. "We know that the VMC are attempting to find us, hence my orders to you to prepare the Dark Heart System for discovery. We in the Rosicrux have agents within StarCom, and they have intercepted an uncoded transmission, sent from this escaped crewman Ramirez to the Blackheath System. It is likely the VMC will respond by attempting to intercept and recover him at Isdalsto."

"I see," said Admiral Adare, thoughtfully.

"We cannot allow this, he could lead them to the Dark Heart System and uncover too much of the Rosicrux plan. He knows of the missiles and the Tears of the Moon, he has seen them. He has seen me. He has seen too much. You must immediately assault House Jorgensson's Isdalsto System and recover the crewman. We cannot leave it to the Salchuzura Mara."

"The plan for that region of space does not include assaults on House Jorgensson," sad Admiral Adare. "The whole point of our operation there is to make it look like Jorgensson are sponsoring the Rose Pirates, to provoke a war with the Levitican Union."

"This is a special circumstance. You will proceed to the Isdalsto System, assault it, and intercept and kill the crewman. This is a direct order. You will also ensure that the Dark Heart System is prepared, should its existence and location be uncovered and all goes wrong."

"The VMC have Reichenburg anyway," said Adare, "That is why I have been preparing up to now. Is it not just as likely that Gavain could obtain the information he needs from Reichenburg and the other prisoners they have taken?"

"No," said the Solar Administrator, "there is less chance. On being admitted to the Dark Heart System, all of you and your crew were submitted to medical examinations, yes?"

"Yes."

"We implanted information into your cortexes which would prevent such a thing. There is a slim possibility that one could mis-fire, hence your preparations so far, but it is unlikely."

Adare felt a sudden anger explode deep within him, as he realised he had been interfered with, without his knowledge. He contained it carefully, allowing no sign of his true anger to manifest itself. "I see," he said, coldly.

"Juan Ramirez has no such controls," said the Solar Administrator. "It is imperative he is prevented from reaching the Blackheath System, and is terminated in the Isdalsto System. The Mara cannot be our only attempt to prevent this. You will set course for Isdalsto immediately."

"I understand, sir," Admiral Adare said, standing. He saluted the Solar Administrator as the figure left his ready room abruptly.

He sat back down in his chair, as Commander Zehra Sahin and Lieutenant-Colonel Iyan Lamans entered his room. He momentarily ignored their requests for information or to assist.

He disliked being spoken to in such a way by the Solar Administrator. Despite his uncharacteristic loyalty to the Rosicrux, to find he had been medically or cybernetically altered during the initiation medical exam troubled him greatly and made him extremely resentful. Added to that, a deep, dark part of him dearly wished for his nemesis, the Admiral James Gavain, to find the Dark Heart System so that he could crush the man once and for all. His higher duty was to the Rosicrux plan, however, there was more than his own vengeance to consider.

He narrowed his eyes, staring at the tortured form of Special Agent Caterina La Rue, twisting and turning in her torture tank. Choices, choices, he thought, beginning to smile to himself.

*

Space ripped open, and numerous starships appeared in the Blackheath System. Identification codes were sent, but they were expected and the Levitican Union military defence forces did not react to the armada that had suddenly arrived in the home system to House Towers.

The starships that were damaged immediately set course for the Kavanagh Shipyards, their repair an immediate priority. Joining them was the *Vindicator*, the battlecruiser belonging to James Gavain. He had much to see to in his short visit to this system. The greater remainder of his ships, those that were undamaged, set course for the Blackheath Stargate between the planets of October and November.

Sat on the bridge of the *Vindicator*, James Gavain stood. <Commander Georgia, you have command of the bridge,> he said.

<Command of the bridge received, Admiral,> Commander Georgia responded smartly.

<Get me Commodore Andersson on comms, we do not have much time,> he said. <Signal Lady Sophia. Inform her I need to meet with her immediately on a matter of the utmost importance, and will take a lander down to her location.>

<Aye, sir,> said Lieutenant Forrest, his communications Lieutenant.

The holographic image of Commodore Harley Andersson was appeared in Gavain's ready room as he crossed to make his customary cup of coffee at the synthesiser unit, never activating it but instead using the real coffee making equipment he kept in the alcove next to it.

"James," said the holographic representation of Harley, "It's so good to see you."

Gavain turned, and said, "You too, Harley." He found to his surprise he did not really feel it. His relationship with Harley had its beginnings back in the days of the Red Imperium, but he wondered if he would ever be able to truly feel something so strong for another person. It was shocking, but the type of relationship Ulrik had with Julia was not something he found he could contemplate with Harley.

He also knew, looking at his old friend and lover, that Harley did not have the same inhibition to his feelings for him.

"Are you coming to the surface?" the hope was there in the voice.

"Yes," replied Gavain, sitting behind his desk. "But I will not have time to visit you, Harley. I am seeing Lady Sophia, and then once all our ships are recharged, we're using the stargate to jump back out. We have a vast distance of space to cross in very little time."

"You will be rendezvousing with General Andryukhin, I understand," said Commodore Andersson, the disappointment on his face obvious. "Why are you seeing Lady Sophia?"

"We have something serious to discuss," said Admiral Gavain. He hesitated, but this was a secure connection, and even if he did not feel as much for his lover as he felt for him, Gavain knew the man was also a co-Director of the VMC and needed to know what his intentions were.

He explained his plan.

"By the Emperors, James," Commodore Harley Andersson exclaimed. "Even in the days of the Imperium you were seen as a genius, a visionary who would go far. But what you are intending is something else entirely. This is fantastic. Do you really think you can do it?"

"If all goes according to plan," said James Gavain.

"What in the name of the Emperor gave you the idea?"

"A conversation with Ulrik," said Gavain quietly. "He made me think of much. I have also been .... dissatisfied with who have I become. This is my attempt to make amends, and to find a better future."

221

"It will be truly amazing if you can pull it off. I have the utmost faith in you James. You do understand the nature of what you're trying to do though? This is nothing like what you have done before."

"I know," said Gavain quietly. "I am as scared as I am determined to do it."

"You will, Jamie, you will," said Andersson confidently. "If anyone can, you can."

"Anyway, Commodore, we have business to discuss," said Gavain, putting the conversation on track. "I have been in warp for a long time. What news is there of my proposition to the various Houses to track down the Blackheath pirates. Have they all agreed to the new contract?"

Andersson smiled broadly. "Yes, James, they have. The Levitican Union, Erdogan, Van Der Meer, Aarlborg Alliance, Hausenhof, they have all agreed to it. Lady Sophia and her Spider have been working on it ceaselessly. The amount of money being offered to us is phenomenal. Contracts are signed and completed, and registered in secret through the Mercenary Bonding Office of the Interstellar Merchants Guild."

"Excellent," said Gavain, "Well done. All we have to do now is find them." He thought of Reichenburg, currently being interrogated along with the other prisoners. He would also have to send the six corvettes out on a hunting mission, he decided, sweeping the Gulf of Medusa. There was little other option.

"Ah, well," said Commodore Andersson, "We may have had a lucky break, there, Jamie."

"Explain," he said with typical curtness.

"Look at this," said Andersson.

The holographic image of Andersson suddenly shifted, minimising slightly and moving to the side. Gavain saw a new holographic image by the side of him, a young man, who looked scared and terrified in some form of cheap communications booth. Instantly, as he looked at the image, Gavain felt the attraction rise. The young man was very handsome indeed.

"Please help," said the image of the man. "My name is Juan Ramirez. I'm sending this urgent recording to the Vindicator Mercenary Corporation, and it needs to get to Admiral James Gavain as soon as possible. I cannot say too much, as I am on an open channel and have restricted funds –" he stopped quickly as a tannoy in the background began to announce a boarding for a passenger transporter.

"- I am on the planet Longshot IV, having escaped from a smuggler ship called the *Nazareth,* working for the Salchuzura Mara. I have been to the homeworld of the pirates that are attacking the Eastern Segment, in the Gulf of Medusa, and have information for you. I have seen Admiral Silus Adare. But I am being pursued, my life is in great danger. I have just enough money to get me to the Isdalsto System in House Jorgensson territory, and will steal if I have to, to get to Blackheath. That's my boarding announcement in the background. I need help if you can give it, even if it's just the money to get me to Blackheath, here's my account details. I have the information you need. Please help me. Please!"

As the image faded and the holographic representation of Andersson took centre again, Gavain frowned. "We must be receiving a number of hoax messages such as this," he said, frowning. "Why do you show me this one?"

"We've analysed it, and there is a possibility it is true," said Andersson. "Admittedly it could equally as likely be a trap. The location and timestamp on the mail all check out as genuine. Voice analysis and image enhancement prove that the gentleman was in genuine distress. In addition, we have been able to verify a number of the statements this Juan Ramirez made. He is actually Juan Ramirez – believe it or not our paths have crossed before, he was on the *Featherlight* when we boarded it and took it – and the IMG records show that he was discharged from a recent job and abandoned on a planet where the *Nazareth* was known to be. He disappeared from all records at that time. The *Nazareth* does have suspected connections to the Salchuzura Mara, and the Longshot System is virtually in the Gulf of Medusa, right on the edges of colonised space in that area. The IMG have also confirmed that he is booked in as a passenger on the ship, and is heading to the Isdalsto System. The Spider Carrington got me that nugget of information."

"To mention Adare and the Gulf of Medusa is also an indicator," said Gavain thoughtfully.

"True, but then we have shared information with a number of House governments," said Andersson. "Our enemies in this Rosicrux conspiracy seem resourceful, they could easily have penetrated any one of those Houses or nations and know what we know."

"It was a risk we had to take," said Gavain.

"Agreed, Jamie. There is a problem though. The Salchuzura Mara own that Longshot System, House Lemans is virtually their puppet, and this was an un-encoded transmission so it is highly likely that they – as well as StarCom CID – have learnt of it. They can make it to the Isdalsto System and be waiting for him as he leaves the transporter, the transporter has a number of stops which means they can get there ahead of him. He will be intercepted. If this is real."

Gavain made his decision. "We must get to him first. Are the biomorphic soldiers ready for field deployment now?"

"Yes."

"They will go with Lieutenant-Commander Bramhall and his corvettes to Isdalsto, insert themselves secretly into the system. I cannot send any of our bigger ships, as they will already be engaged in something else, and besides which, this mission calls for something much more subtle."

"The logic is sound," said Commodore Andersson. "I'll speak to Jason Bramhall now."

"Good. Carry on, Harley," said James, disconnecting the conversation before anything intimate could be discussed.

As he waited for them to near the planet Tahrir so he could speak to Lady Sophia, Gavain found himself thinking of the young Juan Ramirez.

Chapter XVII

Lord Minister Luke Towers found the House Marchenko capital planet and solar system exceptionally strange and uncomfortable. The Khmelnytskyi System was large and sprawling, with nearly twenty planets, and many, many more planetoids within its boundaries. Three stars made the trinary system a hotspot for trade and recharging spaceships, so it was always exceptionally busy. The capital planet within Khmelnytskyi was called Tul'chyn, and it was something like nine times the size of Earth. Heavily industrialised, not much space on the planet was wasted, it being a powerhouse of production.

Being escorted through the streets of the large capital city of Tul'chyn Una was a logistical nightmare in itself. Following the assassination attempt on Caussus Ten, Lord Luke ensured that at all times he had about two hundred Levitican Union Armed Forces troopers around him. About a thousand in all were dedicated to protecting him, with starfighters overhead, battlewalkers roaming the streets, repulsortanks and other military craft keeping the populace away from him.

Lord Gregori Marchenko had assured him that apart from a very small percentage of visitors, every Marchenkan was loaded into the hive-mind consciousness, so there was no possibility of an assassination attempt here.

Lord Luke however, knew that House Marchenko had been introduced to the Union by House Zupanic, the very House which had tried to kill him, so he did not find being surrounded by millions and millions of hive-mind linked cyborgs that reassuring.

Tul'chyn Una was very ordered. It was like being in an alien world. There were signs of Imperial architecture, but there was a strong overlay of Marchenkan artistry in the construction. The immensely tall buildings even looked wrong. People with heavy and cheap, grotesquely obvious cybernetic implants walked in filed ranks across the streets. There were enforcers, which Lord Luke wondered at; why would police be needed on a planet where everyone was linked to a hive-mind. Surely crime would be non-existent.

The heavy industrialisation of the planet had ruined the climate. The skies were dark, heavily clouded, despite the three suns that ensured every minute on this planet was daytime. Very few planets in the Marchenkan system of Khmelnytskyi had a true nightfall.

Eventually, the heavily guarded military convoy reached the vast construction that speared angrily up into the dark daytime sky. The Marchenko Tower Palace was as imposing in real-life as it was in the holovids. It seemed the Marchenkans did everything in big sizes, thought Lord Luke.

"Lord Minister Luke," said Lord Gregori Marchenko, as Lord Luke was shown into the impressive, grand, and oversized throne room, "we are honoured –"

"- to welcome you here to the palace," finished Lady Banuska Marchenko, her lithe and lean form a sharp contrast to her husband's vast bulk.

"We are also very sorry to hear of the assassination attempt on your life," said Lord Gregori.

"It was a phenomenally violent attempt," Lady Banuska said.

Lord Luke's Union military guards were fanning out, joining the House Guards that Marchenko had been allowed to retain on joining the Levitican Union. All Houses maintained a small form of independent military, but the vast majority of their forces had joined together in the LUAF.

"Apart from this, how is your military tour progressing?" asked Lord Gregori, as they walked to the centre of the throne room. Typical of the Marchenkan's, it was much more than just a throne-room. A holographic pit was in the approach to the two thrones, and this was currently flickering between still pictures rapidly, displaying a number of images from around House Marchenko.

"Very well," said Lord Luke, glossing over the assassination attempt. "Polls show that morale is already increasing the LUAF."

"Such a human thing, morale," Lady Banuska commented.

"But a thing we understand," said Lord Gregori smoothly. "Do you wish to discuss the current armed forces positioning, or – " he asked.

"- our efforts within the Ministry of Transformation and Change?" Lady Banuska finished.

"This is a military tour, and I am on a tight schedule, Lord and Lady," said Lord Luke. "If we look at the strategic positioning?"

"Certainly," said Lord Gregori. The display in front of them changed, and converted into a large holo-map of the Levitican Union.

Lord Luke spent some time discussing it with the Lord and Lady Marchenko. As he was going through the positioning of the armed forces, at one point an unsettling thought reoccurred to him. The LUAF was made up of the armed forces of all the member Houses, but after the Levitican War with StarCom, they had all sustained serious damage. The vast military forces of House Marchenko bolstered the armed forces considerably, making up nearly fifty percent of the current LUAF naval fleet alone.

Considering that he had his own doubts about why House Zupanic, who had almost turned traitor to the Union and sold them out to the StarCom Federation, wanted House Marchenko in the Union, Lord Luke had a niggling worry about Marchenkan ships spreading through his Union. There was little he could do to prevent it however, the votes had been cast and he had to live with the political decision. In addition, the extra military force was more than welcome should it transpire that House Jorgensson was about to start a war with them, regardless of whether they had anything to do with the Rose Pirates or not.

As they were going through the positioning and plans, Lord Luke actually physically saw the sudden tensing in Lord Gregori Marchenko and Lady Banuska. It was something he had never witnessed before.

"Is everything alright?" he asked.

"No," said Lord Gregori.

"We are receiving a number of news feeds, the populace is reacting to it," said Lady Banuska.

"Excuse me, what do you mean?" asked Lord Luke Towers.

"Deal with the collective consciousness, Banuska," Lord Gregori ordered. Luke found that interesting, despite his growing disquiet.

"What is happening?" asked Lord Luke again.

Lord Gregori Marchenko turned fully to face Lord Luke. "We are receiving news from the Union capital on Zubrenica XIX. StarCom News Media is covering the story, but now our state media is beginning to respond. It is affecting my people greatly."

"What?" Lord Luke asked yet again.

"Lord Principal Ramicek Zupanic has been assassinated."

Back aboard the flagship *LSS Knightsword*, in his specially converted quarters, Lord Minister Luke Towers had a number of news broadcasts up on continuous replay. The moment of Lord Principal Ramicek Zupanic's death was certainly undeniable, as well as sensational.

The holo-camera had recorded the moment perfectly. He was on his way to that day's Council session, and was being filmed by a presumably uninterested media crew leaving the military barracks that had been converted into his quarters. Zubrenica XIX was after all a military moon, and was only intended as a temporary place of residence for the Council of the Levitican Union until the city on the planet Leviticus could be rebuilt following the war, something that was not too far away hopefully.

As was standard, he was surrounded by Zupanic House Guard, as well as Armed Forces personnel. The overpowered laser shot that had removed his head had snapped in from a high angle, burning through his personal shielding without any issue.

Intelligence reports had started to come through, from his own Ministry. It transpired that the personal shielding of Ramicek Zupanic had been tampered with, to render it ineffectual, some two days before. That made it roughly the point in real-space time that the assassination attempt on Lord Luke had failed. Lord Luke had blocked that piece of information from being released to the media, but some clever person in the SCNM had spotted that there appeared to be a malfunction in the personal shielding so it was already out there in the galaxy.

They had tracked the assassin's firing location fairly rapidly, but no sign of the assassin had been found. He had successfully escaped. The entire moon of Zubrenica XIX was now on lock-down, at Lord Luke's order, with no ships or craft allowed to leave or land.

Lord Brin's Ministry of Justice enforcers were taking over the investigation from Lord Luke's military, and he had officially agreed to the hand-over. There had been numerous hyper-pulse messages going back and forth, and a large number of discussions. The Levitican Union had fallen into disarray.

Only Lord Luke, Lady Sophia, and Elaine Carrington knew the truth at this moment. The Faceless assassin they called Agent Black had successfully carried out his orders, and would remain on the moon for Lady Wyn to arrive. He was not going to attempt to escape; he would wait for his next target to come to him.

Sure enough, earlier in the day, Lady Wyn had been announced as the new head of House for House Zupanic. Lord Micalek was now second in line to the throne. She had made a public speech denouncing the attacks on her family, following the deaths of Vasily and Csarina Zupanic. She was visibly upset at the death of her husband, Ramicek.

There had been numerous discussions between the Houses following the assassination of the leader of the Levitican Union. Lord Luke was waiting for the next announcement to come.

Sure enough, he stopped what he was doing as the holo-cameras suddenly switched from their endless replays of the assassination attempt to show the media briefing room of the Council. Arranged on the speaking podium were Lord Brin Claes, Lady Monique Lapointe, Lad Aria Galetti, Lady Eranisch Marchenko, and Lord Moafa Obamu. Lord Brin Claes stepped forwards and began speaking. Luke thought he looked pale.

"Citizens of the Levitican Union," he began, "on this sad and terrible day, we would understand if you are feeling somewhat disconcerted and apprehensive about the future. Since the inception of the Levitican Union, we have faced many troubles and hard times, and continue to do so. Today is no exception. The assassination of Lord Principal Ramicek Zupanic, by unknown agents for reasons we cannot yet understand, has shocked us all. It is particularly concerning coming so quickly after the attempt on the life of Lord Minister Luke Towers.

"I will keep this announcement brief. Let me reassure you that the Ministry of Justice is doing its utmost to determine who has perpetrated this heinous act. There are however practical matters we must attend to.

"Firstly, let me reassure you, that even with the absence of a Lord Principal the Council of the Levitican Union will continue to sit. Our Charter does not allow for such a circumstance, but we shall take it in turns to chair the Council.

"However, we cannot remain without a leader of our great nation. As according to the Charter, we will immediately call all Heads of Houses to Zubrenica XIX. We will hold a vote for the new Lord Principal as soon as we can, and follow the agreed rules concerning re-voting and re-assignment of Ministries.

"Obviously there is a significant safety issue with the assassin still believed to be on the moon. We do not know where he or she is, or whether they will strike again. Security and protection of the Heads of Houses is of our utmost concern. There will be a further briefing tomorrow, on Standard morning time. Are there any questions?"

Lord Luke nodded to himself, deactivating the holo-feeds. He would have to return to Zubrenica XIX as well, as a serving Lord Minister. Perhaps now was the time he could finally give up his Ministry and pass the political shenanigans to his sister, who had proven to him just how deadly she could play the Imperial game.

*

The Master of the First Circle was in the Temple of Shadow, his customary place of residence. All the other Legates had been recalled to the Temple, and he awaited their arrival. It was time for a formal, face to face convivium, he had ordered.

Stood in one of the temple's towers, he looked out at the scene he saw before him. The existence of the Shadow Council was a strong rumour that had been known by the populace of mankind for many years, since the days of the Red Imperium. Mostly it was connected to the Faceless assassins. Few people, if any, suspected its true power. Certainly no-one except those who worked fully for the Shadow knew exactly where the Temple of Shadow was located, and fewer still of its existence and purpose.

The Legates of the Fifth Circle and Sixth Circle entered the room, the red lines and dark purple lines on their jet black face masks a mirror image of the gold lines on his own. He turned to face them as they approached.

"Hail the Master," they said in unison.

He felt great anger that their missing assassin had been used again, but there was little point in exacting it on these two people. His legendary temper ebbed and flowed, as legendary as that of the True and False Emperor, both of whom were rumoured to be insane in any case. The Master had personally seen to the elimination of those who had propagated such rumours, at least until the insurrection by the Revolutionary Council had put an end to the Red Imperium.

"Our missing assassin has been used again," he said, "on the temporary capital moon of the Levitican Union, Zubrenica XIX. They have locked the system and the moon down, and will not re-open it for some time I suspect."

"The Legate of the Third Circle agrees," said the Legate of the Fifth Circle. "We have spoken of this already, Master."

"It means it cannot escape. We do have some agents of the Fourth Circle in place, but they are ill-equipped to deal with a Faceless. The Heads of Houses have been called to Zubrenica XIX, and they are the only ones who will make moonfall. I want your agents, from both your Circles, to accompany the Lady Wyn onto Zubrenica. Is this understood? It is our only way of inserting our capture force onto the moon. I believe I see what House Towers is trying to do, and believe the assassin will remain in place until he has had a chance to strike at Lady Wyn. That is the point where we take him."

"Why do you believe the missing assassin will strike at Lady Wyn?" asked the Legate of the Sixth Circle.

"Lord Micalek is supposed to become the head of House Zupanic, I believe that to be Lady Sophia Towers' plan. All that stands between him and that is Lady Wyn. Now go do my bidding."

*

<Successful translation achieved, Lieutenant-Commander,> said his helms officer.

<Confirmation from positional scans that we are in the Isdalsto System," said the navigations officer.

<Thank you, people,> said Lieutenant-Commander Jason Bramhall. He could feel the thoughts of all the crew he had on board the corvette *Aggressive* through his connection on the datasphere. <Scanners, have the rest of the corvettes arrived?>

<The last, the SS *Armoured*, has just translated in, Lieutenant-Commander,> came the reply.

Lt-Cmdr Bramhall checked the tactical holo-map himself. They had successfully translated into the Isdalsto System. They were quite a distance out from the system, on the far sides of House Jorgensson territory. The Blackheath Stargate had thrown them into unclaimed territory, and then they had made a series of jumps to reach this system, successfully avoiding all House Jorgensson patrols.

The Isdalsto System was a little different, however. With a decent sized population, it was a system with heavy interstellar traffic. It was also militarised, with Jorgensson capital ships present. This had necessitated all six of the corvettes in Bramhall's squadron coming in at a great distance away from the furthest planet, almost in deepspace.

<Bramhall to squadron,> he addressed them all, <Engage chameleonic fields, and proceed on the designated courses to the planet Isdalsto Primary. We are all running silent from here on in.>

A series of acknowledgements came back to him, and then it was confirmed that all corvettes were now engaging their inhibitor fields and chameleonic shields, disappearing from visual, electronic and other forms of detection.

Bramhall turned to the figure that was standing behind him to the right of his command chair. The figure was tall and impressive, well-built, and looked utterly dangerous and lethal. It worried him greatly, however, as he knew this was all just a facade. Early tests in Tahrir Base had made them realise that the fifty new cybernetic biomorphic soldiers made ordinary Marines and Naval crew – as if the super-human genetically engineered Praetorians could ever be described as ordinary! – exceptionally nervous in the jet black non-skins which was their natural state. The order had been given that when around standard Praetorian borgs, they had to present a certain identifiable image in order to fit in.

This was the leader of the fifty cybernetic biomorphs, and he had sculpted and adopted a particularly powerful image for itself, Bramhall thought. The thing had been granted a rank of Major, which was usually only given to those in charge of a battalion, not forty-nine other people. Bramhall took that as an indication that Gavain intended to produce more of the cybernetic biomorphs, as the first batch had been so successful.

<Major Vantanik,> Bramhall addressed the biomorph, <We will be at Isdalsto Primary in twenty-two hours, and will insert you and your command at that point. You have two full days to make it to the starport, before the passenger transporter arrives. We will remain in our designated positions, ready for your extraction from this system, should all go to plan.>

<Excellent, Lieutenant-Commander,> said the biomorphic Vantanik, who technically although part of the Marine division held a higher equivalent rank. <Carry on.>

*

General Ulrik Andryukhin looked up at the distant horizon, between the tall spire-towers of the city Nimevah. The last of the Erdogan landers was a tiny dot in the distance, and even with strong magnification activated on his helmet it was still little more than a small blur rising into space.

<General Andryukhin, another three Erdogan ships have just jumped out of the Chester System, only two transporters, a cruiser and three frigates remaining,> Captain Delgado suddenly addressed him from his position high in orbit. <Compact ships are attempting to engage.>

<Acknowledged,> Andryukhin replied. <Hold position.>

<The Compact is requesting our assistance?>

<Ignore the requests. Andryukhin out.>

He turned away from the scene, stamping along the rubble-strewn foot-street towards his *King Cobra*. <Sergeant Calaman, take me to the HPCG station, full speed.>

<Aye, sir,> replied Sergeant Calaman, breaking off to give orders to the driver and to recall his squad. She had taken the turret on top of the HAPC, the previous operator having been grievously injured during the assault on the city of Nimevah.

He mounted up into the *King Cobra*, the rest of his squad scant seconds behind him. The ramp doors shut and he felt the HAPC vehicle kick off into the air, turning sharply as it headed back the way they came.

The Erdogan forces in the Chester System had put up some resistance, but had largely folded in the face of the Vindicator Mercenary Corporation assault. They had struck quickly, assaulting the main planet Chestus D and landing directly on top of the main Erdogan defence forces. The fighting there had been the hardest, but they had prevailed, the Erdogan's withdrawing. Once again, General Andryukhin had gained access to their battlenet.

Over the next three days, with Zhou-Zheng Compact forces following in their wake, Andryukhin had stormed into Chestus B, and then Chestus C, the capital world. The final fight had taken place here, in the city of Nimevah, and the Erdogan forces had released their hold on the system. By the time they had landed on Chestus C it was already apparent that the Erdoganites had lost the system.

Star Marshal Ngu had already sent a message of congratulations to Andryukhin, to which he had given the briefest polite response he could manage. Andryukhin had also received a secret message through the Erdogan double agent acting as the Zhou-Zheng liaison, from Feldmarshall Grant, pointing out that he had upheld his end of the bargain and had put up a token resistance in the system. He strongly added that it was now up to Andryukhin to uphold his part of the bargain, and that he hoped the mercenaries had not agreed to the plan as a way of gaining the Chester System with a minimum of damage to their own forces.

In the entire colonised galaxy, only Andryukhin and Gavain and a handful of their senior staff knew the truth, of course. Now that the Chester System was taken, that was about to change.

<We're at the HPCG station, sir,> Sergeant Calaman told him.

<Squad, on me,> Andryukhin ordered, even as he was exiting the *King Cobra* HAPC.

His boots engaged their magnetic locks automatically as they hit the metal pathway. He kept his suit sealed, primarily because in order to gain access to Nimevah, they had blasted through the protective air-dome that shielded the city. The air had hissed out into the non-atmosphere of Chestus C, and the natural low gravity of the planet had reasserted itself with the anti-grav generators targeted early in the assault. He shuddered, as it reminded him too much of the Battle of Mars and the end of the Red Empire.

The squad fanning out behind him, Sergeant Calaman at his side, the two Marines on duty outside the airlock doors inside the compound of the HPCG station saluted as he approached. He ignored them, carrying on into the airlock. A couple of cycles later and he was walking on into the StarCom facility.

He crossed through it easily, being familiar with the station layout. They were all virtually the same throughout the galaxy. There were a number of StarCom Guards' weaponry discarded on the floor, his Marines having taken complete control of the facility. The Erdogan nation had been one of those to allow the Imperial StarCom organisation, which had turned into the StarCom Federation, to continue to maintain and operate their HPCG stations and stargates. The Vindicator Mercenary Corporation, the Levitican Union, and the Zhou-Zheng Compact, were among many that did not recognise the authority of StarCom, and had a policy of removing them wherever they set foot.

Andryukhin confidently walked into the Hall of the Generator, his booted feet no longer magnetically connecting the floor. The station had its own anti-gravity facilities. The vast generator filled much of the room, the powerful equipment capable of sending massive blasts of code and the energy field need to rip holes into hyperspace to a special geosynchronous array far away from the planet, which would ignite the tight-beam field and send the messages all across the galaxy in the blink of an eye. Every time the massive generator thrummed with power, the hole in space would be torn open. Even now, it was like a heartbeat, messages coming in and leaving rapidly on automatic.

When Andryukhin's Marines had stormed the facility, they had prevented the Chief of Station from activating the Armageddon Code, which would destroy the station. It was now running automatically, part of the vast intergalactic web of stations which constantly threw messages across the stars every few seconds. Even the stations which were operated by their own nations and not those of the StarCom Federation remained part of that web, by decree of the new President Pereyra, who was more accommodating publicly at least than her predecessor Nielsen, who had declared the non-StarCom operated facilities blacklisted from the intergalactic communications web.

He entered the control room, seeing the furious Chief of Station Ennis standing between two Marine guards, his red face a stark contrast to the white and regal blue Federation uniform that he wore.

"Are you in charge?" the Chief of Station tremored, "What is the meaning of –"

"Stow it, you fucking Fed," Andryukhin growled, his X-visor helmet retracted back into his suit. "You're going to send a message for me, continuous hyperpulse, to this location." He threw a data-chip across to the Chief of Station, who caught it quickly.

He looked at the chip in his hands. "I can't do that, we're on automatic communication –" he began.

"You can, and you will," said Andryukhin, raising the rotary cannon slightly. The other Marines with him reacted.

"Yeah, okay, sure, sure," said the Chief of Station. The man went across to a console, and slotted the data-chip in. As he read the data scrolling up in front of his eyes, he said, "But this is to an empty starsystem –"

"Just do it," said Andryukhin, crossing the control room to a communications chamber. He stood on the circle, and it automatically lit up, scanning him and preparing to transmit a live holographic image across the stars by continuous hyperpulse.

"Connecting," said the Chief of Station, the unhappiness in his voice obvious. "Dialling for contact now." A couple of seconds later, as the thrum of the massive generator outside had turned into a continuous and annoying background hum, the shock in his voice was obvious as he said, "Connection made, we're getting a reply, the warp-hole is opening. We have full broadcast transmission."

Andryukhin smiled to himself as a holographic image of Admiral James Gavain appeared in front of him.

<James,> Andryukhin greeted him, <We have control of the Chester System. Erdogan forces will be completely evacuated within the hour. The contract with the Compact will be complete at that point in time.>

<How long until your forces can be back aboard their transports?> Gavain asked.

<We can be fully extracted within two hours. The Compact will suspect.>

<Send them a message explaining that we are withdrawing, give no reason. Their suspicions do not matter anymore.>

Andryukhin grinned. <Our ships are fully recharged, so we can jump to the target system in exactly one hundred and twenty nine minutes from now.>

<The clock is ticking then. We will jump in ahead of you and strike in one hundred nineteen minutes time. Good luck, General.>

<Good luck, Admiral. And Jamie?>

<Yes?>

<It is good to see the old you back again.>

James Gavain hesitated, then laughed. <It is good to have a better purpose, Ulrik. This is just the start of it. Gavain out.>

Chapter XVIII

The shuttle lander touched down gently on minimal repulsors, grounding softly at one of the military starports on Zubrenica XIX. Security had increased substantially since the assassination of Lord Principal Ramicek Zupanic, heavily armoured and armed droids, un-augmented Humans and fully augmented cyborgs, including some of the vast monstrosities that were the Marchenko hive collectives, all in vast numbers guarding every inch of the starport complex.

Even in the darker days of the Levitican War, Lord Luke had not seen such a heavy protective presence. The assassinations, both attempted and successful, had shocked the populace in general and rocked the political establishment of the Levitican Union. All was in flux, everything was dangerous.

Lord Luke Towers descended the exit ramp of the lander, booted feet hitting the special metacrete. It had been laced with anti-explosive chemicals. There was a complex series of force fields and shields in active and passive operation. Every guard and soldier on the landing pad had another person or automated weapons system covering him or her. No-one was being trusted, not with a known Faceless assassin on the moon.

Lord Luke hesitated slightly before he entered the droidcar, remembering the near-death experience on Caussus Ten. Even though he knew that the assassin on Zubrenica XIX was Agent Black, in the employ of House Towers, there was nothing to say that there was not another on the planet as yet unrevealed.

As Lord Luke moved through the entrance hall to the converted building that currently served as the Council chambers and temporary parliament building of the Union, he was somewhat surprised to see Lady Monique Lapointe stood there, waiting for him.

"Lady Monique," he smiled slightly, his own tension during the journey making his greeting less warm than it would have been normally. "How are things here on Zubrenica?"

"Tense and dangerous," she replied shortly, falling in by his side. The guards around them fell back, and his trained military mind and eye could guess and see how having two Lord Ministers walking side by side would be stressing the operational commanders.

"It does not surprise me," he said.

"Are we being overheard?" Lady Monique asked bluntly.

He frowned, and adjusted a device on his belt. He knew this would be about the never-ending politics of the Levitican Union. Sophia was so much better at this than he was, he was a military man, not a politician. An invisible force field sprung up around them both. "Not now, we're not, Lady."

"Things here on Zubrenica XIX are bad, particularly since Lord Ramicek was assassinated. It looks even worse, following on the deaths of his brother Vasily and daughter Csarina. Then there was the attempted assassination on yourself. It is like going back to the dark days of the Federation assassinations and the Levitican War."

"It is certainly like that, or worse," Lord Luke conceded. "I understand that all the Heads of Houses are being called here to the moon, for the voting on the new Lord Principal and Ministry heads."

"I am sure that is creating a major security headache for you," said Lady Monique.

"I'm attending to it within the hour," Luke confirmed.

"You should be aware that there are many rumours going through the ministries," said Lady Monique, changing subject. "One of the more persistent is that all these assassinations are part of a vendetta, a secret and quiet disagreement between House Towers and House Zupanic manifesting itself. I thought you should know. What do you think of that?"

He heard the question. "It could look that way," he said non-committedly. "What do you think?"

"I find it coincidental that Erik Towers was assassinated, and now the assassinations are starting again. I find it strange that Micalek Zupanic marries Sophia Towers, and now the only person standing between him and rule of the House is his mother, Lady Wyn."

Luke did not know how to answer. "I can see how that looks bad," he said eventually.

"My only comment, Lord Luke, would be that regardless, Ramicek was the Lord Principal of this Union. I doubted some of his political motives – look at the obvious arrangement he had with Brin Claes, for instance, in voting on Council matters – and that of House Marchenko joining the Union. I suspect him like I suspect every House. But this is destabilising the Union, and many who suspect a House-Towers feud say it has to end, sooner rather than later. Whatever the final outcome is."

"Conspiracy theorists always have things to say," said Lord Luke, nodding, finding that last comment interesting.

"They do," Lady Monique said. There was a long pause. "I do think there is something else you should be aware of. Did you ever wonder why I voted for House Marchenko to join the Levitican Union?"

Despite himself Luke Towers suddenly found himself on safer ground, and he realised she was about to tell him why she had voted so surprisingly in favour of Marchenko joining the Union. He was not prepared for the answer. "Yes," he said, "I did wonder. Considering the humanist leanings of the Lapointe family, it was a little unexpected."

Monique looked distraught. "My mother was killed by the Rose Pirates before the vote," she said. "I was warned, through an anonymous communication, to vote for House Marchenko to join the Union. The death of my mother at the hands of the Rose Pirates was the warning to convince me I would be next. I do not know how, or why, but whoever the Rose Pirates are working for, they wanted Marchenko in the Union."

"I – I'm not sure –" Luke began.

"There are two things there," Monique continued. "The first is that the Pirates are not what they seem, which we are becoming aware of. The second is that the Zupanic family sponsors Marchenko, want them in, and have something to do with it. I will not mourn the loss of Ramicek Zupanic, as I suspect he knows what happened to my mother. Whatever argument it is that your family are involved in with them, bring it to an end before it endangers the Union further, but ensure you win. By murdering Elouise Lapointe, all of House Lapointe now has a matter of vengeance to pursue. I cannot help much, but if you need any assistance, let me or any in House Lapointe know."

With that she bade him farewell, and they parted company.

*

Juan Ramirez felt incredibly nervous as the lander touched down at the First City Starport on Isdalsto Primary. On his journey across the starsystems and deepspace it had occurred to him that there was every chance the Salchuzura Mara or the Rosicrux or both could be waiting for him on the planet. He considered leaving the passenger transporter on one of its stopovers, but knew that he did not have the money to get to Levitican space from Isdalsto, let alone somewhere further away. Also, he had pinned much of his hopes on the Vindicator Mercenary Company coming to meet him here.

It was a disappointment when he emerged into the weak light of First City Starport and did not see the famous red and black uniforms of the Vindicator Mercenary Company waiting for him. All he could see were the enforcers of House Jorgensson, in pairs, at various locations across the wide starport.

He boarded the travellator droid platform, and was carried across the vast expanse of the landing pad towards the terminal entrance. Clutching his shoulder bag, unwilling to let it drop into its hover mode so it was close to him at all times, he stared about him. The enforcers were not reacting to his presence at all, at least, and he could spot no-one paying him undue attention.

The travellator platform came to an end, and he stepped off to sign through airport security. His bag was scanned as he handed over his identity holo-liths. As the person sat in the security booth scanned his holo-lith, he saw the reaction as her eyes widened.

As she passed him back the holo-lith, he saw the vague outline of a tattoo underneath the sleeve of her uniform.

Panicking inwardly but not over-reacting, as it could after all be coincidence, he moved on into the main terminal. He stepped onto another travellator droid, determined to exit the boarding hall and get towards the exit.

As he passed through the boarding hall, he saw a number of men and women were beginning to move, following him. They passed the enforcers, who were not reacting to anything much at all, without any outwardly apparent concern. He counted at least eight of them, and with horror he realised that they were not indigenous House Jorgensson nationals. They were big, muscled, and he was sure he spotted at least one with a possible outline of a weapon under his jacket.

They were the Salchuzura Mara, they had to be.

His heart almost stopped as he realised another two were stood by the huge circular doorway which led from the boarding hall into the main starport building. The travellator came to a stop, and with a confidence born of a life in the gangs he did not feel at all, he stepped forwards to the exit.

As he passed through, they both stopped leaning against the wall and began walking next to him. He looked behind him, and another three had moved up close behind him. Another two were now walking in front of him. There were more spaced out in front and behind. Everywhere he looked, he saw the Salchuzura Mara.

"Carry on walking, Juan," said the heavy-set, muscular woman on his right. "We're walking to the exit, and you're getting into the hover-truck parked outside."

"Who are you?" he asked, stammering, knowing the answer.

"Salchuzura Ma –" she began, but she never finished the sentence.

Another figure had appeared out of nowhere, his hand and arm morphing so quickly before Juan's eyes that he could not believe it, becoming a long-bladed weapon. The blade sliced cleanly through the woman's shoulder, chest, and hip, cleaving her meatily and bloodily into two.

Even as the blood was spraying everywhere, the new figure was dragging Juan to the floor, another figure morphing into a form all in black neatly decapitating the other Mara gang-member who had been on Juan's left.

"Stay down," hissed the figure on top of Juan.

A rotary cannon began to fire, a vast hail of laser shots scything through the Mara gang members in front. The crowd of people were screaming and crying out, panicking. More of the morphing figures appeared, each one neatly intercepting the Mara who were amongst the crowd, scything, ripping, cutting and tearing them apart in the space of a couple of heart-beats.

"On your feet," the figure roared, "with us, if you want to live."

"Who the Emperor are you?" Juan cried, scrabbling to his feet. Enforcers were running towards them, and more of the morphing people were holding them off now the Mara were despatched.

Juan was half-dragged in a run towards the exit, seeing a massive hover-truck outside blowing itself to pieces, the fire blossom raging against the reinforced metaglass windows. The entire starport was descending into chaos, as enforcers engaged with biomorphic beings, and more Mara emerged and tried to fight both morphs and armoured enforcers.

"Major Vantanik, Vindicator Mercenary Corporation," said the black-skinned character, his left arm turning into a large-muzzled weapon. A heavy blast of fire smashed through the emergency blast doors descending across the exit, blowing them to pieces. Juan had to close his unshielded eyes against the glare of the discharge.

Still seeing lights, he stammered, "You came then – thank the Emperor!"

"Into the car," said the Major, limbs morphed back into hands, lifting him up and through the blast doors, and then bodily propelling him into an open topped car. There was a driver already there. The Major jumped in beside him.

The car roared away, not getting into the traffic lanes but coasting below them, at a level dangerous to the pedestrians on the floor. It roared towards the commercial district, another four cars behind them with similar figures in them.

"What are you?" Juan shouted above the slipstream of the passing air. Enforcer vehicles were chasing them, and beginning to open fire. He ducked and screamed, before the force field activated and shrugged away the incoming shots.

"Cybernetic biomorphs," said Major Vantanik. "The best Marines ever made. Admiral Gavain really wants to speak to you, lad."

They were in an industrial district, heading past several warehouses. All of a sudden they made a sharp bank, and Juan screamed again as they passed through a door. It turned out to be holographic, and not solid. Before they passed through, he had looked back and saw a massive anti-aircraft weapon appearing out of thin air on the ground outside the warehouse, heavy thumps pounding the air as they blew the enforcer vehicles into shreds.

"What is that?" asked Juan stupidly, as the aircar smoothly stopped.

"You've heard of strikepods?" said the Major as they disembarked.

"Military starships fire them, usually into other starships or down onto planets for boarding actions or invasions," said Juan, "but that –"

"It works the other way," the Major grinned, obviously enjoying himself too much. "In you get."

There were ranks and ranks of the pods, elongated cone-like vehicles nestled within launch tubes, all of them pointing upwards. The roof of the warehouse was already peeling back.

Juan Ramirez entered a pod, the Major Vantanik strapping himself in next to him. There were twelve seats, and they waited for them to fill, vehicles roaring in. Juan heard other pods filling as more of the mercenaries arrived at the warehouse.

"What's going on?" he asked.

Major Vantanik looked at him. It was somewhat scary, being observed by two completely black eyes. "My biomorphic Marines are withdrawing here. The last in will be the squad left in defence of this warehouse. The pods will fire, and we will be thrown into space, before the orbital defence systems around Isdalsto Primary can react. This entire warehouse will detonate five seconds after our leaving the area. We have ships hidden in space that right now will be moving into orbit, and will collect us. We are getting you out of Isdalsto and to safety, Juan Ramirez."

He blinked. "Thank you, so, so much," he gasped. He wanted to cry.

"Do not thank me. Thank Admiral Gavain by giving us the information you promised."

"I'm going to meet him?" Juan stammered, unable to believe that his hero had saved him.

"Not straight away, he's a bit busy," the eerie Major Vantanik laughed, "but eventually, aye. Now brace, we're about to launch and make our escape." The pod's hatch was sealing.

A second later, there was a massive crump as the spacepod fired.

<Translation achieved ...... we are in the Isdalsto System, Admiral Adare.>

Adare was instantly bombarded with information about the military ships in system. Although a busy system, it was not heavily militarised and there were only a few minor Jorgensson military ships in the solar system. Of greater interest were the six ex-Praetorian Guard corvettes rocketing away from Isdalsto Primary. They were being pursued by two Jorgensson frigates.

He smiled.

<Identify those six corvettes,> he ordered.

<IFFs are not being displayed, visual identification not possible.>

<The corvettes are jumping, will be out-system in five seconds time.>

Adare realised that these were probably the VMC, and that he was too late to prevent their escape. They either had this Juan Ramirez with them or not. Regardless, he was under orders from the Solar Administrator of Dark Heart, and he had to follow them.

He smiled again. He was a dark man with a dark heart himself, and he very much did what he wanted.

Five ships, wearing Rose Pirates insignia, had jumped into Isdalsto under his command. The *Thor's Hammer* dreadnought was the flagship at the head of the V-formation, the *Patriot* P-class destroyer and the *Rebellious* R-class battlecruiser in the row behind, and the S-class strikecruisers *Slaughter* and *Superior* following at the edges of the formation.

<*Slaughter* and *Superior* to engage Jorgensson frigates,> Adare ordered, <*Retribution* and *Patriot* to run interference on Isdalsto Primary defences, and to take the passenger liner. *Hammer* to assume position above First City Starport.>

A couple of minutes later the *Thor's Hammer* was coasting above First City, turning to present its underhull towards the capital city below.

<Target the starport with all planetary weaponry,> Adare ordered coldly, <One full barrage, commence now.>

He felt through the datasphere rather than saw the multitude of weaponry firing downwards at the planetary surface, the terrible dreadnought unleashing a ferocious amount of fire centred on the starport. There would be tens of thousands of people within that starport and the surrounding area, all extinguished in seconds.

<First City Starport has been destroyed,> Commander Zehra Sahin reported moments later.

<All units, withdraw,> Admiral Adare said calmly. <Prepare for jump back to base.>

He sincerely doubted that this Juan Ramirez was down there in the starport, strongly suspecting that the corvettes they had witnessed jumping out of the system had been carrying the witness, but he had followed orders regardless and it was out of his control to influence now. The Solar Administrator would just have to accept that.

*

Kang Li held the Zhou-Zheng Compact rank of Shang Xiao, which was roughly equivalent to the old Imperial rank of Commodore. He was in charge of the reserve forces which had jumped into the Kyiv System, allowing the front-line units to move the battlefront on further into Erdogan territory.

Most of the subjugation of the system was taking place on the planets within Kyiv, not in space. Whilst he had operational control, and even now was sat on the bridge of his ship reviewing reports from various commanders in the field on the planetary surfaces, from a naval point of view all was quiet. Stellar traffic in and out of the system was non-existent, apart from Compact military ships and the 'deathships', the transporters taking Erdogan borgs to work camps further within the homeland.

Kang Li commanded the Compact battlecruiser *ZZCS Jingang*, a Type II Marauder-class capital ship manufactured by A-Zu Industries. It did not match the newer battlecruiser models coming out of the Nihima Corporation, Cervantes Military or Meridian Military Industries, let alone the brand new Compact-designed starships being produced by the alliance of Zhou and Zheng, but it was still a formidable opponent and just as common in many Houses throughout the colonised galaxy.

He had another two battlecruisers in the system, plus three strike cruisers, a star-carrier, and five defensive frigates, not including the various military transporters and support ships. It was a force seen as decent enough in size to protect the system.

He was only due to be on the reserve line for another month, and then was hoping to be given a front-line posting, as he and his ships cycled in to replace those on the forefront of the battle against the Erdogan abominations. He was not a man whose conscience was bothered by the genocide against the augmented freaks.

He was quietly and quite happily reviewing his contribution to the war-effort when he noticed a bit of excitement around the scanners stations. Frowning, he looked up.

The Zhong Wei in charge of the scanners section was already turning to him. "Shang Xiao, we have a problem."

"Explain," he commanded.

"We picked up an unusual signal, a trace which could signify that there is a camouflaged –" The scanners officer broke off, leaning over one of the consoles, "A sustained trace, it may be a ship out there."

<Admiral Gavain, we believe Hostile One has detected us,> Commander Georgia informed him.

Gavain was sat in the flag-chair on the bridge of the *Vindicator*. He and his ships had jumped in-system over two hours ago, coming in at a point where it was believed from intelligence that they would be unobserved. It turned out to be accurate, as the positions of the planets and the suns perfectly hid their translation into the Kyiv System.

The *Vindicator*, *Remembrance*, and *Revenging Angel* battlecruisers, *Queen of Egypt* star-carrier, *Solace*, *Shadow*, and *Snake-Eyes* strikecruisers, *Universal* and *Ubermacht* destroyers, *Kinslayer* and *Kingdom* interdictors, and *Odyssey* frigate had all jumped in undetected to the Kyiv System. The rest of his ships were undergoing repair at Kavanagh Shipyards in the Blackheath System. As Praetorian Guard military ships, and in greater numbers, they easily outclassed the House military starships in the system.

All his ships had engaged their chameleonic fields, and running silent, had approached steadily, speedily, but above all invisibly, heading towards their designated targets. Running silent they were unable to communicate with each other, but the chronometer showed that although it was two minutes earlier than planned, all his ships should be in position to attack now.

He stared at the holo-map in front of him, pinpointing the likely position of his ships, and the known positions of the enemy ships, all of which were tagged as Hostile One, Hostile Two, and so on. Hostile One was the flagship of the enemy, the *Jingang*.

<The command is given to open fire,> he said.

<Fire!> Commander Georgia ordered.

Out in the darkness of space, the peaceful nature of the Kyiv System was torn apart as the torpedoes loaded in the forward tubes of the *Vindicator* burst out into space. The chameleonically camouflaged hull of the *Vindicator* was displayed in searing light as the torpedoes roared away, crossing the relatively short distance towards the *Jingang*.

The *Universal* destroyer opened fire with a blistering barrage of long-range starboard weaponry, as it was actually ahead of schedule and already turned to present one of its flanks for the attack. The *Jingang* was a picture of destruction, its unshielded hull completely bare to the ferocious onslaught that suddenly assaulted it. The *Queen of Egypt* star-carrier joined the assault, firing weaponry, but also launching the first wave of its starfighters and bombers, which immediately zeroed in on Hostile Two, the enemy star-carrier.

<We will have translation into the Kyiv System in one minute's time, Captain,> the navigations officer said.

Jacked in, General Andryukhin caught the announcement made to Captain Delgado. He turned to Enrique, and said, <Let's hope Jamie has the system by now, or we're going to be fried.>

<He'll have it,> Delgado replied confidently.

Ulrik Andryukhin nodded, and then patiently went into parade-ground stance, awaiting the translation back into the Kyiv System. The minute seemed to take an age to pass, but then it was being announced that they were translated back into real-space.

<Confirmed that we are in the Kyiv System.>

<No active hostile threats detected, VMC ships identified.>

<Incoming comms from *Vindicator*.>

<Accept the transmission,> said Captain Delgado, shooting Andryukhin a look which said, 'told you so'.

Gavain had some of his attention on the holo-map of the system, as the communication was established and images of Captain Delgado and General Andryukhin appeared before him.

The *Monstrosity*, *Marvellous*, *Titan of Stars* had all jumped in system. The medical frigate and repair-ship were still out-system, having jumped into another system, and would only translate in if they were informed it was clear for them to do so.

The Zhou-Zheng Compact ships were a mess. They had been caught completely unawares by the hidden and camouflaged Vindicator Mercenary Corporation ships, which had unshielded and attacked with utter precision as soon as the *Vindicator* had fired. All of them had been unprepared for the vicious onslaught by the superior Praetorian Guard fleet. It had ripped through them, the flagship itself being so utterly damaged it had been abandoned by its crew after the first fusillade of fire.

Gavain's ships had taken so little damage it was laughable. The Zhou-Zheng Compact ships had just been torn utterly to pieces. Two of the frigates and one of the strikecruisers had managed to jump out. Most of the action in the system after that had consisted of the mercenary starships mercilessly destroyed the weakly armed military transporters.

<Ulrik, glad you could join us,> said Admiral Gavain. <The system is secure from a naval standpoint.>

<An easy victory, Jamie,> said Ulrik.

<An acceptable one,> Admiral Gavain replied. <Deploy your Marines to the surface. I want those deathcamps shut down hard, no prisoners amongst the Compact enforcers, and plenty of video footage of what was happening there. Use your Erdogan spy to inform the Feldmarshall that he can have his ships jump in at any point he wants, to deal with the Compact military now trapped on the planets, but we're only staying here for a couple of hours. We have liberated the Kyiv System for the Erdogans.>

As Ulrik acknowledged the orders, Gavain was already addressing the comms station. <Lieutenant Forrest, patch me into the HPCG station down there. I want to send a message to the StarCom News Media network.>

*

Star Marshal Ngu sat aboard his flagship, head in his hands. In front of him, the broadcast from the StarCom News Media network was playing, allowing him to see exactly what the traitorous Admiral James Gavain was saying to the rest of the colonised galaxy.

The holo-broadcast was showing pictures of his work camps, which they labelled 'deathcamps', to the entire colonised Galaxy. The heinous Sir Admiral Gavain was speaking.

".... we completed our contracts with the Zhou-Zheng Compact, but in the course of completing them, discovered the atrocities that the Compact was committing against borgs in their war of genocide. It is estimated that in Kyiv alone, already more than two million borgs have died as a direct result of these deathcamps, and another ten million are so badly malnourished that they require urgent medical attention and rehabilitation.

"I could not in good conscience allow this to go unanswered. The Vindicator Mercenary Corporation is a mercenary organisation, but remember that our roots go back to the Red Imperium of Mars and the Praetorian Guard, and we fought against the False Emperor partly because of his endorsement of such genocidal actions against unaugmented. We may be mercenary, but we have a code of ethics, and could not allow this situation in conquered Erdogan territory to continue. Not when we had a part to play in allowing it to happen.

"Entirely voluntarily, and for no payment or recompense monetarily, we have assisted the Erdogan nation in reclaiming the Kyiv System, to undo some of the damage we unwittingly caused. I am also going further than that. I extend the hand of friendship to any borgite Erdogan, any borgite in the colonised galaxy, and indeed any humanist who suffers similar persecution at the hands of a borgite nation, and offer you relief. If you are suffering in such a way as this, make your way to the VMC bases in the Blackheart System, in Levitican Union space, and we shall look after you. We shall provide you with a future.

"I have registered the Vindication Charity with the Interstellar Merchants Guild, which shall be used solely for the benefit of any refugees who need it. The money shall go towards ensuring that you are rehabilitated, saved from persecution, and –"

Star Marshal Ngu deactivated the holo-feed, and then slammed his fist angrily down into the desk.

Raising his head slowly, he called up a large scale holo-map of the Erdogan front-line. It had dissolved into chaos.

They now held the Kyiv System, an easy victory obtained by the deception of the mercenaries. He had thought it suspicious that the Chester System had been taken so easily; it now transpired that the Erdogan forces had returned, striking it hard. A heavy bulk of his forces were in the Odensa System, tired after the hard fighting there, and the Erdogan's had committed some of their reserves.

Ngu could order his own reserves into Odensa System, but it could be suicidal with the fall of Kyiv. He would have to order them into Kyiv again, and sacrifice Odensa. He could shore up Chester, but the fighting there would also get bloody.

He did have other mercenaries in the Odensa System, the Red Legion under the ex-Praetorian General Marcus Zander. His eyes narrowed as he looked at their icon on the map before him. He could not risk another betrayal. He immediately recorded and sent orders for them to be attacked without warning by his own House units. He hoped they were crushed utterly.

He cursed the Vindicator Mercenary Corporation and this Admiral Gavain with all his heart. Apparently they had already jumped out-system, so there was no chance of catching them and making them pay dearly for this betrayal.

His communicator went.

"Yes?" he snapped.

"Star Marshal Ngu," came a familiar and hated voice.

"Solar High Chancellor Zhou?" Ngu was confused. This was an intra-system communication, not a hyper-pulse transmission. "You are here in-system?"

"Oh yes," the delight in the Chancellor's voice was not hidden in the slightest. "The *Hei'an Zhuan* has just jumped in-system. The Primarch and the Primarchess would very much like to speak to you, in person."

Star Marshal Ngu swallowed. His head may not be on his shoulders by the end of the audience.

Chapter XIX

Juan Ramirez felt brilliant. He was free, and safe, and surrounded by his heroes. He stepped out into the cold air of the Tahrir Base, which apparently was a semi-secret installation maintained by the Vindicator mercenaries on the planet Tahrir, in the Blackheath System. He breathed deeply, enjoying the fresh, cold mountain air. It was summer on Tahrir, but here near the south pole, and at such an altitude, it was fairly bitter. Nevertheless, he felt like a god.

The gorgeous Lieutenant-Commander Bramhall and the very intimidating Major Vantanik stood at his side, watching the *Leopard* hoverjeep pulling up in front of them. Major Vantanik had assumed a visage which he assured Ramirez was just an adopted disguise, his natural form being the black devil-like beast he had seen back on Isdalsto Primary.

"Lieutenant-Commander, Major," said Commodore Andersson, returning their salute. He was driving. "Get in, all of you."

Juan Ramirez climbed aboard the back-seat of the *Leopard*, between the two mercenaries. A woman sat next to Andersson turned around and offered her hand. "I'm Doctor Erin Presson, Chief Medical Officer," she said, "and this is Commodore Andersson, commander of the VMC support forces here in Blackheath."

"Pleased to meet you," said Juan, smiling widely. The hoverjeep set off, banking and heading towards the mountain and the access point to what he would eventually learn was a vast underground base.

"I'm going to conduct a quick medical assessment, make sure you're fit and not carrying any implants, spying devices, or any form of device you shouldn't," Dr Presson said. "Assuming you get the all clear, we're then going to have to move straight into an interview."

"An interrogation," grunted Major Vantanik. At that, Juan started visibly.

"It's an interview, Major, behave yourself," said Commodore Andersson sharply.

Dr Presson smiled at Juan reassuringly, but something told him that her nice persona was designed purely to put him at ease. "It is an interview," she said softly, "interrogations are only something we do with prisoners, and at the moment we believe you are on our side, not that of the Rosicrux. If you do not mind though, it will involve a deep-level brain scan. We need to see what you've seen. We need as much intelligence as we can get on our enemy."

"And Admiral Adare," said Andersson pointedly.

"On everything," said Lieutenant-Commander Bramhall.

"Of course," said Juan Ramirez, swallowing his nervousness. "Whatever you need to do. You saved me, I'll help any way I can."

"We need the information rapidly," said Commodore Andersson. "Admiral Gavain will be returning to this system in three or four day's time. He wants the information and intelligence ready by then, so he can make a decision on our next move."

"Admiral Gavain? Will I meet him?" Juan asked.

"Possibly," said Lieutenant-Commander Bramhall. "I imagine he'd want to see you."

"As I said," Juan could not contain his joy, "I'll help any way I can."

As the *Leopard* hoverjeep pulled up, Andersson turned and looked at him. The intelligence of the man was obvious in his eyes and his look. He was weighing him up, Ramirez realised. "Yes, you will," said Andersson confidently, as if he had just passed some form of judgement.

*

Lady Wyn, as the new Head of House Zupanic, stepped onto the surface of the moon Zubrenica XIX. She was as heavily guarded as any head of house, both by Levitican Union Armed Forces and her own personal House Guard. With the deaths of three of her family members, she was taking no chances whatsoever.

Graceful despite her years, wearing all-black to signify her mourning at the loss of her husband, she began to walk across the military starport. News media crews were all around, recording her landing, doubtless hoping for some form of assassination attempt there and then. She paid them no heed, all the time unaware that she was being observed by something much darker.

Agent Black, the Faceless assassin in the employ of House Towers, watched her without any form of undue interest. He had assumed the form of a military guard, killing the previous incumbent of the body-shape he wore and replacing her. It had been his permanent form for some time now, whilst he waited for his next and last target to land on the moon.

As Lady Wyn walked across the specially reinforced and treated floor, he knew his target was now on the planetoid. He just needed the appropriate trigger event, which was the arrival of Lady Sophia and Lord Micalek, and he would complete the assassination.

Walking behind Lady Wyn was one of her manservants, a gentleman who had been in her service for decades. A long-serving member of the family, his real body was back on Zupanica, dead and deconstructed on a molecular level to prevent discovery.

The manservant was in truth a member of the Sixth Circle of the Shadows Council, a cybernetic biomorph, but he was also the leader of the group assigned to track and capture or kill the missing Faceless assassin. The only way to get a significant presence on the moon Zubrenica XIX, particularly as most of the interception taskforce had been on Zupanica, was to attach themselves to Lady Wyn.

The leader of the taskforce, a high-ranking Centurion, knew that a significant proportion of the people accompanying Lady Wyn to the temporary seat of the Levitican Union government were actually members of the Fifth and Sixth Circle. About ten were Faceless assassins, in itself a number not usually gathered in one place, and a further forty were covert operations specialists like him.

He was alert, quietly scanning the crowd, knowing that the missing Faceless assassin would be here somewhere, watching Lady Wyn. His entire taskforce was alert, ready for any attempt on Lady Wyn's life. Whether she was killed was not his concern, but the moment she was attacked, if she was attacked, they would strike against the missing assassin and take it down.

He and his team did not spot the assassin, nor was there an attempt on Lady Wyn's life, but it was surely only a matter of time. They would search in the dark and the shadows whilst they waited, but eventually, at some point, they would find their missing agent.

*

Juan Ramirez looked up into the sky, as the Freiderich-class lander began its short vertical descent onto Tahrir Base. He was at the front of the massed ranks of the mercenaries assembled on the open surface level of the base, stood with the senior staff. He had been given permission after his interviews and brain-scans to have free roam of some areas of the base, but he was not permitted to leave. He had no desire to leave. He wanted to meet the man descending from the sky in the lander.

The lander touched down, repulsors blanking out with deep reverberating thrums, silencers and inhibitor fields currently not engaged. The ramps were already opening, and revealed there was the person he most wanted to meet.

Sir Admiral James Gavain began to stride down the ramp, other officers following behind him.

With a stamp of booted feet the thousands of mercenaries behind Ramirez stood to attention. The thump as they slammed their right fists against the left breasts echoed around the mountains, and they grunted gutturally as they thrust the fists out at an angle into the air. The Imperial Salute was held until Gavain halted at the end of the ramp and returned it. Another massive stamp sounded out as, in one synchronised movement, the thousands of soldiers relaxed their stances back to parade ground rest.

Gavain walked straight up to his senior officers. Juan watched as Commodore Andersson stepped forwards, greeting Gavain quietly in person. He saw with interest how Andersson looked at Gavain, and realised in that split-second that there was more to their relationship than first appeared. He felt a surge of jealousy as he looked at the Admiral. Young, at little more than mid-forties, with centuries longer to live, he was much younger than the Commodore. He was closer to Juan's age than the Commodore.

He was also the most handsome man Juan had ever seen.

Gavain turned his head and looked at Juan. The young Ramirez saw the eyes widen ever so slightly, the hint of a smile on the famously impassive mercenary commander. Andersson turned sharply and looked at Juan, an angry look on his face as he stared at the two.

Then the moment was broken and Gavain was walking towards Juan, the hulking power-armoured form of General Ulrik Andryukhin behind him, Commodore Andersson on the left.

"Juan Ramirez, I am James Gavain."

"I – I know, Admiral – Sir Admiral," Juan stammered.

"The information you have given us is invaluable. You have changed more than you could ever know. My heartfelt thanks."

The pride Juan felt was mirrored only by his intense attraction. As the Admiral's steely grey eyes held his own, he stammered, "It is me who owes you thanks, Admiral."

"James," Gavain insisted. "We are not going to be on planet long, as we will be leaving shortly. I have a conference to hold with my senior officers. But later today, join us for our Last Meal. It is a Praetorian tradition before facing a dangerous engagement."

"I would be honoured," said Juan Ramirez.

"Good. If you're willing to accept it, we can find a place for you in the company. We need good navigators, and your score is exceptionally high."

"I – I don't know what to say," Juan stammered.

"Say yes," Doctor Erin Presson whispered audibly at his side.

"Yes, of course," he said. It was a dream come true.

On the second level, as they walked towards the large briefing room, Commodore Andersson said to James Gavain, "Why did you offer him a berth on one of our ships?"

"I want him close in case it transpires he is a spy," said James coldly, as they entered the briefing room. The auditorium was immense in size, capable of holding several thousand, but the senior officers of the VMC were all sat around the circular table at the centre. This was a briefing for the senior command staff only.

"Are you sure that's the reason?" Andersson asked.

"It is the only reason," Gavain lied.

"Doctor Presson has tested him thoroughly, there is very little probability of him being a plant for malicious information," Andersson said. Gavain did not reply, and they continued on, taking their places at the head of the circular table.

Gavain had Andersson, Andryukhin and De Graaf sat immediately around him, as the co-directors of the mercenary company. There was the traditional empty seat for Lady Sophia, the only other legal director of the group. She was currently on her way to Zubrenica XIX with Lord Micalek.

Gavain began speaking. "Staff, we all know why we are here. We have information about the pirates and the greater enemy we face, this Rosicrux conspiracy. We have agreement from a number of Houses, the mandate to assault and take their base of operations. All repairs to our ships and forces have been affected or shall be complete by the end of today, we have new recruits and new batches of Marines and naval personnel to replace those we have lost or increase our complements to full strength, so we are in the position to strike against the enemy. Captain O'Connor, if you could explain where our information and intelligence comes from."

Captain Jonathan O'Connor, as the intelligence chief, took over. "We have our information from a combination of a number of sources. We obtained some information from the *Vengeance* when we captured it, due to a partial and unsuccessful wipe of the mainframes. We have conducted interrogations of prisoners taken, including Captain Dolf Reichenburg."

Here O'Connor looked very serious. "Unfortunately, Dolf Reichenburg has been reduced to a vegetative state, and we were unable to extract the required information. It appears that there was a genetic malfunction and cerebral data virus inserted deep into his cybernetic cortex interface, which as he came near to breaking, was triggered violently. It is believed Reichenburg will never recover."

"It was particularly nasty," interrupted Doctor Presson, "I have only once before seen its like."

"And where was that?" asked Captain Enrique Delgado.

She looked at Gavain, who solemnly nodded, giving permission for the revelation to be made. "On a Faceless assassin we recovered," she said, "the same Faceless assassin that has formed the basis of the new biomorphic soldiers we are employing." At this Major Vantanik laughed, quite evilly, being fully aware of the source of his existence.

O'Connor continued, "The other primary source of information we have is from a mind scan and brain imprinting interrogation of Juan Ramirez, a civilian navigations officer who was taken to the heart of the enemy system. If you review the data-chips in front of you, the full story of how he came to be in that position and what he saw is presented. Suffice to say that we are satisfied that the information is genuine and we have made the strategic decision to pursue a plan of action based upon it. To the best of our technology, it tests out as being real and true."

As O'Connor sat down, the aged and respected Captain Danae Markos of the *Remembrance* said, "If Reichenburg was imbued with an advanced form of bioartificer technology that prompted a complete bodily malfunction, how can we trust this information from Juan Ramirez? Is it not possible it has been implanted without his knowledge?"

"We can verify some of the story," O'Connor replied, "through various intelligence agencies we have links with and our own information. Some of what he has shown us through his mind scan fits with images we took from the *Vengeance* when we captured it. There is a large part of it which is otherwise unsubstantiated, this is true, but as said, we have taken the decision to proceed on the ninety-seven per cent probability that this is good, genuine intelligence."

"The decision is made," said Admiral Gavain firmly. "Commodore Andersson, if you would explain what we know about this Rosicrux conspiracy."

Commodore Andersson stood, and as he began speaking, the holo-projector began displaying various images. The first one to come up was a symbol, showing a skull and cross, a crown, a rose, a sextant and a swan nestling at its bottom.

"This is the image of the Rosicrux, the party or parties behind the conspiracy affecting the Eastern Segment," he began. "The pirates have used various elements from this symbol to reflect their operations in different regions. The rosicrux has origins potentially going back to the 16th century on Earth, a rosicrucean organisation with foundations in the pseudo-science of alchemy, and links later in life to a secret organisation known as the masons. Such a thing disappeared as the human race emerged into space, so we do not make any link to this historical background, beyond that the conspirators in this modern time and age have decided to adopt it as their cover.

"We still require further details, but it is obvious that the pirates are part of a wider conspiracy to in each sphere they operate within, designed to deliberately destabilise the Eastern Segment, for reasons we are not yet certain of. Here in the Levitican Union, there seems to be some link to creating a war with House Jorgensson, and maybe even possibly bringing House Marchenko into the Union through House Zupanic.

"They have already been successful in sparking the Erdogan-Compact war, and appear to support the Compact. In the galactic south-west, they are stoking divisions between Cervantia, Hausenhof and Korhonen in equal measures. Near Amiens, they are provoking invasion by targeting a number of houses, including House Van Der Meer. They are provoking the war between the Helvanna Dominion and the newly-formed Aarlborg Alliance."

"What possible reason could they have for wanting to completely destabilise the entire Eastern Segment?" asked Captain Zane McDonnagh.

"That we are not sure of," said Admiral Gavain heavily. "Hopefully more will become clear if – when – we take the Dark Heart System."

"There could be any number of possibilities," said Commodore Andersson, "not least that the StarCom Federation has been rebuilding its military heavily, and is currently re-engaged in a small number of hostilities. They could be intending to renew their invasion of the Eastern Segment, with it significantly weakened. The presence of Admiral Adare and a number of supposedly 'ex-' StarCom Federation Praetorians could support that. But it is all conjecture, and we will only truly know once we have invaded the Dark Heart System.

"But anyway, what else we know of the Rosicrux. They may well have political links within the spheres they operate within. We have very recent intelligence from House Towers to suggest that the inclusion of House Marchenko in the Union was specifically sponsored by House Zupanic, and that House Lapointe was effectively threatened by the Rose Pirates into supporting that inclusion. It suggests at the least some influence of the Rosicrux on House Zupanic, or vice versa. Considering the galactic nature of the Rosicrux, it more likely they have some hold or agreement with Zupanic.

"We are also aware of a significant link between the Rosicrux and the Salchuzura Mara crime gang. It appears that certain members of the Mara are also Rosicrux members, and that they have manipulated the crime organisation to their own ends. This appears to widen the reach of the Rosicrux beyond just the Eastern Segment. We cannot be certain exactly what limitations there are on the Rosicrux, how far their power and reach extends, or even who the ultimate members are. What we do have, is this."

An image appeared, of a figure of a robed woman, with a white face-mask. "This character calls herself the Solar Administrator, and is based at the Dark Heart System. It is an old Imperial title. She is a priority target, and Admiral Adare refers to her. Considering also that her face is hidden, we can only assume that she is of a more senior rank in the Rosicrux Conspiracy."

The image changed again, another visual taken directly from Juan Ramirez' mind. "The capabilities of the Rosicrux are truly threatening just in terms of their reach and power, but their military might through the supposed 'pirates' is even greater than we feared. Here they are taking delivery of four InterStellar Hyperspace Missiles, ISHMs which are equipped with Tears of the Moon warheads. We know the Federation recently lost a number of the warheads and missiles with this technology, and that they are being sold on the black-market, supposedly. There is a real problem with the proliferation of these weapons, but to have them in the hands of the Rosicrux and specifically Admiral Adare, the first person to ever use the Tears of the Moon on the planet Alwathbah, is even more dangerous."

Andersson sat down. There was utter silence as the officers absorbed the information.

"This is a very serious and palpable threat," said Gavain, "one I will shortly be discussing with the various Houses that are paying us to pursue the pirates, or privateers, of this Rosicrux. Lucas, if you could explain about The Web, and the Deepspace Stations?"

Captain Lucas De Graaf stood. "The Dark Heart System is an artificial star system, deep in the Gulf of Medusa, surrounded by a cluster of black holes. Very dangerous and nearly impossible to reach, there are only certain approaches that can be made. We were also puzzled by how fast some of the Rosicrux ships were moving from one side of the Segment to another. It transpires that they were using something called The Web.

"The Web consists of a network of Deepspace Stations. Located away from solar systems, in the depths of deep space, the Deepspace Stations look like this –" an image appeared "- each equipped with stargates to enable fast travel. The Web is this network of stations, which all linked together allows access to the Dark Heart System. To travel there otherwise would take months, involve crossing vast distances of uninhabited and empty space, and be incredibly dangerous without knowledge of the flux of the gravitational pulls from the black holes. Virtually impossible, you could say."

"Where are these Deepspace Stations from?" asked Captain Thurman of the *Queen of Egypt* star-carrier. "Are they StarCom? Red Empire? Praetorian Guard? Something else?"

"We are not certain, but they bear very old Imperial designs," Captain De Graaf answered. "There are no StarCom markings on the stargates, either the StarCom from Imperial times pre-Dissolution or StarCom Federation, so we can only assume that the Rosicrux are operating these themselves.

"We've taken a guess on where these stations are within The Web, extrapolated from journey times for ships recognised in multiple attacks, the two precise locations we have for Deepspace Six and Fourteen, and images taken from the *Vengeance*. The Web looks something similar to this." An image appeared in the holographic viewer.

"What of this Dark Heart System?" asked the new Captain Al-Malli.

The image changed to a graphic representation, with cut-outs showing actual visuals of the system taken from Juan's memory. "The Dark Heart System is an artificial system, located in the heart of the black hole cluster. We have heard of artificial systems, in fact they pre-date the Imperium, but they are very rare. Why one should be built here, especially with a web of interconnecting Deepspace stations, we have no idea. There are three rogue planets, held in place and prevented from drifting into the black holes by massive planetary engines the design of which we have definitely never seen, and two artificial planetoids, all linked together by a complicated system of space corridors and space-lifts. Combine with that a large civilian space station, a mining base, two military starbases, an immensely huge shipyards, and a stargate, and we are talking about a large and complex system to assault.

"The system is hidden by a vast array of chameleonic fields of a size we rarely see, so even long-range astronomical arrays could not detect it, even if the black holes aligned in such a way as to provide a small window in from civilised space. There are numerous gun platforms in space and orbital defences on the planets. The planets themselves can support life, can grow food – in short, this is an exceptionally well hidden base system, fully self-sufficient, well armed, and well defended too."

"Phenomenal," breathed Captain Danae Markos. "I have never seen its like." There were a series of agreements from the other officers. "We genuinely have no idea why it was built?"

"None at all," Admiral Gavain answered. At this point he took over the briefing. "What we do know is that we have to assault it, and take it. This is going to be exceptionally difficult, and is without doubt our greatest challenge yet.

"We have significant intelligence on the starships in-system, with identifications on many. There are a large number of civilian starships and support ships there, many obviously abandoned and powered down. There are cargo-freighters, transporters, some fusion-tankers, passenger liners, mining ships, shuttle landers, tugs, barges and more - even no less than five ExCol colonyships centuries old. Some ships are ancient, others are more recent, obvious pirate bounty and salvage. The majority of the ship are not being used. We can also tell that the majority of the planets are not being used anywhere near to their full extent, and one of the starbases is empty. There are some old military starships – again, bearing pre-Imperial and old Imperium markings - which are also obviously unpowered and have been for some time.

"However, the gun platforms are primarily droid-controlled, and they are powered up, as is one of the starbases. There are defences on the planet which are droid-operated and are active, defensive satellite systems which are fully operational, and some indications of a military force both droid and Praetorian borg on the surface of the one planet Juan Ramirez visited. We have no idea of ground forces on the other planets, but there does seem to be a presence of some description on all five.

"In terms of active military ships, specifically the pirates, the news is worse. By piecing together known ships that were out of the system when Juan visited, ships we've seen in other attacks, and ships that he actually saw, we have a rough idea of their strength. Jonathan?"

O'Connor took over, the holo-projector changing to display each ship as he spoke. As he went through the known information on each and every one, Gavain reviewed the data mentally using his cybernetic implants.

The pirates had two dreadnoughts that they knew of, both T-class. They had at least eight battlecruisers, three star-carriers, ten strikecruisers, five destroyers, two interdictors, and nine frigates. It was the equivalent of a fully functional fleet in House terms, and even by Imperial Praetorian Guard standards it was still a small fleet. There were Praetorian Guard-designed military transporters, E-class and M-class, and H-class and D-class armed cargo-freighters, even two spare G-class fusion-tankers - not including the fusion-tankers located at each Deepspace Station. O'Connor finished his briefing.

"It seems like the odds are stacked against us militarily," said Gavain, "but remember that not all those ships will be in-system, as some will be out on raids. There is every chance that the majority will be out on raids, so we may even be a superior force when we assault the Dark Heart System. Unfortunately intelligence in this regard is limited, so we have no way of telling."

"What is the plan of assault?" asked Captain Markos. "How do we attack such a well-fortified and defended system?"

"Ah," and here Gavain gave one of his rare smiles. "There is indeed a plan. We are borrowing a number of fusion-tankers from the Levitican Union, to enable us to cover distance quickly, and for small strike teams to penetrate deep into the Gulf of Medusa. One team will head for Deepspace Six. Another strike team will make way towards Deepspace Fourteen. We will take both simultaneously, before using them to jump our own forces through the Web into Dark Heart ......"

Gavain explained his plan in detail.

Chapter XX

Lord Luke Towers was waiting for his sister as she and her husband, Lord Micalek, disembarked from their shuttle lander. Security was as heavy as it always was these days, and with three potential targets, it was exceptionally strict at the military starport today.

Lord Minister Luke Towers stepped up and hugged his sister, then extended a hand and inclined his head in return to Lord Micalek. "Sister, brother-in-law," he said, smiling, "it is good to see you both."

They began walking across to the aircars waiting for them. "You are last head of house to land on the moon, Sophia," said Lord Luke, without saying that if all went to plan, shortly Micalek would be the head of house for Zupanic. "There will be about two weeks of politicking before the votes is taken again for the Lord Principal."

"We have much to discuss," said Lady Sophia.

"Indeed we do," said Luke, taking a deep breath, "I don't want to be in the Council any more, Sophia. I would like you to stand in my place for House Towers."

There was a pause. "One is not surprised," said Lady Sophia. "One thought you would ask. We can certainly discuss that, and more. We also need to talk about other things –" her gaze deliberately went to Lord Micalek "- and, in addition, James Gavain has yet another suggestion which may well upset the Levitican Union once again."

"Gavain? What plan has he got now?"

"We'll talk about it. We also need to think about the Ministries. If we are to make all of this work to our advantage, we need a well-thought out game plan."

"We have an unexpectedly strong ally in House Lapointe," said Lord Luke, "and of course, House Zupanic." He did not add it would be even stronger once Lady Wyn was disposed of and Lord Micalek was in charge of the House. "Galetti is sometimes amenable to us. Claes votes for whatever Zupanic wants. But you were always better at this sort of thing than me, Sophia. That's why you should be here in the Council, not me."

"Let us get to a secure location, and discuss it further," said Lady Sophia.

"Certainly," replied Lord Luke. Before he got into his aircar, he looked around, knowing he would never spot the Faceless assassin that House Towers was using. Agent Black was out there, though, and the arrival of Lady Sophia and Lord Micalek had just signed the death-warrant for Lady Wyn Zupanic.

Juan Ramirez was on board the *Vindicator*. In one of the tiny crew bunk rooms, with nine other people preparing to get ready for their shift, he had never been happier. He looked at himself in the mirror. Wearing a smart Praetorian Guard Vindicator Mercenary Corporation uniform, he had the junior rank of Midshipman, the lowest possible officer rank. He was to undergo a series of additional implants, upgrading him cybernetically to Praetorian-grade operations. When the other crew got a rest and relaxation period, he was being educated in the way of the pre-Imperial Praetorian Guard. He could not believe how his life had changed.

Smiling broadly, he headed out of the bunk room and to the turbolift. The VMC did have a few non-Praetorian trained crew men in its ranks, and a special exception had been made for him. He was a trainee navigations officer, so had to shadow the third navigations station Sub-Lieutenant every shift. It was an amazing opportunity, especially for some homeless ganger from the dirty, crime-ridden streets of Cervantia.

The turbolift opened onto the bridge, and smartly he stepped through. He looked to one side, and saw Admiral Gavain in his flag-chair. The man looked up at him briefly, and a spark lit in the man's eyes. Once again, Juan felt the attraction.

He crossed the bridge, and sat in the spare suspensor seat next to the navigations station. The Sub-Lieutenant was due to arrive shortly, the Lieutenant of the previous shift still in place. Whilst he waited, Juan Ramirez jacked in.

They were in hyper-space, jumping towards their next destination, an unpopulated system within the fringes of the Gulf of Medusa. Most of the VMC fleet was moving together, before they hit their staging area, a point in deepspace far away from any solar system. There would be strike teams of ships moving deeper into the Gulf.

Juan knew that he might die soon, going into the Dark Heart System with the mercenaries. But it would all be worth it, just for the sake of having made it this far in his life.

He looked behind him, to see the eyes of Admiral Gavain on him again. He felt a warm flush, and turned back to look at the holographic navigations console.

*

Lady Wyn Zupanic exited the hovercar, stepped out into the dark artificial light of Zubrenic XIX moon. The temporary Council building was isolated, other buildings having been removed to provide clear space around it. Battlewalkers stood there on ceremony, but also ready in case there was any assassination attempted today on any of the heads of houses.

She began to cross the open ground, looking up into what passed for the sky on the moon. Most of the moon was covered in an air-dome, a shield to keep artificial oxygen within its confines, layers of defensive shielding resting above it. It was still possible to see the stars and the distant planet of Zubrenica Prime, poking out between the tall skyscrapers and spires that bracketed the Council building and the open approach grounds.

Agent Black was disguised as one of the Levitican Union Armed Forces soldiers, holding a sniper rifle. He had a spotter at his side, and a third guard who was pointing a gun at the two soldiers behind them. No-one was being trusted at the moment, not with a Faceless assassin still suspected to be on the moon.

Agent Black was not given to humour, but he would have laughed at the pathetic attempt of it all. As he looked through the sniper las-rifle, moving the scope slightly so he could identify his target, he realised the time had come.

Leaving the rifle where it was, his left hand morphed into a projectile-firing muzzle weapon, whilst his right arm became a long, thin, but lethal blade. As he decapitated the spotter at his side, he fired at the first of two sentries stood behind him. The second sentry was beginning to react as Agent Black's pinpoint silent shot ploughed through his brain, his right arm already swishing back and cleanly cleaving the last remaining trooper in the room apart.

The room was splattered with blood, but ignoring it and moving fast, he ignored the inferior Union las-rifle before him. His right arm morphed quickly into a far superior sniper rifle, projectile firing with laser bracketing to punch through shields.

He used his telescopic eyes to zero in on the form of Lady Wyn Zupanic, and fired. The shot smashed through her shields, and she collapsed to the floor. He did not stop to watch, seeing from the angle and initial blood-spray that it was a killing shot. He was already turning, body beginning to morph. He probably only had a few seconds to get clear of the building, and he would change and morph several times to escape.

The Centurion in charge of the Shadow Council's force on Zubrenica XIX saw the shot strike, and immediately he was contacting his taskforce. <All units, missing Faceless position identified. Strike, strike, strike, now.>

Agent Black had almost made it out of the largely empty room, an office in a warehouse once used for storing specific military equipment, when the wall at his side exploded.

He turned quickly and ducked as a blade swished over his head, slamming two blades back into the figure that had appeared in a super-human flash, emerging from the hole blasted into the wall, still with a strong cloud of splintering building material disintegrating around it.

Amazingly, the figure did not cry out or shout in pain, merely wrapped around the blades and swung its own again. Realising he was up against another cybernetic biomorph, Agent Black pulled into a back-flip, his feet and legs turning into blades in the blink of an eye and slicing quickly through the limbs of the person.

He rotated back onto feet again, and began a furious whirlwind of an assault on the enemy, cutting it to ribbons. Finally, the augmentation he carried within him realised that he had done enough damage, and he ceased. Five seconds had passed.

It was too long.

He dived through the door, as an explosive series of projectile shells slammed in through the window. His augmetic implants realised it was a thrustcopter, from the Levitican Union Armed Forces, but they were only human soldiers.

As he emerged into the open space of the warehouse, he tracked another three cybernetic biomorphs, two of whom began firing on him immediately. He was being chased by both the defensive forces of the Union and some unknown biomorphic force.

The Centurion was rapidly approaching the warehouse, in another thrustcopter. He thought quickly, but the mission parameters were well defined. Collateral damage was not only acceptable, it was going to be necessary if they were to capture or kill the missing Faceless assassin.

<All units, Levitican Union Armed Forces are not to intercept the target. Permission to engage and eliminate with extreme prejudice is not just given, it is ordered.>

And with that, he quickly shot the three troopers in the crew compartment with him, morphed through into the cockpit killing the pilot and co-pilot, and took the thrustcopter. He drove it towards the warehouse, firing missiles at the three aerial vehicles hovering above the warehouse, and then sent it in a dive towards the ceiling.

Agent Black stood, injured and feeling the physical pain from a number of wounds, five dead biomorphs around him. Another two were firing on him, pinning him in cover, whilst another three were busily hacking the LUAF soldiers who had tried to enter the warehouse into pieces.

If it had not been for the biomorphs, he would have escaped.

With a massive tearing crash, part of the ceiling came in.

Beginning to explode, a thrustcopter ploughed through the roof, a biomorphic figure jumping from it. It was firing at him as it glided down on artificial wings, the thrustcopter vehicle detonating properly behind it. One of the shots hit Agent Black and knocked him back, and then another two from the other biomorphs struck him as well.

Reeling, the figure that fell from the thrustcopter crashed into him.

The Centurion realised he had the missing agent under his feet, and instantly extruded a paralysing implant from his hand. He slapped it down into the face of the assassin, feeling it crush through the fake bone that gave way underneath his attack.

The injury was far from terminal, but the paralysing agent coursed into the biomorph, taking effect almost instantly.

<Missing agent secure, all units extract from the area behind me,> the Centurion ordered. <Provide covering fire for me, it is imperative I get the agent away from this situation.>

The Centurion grinned, using an implant to liquefy the biomorph, pumping the contents into a device he carried within him. It worked by miniaturising the liquefied contents, using advanced technology the Houses, StarCom, the Praetorian Guard, and every other instrument of the Red Imperium of Mars itself could only dream of.

The rest of his squads would die to ensure he escaped, before saving themselves. This moon was about to be torn apart.

*

The Council chamber was unusually quiet, the low chatter from the assembled House Lords and Ladies, their minor nobles, ministry officials and servants entirely missing. Most of them had been in the chamber when the dramatic events this morning had unfolded, and they had been kept here for their safety.

Gradually over the course of the day, as the security threat was considered dealt with, the remaining House members had been permitted entry, under a phenomenal amount of security.

The original plan had been for the Ministers to sit in Council, theirs Heads of Houses behind them, and officially open the discussion on how the Levitican Union was to proceed with the voting for Lord Principal. It would have been followed by at least two weeks of behind the scenes manoeuvring, before the votes and the ministry votes were taken.

The assassination of Lady Wyn had upset everything.

Lord Luke moved around the room, being constantly updated on the current security status. The entire moon was locked down. Even military personnel were not allowed to move freely, which presented some problems with security. Each and every one of them was being checked by House Towers' technology, in an attempt to identify more of the Faceless assassins.

Luke knew that it was their own Agent Black that had eliminated Lady Wyn, but the assault by a phenomenally large and completely unprecedented Faceless force had caught them all by surprise. The target was their stolen Agent Black, without doubt. However they had got on the moon, they had obviously been waiting for the strike, and when it occurred had taken their chance to re-capture or kill their missing Faceless assassin. Some biomorphic bodies had been recovered, but not many and even those were detoriated beyond reasonable attempts at post-humous analysis by some form of virulent destructive defence mechanism.

A number of the interlopers had just disappeared, so were presumed to still be on the moon. The damage the small force had inflicted on his soldiers numbered in the thousands. There had been sporadic engagements throughout the day. At least the Council did not seem to be the target, and a large defensive body, consisting mostly of droids, was providing their protection.

With all shipping embargoed, the survivors were most likely still on the planet.

As Lord Micalek entered the room, looking serious and grim, the entire room fell silent. He traded a glance with Lady Sophia, nodding slightly.

The Ministers went to their seats around the circular table, additional places set out for the Heads of their Houses. Lord Micalek looked lost, and had to be directed to a spare seat by the side of the podium for the Lord Principal.

Not for the first time, Luke wondered at the acting ability of Micalek. Like him and Sophia, Micalek knew more about this situation than anyone else. He knew as well as Luke that the target was Agent Black, and the mother he had betrayed, not anyone in this room. They were most likely safe, as safe as anyone could be in this day and age.

Lord Luke coughed, and stood up.

"In the absence of a Lord Principal, we have no-one to direct us," he began. He was aware that there were holo-cameras recording him, although the footage would not be released for weeks yet. "We must take action for the sake of the Levitican Union. Let me reassure all of you that I believe, although dangerous, the situation out in the moon is now contained. I do have a plan for us, and what we must do. But first, we must confirm who the new House Lord for House Zupanic is."

With that he sat down. Lady Monique Lapointe was the only one in the room who continued to look at him, as Lord Micalek Zupanic stood up.

"With the murders of my mother and father," said Lord Micalek ponderously, "it has been confirmed via pulse-channel that I am now the House Lord of House Zupanic. As Head of House, I will represent House Zupanic in the forthcoming elections."

With that, he returned to his seat.

Lord Luke stood up again. "Thank you for the clarification, Lord Micalek. Now, we –"

"Do you not wish to offer condolences on the death of his mother?" said Lord Moafa Obamu, his eyes glittering dangerously. The accusation was there.

"Lord Luke has done so privately," said Lord Micalek, lying smoothly. "Please, continue."

"How can you guarantee –" Lord Gregori Marchenko interrupted.

"– our protection, considering the current situation?" Lady Banuska Marchenko finished.

"Please, let me answer," said Lord Luke holding his hands up. "Ladies and gentlemen, as I said, the situation is contained but this moon cannot be considered safe. I have arranged for fresh ships from outside the system to jump to our location – they will be here shortly, within two hours. We have technology that can scan for cybernetic biomorphs, and every one of us in addition to our lander crews and soldiers will be tested before we leave this moon for good."

"Why was this technology not revealed and used before?" asked Lord Moafa Obamu quickly.

"We were not aware it would be required," said Lord Luke. That as far as it went was utterly the truth.

"Where are we going?" asked Lord Brin Claes. "Are we returning to our home systems?"

"No," said Lord Luke.

"Where then?" Claes pressed.

"We are heading back to the Newchrist System," and here Luke smiled. "The new city and Council headquarters have been built on the planet of Leviticus. There are new defences there, and we should be safe. During the journey we can discuss the future political organisation of the Union, and I find it fitting that we vote in our new Lord Principal back on the planet where we first formed the Union."

He sat back down, and awaited their reaction. There was a lot of discussion, which dragged on for hours as was so typical of the Union, but by the end of the day they were leaving, heading for the planet Leviticus.

*

Lieutenant-Commander Jason Bramhall heard the acknowledgement that they had exited hyper-space, but he was already focusing through the datasphere on the views outside the corvette he commanded. It was truly scary and frightening.

There was nothing out there, apart from the ships of their small strike squadron.

At some points in his life, aboard military starships, he had occasionally jumped into deepspace. It was unusual, and not recommended as without a proper way to re-charge the stellar vessel, if something went wrong you could be trapped, lost forever with no way of communicating effectively your distress. Never had he jumped so far, so many times, through deepspace like this, without even a layover at a solar system. That it had been their last jump was in some ways a relief, in other ways horrifying.

They were deep in the nothingness of space, but finally near their target. They had jumped to this position, far away from the enemy space station Deepspace Six, so they could approach running silent and hopefully undetected.

The fusion-tanker loaned from the Levitican Union would not be coming with them on the assault, its resources almost fully depleted. The fusion-tanker would only approach slowly behind the strike squadron. If the assault was not successful, not only were Admiral Gavain's plans shattered, but the crew of the fusion-tanker would be trapped in the void forever.

The plan was risky, adventurous, and so typical of something Admiral Gavain would put together. At the same time as they were assaulting Deepspace Six, another strike squadron would be targeting Deepspace Fourteen. There were numerous risks, not the least that one of the assaults would fail, or the enemy would be able to communicate they were under attack. Gavain did not want the full size of his attack force being communicated to the enemy, until they were in the Dark Heart System and it was revealed as they struck.

267

<Incoming transmission from Captain Markos, addressing squadron> his communications officer said.

<Play to the crew on the datasphere,> Jason Bramhall ordered.

<Aye, sir.>

There was the briefest of nano-seconds before Lieutenant-Commander Bramhall saw the image of the old, but incredibly efficient and experienced, Captain Danae Markos in his mind's-eye through his cybernetic implants. She began speaking.

<Strike Squadron Beta,> she said, <I will keep this brief. We have made our final jump, and your commanding officers should now have briefed you on the details of the plan, whilst on our last jump. Our role in this is clear, and the stakes are high. For us or strike team alpha to fail endangers the entire Vindicator Mercenary Corporation, nearly seventy-eight thousand lives in all.

<The order of approach is as follows – the corvettes *Adventurous*, *Aggressive*, and *Arduous*, under Lieutenant-Commander Bramhall will spearhead, and get in closest to the space station. The *Kinslayer* interdictor under Lieutenant-Commander Meier will follow. My battlecruiser, the *Remembrance*, and the *Queen of Egypt* carrier under Captain Thurman will be in the rearguard. At the given co-ordinates we will separate to our attack positions. Our assault must be swift and vicious, and exactly synchronised as planned. From this point on, we are running silent. You have your orders. Now let us carry them out.

< Best of luck to all of you – I know we can do this, in the name of the one True Emperor – and Sir Admiral James Gavain. Captain Markos, over.>

Chapter XXI

Admiral James Gavain was completely impassive, displaying his usual calm demeanour. He knew that his crew admired and respected it, his appearance of confidence allaying their fears and making them feel able to achieve the incredibly ambitious plan he had conceived.

In truth, he was nervous. There was much riding on the success of today, not just the conquering of the Dark Heart System and the disruption of this Rosicrux organisation or conspiracy.

The new Commander Erica Georgia sat at his side. He had every faith in her, her easy-going manner and comradely approach to the crew a distinct opposite of his. His third-in-command, the newly promoted Lieutenant-Commander Chu, was much more stoic, similar to him and somewhat feared by the crew. It was a good combination in the senior leadership team, he felt.

Admiral Gavain watched as the special mission chronometer ticked down. When it reached zero, his two advance strike teams would attack the Deepspace stations needed to get his main force through across the vast interstellar distance in mere minutes in real-time, and on to attack Dark Heart. Once committed, it was too late.

It was too late to stop the strikes anyway. His strike teams were far in advance of his main force.

There were a large number of risks associated with the battle plan, it being officially high-risk in any imaginable circumstances. Of the earlier occurring risks, particular possibilities were that they could not cut the Deepspace Stations off from The Web before they signalled back to Dark Heart that they were under attack, or that the initial fast assaults failed and his main force jumped in unprepared too near to a fully alert spacestation. His strike team ships may not have got into position on time, or the interdictors could activate in the wrong positions, creating a cataclysmic catastrophe as they jumped into an active warp-inhibiter interdiction field. There could be any number of enemy starships unexpectedly at either Deepspace station .....

He stopped thinking like that. They all knew the risks, worrying about them now was pointless. He had back-up plans for all of the possible outcomes, to turn disastrous outcomes into tolerable failures. To fail in this could not, and would not happen, he was determined.

Finally, the mission chronometer hit 'zero'.

<All hands, all ships, this is Admiral Gavain. We have mission time as zero. Operation Dark Heart has begun, and our advance forces will now be striking the Deepspace Stations. We begin our jump to Deepspace Fourteen in two minutes. Gavain, out.>

Gavain sat back, seeing his crew working hard, preparing for the jump. He felt the thrum of the engines through the ship, and knew the preparations were under way to begin the first jump to Deepspace Fourteen.

Right now, the preliminary strikes in the operation would either be working, or failing; if the teams had not been discovered. As with many naval engagements, the first few seconds and minutes would determine the outcome.

*

Lieutenant Sampson, captain of the corvette *SS Armageddon*, watched as the mission chronometer hit zero. Locked into the external viewing sensors, desperate for the first sight of Deepspace Fourteen, the time they had waited stationary here had made her tense and she had spent it pointlessly scanning the apparently empty void before her.

Running silent, and drifting without power for the last part of the approach, they had risked detection by using very under-powered forward repulsors to halt their slow drift towards the location of the Deepspace Station. They were so close to the chameleonically fielded space station, if indeed it was even there, that the risk of detection was inordinately high.

The *Armageddon, Avaricious*, and *Armoured* corvettes were chosen as the very smallest space vehicles, with the greatest chance of getting so close to the target with their smaller profiles and reduced energy signatures.

At the zero point, she ordered < Launch strikepods!>

<Strikepods launched, sir!>

<Shift position now!> she ordered. <Maintain comms silence until we are fired upon, as per orders.>

All three of her corvettes would remain chameleonically camouflaged, until they were successfully located and fired upon. Well within range of the station's weaponry, their only hope to avoid heavy damage was to shift locations rapidly.

Lieutenant-Commander Niesche had been given command of the interdictor *Kingdom*, captured from the Pirates of the Cross of the Rosicrux conspirators. He had once been a captain, of the battlecruiser *Revenging Angel*, which was also part of Strike Team Alpha. Serving in the StarCom Federation Army, he had lost the ship to the Vindicator Mercenary Corporation, but instead of being repatriated to the SCF, he was one of many who had chosen to remain with their captors.

He had been reduced in rank, but had proven himself admirably and had been given command of the captured interdictor on the orders of Admiral Gavain himself. He felt he had much to prove, and he was determined to play his part.

The *Kingdom* had been fully repaired, and was more than battle-worthy again. They had taken a position close to the corvettes, and part of their mission was to draw any fire away from those hidden but vulnerable ships in the immediate part of the battle.

When the mission chronometer hit zero, he was calm in his orders.

<Interdiction field to maximum,> he ordered, <Fire starboard broadside, full batteries, unrestricted fire permission granted.> As an interdictor, they had weaponry that rivalled a destroyer, and at this range such a broadside would have a significant impact on the Deepspace Station.

<Aye, sir.>

<Aye, sir.>

<Forward movement, begin roll, drop chameleonic field, shields to maximum,> he ordered in quick succession. As the interdiction field powered up to full within a couple of seconds, hiding behind a chameleonic field was pointless. The enemy Deepspace Station would know exactly where they were.

Captain Kenzie Viederhaun of the battlecruiser *Revenging Angel* was very popular with his crew, famed for his joviality and approachability. He was masterful, but also popular, with an undeniably wicked sense of humour.

This was one of those times when all his crew were deadly serious. There was no relaxed atmosphere, banter and relaxation on his bridge today.

The *Revenging Angel* as a massive capital starship was the furthest away from the target, but it was still within long-range fire. It could make a major difference to the battle, if the Deepspace Station was where they had been told it was, but it had to reduce range quickly in the first few seconds. At a higher angle than the location of the corvettes and the interdictor, it would come in from the galactic north-north-north.

The mission chronometer ticked to the numeral he had been waiting for.

<Full forward power,> he ordered, <Fore batteries to fire, Marines – strikepods will launch in approximately twenty seconds. Maintain chameleonic fields until we are fired upon.>

Captain Jonathan O'Connor was in his customary seat aboard the *Quintessential* star-carrier, and when the mission chronometer hit the zero mark he felt relief that finally the wait was over. As the commander of the squadron that made up the temporary formation of Strike Team Alpha, and the intelligence officer for the VMC, he was more than ready for anything.

<Launch first wave of starfighters and starbombers,> he ordered. Through the datasphere he felt the instant reaction to his orders, the small attack vehicles roaring away down their magnetised tubes. <Lower cham-fields, shields to full power,> was his next order, as the launches would give away their position all too well. <Fire port broadside. Begin forward movement at quarter-power. Roll on my mark ...... commence roll.>

Then he leaned forward, watching the strategic displays, aware that in this all-important first few seconds of the engagement, firing at apparently nothing, the mission and the overall operation would either succeed or fail.

Now, he felt the flood of tension.

The apparently empty void was torn asunder by multiple flashes of energy and objects, coming from a number of different directions but all focused towards one particular point in deepspace.

Strikepods rocketed at a fantastic speed, the nine vehicles carrying ninety mercenary Marines towards their targets. They would be the first to hit, even before the long- and medium-range energy weapons, the torpedoes, and MAC cannons.

The interduction field spread out in a massive envelope, unseen, although detectable by certain sensors. It was cutting off all access to hyper-pulse, be it ships trying to jump, or more to the point, messages being sent by hyper-pulse. Providing the Deepspace Station was there, it would prevent its HPCG from communicating a distress message back to Dark Heart.

Fire was coming in from all directions, but it was a tense moment for all concerned. Some ships had revealed themselves, others had not.

Then all of a sudden, the strikepods burst through the chameleonic fields of Deepspace Fourteen, and struck into the hull of the station. The Marines on board each strikepod had a nano-second to realise they had broken through the masking stealth field, before the pods slammed into the body of the space station, hard claws biting into the metal, lasers already cutting even as attractor beams pulled them in and locked them in place for added stability. Magnetic clamps fired, and the pods burrowed like ticks through the hull.

Even as that was happening, the chameleonic fields were failing as the fast torpedoes slammed through, dispersing the stealth shields as they detonated with vast explosions on their targets. Heartbeats later the first broadsides slammed heavily into the space station, sustained rates of fire following behind as fast as the individual batteries on the starships could fire.

The howling blare of the red alert signal roared into Commander DeShay's brain, startling him fully awake. He was in his private quarters, a level below the command centre, and had been asleep. Commander DeShay proudly wore the Rosicrux symbol on his converted Praetorian Guard uniform, having fallen asleep without removing the undershirt, only the outer jacket.

<Red alert, all hands, red alert, we are under attack.>

<Commander DeShay to the command centre.>

He was awake in an instant, his advanced cyborg physiology pumping combat drugs into his system. Grabbing the outer jacket from its untidy resting place, Commander DeShay of Deepspace Fourteen was already heading out of his quarters as he jacked fully in. He would be on the command centre in seconds.

<SitRep!> he demanded angrily.

<Under attack by unknown assailants, numbers unknown, ex-Praetorian Guard – two to six corvettes, an interdictor, a star-carrier launching third wave, potentially another two capital ships, positions constantly changing.>

<Warning!> the Major in charge of his Marines virtually shouted across the datasphere, <Enemy Marines aboard!>

<Return fire, drop chameleonic fields, up shields, repel boarders,> Commander DeShay roared as he entered the turbolift.

<Returning fire, aye aye sir.>

<Full shields in one minute thirty seconds, no coverage for fifty seconds, generators are cold.>

<Responding to boarders.>

<More strikepods being launched – battlecruiser detected!>

<Signal Deepspace Six, immediately, HPCG,> DeShay demanded as he emerged into the chaotic command centre.

<We can't sir,> said his worried comms lieutenant, <there is a massive interdiction field in place, and the enemy are preventing us sending a distress call.>

<We will have over a thousand marines on-board within fifteen seconds.>

<They've taken the HPCG Terminal. All ninety of the bastards,> his Major was roaring, <Came in around the HPCG Station.>

<Knock out that fucking interdictor,> Commander DeShay ordered, <And Major, get me back that HPCG Station. We must send a signal immediately.>

He knew from Admiral Adare that there had been a possibility they were compromised, but this was a fantastically choreographed, well-planned, and precise assault. They were sinking already, and sustaining incredible damage all along the main body of the station and the weaponry batteries.

*

Captain Danae Markos watched as Strike Squadron Beta opened up their fire on the position of Deepspace Six, using exactly the same pattern and method of attack as Squadron Alpha on Deepspace Fourteen would currently be doing. The corvettes had all fired their strikepods, to get the first boarding teams onto the space station and take control of the communications mast and station. The interdictor *Kinslayer* had its interdiction field on full within a heartbeat, the massive gravity generators pumping out a sphere of hyper-space disrupting energy. The star-carrier was launching its aerospace vehicles and firing at the same time, and her own battlecruiser was pumping a punishing amount of fire towards the reported position of Deepspace Six. There was a tremendous volume of fire unleashed in this first volley, designed to win the battle before it had begun.

The lasers, torpedoes, missiles, projectile and projection weapons, and the strikepods, all passed through the area where Deepspace Six was supposed to be. They were in deepspace, and there was nothing to stop the heavy weaponry fire, and the ninety men and women on the pods, flying on into deep nothingness.

With a mounting horror she was not used to, Captain Markos opened up the datasphere battlenet for the entire squadron, <Emergency,> she said, maintaining her calm, <Deepspace Six is not where it is supposed to be. We have been misinformed.>

Commander Mamani stood in the middle of her command centre, Deepspace Six's crew and systems telling her all she needed to know and more about the current situation. An ex-Praetorian Guard, she had willingly joined the Rosicrux organisation, a group which seemed to draw both loyalist and traitorous Praetorians to the Second or False Emperor, depending on your viewpoint in the war.

She had been warned by Admiral Adare of the possibility of an attack on Deepspace Six, but had not thought it likely. In the last second, as the reports of heavy weaponry fire, multiple ships both chameleonically shielded and not, and strikepod launches had flooded the datasphere, her first independent and private thought was that Adare had been right.

As a precaution, power-tugs brought in on a special interstellar ferry-ship from Dark Heart had pulled and pushed the Deepspace Station she commanded to another location. All Deepspace Stations that were part of The Web periodically changed their positions, although it was not common. Admiral Adare's precaution had seen to it that they had avoided this potentially dangerous ambush.

<Weaponry systems armed and activated,> her senior tactical officer reported, amongst many others.

<Do not fire,> Commander Mamani said, <they do not know where we are, do not betray our position just yet. HPCG, as soon as we have fired, send a distress call and warning message back to Dark Heart.>

<That will be impossible, one of the ships has produced an interdiction field.>

<Identify it,> Commander Mamani ordered, paying attention to the tactical holomap. The suspected locations of a number of chameleonically shielded ships were displayed to her, but of them, two ship locations were definitely known as they had ceased running silent. One was an interdictor, another was a star-carrier, still launching wave after wave of fighters and bombers.

<Target the interdictor,> she commanded, knowing it would prevent their hyper-pulse communication. <Knock it out quickly once I give the order to fire.>

<Priority target identified, Commander.>

Even as she watched the target, communications were able to identify the location of another ship, possibly a strike cruiser or a battlecruiser, which had begun broadcasting urgently on an open frequency. She knew they would be panicking right now, and she smirked to herself.

Lieutenant-Commander Bramhall thought quickly. The strikepods his corvettes had launched were fast, although some had already begun to fire repulsors to slow their comet-like burn away from the target zone they were supposed to hit. They could easily have carried on, into the depths of space, lost forever.

They had to be retrieved, he knew. Ninety people could not die for nothing.

They also had to find Deepspace Six. It had to be out here, it must be, he thought. They could not have come all this way on a dead end. If it were truly false information that had led them here, and there was no Deepspace Station with its stargate, then all of Strike Squadron Beta had come here to die a lonely, cold death with no way of getting to a safe star system.

Acting with speed, and knowing the vast manoeuvrability of the A-class corvette, he quickly programmed in a series of turns and rolls for his ship, laying over it a fire pattern. It would allow him to fire in every direction by using every weaponry system and quick repulsor and propulsor firing to shift angles. It was desperate, but it was all he could think of.

<Aggressive and Arduous to retrieve the strikepods,> he ordered, <Break comms silence. Helm, tactical, follow this flight and firing pattern simultaneously on my mark.>

<Aye, sir,> came a whole series of responses, and the datasphere told him his orders had been acted upon already.

<Mark!> he said, hoping against hope it worked.

<Corvette identified Commander Manami,> a scanners operator said.

<It's firing in all directions, random shots,> tactical said, <I think they are trying to find us – sir, we've been hit, location revealed to the enemy!>

<All batteries, fire!> Commander Manami ordered.

<Deepspace Six is opening fire, location identified!> said Captain Markos' scanners operator.

<Order all ships to attack,> Captain Markos ordered calmly, realising from the tactical map that the enemy was still in range of the interdiction field. They would not be able to communicate yet, but she watched as the enemy space station deliberately targeted the Kinslayer.

Ironically, the deepspace station's shifted position had brought it closer to her battlecruisers position. <Congratulations to Lieutenant-Commander Bramhall on locating the enemy. Marines be ready to launch, helm bring us in close, full propulsion. Present port broadside. Captain Thurman, get your star-carrier into a position to cover the Kinslayer, if we lose that interdictor we fail our objective here, and may as well go home.>

x

Even as her orders went out, she watched as the *Kinslayer* began to take an incredibly heavy battering from the Deepspace Six spacestation. It was going to be close, she knew.

They were already falling behind schedule, and although she would likely get her Marines onto the station, it may be too late. The timings for this part of the mission were very close, and if the *Kinslayer* was knocked out early, it was over. There were far too many risks in this plan, she felt, and Gavain had been too ambitious.

*

Admiral Gavain watched dispassionately as they neared the end of their weeks-long hyperspace jump. It was one of the wonders of faster-than-light travel, that although he and the majority of his force had jumped a small number of minutes after the simultaneous strikes on the Deepspace Stations were due to begin, in terms of transit time it would take them nearly two Standard weeks to reach their first exit point, even propelled by a stronger and faster stargate in friendly territory. In real time, their journey would take only seven minutes.

<Translation achieved,> his Navigations officer reported. As calm and as cold as ice, Gavain's only reaction was to raise his head.

<Confirm location,> Commander Georgia demanded, <Tactical feed, display acknowledgements of fleet arrival. We stay on red alert until I confirm all-clear.>

Admiral Gavain both watched the tactical holo-display with his eyes, and felt its information relayed to him through his neural link to the datasphere. It was amazing to watch, as the fleet materialised almost together in deepspace, scant nanoseconds separating their arrival.

They were arranged in a four-tined arrowhead formation, with the *Vindicator* battlecruiser at its head. Each of the four lines of ships were set a little further back and away at an angle, allowing full coverage of fire. The *Carnivorous* and the *Vengeance* battlecruisers were in position, and there were two gaps in the line, one for the battlecruiser *Revenging Angel* which was in this locale, and one for the *Remembrance* which was currently attacking Deepspace Six, all being well.

In the next tier were the four strikecruisers, *Solace*, *Shadow*, *Snake-Eyes* and *Scimitar*, the latter fully repaired and re-crewed after its capture from the 'pirates'. Next came the four destroyers, *Undefeatable*, *Universal*, *Ubermacht* and *Paralysis*. At this point, the plan was for the destroyers to move back and the star-carriers and the interdictors to occupy this third line on each tine, one of each also currently assaulting Deepspace Six. The *Odyssey* frigate, the three military transporters, and the lightly armed medical frigate and repair-ship were all in the centre of the formation, and they would be joined by the corvettes. The only ships not joining the fleet were the cargo-freighters, which remained in the Blackheath System.

Gavain surveyed the scene through the sensors; Deepspace Fourteen was revealed, unshielded and not camouflaged. The signs of a heavy firefight were obvious all across its hull, and his communications officer reported that it was broadcasting the coded signal on a secret comms channel indicating that it was mostly pacified.

<We are joining battlenets now .... datasphere meld achieved,> the data-tac officer reported.

<No active enemy detected.>

<Interdiction field deactivated.>

<Signal the squadron to join the fleet formation,> Gavain ordered, knowing that it was too quiet here for there to be an active enemy presence. <Patch me through to the theatre commander and marine commander. All ships to prepare for jump.> He then pulled much of his consciousness back from the datasphere, focusing on the images of the two people who appeared in the holo-display before him.

One was Captain Jonathan O'Connor, in the flag seat of his *Quintessential* star-carrier. The handsome man looked relaxed and happy, a large grin on his face. The other was a marine Major by the name of Chalmer, her helmet removed, and she did not look so relaxed. Her eyes spoke of some form of pain, and had the slightly glassy look of someone on combat drugs. A nasty wound was visible on her right arm, the armour in the area completely melted and scorched on the fringes by what looked like a plasma blast. Sweat was pouring off her, and a field medic marine could be seen temporarily in the background, moving away from her.

<OpRep?> Gavain demanded.

<The theatre is secure,> said O'Connor, keeping it short. <All went according to plan. We have the enemy fusion-tanker captured, and it will be crewed in our absence should we need it. There were no enemy ships in the area. We have control of the HPCG station, the stargate, the command centre, and all other significant targets.>

<Pacification of the station?> asked Admiral Gavain.

<Well under way,> Major Chalmer said. Her voice sounded hoarse. <We have some fighting in the lower decks. Casualties have been at approximately twenty percent – we were facing a small ex-Praetorian marine force. The station is secure. We need approximately three companies to hold the station satisfactorily after the fleet leaves.>

<The medical frigate will remain here until your casualties are loaded, then jump on to Deepspace Six,> Gavain said. <The plan called for five, are you certain three companies is enough?>

<Yes, sir.> There was pride in her voice, <We have exceeded expectation.>

<It will be done. You leave on the fusion-tanker when you receive the signal, as per the plan.> Gavain nodded, and her image disappeared. <Jonathan – what intelligence do we have from the datacore?>

Captain O'Connor grew very serious. <We are still sorting through some of the data, but we do not have full information on the Web of Deepspace Stations. Just one more, a Deepspace Thirteen in the outer ring of the Web, which also connects to Deepspace Six further in the Medusan Gulf. They obviously compartmentalise the data for added security. No real data on the Dark Heart System. We do have ship records passing through, but no identifications of military ships above and beyond those we have made – plenty of civilian ships though, smugglers and the like. No indication as to the location of the InterStellar Hyperspace Missiles, or the Tears of the Moon. I am ready to send the intel we do have back to base, though. Some of it is of interest.>

<You have my order to send the intel back to Commodore Andersson>

< We do have a significant issue, though, James.>

<Which is?>

<They have been using power-tugs to move Deepspace Stations in the inner ring. Deepspace Fourteen had to know so they could connect stargates. Strike Squadron Beta will be firing at an empty location.>

<I see,> was Gavain's empty response, although inside he knew that this boded very ill for their operational assault.

<Shall we jump outside the interdiction field?>

<We still jump as planned. The interdictor will lower its interdiction field at the planned time, in five minutes. It's just as well they have the additional time. We jump to the stargate in approximately two and a half minutes, aid the assault if it is struggling, and prepare for the fact the enemy may have already sent word back to Dark Heart.>

*

Major Edmonds saw the heavy-duty laser blast strike his adjutant to the wall behind him, burning partly through the armour, and quickly turned, diving to one side, his rotary cannon firing wildly. His visor targeted in on the shot and his left arm automatically tracked even as he fell, the projectile weapons stitching up across the corridor deep in the bowels of Deepspace Six, thumping into the enemy Marine that had suddenly appeared.

A missile roared down the corridor from one of the defenders, the entire corridor end turning into a roaring ball of flame. The enemy Marine, in Praetorian Guard armour, staggered out of the blast, still alive.

Having rolled to his feet, Major Edmonds continued to fire. On his left arm he carried a power-sword and an over-under double-barrelled plasma cannon. He fired both, the heavy beams joining the throaty roar of his rotary cannon, and finally the enemy Marine went down.

<Grenade,> he ordered, <ensure his death from a distance, and hold this line.>

He left the squad, down to five Marines, helping his adjutant to his feet. <Stay here, watch this corridor,> he ordered, leaving the injured adjutant in place.

He stamped back into the HPCG Station. Virtually his entire force had launched from the *Remembrance*, and he had led the assault in this section. They were trying to storm the command centre, but failing, being repelled by heavy resistance. At the same time they had taken control of the stargate and the HPCG, but the enemy were now fighting back.

<Major,> Captain Markos hailed him, <The interdiction field is about to lower. Do we still have the HPCG station?>

<Barely,> said the Major, <We need reinforcements, the enemy are fighting back heavily.>

<We can't get them to your location, the shields in your area are still active.>

<Anything, we need it,> said Major Edmonds, as another tremendous explosion rang through the corridors from below.

<I'll close the *Queen of Egypt* in,> Captain Markos said, <*Remembrance* out.> She mentally opened a link to Captain Thurman on the star-carrier. <Thurman, you have to close in on the Deepspace Station, deploy your Marines, now.>

<We will lose shields and take damage.>

<Do it, we are in danger of losing the HPCG station and we're lowering the interdiction field in forty-five seconds. We will have reinforcements shortly. We cannot allow this station to communicate with Dark Heart.>

<By your command, sir.>

<And drop some strikepods directly on that command centre, get it out of the fight.>

The situation was desperate, all hanging on a thread. Lieutenant-Commander Meier's *Kinslayer* had taken heavy damage, and after launching all the Marines on her battlecruiser, Markos had ordered it back as far as it could go, her own battlecruiser protecting it. Some of the space stations shields had failed, but its weaponry had done some damage to her own ships. Jason Bramhall's corvette, the *Adventurous*, was dead in the water and its life-pods ejected. Starfighters were screening them as the other corvettes, fresh from retrieving the strikepods, had returned to collect them.

Commander Mamani could not believe how furiously these Vindicator Mercenaries were fighting. They traded positions, taking up damage to shields before dropping back out to recharge, wearing down her own installations defences as they did so. She had lost shields in certain places, and fresh waves of mercenary Marines had begun to drop in. Even as she watched the tactical display, her tactical officer was informing her that the star-carrier had launched a major detachment.

The enemy had the stargate, and had knocked out a number of her weaponry batteries through marine assaults, meaning her power to damage was severely handicapped. They were determined to hold onto the HPCG, and Commander Mamani knew that especially with the interdictor present, it was to prevent her communicating details of the attack back to Dark Heart and summon help – or send a warning.

Commander Mamani was doing her best, but it was desperate.

A shadow fell across the command centre, through the metaglass, and then suddenly there was a massive thump. She looked up, and shouted, <Strikepod on the observation window, internal blast shutters -> but it was too late.

Even as more strikepods slammed into the metaglass observation windows above her, the first one had cut through. The glass did not shatter, but the piercing tongue of the assault craft had opened up a hole, and enemy Marines were dropping down.

Even as her own Marines, desperately defending outside, tried to leave their defences and come back into the command centre proper, the few that were still present were mobbed, targeted quickly. Some of her crew drew weaponry, she herself pulling out a deadly high-powered hand-laser.

The Marine with the Vindicator Mercenary Corporation badge on his suit of armour zeroed in on her, and with horror she realised it was carrying two chemo-flamers, one on each arm. Even as the multi-laser on its shoulder fired laser shots in every direction, she saw one of the muzzles coming up.

She screamed in pure, instant but short-lived agony, as the chemical flames ripped across the command centre killing numerous crew before it touched her, skin peeling back, eyes cooking, bone crumbling under the pure, unbelievable ferocity of the vicious anti-personnel weapon.

<The command centre has been taken,> Major Edmonds announced. <We only have to hold another twenty seconds.>

He turned as a major explosion sounded deep inside the control room of the HPCG Station, the decking above cracking in. He did not know how the enemy had managed to get this far, but he watched as four of them came down even as the flames from the detonation were slamming one of his Marines to the decking.

The Marine on the floor died with a power-sword being plunged viciously through the back of his head, the helmet and armour weakened in any case by the Rosicrux pirates' explosive entrance.

Firing his rotary cannon, Major Edmonds took out the sword-wielder, focusing all his fire upon that person, correctly identifying it as the leader.

The firefight became desperate, personal shields being engaged and used by the Marines as they fought each other. Major Edmonds at one point was thrown back, a plasma cannon burst removing part of his helmet and completely shutting down one eye. He suspected it was lost, but his augmented body's implants compensated, nullifying drugs pumping into system within a nanosecond of the injury being sustained.

They had taken down the four enemy Marines, but he had lost five of his own in the process. <Plug that hole,> he demanded, <Portable shields.>

He checked the chronometer. <Interdiction field going down,> he said. <Now or never people, hold on, no surrender!>

Lieutenant-Commander Meier saw that the chronometer had hit the designated time. <Deactivate interdiction,> he ordered, mirroring the calmness of the man he had once served directly under when he had been a mere Commander in the Praetorian Guard, James Gavain.

<Interdiction field down, confirm, interdiction field down. All clear.>

Come on, Gavain, he thought to himself.

Lieutenant-Commander Jason Bramhall stormed onto the bridge of the SS *Aggressive*.

The Lieutenant in command stood, moving to the next chair. <You have my ship, sir,> she said.

<Command accepted,> said Bramhall tersely. His brief time in a life-pod, having lost his own ship, had wound him up unbelievably. Even though he was credited with finding the hidden deepspace station, it had been at the cost of his own corvette, the *Adventurous*. It was dead in the water, but could be salvaged if necessary and with time. It was out of the fight for now, however.

Gavain, we need you, he thought.

Captain Danae Markos heard the report come in.

<All starboard shields failing, failing .... gone. Both flank and upper shielding fully depleted.>

<Present the underside,> she commanded.

<Underhull shielding at twenty-one percent of nominal, estimate one minute at current rate of fire.>

She checked the tactical display. The *Queen of Egypt* was pulling back, but had lost some of its shielding, and was taking damage. It was just thankful that her own Marines had managed to knock out so many of the enemy batteries.

<Translation detected!> came the shout, <Massive ship formation coming in! Stargate-powered, fast translation expected, ten seconds. It's large, fits the profile for Admiral Gavain.>

Please, thought Captain Markos. Please, we need this, don't be the enemy.

Admiral Gavain was calm as he was told that the fleet had fully translated in.

Even as battle-nets were joining, he realised that the situation here had been difficult. He could tell from reading the holo-displays. He was surprised only one corvette had been lost, but resisted the urge to wince as he looked at the heavy damage the *Kinslayer* had taken. His battlecruiser and star-carrier had not fared too badly, with what seemed like mainly superficial armour damage, although even that could be telling in what he knew was to come after this assault, the invasion of the Dark Heart System. The *Remembrance* had taken heavy damage to one of its nacelles, and the *Queen of Egypt* had vented variously between three and seven decks into the void from what looked like four heavy torpedo hits.

<*Kinslayer* to raise interdiction field, *Kingdom* to assist,> he ordered. The interdiction field would ensure no interstellar communication could be sent.

He began to demand situation reports from Captain Markos, even as he was ordering his fleet to break formation, and additional Marines to be ploughed into the Deepspace Station. The Rosicrux Marines at Deepspace Six were fighting much better than those at Deepspace Fourteen, but then, they had that crucial element of surprise and preparation at the beginning of the engagement.

Now he had his fleet here, however, and the interdiction fields back up, this could only end with a victory for the VMC.

It had been close, he was to realise later, as they had come within a hair's-breadth of losing control of one of the primary objectives within the station, the hyper-pulse communications generator. Only the superb actions of a number of his senior officers and their daring crew and Marines had prevented advance warning being sent to Dark Heart.

If, he thought darkly, this was not all a trap and Admiral Adare already knew they were coming anyway.

Chapter XXII

The stargate within the Dark Heart Artificial System was undeniably of StarCom design. StarCom had existed for centuries, the primary communications and transport provider of the old Red Imperium of Mars. The design of the stargates had changed little, although to the connoisseur, there were small indications that this was one of the really early Imperial builds.

Commodore Canning acted as the Chief of Station for the Dark Heart Stargate, as well as commander of the heavy ring of defences either side of the immense, circular portal. It was the only real way into the system due to its distance from other systems and even the Web, not to mention the black hole cluster of Dark Heart itself, deep in the wilderness of the Gulf of Medusa. He quite liked his role. He had taken it early in the revitalisation of the artificial system, prior even to the Dissolution of the Imperium, being one of the first to set foot in the system as it was taken out of mothballs.

He knew much of the Rosicrux organisation, more than most perhaps, but he was old and nearing the end of his days. He was happy knowing he was doing his part for something he once believed in, but at close to four centuries old, he had perhaps one more decade of life left. He had reached the limit of genetic engineering and modern medical science. This Rosicrux organisation, although it had an ultimate objective he believed in, was turning out to be something he was not sure he entirely agreed with in terms of how it went about achieving it.

It was early hours Imperial Standard time, although time meant very little in an artificial system with no sun. He preferred the third and final night shift, and always took it, purely as it seemed to suit his body clock.

Sitting in the small command centre of the station, he looked around. It had been upgraded since its StarCom days with ultra-modern and advanced technology, and allowed him complete control of all the defences. He had stationary droid-controlled gun platforms planted all around the two stargate terminus zones, heavy clusters of roving drone minefields outside those zones, a number of slow-moving battery-barges constantly shifting position, as well as two ageing B-class frigates for defence on roaming patrol, not that any of it was likely to be needed. He had heard Admiral Adare's warnings that there was a possibility their existence had been uncovered, but nothing else in the intel reports suggested any immediate threat, and besides which, it was so difficult for even friendly ships to make it to the artificial system, no hostile enemy could make it easily or without detection. He would have plenty of warning.

He did not like Silus Adare. He knew of his reputation, and he did not trust him.

<Commodore, we have a hyperspace pathway-lock incoming from Deepspace Six.>

He frowned, his cup of revitalising energy drink touching his lips. As he drank it and swallowed, he said, <Are we expecting any incoming?>

<No, sir, they hit terminus zone A in five seconds. The hyper-space signature is very large, multiple ships.> Coming from another stargate, even a huge fleet could translate unexpectedly in a few short seconds due to the pathway-lock between stations; if a large fleet jumped in elsewhere there could be several minutes of warning before they landed.

He felt a stab of fear as he saw the read-outs from scanners. An unexpected arrival from one of the deepspace stations was not rare, it happened quite regularly as the various 'pirates' could hit unexpected problems and delays, but this was an incredibly large force. Perhaps Adare had been right. Yet, nothing and no-one could strike them here, surely? This could not be hostile, it did not bear thinking about.

As he thought, he knew he had to follow protocol and sound a limited amber alert, and bring his defences up to battle-readiness. However, while he agonised, time had marched on.

His delay was costly, as the stargate opened and within a nano-second and a bright flash of light, the enemy fleet arrived in-system.

With his ship on red alert for the last half an hour of transit-time, and weeks of transit-time in preparation, Admiral Gavain felt more than ready for this. He had participated in countless large engagements, the largest of which was the Battle for Mars. Possibly though that was also the only other time he had had so much personal interest at stake in his military life. Even the majority of his crew and staff did not know why this was so important to him.

In the last few seconds before they exited, he addressed his ship.

<Remember; we have numerous objectives in this system. Of all of them, our primary, must-have objectives are the Dark Heart Stargate, the military starbase in orbit around Alpha, and the HPCG Station on Alpha. We take and hold the planet Alpha as quickly as possible, and make our stand there against the superior numbers of the enemy in space, whilst our ground forces move through the platforms to the other planets. We must uncover information relating to system defences, and the locations of all the Web Deepspace Stations. Identifying the Rosicrux organisers is a secondary objective at this time. Locating, securing and if necessary destroying the Tears of the Moon-equipped warheads is also a primary objective. We must hold for the given mission time; remember, no matter how bad it seems, however much we suffer, we must, will and can hold. We have the advantage of surprise, we can and we will do this. Good luck all of you, in the name of the one, True Emperor.>

The datasphere went quiet following his address, the social chatter non-existent, itself something highly unusual even when going into a battle situation. The last few seconds drained away.

<Terminus point reached, translating now,> said the helms Lieutenant Vries, suddenly.

<Full fleet translation in effect!> said Lieutenant Agrawal, the scanners officer.

The large bridge crew sprang into action, the entirely quiet bridge suddenly exploding into activity as each man and woman concentrated on their given tasks. Admiral Gavain concentrated on the tactical data being fed through to him, checking first that his ships had all arrived, and then looking at the enemy dispositions. He immediately noticed that the stargate was not even on active alert, which was odd.

<Lieutenant-Commander Bramhall, launch your Marines at the stargate now,> Gavain ordered, <before they get shields up.>

<We're attempting to hack the stargate defences, not being successful so far, they have updated code and defences,> a data-tac officer reported. <No aggressive attacks received yet, only automated passive.>

<Admiral Gavain is a daring bastard,> said Commander Zehra Sahin, on board the T-class *Thor's Hammer*, watching the display as the ships jumped in. <A five second warning, through the stargate – he could only have done that by taking the Deepspace Stations.>

<Indeed,> Admiral Adare smiled, standing up and stretching, before balling his hands into fists. <The game is afoot. Sound the red alert through the system, all defences to go active.>

On the display before him, he could see the disposition of his own ships easily. He could not believe that Gavain had fallen into the weakness of trying an attack on the Dark Heart System. Only seven of the Rosicrux ships were out-system, conducting two piratical attacks. The remainder he had kept in Dark Heart, much to the fury of his Rosicrux masters. Now however, he would be vindicated through that decision he knew.

Jamie, Jamie, Jamie, he thought to himself. You over-reach yourself. Your eighteen ships-of-the-line against my thirty-two, in a heavily defended military base? You do not have a chance.

Being fair, Adare knew that Gavain was very resourceful, and more than likely had some outrageous and daring plan for this battle. Adare could see that he had brought his entire fleet with him, including his military transporters.

<They will be going for one or more of the planets,> Adare predicted. <Squadron One and Two are to combine and head towards the stargate. Squadron Five to form up, prepare to run interference on wherever their military transporters head for. My orders are given.>

<Shall I signal the reserve squadrons, three and four?>

<No, they are running silent. They will assume position around the incoming VMC fleet, we must leave them to it,> said Adare. He always had two of his squadron's hidden, running silent, and two on open display, having expected today to come. <They go on my command only.>

Commander Sahin looked questioningly at Adare, and across their private link, said, <You were expecting him to come?>

<Of course I was. Don't tell the Solar Administrator, but that's why I ordered we jumped later than planned into the Isdalsto System. I wanted Gavain to come, and this was the only way to get him here. We have unfinished business.>

You are truly insane, thought Commander Sahin, but kept the thought to herself.

<Signal the *Vindicator*, I want to speak to my old friend,> Adare said, an evil smile upon his face.

Aboard the *Vindicator*, Admiral Gavain had given the go-order for his small fleet to move on to the first target. They had been in-system for less than two seconds.

Commander Georgia gave the orders to the bridge crew, and they began to respond.

<Moving ahead, full propulsion achieved in ten seconds.>

<Targeting the frigate, positive ID as *SS Brotherhood*.> As Gavain heard the report, he knew that various ships in his squadron were going for the *Brotherhood*, whilst others would be targeting the *SS Brilliance*.

<Shields at full power in forty-four seconds.>

<Weaponry batteries ready to fire in nine seconds.>

Gavain watched the tactical display, seeing that his formation was being maintained perfectly, the result of ceaseless training when not on contracts. He kept his navvies and his soldiers well-drilled. He paid more attention to the enemy, and frowned.

Identifications were beginning to come in, the enemy opening up their Identity Friend or Foe signals. Gavain ordered the same, on the basis that if the fighting became mixed and formation cohesion was lost, at least it would prevent accidental firing on your own ships. The IFFs were coded and not open, but intelligence was able to identify most of the ships out there.

There were a number of frigates moving throughout the Dark Heart System, but already they were pulling back into cohesion, forming into a squadron. The B-class frigates near the stargate were trying to move away as well. Adare had obviously ordered them to abandon their patrol of the stargate terminus zones on the basis they were greatly outmatched.

The ships he could see were roughly arranged into two squadrons, one above the point where Dark Heart Epsilon was supposed to be, the other out at a point where it could move in to cover any of the planets. As the sigil came up for the *Thor's Hammer*, Gavain identified this as the lead squadron. In total, they numbered one dreadnought, five battlecruisers, a star-carrier, four strikecruisers, two destroyers and an interdictor. A formidable force, but nothing like what there should be in-system. The planets in the Dark Heart System, their bases and the shipyard, were all chameleonically hidden, so the void looked empty.

The other ships could be out on raids, but instinct warned Gavain that this was a trap. There were too many of the enemy starships missing, and not enough reported raids on nations and Houses outside the Gulf of Medusa.

The two squadrons were coming in on a heading where they would pincer his fleet as it moved forwards.

<Incoming fire, droid gun platforms revealing themselves.>

<Returning fire, returning fire.>

Gavain saw that the corvettes had unloaded their full complements of Marines, and were now circling the Stargate.

<Incoming hacking attempts, firewall resisting successfully, code and programming unidentified.>

<Hail from the *Thor's Hammer*, Admiral Adare requesting communication with you, sir.>

Gavain looked up. <Ignore the man,> he said, not wanting the distraction or to play any more games with Silus Adare.

<They are ignoring our hail, Admiral.>

"Naughty, naughty, Jamie," Adare actually spoke aloud. <How long until Squadron One and Two meet them?>

<They are accelerating to full propulsion, away from the Stargate. We will have interception in four minutes, at which point they will be fully shielded. Corvettes are remaining in vicinity of the Stargate. We are likely to lose it, they have launched too many strikepods at it.> Commander Sahin replied.

<It does not matter.>

<They obviously do not know where the Dark Heart planets are, they are heading on a course that will bypass it completely.>

Adare narrowed his eyes. He suspected a feint, but equally, maybe they had not got all the intelligence from Juan Ramirez that they had wanted.

In the depths of space, the four-tined pyramidal formation of the Vindicator Mercenary Corporation ships ploughed on, returning fire against the gun platforms firing at them. One of the Rosicrux frigates was successfully powering away, although it was taking heavy damage from multiple VMC starships. The second, the *Brilliance*, was under such heavy fire it was already listing, with power losses and hull ruptures on its still unshielded form marking it out as being the first ship out of the fight.

The frigates had never been intended to take on such a large force, and so they had suffered at the hands of Admiral Gavain.

As the formation continued to advance, striking with unerring accuracy against the static gun platforms thanks to their intelligence, and also making some headway against the battery-barges, the lead elements began to fire in a scattered pattern on the approximate positions of the minefields in their way. The mines detonated as they were caught in the searching fire. The minefield began to detonate in a continuous roil of flame and explosion.

It was like watching an old sea-borne naval fleet advance, except instead of a major bow wave of water, it was preceded by a wash of pure high-explosive flame.

Colonel Petra Raimes had all one hundred and eighty of the corvette-borne Marines on the Dark Heart Stargate. They had left the damaged *Adventurous* at Deepspace Six with the repair-ship, and had doubled up within the strikepods. They had been unsure of how strong the enemy defence would be, but Raimes had discovered that the enemy was not here in great numbers, at least in terms of Marines.

She carried a heavy-duty twin lasercannon on her left shoulder, and it neatly drilled through the Marine before her, punching a hole right through the Rosicrux symbol emblazoned on its chestplate. She jumped forwards and drove her power-sword through the hole and up, driving it through the Marine's throat and into his brain. All around her the fighting had become close-quarters, and although it raged with viciousness and she lost some people, it was all over in seconds.

<We have the first approach to the command centre,> she said. <All squads, report.>

<Second approach ready.>

<Third approach ready.>

There was a long delay, and then <Fourth approach ready.>

<Set thermal charges and detonate on my command,> she ordered. They had to take the command centre first, obtain what intelligence they could, and then systematically clear the rest of the stargate whilst holding the nerve centre of the installation.

Admiral Adare watched as the enemy ships moved closer in. Squadron One and Squadron Two would be joining together soon, rendezvousing before they continued the interception. The delay was in his favour, he felt, as rather than rushing to engage, his ships would be fully shielded and prepared as much as the mercenaries. It also gave longer for his hidden, silent-running ships to get into position.

The mercenaries obviously knew far too much about the stargate defences, as they were ripping through them. The formation of ships had begun to rotate, the four extended tines revolving in a clockwise direction to prevent any ship taking too much damage as the gun platforms were disposed of.

As the two fleets of ships continued their fast advance towards a rendezvous point, Adare began to think to himself that Gavain obviously wanted a head-on confrontation. He was slowing his starships down, falling to half-propulsion and then one-third. They were still heading on a direction parallel to the chameleonically shielded Dark Heart planets and installations.

Commodore Canning gave the order for the data-core to be wiped, even as the thermal explosives went off and huge holes appeared in two doors, the floor, and the ceiling of the command centre. The mercenary Marines came in, guns blazing.

Canning tried to defend, pulling out an automatic shotgun, his shots shredding the armour of a person wearing a colonel's insignia on its helmet. He howled in pain as the demon came forwards, ignoring the heavy hail of fire, and took his arm off his shoulder with a wet, wrenching sound.

Combat drugs prevented the injury from knocking him unconscious, but in his elderly circumstance and prone position, he was powerless to do anything but watch as the mercenary Marines lay waste to his command centre crew.

A mercenary Marine had broken off from the fighting, and before he lost consciousness, Commodore Canning saw and felt in the datasphere that it had successfully penetrated the datasphere and the data-core. The virus that flooded the local battle-net shut him down completely, much as it did everyone else on the stargate.

His last thought was to wonder how much information the accursed mercenaries had been able to retrieve.

Gavain watched the situation carefully, determined to time this to the best possible moment.

Finally, it arrived.

<All ships,> he ordered, <Keep rotation, change course directly to Dark Heart Alpha.>

He sincerely hoped the enemy had not moved the artificial system's planetary bodies using the massive engines constructed on the surface, or he would really be facing disaster. He also felt sure that there were more ships out there, perhaps disguised by the chameleonic fields of the Dark Heart System.

Lieutenant-Commander Bramhall, aboard the *Aggressive* corvette, received confirmation from Colonel Raimes that she had the command centre. His own data-tactical officer was telling him that the enemy datasphere in this region of space had been successfully penetrated.

He commanded a private communication to Colonel Raimes. <Petra,> he said, using her first name, <You have penetrated the data-core?>

<Mostly, they were wiping it. We have some information coming through now, feeding it to you. I must go, we have the rest of the stargate facility to pacify.>

<Understood. Bramhall out.>

Jason Bramhall then stood, nervous despite himself as he accessed the information being fed through from the stargate. Using their greater communications ability, he ordered his comms officer to send the information on to fleet advancing with Gavain, even as they accessed, deciphered and sifted the data-stream for the intelligence they were looking for.

<What are they doing?> Adare virtually screamed.

<They have sharply changed course, avoiding our interception, and are heading directly for Dark Heart Alpha,> reported Commander Sahin calmly. <They also have transmissions being relayed from the stargate, it's safe to say ->

<I don't care about that stargate, I want Gavain. Change course, after him!>

Commander Zehra Sahin gave the necessary orders, but already knew that Gavain had pulled off a superb manoeuvre. As they had changed course, there had been no warning because of the rotation of the fleet formation. They had done so rapidly, the formation pulling apart and re-forming into waves of ships, the military transporters protected in the middle. It was like watching a ball of string unwind as the ships completed the action perfectly, accelerating to full propulsor power with unbelievable acceleration.

They already had a significant head-start on the Rosicrux ships, and even worse, because of the angle at which they had set off for Dark Heart Alpha, it extended the time it would take Adare's ships to catch them. The mercenaries had even more time to assault the Dark Heart System directly.

It was a reminder of why Gavain had earnt the reputation he had.

<Admiral, do you want to order the chameleonic fields on Dark Heart to be dropped, so defensive shields can be raised?>

<No!> screamed the insane Admiral, <I want Gavain caught and dead before he gets there.>

<He is already almost in firing range of the area. We can't catch him ->

<Do it!>

Gavain quickly scanned the intelligence feed coming through, relayed from the stargate through the corvette. There was plenty of information, but sadly the golden nugget of information he wanted was not amongst it thanks to the partial wipe. He had predicted that would be the case, but luck in battle often ran in your favour as well as against, so he had not given up hope.

The *Vindicator* was firing its forward weaponry into the deep void, and within a heartbeat it was progressively joined by the rest of the small fleet as they crossed the pre-determined firing line. Chameleonic fields glittered and in some instances failed as the volleys of sustained weaponry fire broke through the special, disguising energy fields, and the Dark Heart System was revealed in all its glory.

Gavain remained impassive, but inside he was smiling. Their information had been correct, the Dark Heart Artificial System was where they had been told it was. No more of the Rosicrux military ships were revealed, but he saw in an instant that the defences had been re-arranged, added to and strengthened. It reinforced his growing suspicion that they had been expected.

<Gavin to Bramhall, send one of the corvettes back through on a jump to Deepspace Six with this intel, disposition of the enemy as known currently, confirmation that the secondary objective of clearing the stargate terminus zone of enemy defences has been successful, a full report of the engagement so far, and ensure that the information is transmitted via HPCG back to Commodore Andersson.>

<Aye, sir,> came the response.

The *SS Armoured* turned sharply in space suddenly, the other corvettes clearing the area quickly as the stargate began to power up. With a snap of light, controlled by the Marines who had stormed the command centre, the stargate activated and the *Armoured* was pulled into hyper-space, jumping back to Deepspace Six.

1st Lieutenant Abraham Salvador, in his *Great White* super-bomber, was protected by a screen of starfighters as they arrowed at incredibly fast speeds towards Starbase Alpha. The approach of the fleet had been carefully designed and planned to allow a heavy strike by all the fighters and bombers the two star-carriers and various starcraft the fleet's ships carried could manage. Hundreds and hundreds of vehicles were ranging ahead of the fleet, and the starbase had been revealed to them, unshielded, undefended, but with weapons hot.

They had rocketed past the frigates in defence, ignoring their fire as the capital ships of the VMC were already firing upon them with a withering hail of fire. The four frigates were already dropping back, trying to obtain the protection of the starbase and failing miserably. He ignored incoming fire coming from both the *SS Obliterate* frigate and the starbase, and grinned as they hit the launch zone.

<Squad, launch torpedoes on the starbase, I want five firing rounds before we switch targets to frigates>.

Torpedoes whirled away from the super-bombers approaching the starbase, and battle was joined properly. The frigates were in disarray and under heavy fire, and the fighters and super-bombers of the Vindicator Mercenary Corporation were covering the starbase like a vast swarm of blood-sucking insects leaching the life from their victim.

Unshielded the starbase began to take damage, aided in no small part as the destroyers opened up with their blistering long-range fire. The VMC formation began to break apart, Gavain having ordered his capital ships to target the four enemy frigates caught around the starbase.

Medium-range was struck for the starships, and strikepods were launched, carrying Marines towards the starbase before it could raise its shields. Although the starbase was returning fire at a blistering rate, and orbital gun platforms were doing their best to add to the volume of return fire, it was beginning to suffer under the heavy bombardment.

The military transporters *Monstrosity, Marvellous* and *Titan of Stars* had broken away from the formation, zeroing in on Alpha, braving what fire came their way. Within range of the planet, as things were now moving so fast in the engagement, they launched strikepods down towards the surface at known targets. Landers began to detach from the two M-class transporters, slower-moving but higher in capacity as thirty thousand Marines crowded down towards the planet Alpha. The *Titan* was keeping its eight thousand Marines in reserve, ready to drop them in support where necessary.

<Admiral,> said Commander Georgia, <Initial strikes on the planet and starbase successful, Marines aboard. The enemy squadrons will be in range to support in thirty seconds time.>

<Thank you, Commander,> said Gavain. Using his connection to the datasphere, he marked new targets for his forces. He commanded the starfighters and bombers to switch targets, dealing with the enemy frigates, one of which was already dead in the water. He painted several targets for his capital ships on the approaching squadron of Admiral Adare.

<Destroyers *Paralysis* to support ground forces, *Odyssey* to support engagement on frigates,> he ordered, <all ships turn, rear batteries to fire on starbase but prepare for full engagement with Adare's squadron. On my command we move back to the starbase, but only on my command. Hold position.>

This was a risky part he knew, engaging the enemy capital ships whilst the starbase was still active, but there was little he could do. They just had to obtain the intelligence he needed and hold out as long as possible.

1st Lieutenant Chaveux led his squad into the weaponry battery of the starbase. Their strikepod had landed just up the approaching corridor, easily battering through the unshielded starbases armour. Whilst a full two companies were targeting the shield generators, most of the Marines had landed on the starbase in scattered formations, close to the weaponry batteries. It was imperative to shut them down, and then take control of them.

He carried a chemo-flamer and a heavy-duty large yield twin laspulser, a machine-gun version of a laser weapon which spat death towards the enemy as his squad attacked the naval crew inside. Unarmoured, they cut through them. Another squad maintained guard on the entrance to the battery, as his mercilessly butchered the small battery station's crew.

Covered in arterial blood spray, Chaveux confirmed to his commanding officer that they had the battery. The reply he got included some tactical information; amazingly, there were fewer marines than they thought on the base. It was nowhere near full complement, the same story as on the stargate. It appeared the Rosicrux had plenty of ships and naval crew, but less Marines than they required. It would be interesting to know if the same situation was true down on Dark Heart Alpha.

Talking to his squad, he ordered, <Hack into the local system, isolate it from the battle-net. Take full control of the battery – we need to be ready to fire in support of the naval ships. Squad Beta, hold the door, make sure we are not interrupted.>

General Ulrik Andryukhin felt the usual exhilaration of storming into war. It was without doubt what he lived for. With the engagement well underway, and his own Marine force reinforced up to full strength with aggressive recruitment, he felt more than prepared.

He had chosen to descend to the planet Dark Heart Alpha in the first wave of strikepods, rather than take a safer option on one of the landers. He wanted to be in the vanguard of the assault. Even more importantly, he had chosen to lead the attack on the HPCG Station, intending if he were successful to make it into his temporary headquarters building. He wanted to be leading any attack on the *Thor's Hammer*, taking Adare in revenge for the death of Julie Kavanagh, but he had been overruled by James.

<We hit target in six seconds,> Sergeant Calaman said.

The hyperpulse communications generator was one of their primary targets, and with a very good reason. It had been another reason he chose to land there. The strikepod was coming in directly onto the building, its shields carefully destroyed by orbital laser fire and a couple of specially targeted squadrons of bombers and fighters from the *Quintessential*.

He looked at the data the strikepods limited sensors communicated to him, an instant before they hit. The HPCG Station was still operational, but it was open and relatively undefended. The enemy had not expected for them to target this area. His strikepods were coming down within a restricted area of the planet, his landers separating into the seven different drop-zones corresponding to the seven secondary and tertiary targets required.

<We're down,> he said, <fucking do it, people!>

With his unorthodox command, he led the exit from the strikepod.

The specially designed strikepod had landed Captain Zuo's heavy *Executioner* battlewalker on the boundary of the HPCG Station's perimeter, and he forced the machine to smartly step out from its egress hatches. Another battlewalker was carried in the strikepod, another *Executioner*.

Opening fire with automated anti-personnel weapons, he focused more on the main building for the HPCG station. Running the twelve-metre tall machine forwards, the twin-cannon MAC fired heavily at the building, ripping it open, allowing him to use the left arm-mounted power sword to widen the gap even further.

He began to fire inside at the screaming Rosicrux personnel, as he said to General Andryukhin, <Pathway established, General.>

<Thanks, Captain, hold the perimeter,> Andryukhin demanded, using a repulsor-pack affixed to his suit to jump through into the centre of the building, his squad close behind him.

<We are possibly detecting strange signals, potentially a ship approaching on silent, although this not confirmed,> the scanners officer on the *Vindicator* said.

<Keep vigilant, open fire if positive detection is confirmed,> ordered Commander Georgia. <Admiral Gavain?>

<I suspect we are about to be surprised, there are more ships here, there have to be,> said Admiral Gavain. He watched the tactical display, hearing the report that Adare's squadron was almost in long-range firing distance. The starbase was falling more and more silent, his Marines meeting lighter resistance than expected, and every second that passed brought more weapons batteries on the huge military installation under his control.

<Incoming comms from General Andryukhin.>

<Private channel,> said Gavain instantly. An image of the General appeared in his mind's eye. <Ulrik, what news?>

Andryukhin was smiling wildly. <We have the bastards, Jamie. I'm transmitting the data now. We caught the HPCG station unawares, they didn't have time to wipe the data-core. They're strong in naval terms, but in Marine forces, they're running light, even utilising droids. This is going to be much easier for me than I thought, much harder for you. I have the location of the hyperspace missiles and the warheads, they've been moved to Beta. We'll get them with a fast push over the space-lift and space-corridors between the planets.> Here Andryukhin actually laughed. <And we have full details of the Web, every location of every Deepspace Station.>

<Do you have access to transmit the data through hyperspace?>

<Yes, we do, just starting it up now.>

<Excellent,> Gavain nodded, <Use the HPCG Station to transmit the data back to Deepspace Six, and on to Commodore Andersson. Do it now. I'll have a corvette jump out with the information as an added precaution. Gavain out.>

His fleet and Adare's had begun to trade long-range shots. He had ordered the starbase they partially held to restrain from firing until they had targets within short-range, he wanted absolute destructive ability. He then sent a coded message to all his commanding officers, informing them that they had achieved what they needed to.

He had barely finished when the scanners officer roared, <Positive trace, ship detected running on silent – and another – two traces, potentially cruiser-sized!>

<Firing now,> his tactical officer announced.

<No –> shouted the scanners officer, correcting the earlier announcement, <One battlecruiser, one T-class dreadnought!>

Out in the depths of space, a number of the mercenary starships opened fire on the two Rosicrux ships running silent. They had strayed too close, and as the torpedo spreads rocked through their shields, followed closely by missiles, turbolaser, particle acceleration and magnetic acceleration cannons, even disruptor emitters as the two targets were astronomically so close, the chameleonic fields failed.

The Rosicrux pirate ships buckled under the damage, and immediately began to return fire as they lost their element of surprise, but the return fire was weak in comparison. They were taking full broadsides, and only able to respond with forward batteries. The unshielded battlecruiser SS Reverence took heavy damage and immediately showed it, but the immense dreadnought SS Terminator was able to weather the incoming fire.

<Two of our ships are discovered,> said Commander Sahin.

Adare immediately accessed the information on the datasphere, and within a nano-second realised that his two additional squadrons of ships were incredibly close to Dark Heart Alpha and Gavain's fleet.

<Send the signal,> he commanded, <Ships are to open fire and cease running silent.>

He watched as the signal went out, and then clenched both fists, grinding his teeth in pure animal vengeance as he watched the vast number of starships lower their chameleonic fields, firing simultaneously on Gavain's capital ships. It was beautiful to behold.

Outnumbered two ships to one, Gavain did not have a chance. It could be over in minutes.

Adare's trap had worked.

Chapter XXIII

Commodore Andersson was in his own command centre, a purpose-built section within the headquarters level of Tahrir Base in the Blackheath System, in the Levitican Union. He was a fairly large part of the galaxy away from the battle that he knew, right at this very minute, was taking place in the Dark Heart System.

This was quite possibly the riskiest mission they had ever undertaken as a mercenary outfit. A long-serving member of the Praetorian Guard in the Red Imperium of Mars, he was no stranger to this sort of tension and worry, but since he felt his relationship with James Gavain had deepened, this time round it was much more personal. Perhaps not even the Battle of Mars at the end of the Imperial Civil War had caused him this much pain.

When the first message came in, thrown through hyperspace by the captured Deepspace Station Six, he had hoped it contained everything they needed. Unfortunately, although rich in information, it did not contain that little bit they were looking for, the details on the positions of the Deepspace Stations in the Web.

Although hyper-pulse communications were virtually instantaneous, with time-lags so reduced that even an enhanced cyborg would have to focus to detect the time differential, this information was slightly more out of date, by perhaps a minute in real-time. That was because the corvette had to jump from Dark Heart to Deepspace Six to convey it.

The next eighteen minutes and twelve seconds were therefore absolute hell for Harley Andersson, and felt like the longest in his life.

<Incoming message by pulse-channel, Commodore,> someone suddenly announced.

<Feed it through,> he ordered, accessing it immediately. "Yes!" he actually said aloud, as he realised the Web had been fully uncovered. The size of the forces Gavain was facing out there made him pause in horror, but it was unavoidable. He was now the key to ensuring his lover and the tens of thousands of mercenaries out there made it through the hellfire they were now experiencing.

<Coding up the data-packets,> said Commodore Andersson, selecting the launch programmes and orders, <Send them, immediately!>

Tahrir Base sent the information to the HPCG station on Blackheath, and Andersson's part in this was complete.

*

General Andryukhin knew the battle above his head in space was not going well, but there was little he could do. The climate on Dark Heart Alpha was fairly temperate, and it was their false, artificial night-time, so it was actually possible to see through the sparse cloud cover and actually watch the starships fighting each other. At this distance from the action, it was surreal, but it was a sight he had seen before.

He had left the temporary headquarters he had set up in the stargate, and was leading the next part of his force on to the location of the InterStellar Hyperspace Missiles and the Tears of the Moon warheads. As his *King Cobra* HAPC led the attack on the space-lift, breaking through the light automated defences, he estimated it would be another twenty-nine minutes at least before they made it to the immense missile bays that was his assault force's target. It would have been ideal to have the *Titan of Stars* drop its eight thousand Marines on top of the missile bays, but that was impossible with the major naval engagement going on overhead.

His forces were storming through the defences of Dark Heart Alpha. Numerous planetary gun batteries had been seized, and were pumping fire up into the air at the engagement, targeting enemy ships. The Solar Administrator had already been captured in a major offensive on the capital city. The land battle was an amazing success. The naval battle was turning against them, after the initial success.

About four real-time minutes had elapsed since the transmissions had first been sent.

The *Vindicator* was extremely heavily damaged, at six minutes in from the transmissions. Its starboard nacelle was utterly destroyed, and it was trying to engage the enemy by keeping its starboard side away and unpresented, but the fighting was so fierce it was impossible. Despite that, it was leading the fight, taking some capital ships on through a defensive group to target the *Thor's Hammer*. Admiral Adare was only too happy to oblige.

The careful formations of both fleets had fallen apart in short order, and now the entire battle was a very messy skirmish. Starbase Alpha had surprised the Rosicrux when it opened fire heavily, targeting the Rosicrux forces. The volume of fire was heavy, and more than compensated for the outrageous arsenal the two T-class dreadnoughts alone carried. The Vindicator Mercenary Corporation ships stayed close to the starbase and the planet itself, drawing the Rosicrux in, and a further surprise was in store for the Rosicrux when the planetary defences began to open up on them. It went some way towards evening the odds, but did not make it a fair fight by any stretch of the imagination.

The Rosicrux frigates had been caught early in the firefight before the fleets fully engaged, so apart from the *SS Navigator*, which was limping heavily away towards Dark Heart Beta, all the others were dead in the water.

The *Vindicator* finally broke through, with the *Remembrance*, to attack the *Thor's Hammer* at close-range, something which would ordinarily be suicidal against an enemy dreadnought. It helped mitigate the danger that heavy turbolaser shots and torpedoes streaked into the *Hammer* from the starbase, battering its shields and destroying them with a glittering spark on the overhull. Super-bombers peppered the *Hammer* with torpedoes and thermal-bombs, before both the *Vindicator* and *Remembrance* launched their strikepods at the heavy dreadnought. Payloads delivered, they turned rapidly, attempting to retreat back towards the covering fire of the starbase, the *Hammer* engaging both of them simultaneously.

The Remembrance was suffering even worse than the *Vindicator,* with a great many of its decks open to the void and high losses of life. It was about to lose effectiveness, and was certainly reduced in terms of fighting power. The Rosicrux strikecruisers *SS Lightstar, SS Linebacker* and *SS Sabotage* were zeroing in on it. It had perhaps a few minutes more to survive under that rate of fire, if that.

The starbase and planetary defences were making a huge difference, a masterstroke of Gavain's in targeting the batteries and choosing his site of battle beforehand, turning the enemies weapons against them. Adare's surprise with half his fleet running silent was more than enough to tip the balance, and at this point, it was obvious who was going to win.

Thousands and thousands of starfighters and starbombers were engaging one another, screening damaged ships on both sides and leading vicious sorties. The death toll was running high for both sides.

The *Queen of Egypt* star-carrier was heavily damaged, under attack from the *SS Unperturbed* destroyer, *SS Cathedral* battlecruiser and within firing range of the *Terminator*. It had lost half its running lights and power, and was effectively already out of the fight.

The *SS Patriot* and *SS Prosecutor*, both planetary-attack destroyers for the Rosicrux, were attempting to engage the planet below from long-range, but Captain O'Connor had brought the *Quintessential* and the previously heavily damaged *Kinslayer* interdictor in to punish them both.

The Vindicator Mercenary Corporation strikecruiser *Snake-Eyes* took a heavy hit from the *Thor's Hammer* as it pursued the *Vengeance* and *Remembrance*, a full broadside opening up on its deshielded form. With a huge explosion the engine block at the rear was ejected, tumbling away before it detonated spectacularly. Opened up to the void, emergency fields kicking in, it began to lose power. In seconds life-pods were streaming away from the stricken vessel.

The VMC *SS Solace* and *SS Shadow* were being battered by the Rosicrux *SS Quiet of the Void* star-carrier, the strikecruiser *Sanguine* and battlecruisers *Reverence* and *Reproachful*. Suddenly, the VMC battlecruiser *Carnivorous* and *Revenging Angel* were there, firing on the *Reproachful*, inflicting heavy damage and lowering shields. Strikepods were fired from both, and a vicious boarding action began aboard the R-class Rosicrux ship.

The Rosicrux battlecruisers *SS Violator* and *SS Voracious* were viciously pounding the VMC strikecruiser *Scimitar*, and with a flash of light the bow of the ship exploded under several direct torpedo hits, heavily brutalising the forward batteries.

The Rosicrux ships *SS Venomous*, *SS Slaughter*, *SS Superior* and *SS Serpent* suddenly wheeled away from the complicated fighting pattern, pulling together as they broke through the VMC lines. The four VMC destroyers were fighting at long-range, adding their power to the planetary defences and the starbases, battering the heavier Rosicrux ships. The starbase shifted targets quickly, focusing on the V-class battlecruiser, but the faster strikecruisers broke through, obviously intending to close the distance and wreak havoc at close quarters with the destroyers and provide some relief for the beleaguered heavier capital ships of the Rosicrux.

The *Thor's Hammer*, already under a boarding action itself, came within range of the struggling *Vindicator* and launched its own strikepods, throwing Marines at the vessel. Moments later the *Remembrance* and the *Kingdom*, itself heavily damaged and about to be knocked out of the fight, launched more strikepods, this time at its flagship the *Vindicator*, to help repel the boarders.

All was chaos, all was vicious, and the damage being meted out was ferocious.

Admiral Adare was enjoying himself immensely. Although the Vindicator Mercenary Company ships were putting up an excellent fight, two were already dead in the water or partially destroyed, and it was only matter of time until more went. It would be in quick succession when they did, as the attrition of warfare reached the point of no return for the enemy fleet. It was a well-established principle of warfare.

The *Thor's Hammer* had been boarded, and enemy Marines were playing havoc internally, but the situation was contained. Additional Marines had been recalled to the bridge, to help defend it.

It looked as if Gavain had been extremely foolhardy indeed.

All of a sudden, the scanners officer virtually screamed across the datasphere <Warning, warning, stargate activating. Ships incoming, large jump signature detected!>

<More ships?> said Adare. The few ships he had out-system were not likely to be returning now. He felt a sudden sinking feeling. Had he underestimated Gavain again.

<More ships, sir. Sir, translating now!>

Gavain sent out a general message to his entire force, which said very simply, <People, we have held long enough. Our reinforcements are here. Not much longer, just let them cross to join the fight.>

The display showed seventeen capital ships jumping in, of various sizes and models, all of them House-designed and not Praetorian. It appeared that Andersson had done his job well. The entire plan all along had been merely to obtain information on the Web's positions, and then get the real invasion force into the system. The Vindicator Mercenary Company had never been more than an advance scouting force, a distraction and bait to draw the Rosicrux in. It had taken Gavain a long time and a lot of hard negotiation to set this up and make it happen, but now it was beginning to pay off.

With the information they had taken by force from the Dark Heart System, they had found the exact position of the entire Web of Deepspace Stations, as well as uncovering the defences precisely, establishing a foothold in the system, drawing the Rosicrux away from any possible escape route through the stargate. The stargate's defences had been neutered so the incoming House ships would not be harmed, and would arrive fresh to engage the Rosicrux Praetorian ships. Praetorian ships vastly outclassed House ships, but there was no escape for them now and they were all damaged and battle-weary.

<Incoming hail, Admiral.>

<Answer.>

A holographic image of Feldmarshall Grant appeared. <Admiral, we of the Erdogan nation have been able to provide a greater force than I indicated during our negotiations. We received your transmission and orders to use the Deepspace Station your intelligence here uncovered, and did so. I was tired of waiting.> The Feldmarshall laughed. <We are heading for your position full-power, unless as theatre commander you have any counter-orders?>

<No, just get here fast, we're suffering,> said Gavain. <Clear the stargate .... You're not the only ones coming in.>

It all happened relatively quickly.

The half-fleet of Erdogan ships cleared the terminus zone of the stargate, driving at full propulsion directly towards the five planets of the Dark Heart Artificial System and the deadly battle-zone.

No sooner had they moved away than the stargate thrummed again. Seven seconds later it coughed seismically, and a new fleet arrived. These ships were of a wider variety of designs, but there were thirty-five capital House ships. They were all from the Levitican Union, be they originally House Towers, Galetti, Obamu, Marchenko, Zupanic, Claes or Lapointe.

They cleared the area quickly, a second, stronger, heavier wave thumping in towards the battle around Dark Heart Alpha.

The stargate hummed again. It spat forth another small fleet of House ships, these from the Aarlborg Alliance. Twenty-one ships-of-the-line from the three Houses in the Alliance, led by none other than Admiral-of-the-Fleet Jakub Halvorssen himself.

These ships began to move towards Dark Heart Alpha. The stargate went off three more times, initially with eleven Korhonen House Guard ships, and then in another wave, seven House Van Der Meer starships, followed by thirteen Hausenhof nation starships.

It was an armada, an unheard-of joining of House ships not seen since the Revolutionary Council had declared the Civil War and led the rebellion against the False Emperor.

The outcome of this invasion, once looking so much in favour of the Rosicrux, had just rapidly shifted.

Adare found it nearly impossible to believe. Even though the vast number of starships coming in towards the Dark Heart Artificial System were House ships-of-the-line and not ex-Praetorian Guard, they were in such heavy numbers that he knew the tables had turned.

With the mercenaries already virtually in command of one of the starbases, and the majority of Dark Heart Alpha, and in such huge numbers they were easily going to rip through the five linked planets of the artificial system, Adare could no longer see any point in staying. He felt terrible rage as he realised that Gavain had beaten him, using superior tactics and an incredibly risky strategy. Even worse, with the various locations the House ships had jumped in from, it was obvious the Deepspace Stations were compromised and most of the Web would now be unavailable to him. A vast number of ships stood between his forces and the stargate, and there was no guarantee that even if he abandoned the Rosicrux and the Dark Heart System, they could escape through the Web.

A number of his ships had been boarded by mercenary Marines, and Adare had wondered why Gavain was opening his ships up to such close-range exchanges. Now he knew why – Gavain wanted them aboard for this precise moment. Even now, the Sir Admiral Gavain was communicated to all of the Rosicrux ships, demanding surrender. Commander Sahin had called extra Marines to the bridge to protect against the mercenaries already on the *Thor's Hammer*.

They had to try. Only his instinct for survival was stronger than his instinct to conduct murderous mayhem, and his only chance was to take his fleet and make it through the waves of incoming House ships before they consolidated around his position. Survival then would be impossible. It was already only a slim chance.

<Admiral Adare to all ships, break off engagement. We are retreating, heading to the Dark Heart Stargate. This system is lost.> He began to receive protestations from some of those more inducted into the Rosicrux conspiracy, but he ignored them.

<Silus,> Sahin said on a private channel, <Lieutenant-Colonel Iyan Lamans is aboard the *Vindicator*. Are we not retrieving him and our own Marines?>

<No,> said Adare shortly and grimly, <My – our, survival comes first.>

Zehra Sahin paled, but then nodded shortly. <As you command.>

Adare sat back down in his chair, having been stood for most of the battle. He could not believe it was ending this way. Gavain was hailing him personally and directly, but Silus Adare refused the communications.

Suddenly he thought of the InterStellar Hyperspace Missiles. His thoughts had turned to vengeance. He still had command of the military systems, he could order them to fire, send them towards the capital planets of some of this multi-House force arrayed against him.

He leaned forward, about to give the order, when the entire bridge turned into utter chaos.

Major Vantanik stood on the bridge of the *Thor's Hammer*, his cybernetic biomorphic form altered to make him look like a Rosicrux Imperial Marine. He and his forty-nine other biomorphs had been the first aboard the *Thor*, and they had fought through, infiltrating the defending forces by mirroring them. He ensured that when the call came to reinforce the bridge against the normal VMC Marines marauding around the *Hammer*, that a large number of his biomorphic specialists were disguised. They had infiltrated the bridge perfectly, and actually outnumbered the Rosicrux Marines re-called to defend it.

He stood, apparently on guard, but secretly observing the primary target, Silus Adare. All was ready, the bridge was sealed against intruders with the defenders little realising they were already compromised, and he saw no reason to delay on longer.

<All biomorphs,> he ordered, <Order is given, attack now.>

His right and left arms morphed into blades and he viciously sliced through the real Rosicrux soldiers to either side of him. He whirled around, another weapon morphing into his right arm, directing it towards Admiral Adare. Even as the rest of the defenders were being slaughtered with extreme prejudice, he fired the specially-formulated anti-Praetorian toxic dart, designed to complete immobilise advanced Praetorian cyborg physiology.

It struck Adare before he could give any more orders, and the man went down in less than a second, knocked unconscious and paralysed by the toxins.

It was the quickest and shortest bridge assault in the history of the mercenary corporation.

<Major Vantanik to Admiral Gavain,> he said, <I have Admiral Adare and the bridge of the *Thor's Hammer*. Shutting the dreadnought down now. Mission accomplished.>

Chapter XXIV

Gavain stood on the rogue planet of Dark Heart Alpha, looking up at the sky. He did not like being on planets, preferring the environments of starships in space, but his curiosity had got the better of him. He had never been on a rogue planet before, a ball of rock that was bereft of a home solar system. The atmosphere on Alpha was perfect, a largely temperate world and climate. With the false sunlight, held in place by gigantic stationary-engines, it was beautiful.

To think that Alpha was linked by space-lifts and space-corridors to the other four planets in the system truly was a wonder. Two of the planets were also rogue planets, ejected from their solar systems and cast deep into the void countless millions of years ago. Another two were false planets, artificial constructs of unbelievable size.

"So what is the history of this artificial system?" Gavain asked aloud, as they walked down a perfect tree-lined avenue towards the Heart Palace, an immense structure within Primaris Megapolis on Dark Heart Alpha.

A number of people were walking with him. General Andryukhin was at his side, for once untouched by his latest efforts at war. Captain Jonathan O'Connor was there, as the intelligence officer, burn marks fresh on his face and hands where the bridge of his ship had been damaged by a direct and sustained turbolaser strike. Captain Lucas De Graaf, as the other co-director in the VMC was also present, walking serenely along the avenue, looking as if he did not have a care in the colonised galaxy. Captain Danae Markos was there, walking with a confidence that belied her age, the oldest of the group and the most experienced, well-respected amongst all the naval commanders. Commodore Harley Andersson and Doctor Erin Presson were also present, having jumped in with the cargo-freighters from Blackheath, utilising many stargates to get here within less than half a day in real-time and at great financial expense. Lastly, Major Vantanik in his human appearance, the young cybernetic biomorph who had captured the war-criminal Silus Adare and taken the *Thor's Hammer*, who along with Jason Bramhall was being credited as being the heroes of the Dark Heart operation.

Not that the financial expense mattered any more, Gavain reflected privately. Firstly he was no longer focused on how many Imperial Crowns he could earn, and secondly, they had earned a small fortune thanks to his negotiations with the various Houses and nations for this invasion of Dark Heart. The benefits went well beyond purely money, though.

It was O'Connor who answered. He had been accepted into Gavain's inner circle, like Danae Markos and Major Viktor Vantanik. His advice and capabilities and even friendship were highly regarded by Gavain. Only Lady Sophia of the few he counted as his friends was absent, but then, she was in the Newchrist System, on the planet Leviticus, attending to the political machinations of the Levitican Union.

"We've been able to piece together some history from the data-cores in-system," said O'Connor. "It dates back to shortly before the Droid Wars, when Alpha, Beta and Gamma were pulled together by the Intelligentia. They built the additional two artificial planetoids, Delta and Epsilon. They used advanced technology for all of it, which apparently the True Emperor was later to learn of when he discovered the system very early in his reign. It appears the True Emperor broke his father's command, and his own Imperial Edict, that Intelligentia Droid technology was never to be employed by the human and borg survivors. The Droids had long gone, the Intelligentia having extinguished themselves in the wars much earlier, and it lay abandoned and empty for a long time. It was discovered by accident by the ExCol division of the Imperium, the Emperor returning later with precursor to the Praetorian Guard.

"The True Emperor outfitted the system, building the space-lifts and corridors to connect the planets. That's why we see so much of the Imperial stamp on the system. He added both military starbases, converted the original Intelligentia shipyards, built the mining base, terraformed some of Alpha and began early terraforming on Beta. It was the True Emperor who constructed the Web.

"Sadly, when the Imperium hit the Decades of Restriction following the Unification War, he ordered it abandoned due to cost reasons. It lay empty for another two centuries, abandoned. Apparently Imperial Intelligence knew of the Web, using it to cross the Medusan Gulf quickly, but they never knew of Dark Heart.

"Then suddenly, in recent history, at the time of the Revolutionary Council, the Solar Administrator appeared. The Rosicrux organisation suddenly took it over. How they knew of it I do not know yet, but maybe the information will come out as we interrogate her. It truly is fascinating, I'm sure this must be one of the wonders of the Galaxy."

"It explains the different melds in the architecture on this planet, anyway," said Commodore Andersson as he looked around. It was certainly true, Primaris Megapolis was a strange aggregate of many different architectural styles, from the functional Droid Intelligentia through to the austere but proud and inventive early Imperial and then the increasingly sweeping and grand middle Imperial architectural styles.

They had reached the large parade ground before the Heart Palace, and began crossing it to the inner defensive wall. "Well, to work, ladies and gentlemen," said, "Jack in." Their own datasphere was already up and running within the Dark Heart Artificial System, the naval data-tech specialists having set it up almost immediately after the battle. Within a heartbeat, every one of the cyborgs had used their internal modems to connect.

<Current dispositions of the House fleets?> asked Gavain.

Images appeared in all their minds, along with data records and a display map. <The House and nation fleets have almost all left the system. The Levitican Union is now all that's left, having recalled some of their ships, but some twelve ships-of-the-line are still here in-system considering our dilapidated state. There are still about seven or so Rosicrux ships that are unaccounted for, being out-system when we invaded, and there is still a possibility they may return. The damages we sustained were high, we need the assistance to resist if the missing Rosicrux ships come back,> Captain Danae Markos reported.

<And how is the pacification of the planetary bodies and installations going?> asked Gavain.

Ulrik Andryukhin took that one. <We have complete control of Alpha, Beta, Gamma and Delta. Only Epsilon remains. One Imperial Standard day to take four planets, I have set a new record,> laughter was heard across the datasphere at that one, <We have the second starbase under our control, after some very hard fighting. The mining base is ours, as is the shipyards. All the system defences are now operating for us. I am having them re-slaved to a central operations room here, within Heart Palace, just to make control easier. We also have the InterStellar Hyperspace Missiles and the Tears of the Moon.>

Gavain was very serious as he spoke. <Out of all my negotiations with the Houses and nations, that was the most contentious point. Each one of them wanted the technology. I refused of course, but said we would destroy them, and record and provide evidence. Jonathan, Erin, you have about a week to break the Tears of the Moon secrets and make sure we can manufacture our own, before I will have to provide the evidence of their destruction. Add it to your list of priorities, I want that technology.> Both of them confirmed with affirmatives at the surprising order.

<Breaking a contract, Jamie?> said Ulrik lightly, providing a moment of relief. All of them here knew that he was teasing over the Compact-Erdogan contract, although few knew just how close him and Gavain had come to a serious disagreement on it.

Gavain's tone lightened, in response to the friendly jibe. <Not the first time in my life. Ulrik, your priorities are to finish the capture of Epsilon, make sure that this system is secure, and within two days have Marines and naval personnel on every Deepspace Station in the Web. Danae, we know from visuals from the House ships that there is all manner of starships and more at the different Deepspace Stations. I want them all skeleton crewed and brought back here to the Dark Heart System, as soon as possible.>

<Aye, sir,> said Danae.

<When it's just us, it is Jamie,> he corrected, <even in serious meetings such as this.> He gave a rare smile. <I am aware of the damage to our assets, and our terrible casualty and fatality figures. What I need to know is projections for the future. How long to repair, and how long to recover strength.> He had addressed the question to Harley Andersson and Erin Presson, who had taken control of the recovery efforts.

<The damages to our assets were exceptionally high,> said Andersson, <in terms of naval ships, we have not permanently lost any ships, which is somewhat amazing – but you should all be aware that had the battle continued on for just another two minutes, our losses would have been high. Nearly three-quarters of our ships have such high levels of damage that they would have been counted as destroyed, irreparable. Even using the massively advanced shipyards here, it is going to take at least two to three months to fully repair and become operational. Until then, we are reduced to a few capital ships-of-the-line.

<In terms of ground assets and Marine assets the news is somewhat better, as resistance on the planets and in the space installations was much lighter than we expected. We outnumbered the enemy. Even the military transporters are relatively undamaged, and can still be considered operational. We are still fully capable in that respect.>

Andersson finished, and Dr Presson took over. <Casualties and fatalities follow the same pattern, in that we took heavy losses amongst the naval crew and very light losses on the Marines. Our medical facilities, even the ones we have taken here in Dark Heart, are vastly overstretched - we really need help, Jamie, I'm telling you now. In terms of fatalities it follows the same pattern. We are now considerably under strength when it comes to naval personnel.>

<We will hold a memorial service; Harley, add that to your task-list. But what of replacements, back to our former strength?> Gavain asked. They were still crossing the large parade ground, but he sent a mental command ahead and the huge triple-reinforced gates began to retract either into the ground or into the walls either side, to allow them into the expansive courtyard inside.

<We emptied most of those who were waiting in the Blackheath System for us to take them on. There are a lot more who have applied but have not made their 'pilgrimage' to Blackheath, both Praetorian and ex-Praetorian. We still get a lot of interest. Our media appearances and reputation ensure that. We can ask them to come in. We can also advertise.> Harley hesitated, knowing Gavain's preference on this. <Perhaps the time has come to accept non-Praetorian borgs and upgrade them with Praetorian technology and training?>

<Praetorians are still first choice for front-line posts, but we will take non-Praetorian borgs as well. Unaugmented too, for non-military posts,> said Gavain. Andersson smiled, in on the secret, guessing why he had allowed that particular exception.

<Non-military posts?> asked Danae Markos.

<I will explain shortly. Erin, what about the replacements we are growing in the accelerated growth biovat tanks on Tahrir? And, if we were to use the facilities here in Dark Heart?>

Doctor Erin Presson frowned at the implication there. <The next batch will be ready in about three week's time. As you directed, five hundred biomorphs, a thousand Marines and a thousand naval officers. The facilities here in Dark Heart are amazing – the True Emperor had two full Medical Biovat Manufactory built, one on Alpha, one on Beta. We would need to upgrade them with our updated technology, which would take -> she stopped as she computed <- about two weeks Standard, but then we would be able to produce thirty thousand every three months.>

<Do it,> Gavain commanded, <Switch Tahrir Base to producing biomorphs only on the next batch, look at our new naval and military strength, and get me a proposal for the quantities in the next three hours.>

<Aye, si – yes, Jamie,> she caught his look.

<We will also consider the junior-level Rosicrux prisoners we have taken as replacements, but only after a strong series of vetting and testing for loyalty to the Rosicrux. Now,> said James Gavain, as they crossed into the palace grounds and courtyard, <What of the Rosicrux? What have we learnt so far from the data, prisoners, and other intelligence, Jonathan?> The Heart Palace was now towering over them, a gargantuan construction of pure early Imperial architecture.

O'Connor sighed heavily. He was working without stop, co-ordinating a massive intelligence gathering exercise across tens of thousands of prisoners, five planets and multiple space stations. <We're still sifting through all the data intelligence, it will take weeks even with all my resources placed onto it, the sheer volume of data throughout the centuries is phenomenal. We're finding hidden caches, isolated data-cores, disguised trap-doors into ghost systems, all sorts of things. A number of booby-trap viruses too, we have to be careful as we proceed.

<As for prisoners, well, we're still transferring them. Dark Heart Gamma has a large prison facility, so we're making use of it. Interrogations have begun on the more senior officers already, but for example, high-priority targets like the Solar Administrator are confusing us greatly. We cannot track her origin, background, identity, or anything, or even penetrate the mental defences she has built into her brain. She is an advanced biomorph, by the way, the same as Viktor Vantanik here.>

<There is a possible link to the Faceless?> asked Commodore Andersson disbelievingly.

<No comment, not until we've broken her,> said O'Connor. <We are being careful – we have found a number of disguised biomorphs amongst the prisoners. The Rosicrux are using them, so it explains how they have remained undetected in their operations against the Eastern Segment Houses.>

<We see the difficulties with the intel sources,> said Andersson, <what of the information we have obtained on the Rosicrux?>

<They are called Rosicrux, but do not trace their origins back to the masonic organisations of old Earth. It is another blind, a name they chose possibly at random. We have found links to other organisations operating the same as the Rosicrux – it seems to be a codename for their operation here in the Eastern Segment, rather than an organisation. We have no real clue as to who they are, or why they were doing this. Yet.>

<Wheels within wheels – first the fucking pirates, operating in secret reporting to the Rosicrux, then the fucking Rosicrux reporting up to someone else. What have we stumbled on here? What was the bastard's ultimate purpose?> asked Andryukhin.

<Their given aim was to completely destabilise the Eastern Segment, tear it apart in multiple wars. The organisation interestingly appeared before the Dissolution of the Imperium, some years before, and they already knew of Dark Heart somehow. They had entered this system approximately two years before the Battle of Mars, and then started recruiting ex-Praetorian Guard following the Dissolution Order, bringing the artificial system into limited use again. The Rosicrux do not appear to be linked in any way or a result of the end of the Red Imperium of Mars, they merely begin active operations once Dissolution had taken effect.>

<That suggests they were set up by someone, or a group of people, who saw what was about to happen, and prepared for it,> said Gavain. <Either in the Imperial Senate or the Revolutionary Council. Plans within plans, as you said so eloquently, Ulrik.>

<There were a lot of biomorphic Rosicrux in this system, but before the Dissolved Praetorian Guard began to arrive, the majority of them had left. This Solar Administrator was the head person of the Rosicrux project – interestingly, there are never any communications out of the Dark Heart Artificial System to some higher authority, but plenty of visits by a number of ships of a design and make we have never seen. Her orders were relayed verbally.>

<We will have to examine those ship scans in detail,> said Gavain. <Do we have any idea how far the Rosicrux conspiracy stretched? How far they had penetrated?>

Here O'Connor looked disconcerted. They were at the entrance steps into the Heart Palace, and they had now stopped beneath a small grove of trees just to the side, a number of suspensor-benches rising up to meet them as they sat down. Ulrik Andryukhin and Viktor Vantanik took the grass, hunkering down comfortably.

<Oh yes,> said O'Connor, <It was wider than we could have imagined. Firstly, this unnamed Solar Administrator was receiving intelligence from her superiors. From what we have seen, and we are still in preliminary investigations, they have access to the StarCom Federation Central Intelligence Department, News Media, Communications Division, Stargate Operations Division, Exploration and Colonisation Corps, the StarCom Federation Army. They have access to the Interstellar Merchants Guild, and all its various branches of operation. They have intelligence coming from the Faceless and the Shadow Council that run it. Intelligence from the other operations and divisions that survived the Dissolution in other parts of the colonised galaxy. They have vast resources or contacts.>

<So much, much bigger than we ever suspected,> said Harley Andersson.

<Oh yes,> said O'Connor. <In terms of people directly within the Rosicrux organisation, they have several criminal gangs, all manner of dignitaries, ambassadors, military personnel – they have penetrated virtually every nation or House in the Eastern Segment. Which in itself has brought the biggest revelation.>

<Which is?> asked Gavain.

<We thought that it was the Rosicrux who were trying to make it look as if the various nation states and Houses were sponsoring them, as a cover. In truth, the Houses knew. We have complete details of their plans. The Zhou-Zheng Compact was pumping billions of Crowns into the organisation, in return for crippling the Erdogans, with the full knowledge of the Star Marshal, the Primarch and Primarchess. Cervantia is sponsoring the attacks on Korhonen and Hausenhof. The Helvanna Dominion was paying the Rosicrux for privateering work on the Aarlborg Alliance, with the General of the Helvanna Dominion authorising the payments personally. The Rosicrux have stoked the animosities, and then profited from it by approaching the nations asking for the funds in return for weakening their enemies. The Rosicrux have been playing the nations, states and Houses here in the Eastern Segment. We know their methods, but we do not know why. It is certainly not for the money, it was re-invested into their operations.>

<We must consider carefully whether or not to release that information,> said Gavain quietly. <Such a revelation would spark many wars immediately, if it is not already inevitable. What was the story in the Levitican Union?>

<Surprising,> said O'Connor. <We thought it was to spark war with House Jorgensson, and indeed it was. But it was House Zupanic, under Lady Wyn and Lord Ramicek, and House Marchenko, under Gregori Marchenko, who were paying the money. The plan was, and still is, for the Union to go to war with House Jorgensson, conquer it, and then for Marchenko and Zupanic to unite together and conquer the smaller Houses in the aftermath. Even worse, Lord Micalek Zupanic was aware of it, so think of the political ramifications for Lady Sophia. He has willingly killed his mother and father.>

<Unbelievable,> said Andersson, shaking his head.

<That is serious. Micalek's involvement with the Rosicrux is something I may reveal to Lady Sophia,> said Gavain, <I will think about it. I am taking the *Thor's Hammer* to the Newchrist System within twenty-four hours, it is hardly damaged.> He laughed, <Use a pulse-channel to tell them I am coming in Adare's ship, and to hand Adare over, so they don't fire on our appearance in-system.>

<I am so glad we got the fucker, Jamie,> said Ulrik with feeling. <It's a shame you did not kill him, Viktor.>

Viktor Vantanik shrugged, a learnt gesture from the non-human biomorph. <He will face execution for his war-crimes, he is as good as dead anyway.>

<James,> said Danae Markos, <why are you going there?>

315

<Ah, of course,> and here James Gavain smiled brightly. <Lucas, Ulrik, Harley, they all know why. It is time you all did, and in fact, the rest of our organisation too.>

Slowly he began to explain, to the increasing disbelief of the people before him.

*

Lady Sophia walked through the new observatory gardens in the vast underwater city of the new capital of the Levitican Union. The original had been destroyed in the Levitican War against the StarCom Federation, but this new replacement had been built. The Levitican Union Capital City in the water-planet of Leviticus was the only city currently re-built, but there would be many more.

As she and James Gavain walked through the observatory gardens, they both looked up as a gigantic sea creature, long and sinuous and reptilian, swam overhead, desperately hunting a smaller prey. Both of them hit the defensive force-fields, and bounced away harmlessly, the prey using the chance to escape.

There is a metaphor there, thought Lady Sophia. But who is the prey and who is the hunter?

"Is it not strange being aboard the *Thor's Hammer*?" she asked, "Silus Adare's ship?"

"Somewhat," James Gavain replied honestly. "But the *Vindicator* was so heavily damaged, she will not be sailing again for at least a month. Our damage overall was extremely serious. I almost lost my fleet."

"But you have gained so much more," said Lady Sophia.

"Good negotiations," commented Gavain. "I had an excellent teacher, Sophia."

Lady Sophia laughed gently. "One thinks you have outstripped even one's capabilities in that regard. What exactly did you gain from this latest series of contracts to invade Dark Heart, again?"

Gavain was typically blank-faced as he matter-of-factly said, "Imperial Crowns measured in the billions, a contract pay-out bigger than some of the annual gross domestic product of the smaller House territories in the Union, my Lady. All the ships that we fought in the Dark Heart System, plus all the ships that were either civilian and in use, or military or civilian and mothballed in Dark Heart. All the Deepspace Stations in approach to Dark Heart."

"And of course, the biggest treasure of all," she said.

"The Dark Heart Artificial System itself," said Gavain, nodding. "A wonder of the galaxy, as some of my people are already calling it. A lost treasure. The facilities there are truly beyond the scope of what I had imagined we would find. In the black hole cluster, it is a fortress like none other I have heard of. There is more than enough there for me to realise my aims and ambition."

"Well, one has to attend the Council meeting, to elect the new Lord Principal and arrange the Ministries," said Lady Sophia, "then you will be called in. Are you ready?"

He exhaled heavily, nervous despite himself. "This is far outside the realm of my experience, Sophia. I will need your help, and your support. I greatly appreciate it."

Lady Sophia stopped, turning to him. "Jamie, you have come so far. What you are about to do elevates yourself, but is without doubt one of the most courageous things one has heard of since the Dissolution. You are capable of so much. One will help you through the politics, and the setting up of your new goal."

"As I said, I appreciate it, Sophia. The politics is so .... alien to me."

"You coped with emerging into the real world from the Praetorian Guard," said Lady Sophia firmly. "You learnt in very short term how to be an excellent mercenary, trading on your skills. Now, you will learn something new. You have already displayed that you have the nous and instinct to deal with the politics you will encounter. When it comes to running the system, one will of course help."

Gavain nodded. "Thank you. I owe you much, I will not forget it."

She grinned, eyes narrowing. "Do not forget, one has given up her directorship in the Vindicator Mercenary Corporation for this."

Gavain looked her straight in the eyes, "And gained something you need much more. A strong military, and now political, ally."

"We need it," said Lady Sophia, "The Union needs it, if we are to survive." Her face fell, becoming hard. "One has not confronted Lord Micalek about his knowledge of the Rosicrux organisation, and his knowledge of the Marchenko plot. If one had not seen the evidence you pulled from Dark Heart, one would have refused to believe it. He willingly used one to kill his family. The man is truly a beast and a butcher. One participated in the assassinations to end the threat of House Zupanic to the Union and my family – it appears that like the hydra, chopping of one head of the beast has only allowed another, more dangerous one to grow in its place. All one's efforts to protect my child –" here she rubbed her belly "- appeared to be for nothing."

"At least you know of the plot," said Gavain, "Well, we know of the plot. Remember you have an ally in this in me, now. As we discussed, say nothing, wait and watch to see what he does. He did not tell us of the Rosicrux, but he may abandon it."

"No," said Lady Sophia, "he cannot be trusted, it is proven to one now."

"Do not jump to conclusions, wait and see," said Gavain. "We will be watching him, anyway."

"That gives me the greatest confidence of all," said Lady Sophia, smiling brightly, but without feeling at all. A note sounded out, ringing again and again. "That is the call to Council," she said. "We take the vote, decide on the ministries, and then one will call for you."

"Good luck, my Lady."

"And to you."

Chapter XXV

In the Council Chamber, Lady Sophia was the last to take her seat at the circular nahalwood table, the setting before draped with the flag of House Towers, next to the flag of the Levitican Union. All the Heads of House were present, their former Lord or Lady Ministers behind them if they had not been the Head of House, and every House had their own flag laid out before them.

As she sat, Lord Micalek nodded at her, and smiled. She returned it, using the best of her ability to hide how she truly felt. The man was a monster.

Servants came forwards, bring expensive Fomalhaut champagne, for the toasting after the voting was concluded. They served them in equally expensive crystal glass, mined from the frozen planetoid of Pluto, in Sol.

Lord Micalek coughed, and then spoke. His eyes went to the slightly more ornate seat where his father had sat as Lord Principal. It remained empty, a stark reminder of why they were here. "Council, heads of House," he said, "We are all gathered here as described in the Charter, to elect a new Lord Principal. The voting procedure will be the same as when we first met, on the day of the birth of the Union.

"We have all named our first and second preferences for the Ministries. We will now cast our secret rounds of voting to elect the next Principal, the second of that title to lead the Union forwards in these difficult days post-Imperium. Every house is eligible to become Principal, but we are not allowed to vote for ourselves. After the Principal is elected, we will then refer to first and second preferences for the Ministries. Are we all ready to begin?"

There were several murmurs of assent. Holographic black screens appeared in front of the small visual displays projected for each House Lord or Lady, to allow the votes to be cast in secrecy. "Then let us begin, cast your votes now."

House Lady Sophia leaned forwards, seeing the six holographic panels hovering in the air, one for each of the other Houses. There had been weeks and weeks of manoeuvring and jockeying, but this was the point of ultimate test as to whether or not the politicking had been worth it. She tapped the button for House Lapointe.

As Sophia waited for the voting to finish, she reflected on how much had changed. Three Heads of Houses who had been in the first ever vote to elect the Principal were no longer alive, and there was another House in the Union.

The results flashed up in the air, at the centre of the table. Lord Micalek stood, and said needlessly as they could all see it, "House Marchenko, Obamu, and Galetti have no votes, so they are eliminated from consideration. House Lapointe has one vote, House Claes has one vote, House Zupanic has one vote, and House Towers has four votes." There were a series of murmurs around the table, and Sophia felt everyone's eyes upon her. This time, there was already a clear winner.

Sophia knew her votes had come from Lapointe, Zupanic, Marchenko and Claes. Claes were always working with House Zupanic, and Marchenko owed their existence in the union to House Zupanic, so Micalek had used his influence to affect their voting. Of course, both Sophia and her brother Luke stood behind her now knew the truth behind the Marchenko inclusion in the Union.

"We proceed to the second round of voting. In this round, only the two leading Houses go through to the third and final round of voting, unless there is a tie and we have to extend voting, or if there is a unanimous decision. Please, cast your votes."

Lady Sophia was patient as she waited, casting her vote as an abstention as soon as the voting opened. There was a long pause, and then the voting came in again, flashing up on the screen. Lady Sophia's eyes widened, and she breathed in. Her brother rested his hand on her shoulder.

Lord Micalek stood, smiling his actor's smile widely. "Congratulations to House Towers. We have a unanimous vote in your favour. The decision is made, the Union has spoken. Would you please take your seat as the head of government, Lady Principal Sophia Towers."

Lady Sophia Towers stood, looking back at her brother Luke. She knew he was not disappointed at all to be losing his position as a Minister, because as a Towers, he was now debarred from representing the House in a Ministry. She sat in the Principal's chair, and then raised the fluted champagne glass. "A toast, to the second government of the Levitican Union," she said. They all sipped from the champagne, and then a round of old-fashioned applause began.

"We now need to elect our Ministers," she said. "If we go around the table, naming our first preferences."

It was reasonably straightforward, in that House Marchenko requested the Ministry of Transformation and Integration, the behemoth form of Gregori choosing his daughter Eranisch. Lady Aria Galetti wanted Domestic Affairs again, and she took it herself. Brin Claes went for Foreign Relations, and won it without challenge. Monique Lapointe took the Ministry of Justice. The only point of contention was over Military Defence, with both Micalek Zupanic and Moafa Obamu selecting it, leaving the Ministry of Economic Affairs and Trade unselected.

They had a vote, and predictably with the power block forming in the Union in relation to the voting, Zupanic won Military Defence. Only Sophia and her brother Luke knew how dangerous and precarious their position was; both Claes and Marchenko voted with Zupanic, not Towers, and Micalek was most likely only pretending to follow House Towers.

Either way, Moafa Obamu looked furious.

As the toasting finished, Lady Sophia tapped the metallic ball on the dais before her to command attention, sparks flying into the air. "This has been an historic day, my Council," she said. "But, Lords and Ladies, all is not finished. In a moment I will ask for any other business to be raised before we adjourn, but firstly, I wish to call a special visitor to address the Council." She cleared her throat, and commanded, "Send for Sir Admiral James Gavain."

She had only confided in Lady Monique Lapointe as to what was intended. The rest of the Lords and Ladies knew that the *Thor's Hammer* was in orbit, with Gavain aboard, but that it had purely been to deliver Silus Adare and his crew for judgement and in all probability, sentencing to the executioner.

There was a short wait, and then James Gavain entered. He was dressed completely differently, wearing highly expensive clothing, high-collared in Imperial fashion but coloured red and black. There were many different shades of red in it, and the material was of something that no-one in the room, Sophia included, recognised. With his martial reputation and bearing, he looked like a barbarian conqueror approaching his defeated opponents.

"Sir Admiral James Gavain, the first knight of the Levitican Union, ward of House Towers, protector of the Blackheath System, master of Tahrir, you have the floor," she said. "Please, address the council in your own time and at your leisure."

James Gavain stood there for a long time, impassive, unmoving before them all. It was impossible to tell how nervous he was, because of the confident stare he gave to every one of the Lord and Lady Ministers around the table, but it was a confidence masking fear of the unknown. Then he began speaking.

"Lords and Ladies of the Levitican Union," he said, "I come here before you as the deliverer of the war-criminal Silus Adare. You have all read the reports of my action against the Rosicrux, and you are aware that the Dark Heart Artificial System and its entire domain now belong to me. I am here to inform you of my intent.

"I now command a vast military fleet and army, compromised of ex-Praetorian Guard, the finest military personnel in the colonised galaxy. We are re-organising, and as such, I am now adopting a rank you have not heard since before the Dissolution Order. I am becoming Commander-In-Chief, taking the title of the highest rank in the Praetorian Guard.

"But I come to ask of you a major boon. With my own territory, and in accordance with Imperial Decree and Imperial Law, I come before you as much more than just a mercenary. In the old Imperium, if more than ten Houses supported it, a new House Lord Senator or Lady Senator could be elected into the Imperial Senate. The Imperium might be dead, the Senate might be gone, but many still recognise the Imperial Law and hold to it. I have the support of many Houses outside the Levitican Union, but ask you to recognise me officially as the new House Lord of the Vindicatus nation, and House Gavain."

He continued to outline the benefits to the Union, that if he were recognised by all the Houses, he would enter into a mutual defence pact with the Union, lending his military forces to its defence. The Vindicator Mercenary Corporation would still exist, he would hire out his military as mercenaries as his primary export as well as defending his own territory, but there were many more things he could trade once the Dark Heart Artificial System was fully functional. He would offer favourable trading conditions. He would engage in a level of intelligence sharing not seen with any House outside the Union.

Utter, shocked silence met his announcement; and then the questions began.

James Gavain sat in front of the holo-camera crews and news media in the official briefing room of the Council. The StarCom News Media were of course present, as were the Levitican News Media, between them dominating the room, but there were also many more from all over the Eastern Segment.

The Levitican Union Lady Principal and her Lord and Lady Ministers had conducted the initial announcement, confirming the outcome of their voting. And then, James Gavain had been introduced. Already it was a fantastic day for the newshounds, but it was about to become even more so.

"Ladies and gentlemen of the colonised galaxy," said Lady Principal Sophia Towers, "allow me to introduce the new House Lord of House Gavain of the nation of Vindicatus, Commander-In-Chief of the Vindicator Mercenary Corporation and Vindicatus Army, Sir Knight of the Levitican Union, ward of House Towers, protector of Blackheath, and master of Tahrir."

Dressed in all his finery, James stood before holo-cameras. His nervousness was already gone, his adaptability giving him all the reassurance he needed.

"I address you as Lord James Gavain, newly recognised as a House Lord by numerous Houses in the Eastern Segment. I am not at liberty to discuss how or why, although in time doubtless the truth will come out, but I am now the Lord of an artificial system constructed in the heart of a black hole cluster, deep in the Gulf of Medusa. I am using this system as my new landholding and base of operations, but it is due to become so much more than that."

A graphic appeared before him, the holo-display bringing up a starmap showing the location of the Dark Heart Artificial System. Slowly, the Web began to appear, the Deepspace Station positions marked out with galactic co-ordinates.

"I am naming it the Vindicatus nation. Entry to the Vindicatus nation can be achieved through the Web, a series of Deepspace Stations equipped with stargates, which enable us to be reached from a number of different points on all sides of the Gulf of Medusa. We are also extending the Web into the Levitican Union, connecting it through a House Zupanic stargate to the Blackheath System.

"The Vindicatus national army, will be known as the Vindicatus Mercenary Corporation. We are all ex-Praetorian Guard, and whilst I will defend my nation from aggressors, we a very much for hire in about two months time.

"But, the Vindicatus nation as led by House Gavain will be more than just a new state. Subject to a series of background checks and provision of a nationality identification holo-lith, I open our territory and our land to any and all Praetorian Guard who wish to join. Be aware that you do not have to join our army, but if you no longer wish to fight, you will be expected to contribute to the well-being of the nation through employed work. We have manufactories to populate, agricultural fields to maintain, entire industries to build.

"I also open our borders to anybody, be they cyborg or human. Many of you will remember how we turned on our former employers, the Zhou-Zheng Compact, at the end of our contractual obligations and following our horrendous discovery of the deathcamps they were running to systematically and genocidally eliminate all borgs in their conquered lands.

"It was this that created the desire within me to set up a safe haven for all. In my time I have seen many horrific war-crimes, which includes the deathcamps for unaugmented humans that the False Emperor instigated, and led to me rebelling with the Revolutionary Council and much of the Praetorian Guard against his tyranny. I am a free-thinker, taking or holding neither the borgite nor the humanist view. I no longer wish for people to suffer at the hands of the tyrant, to be persecuted for who or what they are.

"So, I have established the Vindicatus nation. We have registered the Vindication Charity with the Interstellar Merchants Guild, to collect donations from around the galaxy for any who wish to donate to this cause of providing a home for refugees from persecution. The Vindication Charity will also provide applicants with the funds to make it to one of our stargates, either those in the Web or at Blackheath. Once there we can transport you to our home system, Dark Heart, where you will be provided protection from your persecutors in return for the promise of employment for the benefit of building this new nation from the ashes of war, into something we can all be proud of.

"People of the galaxy, for too long have we suffered, and for too long have I watched and made my own money from the end of the Imperium. Now is the time for me to use that money to good effect, to use my capabilities and my drive, and that of my people, all of my resources in fact, to build a new future. That future is the nation Vindicatus, of House Gavain.

"Truly, and in every sense of the word, welcome to my own vindication. Now, are there any questions."

*

Lord Micalek moved purposefully through the noble barge of House Zupanic, the LSS *Divine Right*. He had taken a shuttle lander back to the spaceship, roughly a day after the announcements and momentous decisions of the Levitican Union elections and Gavain's amazing revelations. The mercenary had a heart and conscience after all, it appeared.

House Lord Micalek did not dwell on the thought, his usual disdain for what he perceived as such a weakness fading as he thought of Lady Sophia. He felt the stab of pain whenever he did so. Even worse, he was the one helping to twist the knife.

He entered the highly secured central reception chamber, which had been isolated from the rest of the ship. Most of the crew did not even know the truth of what or who they carried within the *Divine Right*, and they would never know.

As he entered the reception chamber, he was scanned by the security guards before being admitted, his identity confirmed. He then continued his powerful stride through the anteroom into the main audience room itself.

The audience room had been converted into what amounted to a medical bay. A number of masked and unidentifiable medics moved around the figure held suspended in the biovat in the centre of the room. The figure was twisted, the body contorted beyond normal parameters, and half of its head was missing. The eyes remained open though, and the brain within the shattered skull was obviously still cognisant, as those eyes narrowed in pure hate as they saw Lord Micalek.

There were bed-chambers converted from miscellaneous rooms off this main audience room, primarily for the medics held hostage here. There was a larger private room at the back, where the woman who stood by the biovat tank rested and hid from the watchful gaze of the galaxy.

"Mother," said Lord Micalek.

Lady Wyn Zupanic, very much alive and in very good health, turned to face him. One hand still rested on the cool glass of the biovat tank, Xavier Zupanic's hand reaching out to touch the glass internally.

"Micci," said his mother. "Me and Xav are so pleased to see you. I fear we will not be able to meet often now, considering I am supposed to be dead."

"Can he hear us?" asked Lord Micalek, looking pointedly at his half-dead and mostly insane brother.

"Oh, no, not yet," said Lady Wyn, "but he will be fully revived soon."

"I cannot wait."

"Contain your jealousy, Micalek!" said Lady Wyn sharply.

"Yes, mother," he said, sounding not in the least sorry. He changed subject. "You have still not explained to me how you managed to get such a convincing double into your place for the assassination attempt. She passed all the security and identity checks."

"Just know that I did it," said Lady Wyn. "How is not important. It is enough that I live, and can be there behind the throne of House Zupanic as you lead us to victory. After all, look at Elaine Carrington, I am hardly the first mother of a noble to come back from the dead and live in the shadows of her children."

"Yes, mother," said Lord Micalek.

"Between us and House Marchenko, we shall carve the Levitican Union apart."

"As you say, mother," said Micalek subserviently. "The Rosicrux plan suits our own, and even though they are now gone, we can still continue. All the pieces are in place. We provoke war with House Jorgensson, and in the ashes afterwards, we break the Union apart and take full control of our 'unified' territories."

"How goes it with Lady Sophia?" asked Lady Wyn.

"Well," said Micalek sharply. "She still hides the pregnancy from me, but he or she will be born in another five months. I assume she does not suspect artificial insemination with my sperm, to ensure the child is born."

"Excellent," said Lady Wyn. "And of course, her complicity in your murdering of your uncle, sister, and father will only tie her closer to you."

"Just remember mother," said Lord Micalek, "I have warned you. I love Lady Sophia, and nothing is to befall her. When the time comes, I will find a way to convince her to renounce House Towers territory to me, our secret bargain beforehand notwithstanding. She is never, ever to be harmed."

"As you say, my son."

"Mother. I love her. I need your word on this."

"Of course," said Lady Wyn, "You have my word, my son. No harm will come to her. Just make sure you manage to get her out of the way."

"I will. If you cross me, though, another bout of murder will break out inside the House of Zupanic. Have I made myself clear?"

Lady Wyn raised her eyes at the threat, but did not respond. "If you don't mind, you have to go be the Minister of Military Defence, and I have to look after Xav."

"Yes. Have a good journey back to Dalcice." With that, Lord Micalek turned around and smartly marched out of the converted room.

Lady Wyn stroked the biovat tank of the son who was technically more insane than the rest, the wife who had mercilessly killed her husband through the most artful of deceptions, and said, "Micalek is just like his father, poor boy. Falling in love is always a fatal error."

*

Gavain lay in the bed of his spacious room aboard the *Thor's Hammer*, hands underneath his head, staring at the ceiling.

Juan Ramirez had left a couple of hours earlier, his shift at the navigations console of the *Hammer* about to begin. Gavain had transferred all of his surviving crew from the *Vindicator*, plus a large number from the *Remembrance*, across to the *Hammer* for the journey to Leviticus. Now he had achieved all he wanted there, they were jumping back to Dark Heart. He had a government to put in place, a nation to build.

326

He had resisted Juan for as long as he could, but the attraction was undeniable. For the first time, he understood how General Andryukhin had felt about Julie Kavanagh when she had been alive. It was an amazing feeling, something Gavain could never have imagined, and certainly something he had never felt for Commodore Andersson.

The thought of Harley made his unusual smile dip a bit. He knew how Harley felt about him, although he had never returned it. Up until this journey to and from Leviticus, Gavain had thought he would never understand that depth of emotion, felt he would never be able to experience it himself. It was difficult on two counts; one, because Andersson was also a good friend and was likely to take a very senior role in either the government of the Vindicatus Mercenary Corporation army, or both, and second, because James genuinely did not want to hurt the man. He had confided in Lady Sophia before he left Leviticus, and she herself had been amazed at his predicament, and warned him strongly in no uncertain terms to be careful. The jilted reacted badly, she had said, adding that she had forgotten how alien the Praetorians could be sometimes, but she was also certain that their human side would lead to the same reaction from Andersson.

Putting it out of his mind, he swung his legs off the bed and went to make himself a cup of his real coffee.

He was turning many things over in his calculating brain, thinking of how to structure the government of Dark Heart. What type of nation did he want to build, how was he going to manage the structure. How did he start a government, and keep the army separate, considering their martial background? Lady Sophia had suggested that he acknowledge it, but also remember that his nation would change him.

There were many concerns, not least that as a condition of relinquishing her directorship from the VMC, Lady Sophia had insisted on a strong political tie to the Levitican Union, and to House Towers personally. Gavain had agreed, and had only just realised the challenges it was going to bring with the vicious plots of House Zupanic and Marchenko. He would have to find some sort of solution before it all went too far, and the Union was torn apart.

His motivations for declaring himself House Lord were genuinely personal. His argument with Ulrik Andryukhin, and discovering the horrors of the atrocities that the Zhou-Zheng Compact, had really opened James's eyes to the truth of what he had become. He had become a money-soldier, ignoring the ethics of what was right and wrong. It was a sense of morality and what was best that had led him to participate in the revolution against the False Emperor and his pogroms against the human unaugmented, and he had been shocked to realise that his actions in helping to end that terrible reign had actually plunged the colonised galaxy into worse turmoil in many regions. The atrocities being committed now were just as bad or even worse, with borgites targeting unaugmented, and humans persecuting the augmented.

He was a free-thinker, and genuinely took the middle ground, wanting all to live harmoniously, at least accepting the other's existence even if they did not like it. He knew that was impossible however, particularly with the venomous and deadly politics that ruled the surviving nations and Houses less than two years after the Dissolution of the Imperium. Old hatreds had come to the fore, both personal and intra-familial and based on modification.

It had led to the desire to create the Vindicatus nation, a genuine home and refuge for all those who faced persecution. It would doubtless be portrayed by some as aggrandisement of his position on his part, but he did not hunger for power. He genuinely wanted to bring some relief to at least some people, atone for his actions and selfishness since Dissolution, and undo some of the damage that had spiralled out of control across the galaxy since the False Emperor had been removed.

He continued to change and develop, he realised. He had made the effort to widen his circle of close friends, he had accepted more people in towards himself. He was doing his best to improve the lot of both borgite and humanist. He was about to delve into hard politics at a high level for the first time. He would continue to grow and change, not just in a professional and charitable way, but also on the personal when it came to his friends and even his romantic life.

As he looked at the holographic mirror before him, bare chest reflecting the starlight outside, for the first time in a very long time he liked what he saw looking back at him.

*

In the vast construction of the Temple of Shadow, hidden in a location that very few knew and even less would have been able to actually reach, the Master of the First Circle sat in his own private quarters. He was a permanent resident of the Temple of Shadow, unlike the rest of the Circle Legates, some of whom had their own identities and lives to maintain.

He had no life outside the Shadow Council, not yet. He was determined that was not going to continue to be the case forever, as one day, he would burst into the colonised galaxy, and demand his due.

A mechanised voice announced, "Visitor for the Master." His own personal droid stood at the doorway, powering back up as it spoke, suddenly invading his period of unusual reflection.

"Who is it?" he asked quietly. This melancholic mood was unlike him. He sat there at the desk in his own audience chamber, the usual shadows of the Temple cast away, the ceiling and walls transparent and allowing the weak sunlight in. Compared to the environs of the rest of the Temple, it was positively bright. The distant M-class star the Temple of Shadow orbited was such a way away it made little real difference to him. Perhaps a journey outside the Temple of Shadow was needed, but there was so much to do.

"The Legates of the Second and Third Circle," replied the droid.

He looked at his desk, where his protective jet black face-mask with its straight golden lines highlighting the eye brows, rectangular nose and mouth lay. The Legates knew the truth of his identity, however, and there was no need to hide it. He knew the identities of everyone in the Shadow Council, as a matter of course.

Becoming the leader again, and in a much stronger voice, he commanded, "Enter."

The Legate of the Second with the silver lines on her face-mask, and the Legate of the Third with the white lines on his face-mask, both entered together. They approached his ornate and ancient desk, taken from old Earth in the tail end of the second millennium.

"Hail the master," they both intoned in unison. Both blinked through the eye-slits in the face-masks, surprised to see his full face revealed. There was no denying his lineage, or who he was.

"Has the wayward Faceless assassin arrived yet?" the Master demanded.

"Yes, Master," said the male Legate of the Third Circle. "We have it reconstituted, and it is undergoing full debrief. We will fully liquidate it if you so command, but there is much to be learnt from it. The Legate of the Fifth Circle even hopes to return it to active duty at a higher rank."

"I will read the reports and decide," said the Master. "What of the Rosicrux operation, following the disaster at Dark Heart?"

329

"Elements still survive, Master," said the Legate of the Third Circle again, "but it is effectively dead. We have lost the heart of it, so to speak. My recommendation is to cancel it, terminate it in some instances to prevent further discovery. We are still not sure how much this Gavain now knows, but he will in all probability continue to search for clues. They will have references speaking of the Shadow Council's involvement, but nothing overtly suggesting we were ever in control."

"This James Gavain is becoming a major problem," said the Master, thoughtfully. "The Legate of the Fifth may yet have to terminate him."

"It is of Gavain that we wish to speak to you, Master," said the Legate of the Third.

"I was coming to what brought you here, invading my sanctum," the Master said. "Speak."

"We came to inform you of a concerning development, in the Levitican Union," said the Legate of the Second. She had a strong voice, and was commanding. In the times to come, she would be the star of the Shadow Council as its more dangerous elements emerged from the Shadows, the Master knew. "Please, review this," she handed over a data-chip.

Using the cybernetic implant built into his right hand, the master accessed the data-chip. The two Legates remained motionless, and knew that he had absorbed all the information when he suddenly smashed the chip into pieces, picking up the desk before him and throwing it ruthlessly to one side.

"How dare he!" raged the Master. "Who does this Gavain think he is! He calls himself a House Lord, names himself Commander-in-Chief!" There was clatter as a number of biomorphs entered the room, weapons-ready, but the Second Legate ordered them back quietly with a hand signal. "The man goes far too far!"

"Please, my Master –" said the Second Legate.

"No!" he roared. "It is not to be tolerated under any circumstances. Contact the Fifth Legate, I want the Faceless in Dark Heart and Gavain dead! Send our very best! I hereby order it by Imperial Edict!"

The words were said.

Both the Second and Third Legate smashed their right hands into their chests, then extended them in the Imperial Salute, fist closed, arm at an angle and upright. They then bowed their heads and went to one knee. An Imperial Edict had been given, and it was a death-sentence for James Gavain.

"It will be as you command, Third Emperor –" the Legate of the Third Circle said in error.

The roar made the Legate silent in a nano-second, and he suddenly found himself on the floor, a long, extended blade at his throat, pricking in underneath the face-mask. The pure raging fury on the face of the man who called himself Master, made him look just like the True and the False Emperors at their very worst.

"*Never, ever, call me Emperor!*" the man hissed. As soon as it flared, the infamous rage of the Emperor family line had faded, and he stepped back, withdrawing the blade.

"Not until I am Third Emperor, and the Red Imperium of Mars has arisen again," he said.

Liked The Book?

Age of Secession

I would love to have your reviews and feedback, if you would like to post this in the place where you bought the book. It all helps to spread the news about the Age of Secession.

Visit the website www.ageofsecession.com, for lots of new content and Age of Secession-related material. News, new releases, background to the series, and more being added all the time!

Roger Ruffles himself would love to hear from you, so either follow him on Twitter @RogerRuffles, or write to him at ageofsecession@gmail.com

If Facebook is more of your thing, there is also the Age of Secession page, at www.facebook.com/AgeOfSecession.

The Age of Secession Continues .....

SHADOW
Part III – Vindicator Trilogy

OUT NOW

The Lord James Gavain has surprised the galaxy with his actions, and is seen very much as a hero. He attempts to build a new nation and a better future, taking in refugees from the many battles and wars throughout the seceding Houses, trading on the mercenary ability of his comrades and what appears to be the advanced technology he has recovered, yet he finds that there is a limit to how honourable one can be and still rule a post-Imperial House.

Beset by enemies jealous of his avarice, engaging in the murderous politics of the Levitican Union, he struggles to discover the truth behind the mysterious masters of the Rosicrux. They are about to emerge from the shadows explosively, and in the process, the galaxy will once again feel the wrath of a threat it thought had disappeared for good. The Shadow has arrived, and what he intends for the people of the galaxy is far worse than any of his predecessors visited upon mankind.

Gavain is a changed man, but he is about to face yet another life-altering challenge. Ultimately, it is a dire choice. Does he intercede and fight a monster with equally evil and heinous methods, or does he take the moral and ethical approach, and watch his attempt to halt the shadow casting itself over the galaxy fail? Whatever the choice is, it will cost him, and he will never be the same again.

Coming Soon to the Age of Secession .....

PAY DIRT: DISHONEST INTENTIONS

IN 2018

Life is tough for many in the Age of Secession, and for some it has become much tougher since the Emperors of House Constantin fell from grace.

Iain Briggs is a con-man, along with friends Dominic Gaiman and Marin Todor. They have moved from trick to trick, from planet to star system to intergalactic House since the Red Empire of Mars fell, each scam being bigger than the last.

The rise of the Vindicate Empire offers them their biggest and most dangerous opportunity yet, as this Fifth Empire looks to build landgates and starterminals across the colonised galaxy in every direction. It will revolutionise space travel, allowing trade to pass from one side of the colonised galaxy to another within a day, rather than in years.

Constructing a pathway across the stars, they will face the jealousies of leaders, the murderous intent of criminals, the hidden and dangerous motives of pirates, the wrath of the security forces of the nations they are working both for and against. This is the biggest job of all, and if any of them are to escape with their lives, they will have to succeed in a way they could not imagine when they started.

Most would see pay dirt as succeeding in one of the biggest construction jobs in mankind's history. They will see pay dirt as escaping with their lives, from an ever-deepening web of dishonest intentions.

Out Soon!

Go to facebook, twitter, or www.ageofsecession.com
for more details

Coming Later to the Age of Secession .....

In 2018/2019

Augmented Genocide

As the billions of Erdogan refugees make their home in the growing systems of the Mercenary Lord, back at home the Zhou-Zheng Compact have opened their deathcamps and are slowly exterminating their conquered people. There is not a single Erdogan family who has not suffered a loss, a relative dying in a work-camp.
This is the story of those who fought, against the Genocide of the Augmented.

The Lost Kindred

The Lost Kindred were abandoned.
It all began centuries before the Age of Secession started, but it will come to a head now. As the colonised galaxy turns upon itself, the Thirteen Kindred will return in greater force than ever before.
And the Kinsmen are angry that they were ever abandoned in the first place.

Adare's Legacy: Kingdom of Blood

It is to the Bandit Kingdoms of the Badlands that Caterina arrives with a child she did not want, but is now determined to protect whatever his origins. Abandoned by her former nation, all alone in a harsh and hostile galaxy, she finds she has to be as black-hearted as the pirates she now keeps company with.
She will stop at nothing to ensure that there is a legacy for the child of Silus Adare.
The Kingdom of Blood.

Collective Misdirection

It began with a virus, a simple line of quantum-locked code. It spread silently, the interconnected hive minds of the Nacrimosa Collective being a perfect breeding ground. Then one day, someone somewhere pressed a button, and an entire nation froze in terror as their minds shut down.
Who brought the Collective to its knees? The galaxy is being lied to, misdirected somehow, and what appears to be an opportunity for some might be more of a poisoned chalice than it first appears.
The Collective Misdirection must be exposed, before it is too late.

Printed in Great Britain
by Amazon